CW01510118

BLACKWICKET

BEA NORTHWICK

Copyright © 2025 Bea Northwick

All rights reserved.
No part of this publication may be reproduced, distributed, or transmitted in any form or by any means, including photocopying, recording, or other electronic or mechanical methods, without the prior written permission of the publisher, except as permitted by
U.S. Copyright law.

The story, all names, characters, and incidents portrayed in this production are fictitious. No identification with actual persons (living or deceased), places, buildings, and products is intended or should be inferred.

Book Cover by Lena Yang Edition 1. 2025
ISBN-13: 9798988473879

Dedication

Here's to the broken and the broken-hearted. May you find power in that deep darkness, and may the sun rise again. Someday.

PROLOGUE

T he sound of crying woke me, growing fainter as it receded down the hall. I sat up and peered into the gloom, fractured by small wafts of moonlight that had slipped through the wooden shutters. I was alone, my sister's bed empty, the creature that had taken up lurking in the slanted dormer alcove at night, absent.

My sister missing wasn't strange, but the Drudge being gone alarmed me. It only moved when there was danger in the house.

I climbed from bed, following the sound into the moldering hallway that smelled of mildew and damp, the cool ocean air stealing in from windows no longer able to shut in their swollen frames. The usual thrum of the house had lessened, and the stillness felt odd in my bones. I caught sight of candlelight flickering in the stairwell, followed by a gulping sob.

Fiona.

Two flights brought me to the foyer, shadowy and unwelcoming. The heartbreaking noises continued in the parlor, a room I hadn't set foot in since the day I'd made the mistake that broke my family. But I hadn't heard Fiona cry in years, and I needed to know what event had caused her tears.

I found her slouched against the wall near the Narthex, a hidden doorway between here and the realm magical law prohibited anyone from entering, the one leading to chaotic corridors crafted by Curse Eaters over generations.

When she saw me, she startled, wailing slightly, huddling into herself.

I hurried to her, kneeling to place my hand on her knees, which she'd drawn to her chest. She was two years older than I, eighteen this past summer, but she looked like a little girl again, curled up like this.

"I wasn't going to wake you." Her voice trembled.

"What's happened?"

"Mother's gone," she whispered.

"Gone where?" I asked, prepared to act, assuming she'd wandered into the night again to walk the cliffs, an unsafe excursion in her state. We were always worried she'd forget to look for the edge.

Fiona gripped my wrist, fingernails digging as she forced my palm against the surface where the portal had always existed, giving my family forbidden access to the place where magic was born.

"Dark Hall," Fiona replied. "She went to Dark Hall."

The house moaned, like the mortally wounded begging for death.

There was no telltale vibration beneath my hand, no softness in space growing ever more pliant as my magic unfurled to touch it, only an inflexible wall, the portal sealed shut. I stood, panic returning tenfold.

"You didn't try to stop her?" My voice rose, wild, disbelieving.

"What was I supposed to do?" She yelled in return.

"Grab her, hold her, beg her not to leave!" I clutched my chest as my heart raced painfully. Mother was gone. Not just gone, but good as dead.

"She wanted to go, Eleanora," Fiona said, rising unsteadily.

"Well, so do I." The words were out before I'd considered them, and once they were free, the rest followed. "I hate this house. I hate Grigori and this filthy town. I'm scared all the time. People *hate* us."

Faced with my rage, my sister's demeanor changed from the mournful bewilderment of loss to one of insult. She'd always taken our duty more seriously.

"It's our burden to bear. What will the people of Nightglass do without us?"

"Die too, for all I care," I choked out, "Like mother. She's dead, Fiona. You don't walk into Dark Hall as cursed as she was and leave."

My sister struggled briefly with her turmoil before crumbling beneath it.

"This is all your fault!" she shrieked, her body shaking with the effort. "You should have kept out of mother's business!"

"I was trying to help," I cried, stunned by both her animosity and the accusation.

"No one wanted your help, Ellie." Fiona wasn't screaming anymore, her voice dropping into the exhausted register of a young woman who was finally giving in to fate.

"Grigori had our family by the throat."

"If it weren't Grigori, it would be the Authority."

My anger flared, fueled by the cataclysm of sorrow and hurt.

"You're only complacent about Grigori's wickedness because you're hoping someday the hand around your throat will be William's," I snapped.

Even in the paltry circle of candlelight, I could see the furious flush on my sister's face.

"Fiona," I said softly, regretting my remark. "Why are we still trying to hold up this town, this house, when the people we help don't even want us to exist?"

"*We* don't hold it up." I'd never heard such venom in her

voice, and it penetrated deep. "You spend all your time in the garden, pretending nothing ever happened."

"Mother started that garden to help with the curses, to…"

"You should go," she said abruptly. "Somewhere far away, like you've always dreamed of."

"I want us to leave *together*," I reached for her hand, but she pulled away.

Fiona shook her head, hugging her arms around herself.

"The Authority will find us. If you're alone, you'll have a better chance, and so will I. Grigori has offered to sponsor my license."

"He knows you can eat curses?"

"He has for a long time, Ellie. He's cruel, not stupid."

"You have to refuse!" If Grigori Nightglass sponsored Fiona, her life would belong to him, just as our mothers had.

"It means protection for the house and the town."

"At what cost?"

"I don't have the luxury of considering the price I'll have to pay because of you!"

It was the final slap, the severing of everything we were, of all the dreams we'd once had to escape this life. I withdrew, simmering with offense and grief, and rushed back to our shared bedroom in the eves to pack a small bag, filled with enough things to sell for the money I'd need to start somewhere else.

Fiona was in the foyer when I came down, and it looked as though she might say something. I waited, pleading silently for her to change her mind and go with me, but she only stepped to the front door and opened it to the night.

With tears on my cheeks, I left Blackwicket House and my sister, beginning the long walk into town, where I'd catch the first train, no matter its destination. When I reached the gate, I paused, looking up the cliffs, dressed in their white autumn thrift, toward the house. The full moon hung proudly above it, my mother's garden of peculiar flowers drinking in its glow.

In my sixteen years, I'd learned enough to know that the darkness that devoured people from the inside out was often their own. But for a Curse Eater, for my family, it was the darkness that didn't belong to us, the darkness we borrowed. My sister had chosen this future, but I refused.

I would never come back to this house again.

CHAPTER ONE

Galton's department store, the largest in the city of Devin, roiled with chaotic life, each of the five floors packed with last-minute shoppers and onlookers who'd come to ogle the enchanted displays. Every year, alongside the first icy promises of snow, winter brought the temporary softening of laws prohibiting the use of magic. With the proper licensing and plenty of donations, Galton's had obtained permission to provide a bit of extra wonder to the season and more than a bit of additional profit to the store. Not that it needed any more money.

My uncharitable thoughts rankled me, and I fiddled with the ruffled collar of my blouse, laying the starched white frills neatly over the uniform jacket assigned to all of the girls in the cosmetics department. I had been working the perfume counter for a year, condemned to wear the heinous Galton Girl ensemble: a stiff skirt and jacket set in variations of soft blues and grays that did nothing for my complexion, which a recent Authority report had described as *wan*.

I tilted my head to dislodge the memory, but it held tight. My powder blue kitten heels were pinching, and I had a run in my stocking, dangerously near the hem of my skirt. I willed it to remain content in its place and venture no farther south. I was poised to spend the evening uncomfortable, contemplating all the ways my life had recently gone terribly wrong.

Sleep had eluded me for weeks, and my appetite was inconsistent. Yet to anyone looking, I was chipper-faced and clean, my hair freshly curled and pinned into controlled waves at my neck, no strand amiss. I'd kept my makeup subtle to avoid attracting unwanted attention from husbands who'd wandered away from their wives in Women's Clothing across the aisle, and I wore no scent on my skin but lavender soap. Galton's dress regulations prohibited perfume, and I was tempting fate with the lavender, but being the best saleswoman they had came with some liberties. I mulled over my status as the lead clerk, such a normal, safe thing to be.

Humanity undulated around my counter: youths hunting for small tokens to give to sweethearts, men in their trilby hats and wool suits rushing to purchase gifts they had left for the last minute, and women in their best winter day dresses, pulling behind them sugar-addled children, faces still sticky with sweets from the confectioners one floor below. I visited the sweet shop often myself to enjoy their enchanted display. It consisted of red licorice and cream taffy, stretched and molded into the form of a Clydesdale-sized candy elephant, which periodically raised its trunk to trumpet sparks through the air. This golden glitter transformed into wrapped tarts and jellies, raining in pinpoint form into perfect rows of silver foil boxes. Magic of this complexity was the work of dozens of people, all from various prominent families whose abilities hadn't completely atrophied over the decades since the ban. They'd each offered what they could, but it was still the barest of scraps. Though I craved an opportunity to participate, to stretch muscles long unused, there were rules for people who lived their lives in hiding, ones I'd chanced breaking a few too many times already.

I spared a glance at the disappointing spectacle constructed for my department: a series of poufs rising from their gold compacts in graceful arcs, twirling to release a powdery scent before descending again, compact lids snapping shut and reopening to repeat the performance. I'd have wagered it more a feat of engineering than magic, but a faint power still buzzed pleasantly, and I lowered my guard a little to enjoy it.

Immediately, a cold tremor twitched through me, slinking into my shoulders, an unfortunate sign that more than whimsy visited Galton's today. I shut myself up again hastily.

Unpolluted magic was a rare and tempting resource, attracting many types of wickedness. The Authority were undeniably present, dressed as civilians and monitoring each floor for attempts to steal the displays and for any signs of Drudge, cursed magic with enough juice to twist itself into something corporeal. Since the prohibition, Drudge were rare but a threat nonetheless, and Authority prolific. I had a history with both and no interest in running into either.

With cursed magic lurking nearby, I'd need to keep my head down.

Faking illness was tempting, but I'd already taken my entire year of leave following the summer incident that haunted me. Even one more day might cost me my position, best saleswoman or not. I arranged our most expensive bottles to catch the light and pasted on a smile to tempt passersby to stop and distract me from my thoughts. A few eyes slid my way but didn't linger, and I sighed through my teeth.

"Lizzie!"

My counter partner Magdaline Shaw called out to a friend in her chirping soprano, joyful and excited as always. Everyone was Magdaline's friend, a trait equal measures endearing and nauseating.

"Lizzie, has your brain clocked in?"

Magdaline appeared at my left elbow, dressed in the Galton Girl uniform, her sweep of ash blond hair worn with a cobalt pin. She was peering at me with those cornflower-blue eyes, lips upturned, bemused.

With a jolt, I shifted back into my present. *Lizzie*. That was me and had been for two years. Before Lizzie, I'd been Joan; before Joan, Carrie; half a dozen names, all fitting me worse than a secondhand girdle.

"Sorry, Madge," I replied, "I was daydreaming."

She pulled a sympathetic face, a small crease appearing between her brows. "I know it's rough whiling away the hours here when you've got such a fine night to look forward to. I'd be daydreaming too."

I had no plans tonight.

"Dolly Pier is going to be a thrill," she continued. "I still can't believe Ben's taking you there, the cab costs an arm and a leg…"

As was her way, my friend went on talking, amiably rambling with hardly a breath taken, while my stomach curdled with guilt. I'd forgotten tonight. Forgotten Ben. I'd been doing that too much lately. There'd barely be time to change after shift, but my worries were likely wasted. Ben was too sensible to care about my looks and never noticed any effort I put into them.

As Madge chatted on, she chose a bottle of our most expensive scent and spritzed her wrists. Now, she smelled the way she looked, like a starlet waiting for her big break, all sun-kissed skin, pale hair, and excessive, vulnerable optimism. She was summer in human form.

"Have you talked to Wendy?" she asked, breezing into a new subject. Heat surged to my cheeks. "She never answers the phone when I call her flat."

Wendy never answered because she was long gone and never coming back.

Resentment unfolded in my belly. My life had been settling. I'd gotten used to being Elizabeth Knoles, the woman from a quaint farm town, a two-day train ride away with happy, simple parents who missed her and sent her letters and some money every now and then. *Lizzie* had a one-room flat in a safe part of town, a library card, a decent boyfriend, and a steady job. She was even due a promotion to department manager. I'd finally been wrestling my life into submission.

And then Wendy Mofton happened.

Sweet, quiet, Wendy and her dreamy white-collar husband, ten years her senior, with his big goofy smile, bigger laugh, and a talent for leaving bruises where no one was likely to notice them. If I'd minded my business, the Authority wouldn't know I existed, and Wendy's husband would still be alive.

Anxiety jumped in my throat.

"She hasn't been in touch with me since Brock passed," I said. Not since she'd hinted to the Authority I might be involved, resulting in the investigation, the interrogation, and the end of my anonymity in this vast metropolis where I'd once been blessedly invisible. Now, I felt eyes on me at every turn, jumped at any sudden movement. I'd been keeping my nose clean, for the most part, but trouble sought me out, and I had a damnable empathy for it. But at least Wendy was free. Really, there was no one to be angry with but myself. After all, she hadn't made me kill her husband. I'd done that on my own.

"What an asshole," Magdaline proclaimed fervently, placing the perfume down a little too hard, the high clink of glass emphasizing her distaste. "Good riddance if you ask me. Gosh, I hope she's okay."

I was proud of my friend for having enough sense to detect Brock's hidden ugliness. At twenty-three, she often seemed much younger, but that might have been more show than I thought.

"Anyway…" The brightness was back in her voice, gloom pushed aside. "I've been dying to talk to you about this knockout

I've been seeing around lately, tall, devilish, so handsome. He could probably throw me over his shoulder like a rag doll."

"Madge, *I* could throw you over my shoulder like a rag doll."

Her giggle fizzed, high and sweet as champagne. "You'll see what I mean. I'll point him out. I thought he might be shopping with his wife, but I've never seen a lady with him, and he's always looking this way. I bet he's working up the nerve to ... oh."

Magdaline stopped short, voice pinched into silence as though someone had taken her by the neck. She was looking over my shoulder, expression collapsed.

"It's Ms. Rosley," she said with a mournful twist of her hands.

This was jolting news.

Once upon a time, Ms. Rosley had been a regular at our counter, dressed to impress no matter the day or time. In her forties, she was attractive, self-assured, and very hard to read. She knew exactly what she wanted but would never tell you. Her favorite pastime was making the shop girls guess, offering no clues besides a slight rise of the brow or curl of the lip.

She was notorious at Galton's for being the most difficult-to-please woman alive, but we gave her sympathy and the benefit of the doubt. The woman had lost three of her four children to illness, the youngest escaping with his life but not his health. Despite her lavish monthly shopping trips, she was most often nursing her delicate son at home, rarely making appearances elsewhere but in the department store. I'd begun making extra time for her, and a tenuous, strange respect had formed. We weren't friends, just two people, scarred by loss, recognizing that feature in each other.

Three weeks ago, her young son had joined his siblings, and no one expected to ever lay eyes on Ms. Rosley again. But here she was, disheveled—her distinct curled pompadour style lank with grease, pinned only halfway. Her coat had been buttoned askew, the pale collar stained by something green and gelatinous. Sorrow had done its work on this woman. She approached the counter like a broken windup toy, eyes glassy and distant, carrying bags from various departments, a fair number more than usual. There was something decayed about her, skin sagging on bones as though she'd begun to rot beneath, like a wooden doll plagued with mildew.

A pit of dread opened in my stomach. I was bitterly familiar with this look. As she neared, she stumbled under the weight of her things, and I noticed the same green substance clinging to the corner of her mouth—it was candy.

I could sense Magdaline retreating, turning to find something else to do, an excuse to leave so I could deal with Ms. Rosley alone. The woman placed her sacks on the floor, filled with children's things: clothes, toys, and several bags of sweets. With some dignity, she raised her chin but didn't speak. I returned her intense gaze.

"Ms. Rosley, you've done quite a bit of shopping," I ventured.

She shook her head as though to say no before answering. "Yes."

The glob of candy slipped from her mouth and onto the glass-top display. I prepared to ask what perfume she wanted to try, but she anticipated the question.

"I want a bottle of Joyeux."

"Oh yes," I said, trying a light-hearted approach. "The one that smells like sugar."

"David loved that smell," she said, voice wistful.

Her little boy. My heart ached.

"This was his favorite time of year, you know," she went on dreamily as I retrieved the test bottle and readied it. I went slower than typical, and with a steadying inhalation, I reached, not with my fingers but with coils of forbidden magic rising from the slow-turning universe tucked away in me, the part belonging to where we'd all come from and were no longer allowed to return to.

"It's a beautiful time," I conceded while, with senses long decried as corrupt, I searched for the telltale sensation of wrongness that would prove that what I suspected was true. More than grief was responsible for Ms. Rosley's alarming state.

"The enchantments were his favorite. He was always telling me someday, maybe he'd be able to craft them too. Swore he'd find a way to use magic to heal instead of hurt." Her lip quivered. "Children never understand the danger of things, do they?"

I attempted to take her hand in mine, so I might turn her wrist and dab the scent on it as I'd done many times, but she jerked away, the movement unbalancing her.

I withdrew my invisible prodding, worried she'd sensed it, though most people had long lost the ability to.

"Ms. Rosley?"

"I'm going to visit my children today. I bought them gifts," she said, motioning to the cluster of items at her feet. It was far too much to leave on the graves of loved ones. No groundskeeper would allow it.

"Is anyone going with you?" I asked delicately, hoping she'd say her husband, a relative, a friend, someone to hold her as she stood in the face of her greatest pain.

"No. It can only be me." Her dreamy countenance hardened, turning testy. "I just need the perfume, and I'm in a rush."

"All right," I agreed. "Do you want to try it?"

I needed to touch her.

She offered her wrist with an impatient huff, and I took her fingers, bone-thin and filthy, the smell of her unwashed skin sour. As I pushed back the sleeve of her coat, I brushed her gold bracelet and flinched, a metallic sting of malice biting into me.

"It's candy residue, for goodness' sake." Ms. Rosley scowled, prepared to pull her wrist away, but I held on tighter than necessary, and she didn't resist.

"I'm sorry. Your charming bracelet—it's cold." I kept my voice even, almost cooing, taking my time dabbing the scent on, trying to decide what to do. "I've never seen you wear this one."

She considered the jewelry, wary, in awe, as though seeing it for the first time.

"It's always cold," she replied, breathy, "but I won't take it off. Some good friends gave it to me. The jewels, you see…one for each of my children."

A disturbed look crossed Ms. Rosley's face, eyes wide, filled with tears, and her breath came in shallow pulls. My attention was equally locked on the accessory, its gold plating clouded by more than the fingerprints of an admiring hand. A faint, stringy, miasma trailed to her lamé handbag on the counter.

Abruptly, Ms. Rosley clapped her other hand over mine, holding with an impressive grip for such an emaciated frame.

"Do you believe in ghosts?" she asked, a tear falling onto my knuckles, slipping into the warm space between our joined hands.

"Do you?" I asked quietly in return.

"I hear them. My babies. They're calling to me, and they sound so afraid. They need me."

If voices were tormenting her, they weren't those of her children.

"They're in Dark Hall," she whispered, raising her eyes to meet mine, determined, afraid. "It's all my fault, so I'm going to get them back. They promised I could."

Time slowed, the white noise of blood and horror pumping in my ears.

"Who did?"

Ms. Rosley released me, returning to business as usual. I reeled, trying to keep pace with her rapidly fluctuating moods.

"You've kept me long enough," she said, opening her handbag and rifling inside. "I only came for this perfume, not to chat all day."

She retrieved her pocketbook and set the purse on the counter, open, and there it was, wrapped around the barrel of a revolver. A Drudge. It was small and newly formed, gawping up at me, distressingly infant-like. Its chosen physical state was still unstable, shifting in and out of view like a shadow caught in firelight.

"Where are you off to next, Ms. Rosley?" I inquired carefully.

"Aren't you full of questions?" she snorted, handing me enough bills to pay for five bottles. "I'm going to the cemetery. Don't bother with my change. I don't need it."

She was going to walk away with the end of her life tucked neatly in her purse. She'd take her gifts, spray her youngest child's favorite scent, then leave this plane of misery in hopes of being reunited with all she'd lost.

The infant Drudge would feed on her dying magic. Then perhaps it would fold itself back into the bracelet and be sold at auction, passed to a relative, making its way from one person to the next, filling each of them with its pain, forcing its suffering onto others until it was strong enough to fully walk on its own. I could let it be and continue my borrowed life without worrying about the curse or the people it would ruin. I could let her go and say a silent prayer that she found peace.

I could.

"I don't have all the time in the world," Ms. Rosley snapped.

I seized her wrist and flipped open the clasp with my free hand, a trick I'd learned my first year away from home. It fell into my palm with the hiss of a hot brand in water. Immediately, the claws of the diseased magic unhooked from the poor woman, more interested in the unexpected salvation it sensed in the cradle of my magic.

Ms. Rosley loosed a piercing howl, as though her soul were being forcibly removed. Depending on how long she'd been wearing the bracelet, part of it had been. Now that I had the vessel, the Drudge would have no choice but to follow, but for good measure, I snatched the purse, handgun inside, and I ran.

CHAPTER TWO

"Lizzie!" Magdaline gasped as I shoved past her, clutching the items to my chest. I hoped Ms. Rosley's shrieks would cause enough pandemonium in the crowd that I could escape undetected through the staff corridors, but I'd been stupid to wish for chaos. It was the one thing that always came when called.

The Drudge thrashed inside the clutch, yanking its tether with such force that the bracelet slipped from my hand, and in my haste to catch it, I lost grip on the purse. It fell to the ground, discharging the revolver. The blast shattered the perfume counter, and Magdaline cried out, crumpling into a heap.

"Madge!"

The crash of noise drove the already alarmed masses into hysterics as people attempted to flee, purchases abandoned, children wailing as they were snatched off their feet and from their prams into the arms of terrified parents. Ms. Rosley had fallen, her prone form convulsing. I couldn't know if I'd done right. She'd been so far gone.

Ejected from the bag, the Drudge squelched through the debris and began clambering toward the cosmetics display. Its ferocity was aided by the instinct to cleanse itself in pure magic, even though the promise of liberation was a lie. Human terror had already tainted the exhibit, turning the sparkling edges of the enchantment dim and gray. Such paltry offerings would never be enough, and the curse would only pollute what it absorbed, growing in power and misery until strong enough to break from its vessel and walk the world.

What I needed to do now would cost a pound of flesh and more, but from the moment I'd touched the curse, I'd condemned myself to it.

Grateful the panicking hordes were giving us a wide berth, I took a stabilizing breath, withdrawing my senses from the mayhem and reaching for the heart of the creature buried deep in the bracelet. The tendrils of magic I'd employed with Ms. Rosley began their hunt through the tightly wound darkness until they grazed upon an electric thread. I seized it and pulled.

The Drudge flipped onto its back, the size of a rabbit now, with a grotesque flailing of stunted limbs, features clay-soft and malformed. I drew it closer through the wreckage of the shattered counter, the rivulets of perfume thickening the air with cloying scents. On the third drag, it accepted its odds. Choosing me was its best option.

It fumbled onto its stomach, skittering closer blink by blink, and I lowered the barrier I'd grown so accustomed to holding in place, ready to let it in. A hand on my arm startled me. Magdaline.

"We have to go," she said, shaky, clutching the top of her right shoulder, the blue of her jacket stained a vivid, angry red. The bullet had grazed her. Despite her injury and having witnessed what I'd done, she'd stayed to ensure my safety.

The Drudge leapt, clawing its way up my chest and throat, small hands hot as dying embers. Reaching my face, it burrowed into my mouth and stretched the delicate corner of my lips, which tore from the force. But as my jawbone gave a warning groan, the Drudge collapsed into a murky cloud of rust-hued ashes. The inhalation that followed was involuntary, a reflex bred into me by generations, practiced since childhood, and suppressed for years. The curse wasted no time tangling itself in the branches of my ribs, burning like fire smoke and leaving the taste of smog and expensive perfume on my tongue.

It was an eternity lasting no more than a second, and my next breath came ragged.

"Oh, god," Magdaline said. The fear and betrayal in my friend's eyes anguished me. "You're a Curse Eater?"

As she retreated a haphazard step, she slipped on broken glass and fell, landing on her injured arm and leaving streaks of gore on the terrazzo.

I moved to help her.

"Stay away!" she screamed, kicking at me so fiercely that a kitten heel dislodged, hitting my shin. This was horror, and I was the monster that had inspired it.

An apology would mean nothing. I couldn't take back the choices I'd made, so I did the best I could for Magdaline and left her alone, turning to begin my run to the staff door. Hidden by a glass brick wall, it separated the cosmetics department from the rest of the east floor and remained the only exit free of the crush of people trying to escape. But as I rounded the destroyed counter, my eye caught an oddity: an imposing figure standing stock-still amid the panic. The mob gave him ample room, instinctively aware that to touch him would be a fatal error. He was too far for me to see the color of his eyes, but I knew it all the same, knew the plane of his cheeks, the juncture of his jaw and neck scarred with law-sanctioned violence. I recalled his voice, low and mocking, following the final time I'd insisted I knew nothing of Brock Mofton's death.

The Authority has a procedure to handle dealers of black-market magic. Do you know what Annulment is, Ms. Knoles? Do you know how much it hurts?

This was Magdaline's handsome stranger. Not a stranger at

all. He hadn't been working up the nerve to flirt—he'd been watching me, waiting for a mistake like this.

The poorly stacked house of cards that was my borrowed life came tumbling down as I fled. The Inspector made no move to pursue, perhaps knowing there was nowhere I could go in Devin where he couldn't find me.

The chaos I'd unleashed had made it onto the street, frantic shoppers and bystanders gathering to ogle the flood of people pouring from the most distinguished department store in the city. Authority sirens blared, punctuated by exclamations of dread, each more extravagant than the last.

Cursed items in the store.

Someone murdered by a Drudge

Dark Hall is open.

The weight I carried spread, a languid toxin, making my limbs heavy and my mind sluggish. It entreated me to slow, to give in, and be emptied. I'd never consumed anything this strong so far from a place of safety, from a person who could offer help if I began to drown.

The heady charge of corrupt energy made forward movement a labor, but I kept my spine straight even as I was forced to shoulder past people, no one shifting even a fraction to the side. Frustration rose, mixing with the dark taint of the magic, turning it to rage. The high scream of fire engines had joined the cacophony, but the crowd continued to block the street, preventing assistance from reaching its destination, reaching people who might be hurt.

Poor Ms. Rosley. Poor Magdaline.

"Move!" I bellowed, gambling my strength on the outburst. Several stunned faces turned my way, and a small path opened. I made it to the sidewalk, the assembly of people more malleable here, and spied the entrance to the narrow alley system I often braved on rainy days. It was a shortcut to the parallel street on the opposite side of the entertainment district where I lived.

An inch closer, another, until my progress was cut off by a handsome woman in her sixties. Pearl earrings hung at her lobes, like snowflakes suspended, the somber navy of her wool overcoat contrasting with starry silver hair, brushed in a perfect chignon. She was too close, and the bright fragrance of lilacs and greenery filled my nose, the scent clashing with the frigid fold of winter.

"Oh, darling, are you alright?" she asked, clearly prepared to make a fuss. "Your poor mouth is bleeding!"

Hazily, I swiped my knuckles across my sore lips, and they came away smeared red. I hadn't been able to separate the tang of blood from the foulness the Drudge had left behind.

"You've come from the department store, haven't you? Here, follow me, we need to find you a place to sit, assess the damage."

The kindness stalled me, and she clasped my hand in hers, patting, offering an assured smile. Her fingers were warm, skin soft, and for the smallest of moments, my heart beat slower, jumbled thoughts melting and turning wooly. Everything grew quiet, she and I the sole people in existence. The only other person who'd ever made me feel so contented in a moment better suited for panic was my mother. I'd been climbing the porch railing, trying to get to the roof to help a bird that had flown into the foyer window, when the rotted wood splintered and I fell, breaking my wrist. Mother had stroked my hair and murmured words that spread sweet as sunbeams, and the pain of her setting the bones into place was reduced.

This long-ago memory prevented the bewitchment from doing its intended work, and my wits returned to me. I forcefully severed the connection, even as her magic began searching mine, seeking out the Drudge. She pulled back, grimacing as though I'd struck her.

"Please, don't be frightened," she said, coaxing. "I want to help you."

I couldn't give this woman any more reason to think she was dealing with a vulnerable target, so I risked a threatening step towards her.

"You know what I'll do if you try it again," I replied.

Compassion drained from her eyes, the facade of care cracking under pressure. She observed me with dispassionate, almost medical, interest.

"Don't let them trap you, Eleanora." Her use of the name my mother had given me was disorienting. "Let me take it. I know what to do with it."

"Fire! Fire! Everyone, back up! The place is on fire!" The roar rose above the droves, and at last, they broke apart in all directions, separating me from the old woman.

I took my opportunity, using the surge as cover and slipping into the eerie stillness of the alley, the fastest route home. All I needed was time enough to safely rid myself of the curse and shove it into its old vessel, but already I heard the sound of footfall behind me. I'd chosen wrong, my desperation making me stupid. There were only two more turns before I reached another main road, another swarm of humanity I might hide myself among. I picked up my pace only for the heel of my uniform shoe to wedge itself between crooked cobblestones, sending me to my knees. The footsteps grew louder, then slowed, the beasts always at my back catching up to me at last.

I was unwilling to die in an alley of a city I didn't even like, ripped to bits by the type of people who'd ruined my life to begin with. I stood unsteadily. Unlike forcing the Drudge into a lifeless host, the unforgivable crime I was going to commit wouldn't be difficult work. The Drudge was already willingly rising, begging to be shared.

"Eleanora." A man's voice.

I whipped around, abandoning my shoe, hands raised to grab hold, mouth open to release the vile toxin onto its next victim. Transferring the curse so aggressively would wreck me, but I would be free of it. I would get away, and my pursuer would likely die of shock.

But he'd predicted this. Catching both of my wrists, he drove his knee into the soft hollow beneath my ribs, hard enough to knock the air from me. I buckled, but my attacker held tight to my arms, preventing me from toppling over. The jolt of the impact discouraged the curse from advancing, and it made a morose retreat.

"Whoa there, Cricket. Got you a little too hard. Up you get."

I coughed, looking into the face of the man I'd failed to murder.

"Darren?" I choked out, disbelieving.

"Still calling me by my given name, huh? Okay."

I certainly wasn't going to call him *Dad*.

He stabilized me, drawing my arm over his shoulder, "Damn, that's a lousy one you've got there. Even I can feel it. I don't know what the hell you were thinking, but we'll talk about that later. You've got to transfer it, or the rot will get you."

On any given day, feelings for my father tipped precariously toward detestation, but relief wounded my will to hate him, leaving space for the child I'd been the last time we'd seen each other.

"Maybe it should finally," I replied. The sentiment was honest, but sounded petulant. I was sixteen again, equally afraid and full of pride.

"Don't pout," he said, nudging me forward. "And move your feet. Your exit wasn't stealthy. The Authority will be looking for you."

The Authority and something more sinister. I recalled the woman in the street, her detached interest and powerful magic.

"The Brom know I'm here," I managed as we took our first step.

Darren halted. I couldn't meet his eye.

"Well..." he said after a beat, starting us off again, bearing most of my weight. "If this is your way of 'escaping your tainted family legacy,' I hope you're open to some critiques."

CHAPTER THREE

The journey through the alleys leading to my tenement was excruciating, Darren recommending we take every wrong turn in case the woman or her cohorts were tracking us. I had less time than ever to assemble my belongings and get gone, but when we emerged from the labyrinthine backstreets, we were in a part of Devin I didn't frequent. Oldtown. This district was downtrodden, known for its seedy bars, cheap motels, and easy access to carnal entertainments you wouldn't find on the Galton side of the city. People here wouldn't blink an eye at a battered woman being half dragged down the street.

"This isn't right," I said.

I feared we'd taken a wrong turn. At this rate, I'd never make it back to my apartment to retrieve the items that wouldn't help my case once the Authority had them in custody.

"We can't go back to your place, Cricket," Darren said. "The Authority know where you live."

"There are things I can't leave," I protested as he continued to guide my steps.

"We'll talk after you feel better."

He helped me navigate across the street, steam rising from the sidewalk vents like fog. We arrived at a four-story motel, squatting between two taller buildings, whose windows were long boarded. A balding man in a suit jacket several sizes too small sat at the front desk, absorbed in yesterday's newspaper. My father waved a set of keys, but the clerk didn't even raise his eyes.

Following two grueling flights of stairs, Darren unlocked a pinewood door and led me inside. I shrugged him off the moment we crossed the threshold, stumbling to the dingy yellow bathroom to vomit into the sink. At least now my mouth tasted of acrid bile instead of Drudge. A consumed curse often granted its new host a surge of magical ability, a temporary rush of psychic strength, along with a nagging sensation of a toothache in your chest. Drudge didn't function this way. They didn't trickle poison, but spread like blood in water.

"Do you still have the vessel?" Darren asked from the other room as I finished gagging and rinsed my mouth with tepid water, feeling little better than dead.

I retrieved the bracelet from my skirt pocket, raising it wordlessly over my head as I wiped my face on a stained towel.

"Right. Do you need me to...uh." My father fumbled his words, doing everything in his power to avoid offering his help.

"Don't bother, Darren," I grumbled, still queasy. I'd done this so many times without him.

He rubbed the back of his neck.

"You should give this one to Dark Hall."

The suggestion was ridiculous. Placing a curse in Dark Hall was reckless, and getting caught opening a portal was punishable by Annulment.

"You know I can't reach Dark Hall."

"If your mother could..."

"I'm not her."

"Well, what do you plan to do with it?" He threw his hands out, frustrated with my mulishness.

The curse twisted deeper, searching for a permanent home in my breast. I couldn't afford the gentler route, like soaking a bandage before removing it from a wound. Hasty action was required, and I'd have to endure the void it left behind. I staggered to the bed and sat heavily, the mattress eliciting a distressed creak. Something dripped onto the floor beneath the frame.

Pressing the jewelry to my chest, I closed my eyes, the ache settling in. I groped for the edge of the magic, peeling at it bit by bit. Sensing my intentions, it cringed away. Curses didn't appreciate cold, lifeless things. I'd often imagined being trapped in a lifeless host was similar to being confined in a casket with no promise of death and no knowledge of when you'd be free again.

Desperation made me callous, rough, but the harder I tugged, the stronger the curse fought, its teeth sinking deeper, the fiber of who I was warping around it. Panic rose until all I was doing was feeding this Drudge the noxious nutrients it required to stand its ground and take permanent residence. I should have stopped, admitted I needed help.

"Cricket." Darren's tone was uneasy.

My ribs contracted, accompanied by an audible pop of shoulder joints as the curse wrenched inward.

"Eleanora!" he barked, lunging, one hand eclipsing my folded ones. His magic was as welcome as cool water on a feverish face. Though he possessed little, he'd learned to leverage the momentum of others.

The extra force was all it took, and the Drudge lost its grip. It ascended from my throat like a wail, its vaporous form drawn back into the vessel, taking a piece of me with it. The fragment it stole was small, perhaps no larger than a teardrop, and in its place, an equal portion of the curse remained.

"That was real stupid, kid," Darren muttered, pressing my forehead against his chest, anticipating the next unavoidable event: my swift descent into the gray realm of unconsciousness where curses and absent fathers didn't exist.

Awareness crashed through me, and I sat up, sucking in air. For a bewildering second, the world spun as I tried to piece together my location and the state of my safety. A hard blink brought the spinning to heel, and I remembered.

"Welcome back to the world of the waking," my father's disembodied voice rumbled.

"I'm on the floor," I managed, coming to a stiff seated position a few feet from the bed. Darren had rolled his coat to place under my head.

My father sat at the rickety table in its single chair, a takeaway bag filled with waxy boxes of food nearby. He was scoffing a pile of greasy noodles, unbothered.

"I wasn't going to tuck you into that infested sack," he said, mouth full. "Come eat."

"You could have killed me."

We both knew I wasn't referring to where he'd put me to recover.

"Could have. Didn't." He pointed his fork at me to emphasize the last part. "Anyway, you were doing a pretty decent job of it yourself. You got all soft in the collarbones. I've seen that a time or two. It's never pretty."

"I assume you didn't offer your gallantry then."

"You're my kid," he replied brusquely.

My father had watched people die of curse rot and likely scalped the magic off their still-warm bodies. He'd saved me out of guilt or, more likely, self-interest, another reason to remain wary.

Skewering another bite of noodles, he added, "I remember you wrestling bigger monsters with much less effort back when you still had baby teeth."

"That's an exaggeration." I rose to my feet, balance still dubious.

"An observation," he rejoined.

"There were things I needed from my apartment." I chose condemnation because I didn't know how to express gratitude for this. By now, the Authority had discovered my collection, and they'd be eager as ever to administer their justice.

Continuing to use his fork as an instructor's pointer, he gestured to two carpet bags pushed against the wall.

"Didn't get it all, but I grabbed what would earn you a ticket to having your magic yanked out your ass by the Authority."

"Your world-class charm appears to be intact."

"It's the truth, no charm required. So," he segued as I rushed to assess my belongings. "How many you got in there? Ten? Fifteen?"

I opened the bags, rummaging, pushing aside the remnants of my most recent life until my fingers brushed the smooth surface of a plain wooden lockbox, festering with vessels full of foul power. I'd been gathering these artifacts for years, snatching them from shop shelves and off employers' bookcases and desks. Two had come from my early days of pick-pocketing when I'd been Carrie Holt in the small city of Weston.

I hadn't intended to answer my father's question, but a strange sense of guilt encouraged the response.

"Thirty-three."

He whistled low.

"That's a goddamn felony ten times over. Not too different from your old man after all."

"I don't sell them."

"Neither do I." He offered me an unaffected smile.

"Of course not," I said.

"Ah, cut it out. You've been on the wrong side of the Authority recently yourself. That guy, Mofton..."

"I didn't have anything to do with that."

"Of course not," he replied, echoing me.

I eyed him. My father had always been a dandy, concerned with appearances, but I noticed the stubble on his chin and the faded glory of a once-expensive suit. There was gray at his temples, but the new bulge of his belly aged him most. For a white-hot moment, I wondered how my mother would have looked if she'd lived long enough to turn soft and gray.

"So, what, you're keeping the curses as pets?" Darren asked, tossing his empty food container back into the paper bag. "That's depressing, Cricket."

After leaving home, I promised myself I'd never curse eat again, and I hadn't, but as I came across curses out in the world, it felt wrong to ignore them. So, I became a collector. Every night, as a minor concession, I infused the box with a meager portion of my magic to prevent the curses from growing too restless and turning on one another. As I accumulated more, the amount of magic necessary to keep them subdued increased. Soon, I wouldn't be able to pacify them. But I didn't owe Darren an explanation.

Ignoring his question, I appraised what else had been gathered. The pocketbook I'd hidden in the ceiling vent was present, filled with money I'd saved for a hasty exit. I'd grown too comfortable, daring to think I'd be in Devin long term, and there was very little. I also found a chaotic assortment of clothes, items yanked from my closet and drawers at random. There was a coat I'd meant to get rid of, a pair of trousers and a winter skirt, a vest, no stockings, no shoes, and nearly all the blouses for warm weather. Most of the savings I'd managed would have to go toward replacing items. If I traveled stockingless, dressed in a thin summer shirt, I'd attract attention, and attention was my eternal nemesis.

The other items were sentimental, and I was surprised by Darren's inclusion of them: a birthday card from Madge and a small book of terrible poetry Ben had given me, with pressed flowers in the pages for no other reason than I liked pretending I was a romantic woman. There was also an intimate letter tucked inside. Ben was a civil engineer, frequently traveling to remote areas struggling to adjust to a world devoid of magical energy that once drove economies and households. His frequent absences suited me and my need for space and privacy to deal with the curses I'd accumulated. When he was away, he wrote to me and returned with enough entertaining stories to keep our conversation light and free of talk about what I'd been up to. It was possible he assumed I never got up to anything. I'd convinced him I was a woman of very few interests: a competent dance partner, an avid listener, a terrible cook, and a willing bedmate. It's all he seemed to want and all I had the energy to provide while balancing a counterfeit identity and an illegal pastime.

The final non-essential item I uncovered was the only photo of me I'd kept, taken on my twenty-sixth birthday, a month before the disaster that triggered my Sisyphean tumble: Madge, Wendy, Ben, and I sitting together on the bench of a picnic table, the sun shining a spotlight on our happiness. Ben's arm rested around my waist, while Madge and Wendy leaned together, faces bright with laughter.

I swallowed the lump in my throat and tossed the mementos into a sad pile. Then, sparing energy I really couldn't waste, I drew on my wrecked magic. A feeble spark ignited, and I wove in instructions to burn only these memories, bringing the diminutive flame dancing on my fingertips to the photo. When it was all alight, I claimed the trousers and knit sweater from the trunk and changed quickly in the bathroom. I smoothed my hair, but there was nothing to do for the tear at the corner of my mouth, which had stopped seeping but was swollen and red.

When I exited with my ruined uniform, Darren was still sitting at the table, finishing his food, as content and peaceful as though this were a routine. A casual drop-in.

"Where's the bracelet?" I asked.

"Safe."

"I know what you do with curses, Darren."

With a long-suffering sigh, he produced the bracelet and tossed it to me. I caught it by a small miracle, dropping the clothes in the process.

"Would fetch a nice price. You could go anywhere."

"This almost killed a woman. I'm sure it's killed others."

I considered Ms. Rosley's children, all falling ill, dying within weeks of each other.

"All the more reason to part with it," Darren said.

"I won't condemn others to death for money. It'll only end up with the Brom, and they don't need any assistance in the death department."

"That sounded like Isolde Blackwicket talking." He shook his head, rueful.

"Why are you here?" I asked, exasperated, using my foot to shove the Galton's regalia closer to the magical fire.

"Can't a father just want to visit his little girl?"

"No. That wouldn't explain why you broke into my apartment to pack everything, or why you were at Galton's waiting for me. It's been ten years. I'm surprised you even remembered what I look like."

He glanced at me briefly.

"Couldn't forget that. You've got your mother's face."

He was dodging, trying to turn the conversation. But I couldn't stand around and play these pointless games. Neither the Authority nor the Brom would be satisfied when they found my apartment deserted. I made a sound of impatient disgust as I stalked to my belongings, fetching the pocketbook and closing the carpet bag's hinged frame with a snap.

"Good, you're ready," Darren said. "I'm surprised no one's

guessed where you are yet. I'll bring the food. You should eat. You're still a little pale."

He motioned vaguely around his face.

"You're not coming with me." I lifted the bags. "You've seen me. Now let's say our goodbyes for another ten years."

"Truth is." He stood, intercepting me at the door, "I've come to take you home."

Home.

I gave a harsh bark of laughter directly in his face.

"In a body bag? Because that's the only way anyone will ever get me back there."

"Eleanora."

My father's voice was heavy, filled with something terrible.

"Fiona's dead," he confessed softly.

Reality shifted, closing in to suffocate me before expanding, stretching into a vast, black nothing with me in the center. There was a ringing in my ears, growing louder, engulfing me in its high scream. Something moved in my periphery, the retreating head of a girl, blond curls bouncing, step light and carefree. She faded, becoming gloom, reappearing as her older self, tall and lean, already beautiful with a smile that invited love but received only pain. Ghostlike, she moved through me, and I turned to find we stood shoulder to shoulder at the entrance of that house. She was a young woman now, eighteen, quiet and sad, watching the retreating form of her sister as I left for good. The burdens of her life had already etched themselves on her features, making her even more striking. In the space of a heartbeat, my sister's phantom became the woman I'd seen a few short months ago, when she'd finally answered one of my letters and met me at a café on the outskirts of Devin, only to tell me to stop writing, to forget her, and to never come home.

Live your own life and let me live mine, Eleanora.

Her voice echoed in my ears as she closed the door, separating us forever.

Memories dissolved, leaving only misery behind.

"You're lying," I said, voice hollow.

"Not about this." Darren's eyes were misty with difficult emotions.

"How?"

"She went too far, Cricket. Got mixed up in stuff even I wouldn't touch."

It wasn't true. Not the timid girl, sweet as spun sugar and just as delicate, who flinched at thunder, and always spoke kindly to those most likely to spit on us in town or call the Authority to report magic use despite my mother's license.

"It's not their fault, Ellie," Fiona had whispered at night, both of us unable to sleep. "What we can do, most people forgot how to. It hurts them too much to remember."

Darren's sadness spilled onto his cheek, and he swiped at it, self-conscious.

"You have to come home, Eleanora," he said. "She wanted you to come home."

She *hadn't*. She'd wanted me to stay away.

"No," I replied, the words barely a mutter. "I won't."

He took my shaking hand. "Sweetheart, look at yourself. You're out of options."

CHAPTER FOUR

I stepped down the hallway, careful to avoid the floorboards I knew to be the most contrary. My mother and sister were asleep, and I wasn't supposed to be out of bed this late. My next footfall brought with it a stab of memory. No one was asleep. They were all gone.

I halted, a decade of memories converging. How had I gotten here? I barely remembered boarding the train.

A soft mewling sounded up the corridor from a door that poured firelight onto the faded runner. Someone was in the parlor, the place where all my warmest, most tender memories had been made, and where they'd all been so thoroughly corrupted. I wanted to stumble back to my room and confront these terrible feelings in the light of day, but a figure moved in the shadows, drawing my attention.

Fiona.

She was alive. It had all been a hideous lie.

I sucked in a breath and hurried toward where she paused at the parlor threshold, pale hand lighted on the doorframe, only daring a peek. She was so near, and I reached to touch the shining braid of her hair, a style she hadn't worn since we were young.

I didn't notice her turn, but suddenly she was facing me, snatching my wrist in her icy fingers, shushing. She tugged me forward and relinquished her spot close to the door so I could look inside. There were two people there, in the center of the room—a prone child and a crouching woman. By the soft curl of the chestnut hair, I knew the woman to be my mother, and the child…a scream stuck in my throat, strangling me, as the hallway breathed, writhing with invisible life. The boy's head lolled sideways, copper smoke billowing from his small nose and chapped mouth, his hazel eyes devoid of life. The woman scuttled around, resembling an animal guarding its kill, and I found it wasn't my mother. It was me.

Reeling back, I bumped into a weeping Fiona. Instead of tears, that same red vapor rose to halo her golden head, and a sound intoned, deep and doomed as metal creaking underwater.

"Dark Hall is open," she whispered, her mouth filled with ashes.

A slurry of tentacles surged from behind, overwhelming her. Her neck, clavicle, and shoulders snapped in sharp succession, echoing like gunshots as the Fiend of Dark Hall twisted her body into an impossible shape.

I jolted awake in the train car, the rumble of the tracks grounding me, and waited for my heartbeat to slow. Watery light streamed through the window, and I observed the passing landscape, the expansive fields, fallow and snowy, and the distant hills of bare trees. Here and there, a break in the woods revealed a stretch of water glinting beneath the apathetic winter sun. We were nearing Nightglass.

The door slid open, and Darren appeared, holding a paper-wrapped sandwich. I hadn't asked how he'd afforded a private car, because I'd been too grateful not to have to share this distressing trip with strangers. Sharing it with my father was bad enough.

"Feeling sick, Cricket?"

"Not looking forward to our destination."

"You're going for your sister. Lay her to rest, clean out the house. Then you can return to your"—he waved his free hand dismissively—"*normal* life. Here, I brought you food. You're looking like a revived corpse."

My stomach turned, the image of Fiona flashing, bright as lightning.

I didn't take the sandwich.

"Clean out the house?" I repeated, and he sighed, realizing I wasn't going to accept his offering.

"Yeah." He unwrapped the food. "Get rid of all the stuff your mother and sister left."

He was talking about the curses, the ones buried in the bones of Blackwicket House.

Once upon a time, they'd been deposited there to begin the slow, languid process of unweaving. Their rotted threads would be plucked away, then filtered through unadulterated magic until it remembered how to be itself again. Our home had boasted a Narthex, which mother had painstakingly built to connect us to the living power of the world beyond ours, where magic lingered. The proximity had kept the curses docile, but that Narthex had been closed, and magic was scarce these days. Most of what remained was damaged, and the small amount belonging to each of us by natural order, too insignificant.

Clearing the house of its burden required more than a single Curse Eater. Even two were woefully deficient. A familiar guilt nauseated me. I'd abandoned an impossible job on Fiona's shoulders all so I could escape the house, the shame, and myself.

"I'm not staying long enough for that," I replied.

"The house shouldn't be left the way it is. D'you know how dangerous that would be?"

"What do you know about it? *Any* of it?"

"Cricket, your mom and I weren't married, and sure, I was gone a lot, but we loved each other. She confided in me. I know how it works, how the place runs. I couldn't help, but..."

"*Wouldn't* help," I corrected. "You never wanted to and made sure you weren't ever around to be asked."

He crumpled the paper around his uneaten sandwich and tossed it onto the bench seat beside him, rubbing a hand across his face, angry.

"I can't change the past, Eleanora," he said.

"No," I replied, bitterly. "You can't."

An uncomfortable silence followed, and I focused on the world passing outside, the gentle rocking of the train, wondering how I could manage everything I needed to do and leave before the house sank its claws into me again. Another glimpse of the coast encouraged a memory of the cliffs overlooking a glorious sea.

There were many dangers in returning to Blackwicket House, but it was the tug in my heart, the unwelcome, undeniable yearning for home that disquieted me most.

We arrived at Nightglass Station at noon. The platform, long ago decorated with only a sagging bench and an empty planter, now featured an array of seating and bright lampposts, modest comforts for the hordes of tourists disembarking.

The scent of travel clung to the throng of bodies that jostled us, mingling with stale perfumes layered thickly over furs and expensive wool. I watched for a familiar face among the congregation, the piercing eyes that saw through my lies.

Emerging from the station proper, we followed the lively exodus to the main street. There had never been so many visitors during the bleakest season of the year. The bareness and cold were as inviting to most sensible people as an invitation to lie in a grave. I hugged my bag close. After living in bustling cities, the crowd shouldn't have bothered me, but my skin crawled, stomach knotted. The people felt unnatural here in this wintery port town.

Tired of showing patience for my hesitation, Darren took hold of my upper arm and began hauling me toward the road, raising his hand and whistling at a black cab that had pulled to the curb, eager for a fare. The man who emerged was stocky and grim, his driver's cap positioned low over a heavy brow. This line of work fit him strangely, his shape and demeanor better suited for the docks that had once groaned under the weight of imported textiles and goods imbued with magic from all corners of the globe.

"Where to?" he grouched, turning to me to retrieve my bags, which I handed to him with reluctance. I'd have preferred to keep them in my lap, but drawing attention to my attachment to them wasn't worth the risk.

I prepared to give him directions to a street at the edge of town, where the road forked and led travelers to either the rocky coastline or up the tree-lined hills to the crag where an old estate towered, haunting the town. If I told him where we were going, he'd refuse.

"Blackwicket House," Darren declared, extending a fold of bills, more than needed for a trip to the opposite end of town.

The driver's ruddy features contorted with distrust as he pushed the monetary offering away with two fingers, as if it were contaminated.

"Ain't a soul going to take you up there. Enjoy your walk."

"Please," I said, taking a small step forward to waylay his departure.

He fixed his stormy grey gaze on me, ready to snarl, but instead, he released a gruff breath, lifted his chin, and studied me. His attention idled on the metropolitan hairstyle popular in Devin, brunette locks pinned from my temple, brushed into a series of well-tamed waves at the nape of my neck. I wasn't dressed in finery, but I was a woman from the city, that must have been acceptable.

"I'll take you to the corner block," he conceded. Darren offered him the money again. He eyed it with disdain. "No charge."

"That's kind of you," I said, receiving a grunt in response.

I spared a frustrated glance at my father, and he returned his own.

"You're always willing to take the least you can get," he grumbled, opening the car door for me.

"And you're always after the most," I replied, climbing inside.

"Someday, I hope you'll put your hatred of me aside. We're all we have left."

I set my attention straight ahead.

"Then neither of us has very much."

My father remained quiet as we crept along the first few blocks, pedestrians slowing our progress. I felt him next to me like a hope you're too afraid to embrace, one that's slipped from your fingers so many times you become wise and stop grasping for it. But I was myself, forever trying once more, damn me.

"Nightglass seems to be doing well," I said.

"Better than well," Darren replied readily. "Grigori did a number on this place the past few years. Made it a real appealing spot for people with plenty of free time and too much money. New hotels."

He pointed through my window at the *Orville*, formerly a well-kept, but modest block of apartments for dock workers. It had been joined in a marriage of extravagance, exhibiting both a large glass entryway and a doorman.

"There's a top-notch lounge here, too, great entertainment and food isn't bad either. Honestly, it's a little too hoity-toity for me."

A woman laughed, high and loud, as we passed the town crossroads where the village green had been, peaceful and rarely disturbed. Presently, at each of the four corners, a bustle of well-dressed people filled the streets, which were lined with restaurants and lounges where grocers and chandlers had until now held pride of place. I browsed the recent additions as we made our slow way down the avenue—milliners, tailors, beauty salons, luxury stationers, and a prominent lounge, its arched marquee glittering with blinking lights.

THE VAPORS

In my absence, Nightglass had flourished, and the transformation was both troubling and captivating. I compared the evolution of the town to the stagnant life I'd been leading, plagued by ghosts of my own making, and experienced an uncomfortable bite of envy. The car moved from the center of town, and down familiar side streets, I was likely still capable of navigating in total darkness, where new luxury row houses, with their tidy front gardens and stylish balconies, gave way to older cottages, many reconstructed and unrecognizable. As we approached our destination, the driver slowed, perhaps worried the estate would sneak up on him, or just as likely because the cobbled street yielded to crushed stone. I found that the quaint timber houses that had once lined this road had been demolished, creating a stark chasm between the town and its most detested family: mine.

The hired car came to a stop at the wrought iron carriage gate, chained closed, its red brick faded and overgrown with bare wisteria vines.

"This is where I leave you," the driver proclaimed.

"You're not serious," Darren argued. "That's a half-mile walk, and it's the middle of blasted winter. Just drive us up the hill to the front."

"No one who knows what's good for them goes near that

house," the driver said sternly. "I'd warn you yourselves not to go, but I recognize those eyes."

He glanced at me in the rearview mirror, and our gazes touched. Held.

"Blackwickets always come home."

He climbed into the cold and retrieved my bags from the trunk, and even went as far as to set them by the porter's gate, which was unlocked and partially ajar.

As he returned to the cab, he hesitated, muttering, "It's a shame about Fiona. We all thought she was a good sort."

This man had known my sister. Curious, I tested the air between us, seeking signs of the telltale buzz, the sensations of chaotic electricity, of magic gone wrong.

"I'll ask you not to do that, miss," he barked, and I snatched my senses back, startled and embarrassed. The sensation accompanying someone searching for strings of magic was subtle and difficult to detect without considerable practice, yet this cab driver sensed me before I'd even gotten close.

"I'm sorry," I managed.

He shoved a finger in my direction. "Don't go poking where you haven't been invited. It'll land you in more trouble than you can handle."

"I didn't catch your name," I said, the pitch of my voice false with friendliness.

"And you won't," he replied, gruff. "I mind my business, now you mind yours."

He climbed behind the wheel, and the engine roared to life. Though he didn't speed as if the hounds of hell were on his heels, his haste was evident by the way the car bounced too heavily over the deep divots in the broken stone.

Darren hoisted a bag off the dormant grass.

"Making friends already. That's my girl."

I watched the car disappear down the road, the whetted

point of anxiety threatening to slit the barrier that protected me from my most raw, unpleasant emotions. I retrieved the remaining bag and approached my fate, peering through brown ivy and wrought iron bars to the cliffside, where the house's daunting silhouette loomed. Darren remained at a distance, silent, allowing me privacy as I was swallowed by the gravity of what awaited me on the other side.

With great resignation, I pushed open the porter's gate.

CHAPTER FIVE

Blackwicket House was anything but demure. It stood resolutely on a square foundation, three stories high, crowned with sloped mansard roofs and gray stone chimneys that reminded me of horns. A covered porch spanned the length of the house, once conveying welcome, but the elements had rendered its railings and carved arches splintered, baring sharp edges to visitors. Ornately trimmed windows, set beneath slate gray dormers, glared at us as we approached, their murky panes filled with judgment, and at the heart of it all rose a central tower, dark and forlorn as a forsaken lighthouse the world had forgotten it needed.

The trek was dismal, spent battling blasts of frosty wind cresting the cliffside and sweeping across the dormant meadowland, crashing into us as ferociously as waves seeking sailors to savage against rocks. Every step invited my history to fold me in an embrace I'd shunned, and the baleful energy of Blackwicket House grew stronger, vibrating in the marrow of my bones. It urged magic users to draw closer, to give a little, or even all of themselves, for the promise of nothing in return.

I ascended the porch, my gaze steady on the weathered oak door, its curved transom inlaid with green and blue lead glass. Hanging in this window was a sign, once reading:

REST YOUR BURDENS HERE AND LEAVE FREE

Worn by salt air, neglect, and undoubtedly some creative vandalism, it now read only:

BURDENS HERE ... LEAVE

This edition rang truer.

I had no business being here, but where else could I go? I was destitute, friendless, and a wanted criminal who'd lost the last real thing she'd ever loved.

Fiona.

Grief replaced my anxiety, and I braced myself, unwilling to indulge in a breakdown in front of my father.

"It's a shame how far this old lady's fallen," he sighed.

"It looks worse than I've ever seen it."

"Fiona struggled the past couple of years."

Guilt coiled tight around my lungs, shaming me for my absence.

"I used to come up here to flirt with your mom between dock shifts," Darren continued, surprisingly sentimental. "Granny Fora liked to chase me off with a fire poker. Got me solid in the shoulder."

He rubbed said shoulder for emphasis, grinning. "Didn't stop me, though."

I regarded my father, attempting to see a man worthy of Isolde Blackwicket's attention. But all I discerned was an aging black-market crook who couldn't accept the love given to him or offer any in return. My grandmother, who'd died before fifty and left her daughter to fend for herself in a world growing ever more cruel, had sensed this aspect in him and reacted accordingly.

"I'm sure you didn't deserve it," I replied.

Grasping the front door's brass handle, worn shiny by a

thousand hands, I waited for the telltale thrum of energy, the rush of greeting, but it remained a lifeless piece of metal. I tried it. Locked.

"The key," I said.

"Oh, uh." Darren rummaged in his pocket. "I don't think there is one."

"Then why are you looking for it?"

"Nervous. This place, you know, it…"

A surge of static jumped from the handle, raising the hairs on my arm, followed by the sound of a bolt retreating. The heavy wood door swung inward a few inches, hinges singing. The house remembered the girl who'd turned her back on it after all.

"Does that," Darren finished with an uncomfortable chuckle, sticking his hands deep into his coat pockets.

"The latch wasn't set," I said, the lie unnecessary, as my father was acquainted with Blackwicket House and its machinations, but some habits were too deeply ingrained.

As I entered the foyer, I was greeted by the familiar fragrance of aged cedar and salty damp. Here, guests would have been welcomed by a sightline that drew the eye along a lushly carpeted front hall to the grand window overlooking the cliffs, offering a sense of being suspended in the air. But the brocade draperies were closed, blocking the light, shrouding the hallway in forbidding shadows. Another step produced the creak of a loose board, one I'd pressed repeatedly as a child just to hear the varying notes of its protest until my mother's stern, affectionate voice called

Eleanora, please. Even the dead can't rest!

The ghost of her voice echoed in my ear, and despite myself, I leaned my weight back to make the board squeak again, but it was silent, giving me no more welcome.

This and many other rooms besides had once brimmed with plants, flowers of all kinds, spilling from pots and hangers, the verdant green of it livening a space often wreathed in darkness. Our mother had taught us to nurture them with the lightest touch of magic. It had been her quiet mission to secretly sharpen our senses without exposing our abilities. Organic magic was rare, and the people capable of calling upon it rarer, encouraging the eyes of greed to fall on natural users, no single villain more troubling than Grigori Nightglass. His strange, clinical fascination with Curse Eaters made mother fear he'd discover Fiona and I were gifted.

These plants were gone as well, and in their place, pulpy water scars remained, boards stripped of their stain. The proud formal stairwell, its hand carved banister still stubbornly beautiful, rose to my left, tufted runners removed, steps worn with the nicks and scrapes of use. My gaze slipped next to the wide mahogany counter where arriving guests would have checked in, back when the inn was still well-loved and full.

As nostalgia softened my heart to it, I finally felt the pulse of Blackwicket House. It encouraged the terrible adoration I'd never fully rid myself of, the sort that had accompanied me into every new city, on every train, in every car, tethering me to my bleak heritage. Overwhelmed, I turned to my father for support, hoping to rest my head against the cool collar of his jacket, to be held by someone who'd known me my entire life, who understood what this meant. But he hadn't come inside.

He stood on the porch, gazing in, wary.

"You're not coming?" I hated the way my voice clogged in my nose.

"Aw, Cricket." He hesitated. "I can't."

I dropped my bag onto the floor and stormed back to yank the other from his grip.

"You've never been needed before," I said, re-entering the foyer. "This isn't any different."

Damn the tear that slid down my cheek.

"Eleanora."

I attempted to shove the door closed, but my father slapped his palm against it.

"Wait, wait, you need to know something." He pushed, and I relented enough to see his earnest expression.

"What?" I spat.

"Fiona's funeral is in two days. At the Nightglass estate."

The mention of my sister's funeral landed like a punch. For a moment, my anger had made me forget.

"No," I responded.

"What d'you mean no?"

"Her funeral won't be at the Nightglass estate. She hated that place. I'm here, so I'll take over the arrangements."

"But it's already done."

"You can't make those decisions. You're not even on her goddamn birth certificate. As her last legal living relative, it's my responsibility. The funeral will be here. She'll be buried in the family plot."

"Eleanora, find some sense, nobody will come to this house anymore. The kids in town recite rhymes about it, for fuck's sake."

"Then I'll bury her myself."

"That's just plain stupid, Cricket."

He was right, but heartache enhanced my stubbornness.

"Appreciate it as proof that I inherited at least one of your qualities, Darren."

I drove my shoulder into the door, the sudden force giving my father no chance to react. He'd never dare knock, let alone barge in, but I turned the bolt anyway, just to underscore my hurt. It secured itself with well-oiled ease. Fiona must have locked it often.

My eyes burned, tears threatening to start and never stop. I knew if I didn't address my grief soon, it would harden and become something worse, but I needed a bit more time.

I raised my eyes to the high coffered ceiling two stories overhead, where the seven-bracket brass chandelier still hung, its arms adorned with lacy cobwebs. Many of my winter days had been spent lying in the warm pool of sunlight that streamed from the high window, tracing the curves and coils of the fixture, pretending to stroke the fern-shaped fronds of the medallion with my fingertips.

"Hello," I whispered, and the house creaked, releasing a long-awaited breath.

"I'm not staying," I added, wanting to make sure it understood that I wasn't its salvation, that it couldn't depend on me.

There was a shudder in my soul as everything fell silent, a deep, fathomless noise. My ears ached from the pressure of it.

Leaving my bags on the parquet floor, I moved to the old front desk, running a touch over the top where the edges of gold filigree had faded. Here were the memories of early years, of a pair of little girls sitting on high stools, drawing pictures, and welcoming the rare visitors with bright smiles meant to lift spirits, already aware of what was being brought to leave behind in our mother's care.

Next to a wall of slats for letters and correspondence was the small square board for keys. Blackwicket House boasted twelve rooms, ten designated for guests and two for family. All the keys were present, still hanging on their hooks. The back wall beyond this was bare, grass cloth wallpaper faded, gold vines and emerald leaves dusty and sun-bleached, evoking fairytales from my youth, however dim. I'd occasionally broken the rules and used magic to bring the metallic threads to life, stirring them in a bewitched breeze, winding them through one another until they formed silhouettes of castle turrets and forest cottages. Fiona had never caused mischief, but loved it when I did, and though such magical larks were kept small, lest the Drudge grow too curious, they were cherished moments.

Moments now turned to thorns in my heart.

A heaviness descended around my shoulders, eager to crush me beneath the weight of loss. To battle it, I decided to take stock of the damage a decade of neglect had done, to gather the stories of Fiona's struggles and what she endured to be driven to do the things my father accused her of.

I couldn't face the first floor. Not yet. So, I climbed the stairs, my footsteps falling louder than they used to. The paneling from downstairs continued, the yellowing cornices following the slope of the ceiling. I came to the hushed landing of the second floor, knowing it was illogical to begin here. I needed to go where Fiona had most likely spent her hours: the family wing. The stillness I found atop the last flight was eerie and uncommon. There was no natural light besides the watery sun shining through diamond windowpanes at either end of the hall. To combat this dreariness, the walls had been lined with sconces, their white globes resembling a parade of full moons guiding a weary traveler. I flipped a switch. There was a buzz and a pop, the lights coming on in slow succession, as if struggling to remember their function. Finally, they found their footing, and the hall grew luminous with the insincere glow of artificial light.

Energy anomalies were not unusual, not with what lived here, but the audible buzzing served as a sign that the issue was mundane, not magical. I could ignore it. Let the house catch fire with faulty wiring. Let it burn.

Ten years ago, a mere three rooms in Blackwicket House were livable, and even those barely so. The walls and ceilings had become wrecked with mildew from cracked windows and the poor state of the roof, which let in rain. The linens and rugs had soured and browned with water, paper peeling, windowsills becoming soft with rot. Isolde Blackwicket had closed each door, never to open them again.

Delaying a confrontation with these rooms, I wandered to the tower door, tucked away in a small alcove, goldenrod paper wrinkled with damp. I imagined the stairwell had completely caved in. I reached for the doorknob, but it was locked. The keys. They were downstairs. Aggravated at the thought of the journey up being in vain, I cursed under my breath, then quieted as an instinctive urge tingled at the base of my neck. I withdrew my hand until only fingertips remained, searching for the fluttering hum of life. There it was, soft as a sleeping breath. I could open the door without a key, just this time, but as I dipped into my neglected magic, searching for a connection, the humming swelled, transforming into a piercing electric scream. The globe of light nearest me exploded, glass scattering in all directions. I guarded my face, ducking away with a startled cry.

Sparks convulsed and the fixture crackled thrice before dying out even as the other bulbs brightened, leaving me squinting. I choked on the scent of scorched metal and something else I couldn't place, nauseatingly oversweet, until the chaos calmed, lights dimming. Shards fell from my sleeves as I lowered my hands and began my race down the stairs, planning to collect the little money I had and leave everything else behind before I was forced to brave anymore of this bullying. But as I tripped towards the bottom step, barely catching myself on the banister, my strategy was derailed by something unexpected—the dominating figure of a man I knew all too well, waiting for me in the foyer.

CHAPTER SIX

He towered over the check-in counter, melted snow dappling the shoulders of his earth-brown overcoat, which he'd unbuttoned, signaling he'd been inside for some time. His hands were tucked in the pockets of his well-tailored wool trousers, casual as a commuter waiting for a train. I'd only ever seen his coal-black hair styled in a precise, sleek wave at his temple, the fashion as buttoned up and controlled as the rest of him, but the sea gale had abused it, curling the ends around his ears. The effect did nothing to soften his features, serving instead to draw attention to his stern brow and the aquiline arch of his nose, unarguably broken, perhaps on multiple occasions. More than these aspects, it was the violent scar that drew my eye, a testament to his infamous line of work. It ran from the apex of one high, tawny cheek to interrupt the severe line of his jaw, skipping the jugular only to begin again an inch above his shirt collar. The wound had likely been deep, magically cauterized by a hasty hand, leaving the skin puckered and shining, blanched of all color.

He'd been considering my abandoned bags when I'd come nearly crashing down and raised his eyes to me, dark as his history of tormenting magic users in the name of order.

"Inspector Harrow." The words emerged strangled.

"Ms. Knoles," the Inspector said, drawing the name out in his gravely baritone. He made a small show of wincing, "Oh, that's right. It isn't Knoles, is it?"

My foot rose to retreat up the steps.

"If you run," he cautioned softly, as though speaking in a sacred place, or perhaps a damned one, where evil is easily disturbed, "I'll chase you. If you fight, well, you're a delicate-looking thing, but I'm plenty aware you pack a nasty punch, so I'll take no chances."

He shifted his coat aside with a flick, revealing the grip of a revolver holstered at his hip. But it was an empty threat. This man possessed the power to do far worse than shoot me. Inspectors like Harrow were trained in Annulment, the merciless act of severing the natural magic from a body. Unlike Curse Eating, which carried the risk of tearing away fragments of the soul along with diseased magic, Annulment was the deliberate removal of a facet of humanity impossible to survive without.

"How did you get in?"

He glanced at the door. From this angle, the scar was in full view. When we'd first met over an interrogation table, he'd caught me noticing it.

"Brom." He'd tapped it. "I wasn't lucky enough to be dealing with an adept like yourself, Ms. Knoles. The fool didn't know how to use the magic he'd stolen, so he pulled a weapon. It was undoubtedly less painful than what you did to Mr. Mofton."

"Brock was my friend."

"Liar liar," he'd murmured, fixing me with his icy gaze, piercing and fathomless with hatred.

"Door was open," he said, amusement in his voice, though there was no smile on his broad mouth.

I'd bolted that door. Even if I hadn't, the house was experienced with thwarting attempts at lock-picking, which meant it had invited him in, the worst person it could have welcomed outside of Grigori Nightglass himself. There was no longer any question about where I stood in its favor. His presence was punishment.

"I figured you'd be scurrying out of Devin. Went to your flat and found it ransacked and thought someone else got to you first, but then a tip comes in: Darren Rose is in Oldtown at some rattrap with a cagey, bloodless looking dame."

Somehow, I still found the gal to be offended by the fact the Authority assumed the woman to be me before being outraged that my father hadn't disclosed he was on their radar. Admitting to being blood-related to Darren wasn't an excellent card to have in my hand, but other implications were worse.

"Darren's my father."

His right brow twitched upward.

"I haven't talked to him in ten years."

"That long? How lucky he shows up to help you in your hour of need."

I had no rebuttal. The timing of Darren's arrival following my foolish decision at the department store was too unbelievable. The Inspector would never accept it as a coincidence.

"Oh," he added as an afterthought, "You might be interested to know that the woman, Ms. Rosley, didn't survive the stunt you pulled at Galtons."

A shock of regret jarred me. All of this, and I hadn't even been able to help her.

"I was trying to save her life," I said, gritty and uneven.

"An interesting way to go about it."

Scorn handed me back my spine. I released my white-knuckled hold on the banister and took the last step down to prove I didn't always run, that I was capable of standing and taking ground when necessary.

"Let me make something clear, *Inspector*. What happened at Galton's was the result of someone else's wrongdoing, not mine. Whatever Ms. Rosley was involved in had nothing to do with me."

The Inspector rose to my meager challenge and took a few relaxed steps forward, bringing us ever closer. My pulse jumped and I considered what he might do to me now that we were no longer in Devin, divided by a metal table, with no other Authority to observe or inhibit him. The most effective weapon at my disposal was angry with me, and I wasn't sure if the house would come to my aid if called. He drew close enough that I was forced to raise my chin to maintain eye contact, and the pride keeping me from opening to the house bowed.

"I think it has *everything* to do with you, Eleanora Blackwicket." He raised a hand toward me, and in a flash of blind panic, I dropped my defenses to let Blackwicket House in. But no response came, no flood of cursed magic, no rippling of the fabric of the shadows. Only static, empty, nothing.

The Inspector's fingers brushed along a wayward curl at my forehead, and when he withdrew, he held a shard of frosted glass, curved and sharp as a sickle. I'd forfeited my self-respect for nothing, but at the very least, I'd maintained physical composure, denying the Inspector the satisfaction of knowing he'd frightened me.

"I didn't murder Ms. Rosley." I was proud of my even tone.

"No," he said, looking at me as if he thought that was a shame. At last, he gave a regretful shake of his head and turned away, examining the sliver as he went, a piece of a puzzle he couldn't place. "The curse you so charitably removed caused Kate Rosley's death. You stealing it is a separate crime, but I won't jump to any conclusions until I learn a bit more about you and your unusual family. I especially have questions regarding your sister, Fiona."

Here it was—the moment when the consequences of the lives we'd lived, the secrets we'd wrapped ourselves in, all the wretched, dreadful mistakes, were finally coming to call. The Authority knew about Darren, Fiona, me, and if I didn't tread carefully, there'd be no stopping them from discovering the scar of the Narthex etched in the wall of the parlor.

"My sister is dead, Inspector. That's why my father was there, to fetch me and bring me home for her burial."

"I heard." Sympathy fit in his mouth too poorly to be sincere. "My condolences. Was she involved in anything untoward, Ms. Blackwicket? Something that might have had a hand in her untimely end?"

"Like my father, Inspector, I haven't spoken to Fiona in a decade. I have no insights into her life."

"But that's not true." He set the shard on the desktop next to the guest book, arranging it like he expected future visitors to prick their fingers and sign their names in blood. "She met you in Devin several weeks ago at that tedious new cafe near the University district."

He'd been tailing me, haunting me for weeks after my arrest.

"You had no right to follow me." My voice rose despite my efforts to remain placid. "I was absolved of all wrongdoing in that case."

"You *were*," he conceded, "An oversight on the Bureau's part, but in any event, they don't let potential Curse Eaters back on the streets without monitoring them, acquitted of murder or not. Plus, I had a feeling. You didn't quite fit the bill for a displaced country girl, far from home, a victim of circumstance. And the curse that got Brock Mofton?"

He offered a low whistle.

"All I want to do is bury Fiona. She deserves that. Then I'll leave and you can stop wasting your valuable resources attempting to soothe your bruised ego."

This encouraged a tight smile.

"I didn't just track you out here for a good time, Ms. Blackwicket. I was assigned by the Authority to this backwater hole to investigate several disappearances, all involving some powerful, well-connected families. We have reason to believe your Fiona was involved in these cases and perhaps taking part in a few more unsavory things besides."

"What reason?" I demanded, hoping I sounded like a woman outraged by the accusation rather than one who feared it could be true.

"I'm sure it's all a misunderstanding, and we can clear her name." He evaded the question, his placating tone rankling me, then scratched his cheek and feigned contrition. "That reminds me. I'll be staying in town a while, and the recommended hotels are a little too crowded for my tastes. So, I'll thank you for renting me a bed for the time being."

Laughing in his face seemed like an unsafe route, so I refrained.

"You can't stay here. This isn't a functioning inn. it hasn't been for years."

"Your sister would have disagreed," he replied, watching for my reaction. He knew something I didn't, and so did Darren. Fiona's secrets belonged to everyone but me. "Don't bother yourself with the details, I've already chosen my room."

He held up his hand, clasping in his previously empty palm a set of keys taken from the cabinet. I spared a look at the board. The key missing belonged to the room near the top of the third-floor stairs. Animosity spread through my limbs, dampening the heartache and fear that had been keeping me off balance. My cheeks grew hot with the impotent rage bounding behind my ribs, nowhere to be safely expressed, doomed to feed the scraps of the Drudge I hadn't yet dislodged. Said creature twisted, its maw opening to swallow my fury. If the Inspector was so eager to stay, to stick his hand in corners where vicious things were hiding, I'd allow it. Blackwicket House wasn't inclined to protect me, but it would most certainly protect itself, and, like Brock Mofton, I'd be happy to see curses do their work on the Inspector.

"This is an opportunity, Ms. Blackwicket. Two people with a history like ours," Inspector Harrow motioned between us, indicating a connection, "are owed a second chance to get it right. We have another opportunity to get better acquainted because, as it turns out, I don't know you at all. I look forward to remedying that."

Another man might have accompanied these remarks with a gamey wink, but even this was too human a thing for Inspector Harrow, whose countenance remained dispassionate.

"I already know everything I can stomach about you," I said, venting my anger.

"Hm," was his dismissive response as he tucked the room key into his pocket and began buttoning his overcoat. "I have some business to see to before I beg further hospitality, but I'll ask you to refrain from padlocking the main gate, it was a bitch to get open."

"I wasn't expecting company," I snapped.

"An honest mistake. You make a lot of those, don't you?"

"Inspector…"

He was already leaving. As he gripped the door handle, the house made its first move since I'd been upstairs. It shuddered. Inspector Harrow paused, turning his head a fraction, eyes lowered, listening.

My breath stuck in my throat. I could accuse the wind, the shifting of the old frame on an even older foundation, harassed by the weather, but any word from of my mouth about it would only draw further attention. I turned to distraction.

"Don't expect me to feed or clean up after you, Inspector. You're here against my wishes, and I'm not an innkeeper."

"You're not," he agreed, opening the door, allowing in a rush of winter air that cooled my hot skin. He yielded the ghost of a smile, smug. "You're a Curse Eater."

I watched through the white muslin curtains as Inspector Harrow entered his sleek, long-bodied car, the ivory white of natural pearl. Chrome flashed on the fender as he circled the drive. It was a far cry from the utilitarian unit that picked me up in Devin, and I wondered how an Inspector afforded such a luxury. Cruelty must pay well. I stood there as he drove through the distant gate, despising him every second.

I was trapped here, caught like a fly in the jaws of a languorous sundew. There was nowhere I could go short of swimming across the sea to escape the Authority's attention now that they'd linked my face to a name that interested them. My life was in shambles and my heart present merely to remind me it hurt. I touched the windowsill but didn't lower my defenses again.

"You've really done it," I muttered to the house, to myself, to the spirit of my dead sister whose body was waiting in a morgue, a body I'd have to identify. I floated the argument that viewing Fiona's remains wasn't necessary—both my father and the Authority had corroborated her passing.

However, a nagging suspicion remained. There was something I wasn't being told, some vital information being withheld for the benefit of everyone but Fiona. I pressed my knuckles against my eyes until bursts of white light exploded behind my lids, then grabbed my coat. The house didn't resist my departure, but walking over the threshold wasn't as easy as I'd imagined. Leaving Blackwicket House always came with the sensation of pressing through a bubble, abandoning the comfort of familiar dangers to confront a world filled with people I couldn't predict, who often surprised me with their capacity for both spontaneous kindness and animosity.

I glanced back toward the gloomy memories of my childhood, then along the arching drive that gave way to the gardens, once my mother's point of pride, wishing wishes that were far too late to make.

CHAPTER SEVEN

T he cold made white veils of my breath as I meandered to the gate, keeping watch for the gleam of a returning car. Although late afternoon, the sun was already setting, winter urging it to an early rest and darkening the snow-filled sky. I made my way along the overgrown sideroad, shivering in my city coat, insufficient against the oppressive wind of the coast. Wooded shoulders gave way to the open tumble of earth leading to the shoreline, and I paused, taking in the vista. White waves crashed around crumbling docks and along the stretch of pebbled beach that would tempt tourists come summer. My fingers tingled with the cold. I'd forgotten my gloves.

I turned toward town, apprehensive. Even from here, I could see the lights, hear the seething streets. What had these people come for in this frozen wasteland of skeletal hills, cold water, and gray sky? Nightglass offered nothing in this desolate season. Even the prospect of a few upscale restaurants and novelty lounges would fade in the face of harsh snows already threatening to roll in. The closest city was an hour's train ride away, far more palatable, providing pampered warmth and a myriad of better entertainments to make the gnawing of winter bearable.

I followed the path from the outskirts to the cobbled road that led to the center of town. I expected at least a few people coming and going from the houses here, but the doors were shut tight, the curtains drawn in every window, eerily quiet compared to the bustling avenue ahead, where lively people flowed like water bursting from a dam.

I emerged onto the main thoroughfare, no shortage of visitors milling around the sidewalks, wrapped in their expensive overcoats, hands tucked in suede gloves, shoes gleaming with a fresh shine; the women were the prizes on men's arms in their silk, crepe, and fur. They each walked as though every eye was on them, but in truth, no one was paying attention to anyone but themselves.

Still, I worried my sober brown coat and plain tweed skirt suit made me conspicuous, and though I'd applied red to my cheeks and lips, I wasn't made up enough to blend in with this society. I raised my chin and focused my eyes ahead as I neared the crossing that would take me through the four-lane street toward the marquee-lit entrance of the Vapors. The road was congested with automobiles, all varying degrees of luxury, and even the taxis gleamed, black as summer beetles.

A small crowd waited for the traffic official to allow them across, and I joined them, feeling claustrophobic. The aura and odor surrounding me was putrid as a spoiled rag drenched in perfumed oil: pungent, botanic, and lingering. This wasn't the natural scent of human bodies, but the psychic reek of magic gone wrong. I couldn't pinpoint its exact origin and was too cautious to lower my guard and investigate. I repeated to myself in a slow, grounding rhythm: *This town is not mine.*

The traffic whistle blew, sharp and long, and I allowed the crowd to surge head, straggling back in search of fresher air.

A slender man in an unfussy black cap and twill work jacket approached from the opposite direction. Despite the ample space, he walked close, either too distracted to notice me in his way or too indifferent to care. I attempted to sidestep, but wasn't quick enough, and our shoulders collided.

The discomfort of the impact wasn't what halted me in my tracks or made me turn my head to glare into the eyes of the stranger. It was the tug of invisible, searching hands seeking signs of corruption to pull free.

"Get off," I commanded, employing the same tone I'd once used with a fellow who'd become overly familiar with the hem of my skirt on a city streetcar.

If the stranger was surprised, it didn't register beyond the slight narrowing of his eyes.

"Sorry, miss. Didn't realize." Grinning, he tipped his hat and continued on his way as if he hadn't just tried to psychically assault me.

I watched him go, brow furrowed, until a car honked. I was still standing in the road.

"Move on!" the traffic officer shouted, and I completed crossing, regretting what I'd done to the cab driver. Though my intentions hadn't been nefarious, the invasion was the same.

I proceeded more carefully, wary of brushing too close to anyone, and when I reached the walkway, I exited the persistent flow of people to get my bearings, pretending to pause and admire the display window of a men's hat shop. As I stood there, stalling, a car pulled up to the nearby curb, splashing slush onto the walkway and feet of those unfortunate enough to be standing nearby. Several cries of dismay rose, quieting again as the door opened and a woman emerged from the passenger side. Apologies were uttered, and foot traffic halted, creating a clear lane to the ornate golden doors of the lounge. They swung wide and welcoming, pouring forth warm light and the sweet scent of jasmine. While working at Galton's, I'd grown accustomed to the fine costuming of the wealthy but was never immune to the sight of someone truly stunning.

The woman wore a coat as white as a fawn's underbelly, her short hair styled in finger waves, two curls meticulously placed at her temple near the elegant arch of her brows. Accentuated with powder and rouge, her umber skin sparkled like a diamond under a spotlight, smooth as glass. The pillow of her lips were brushed with a generous coat of carmine, but her eyelids were bare of all makeup save for a dark, bold line along her lashes.

Aside from her elegance, it was the nimbus of hypnotic power she radiated that entranced the hovering crowd. This woman was magic, the way people were before fear and gluttony had driven it away. Displays of this kind of ability got people killed, but she wore it like a fine stole. Onlookers leaned in her direction, shuffling their feet to inch closer without breaching the halo of her light, aware that doing so would invite a swift correction from the man who'd emerged from the driver's side to stand as a sentry beside her. It was the cab driver who'd brought me to the gate of Blackwicket House only a few short hours ago.

Although the boundary held firm, the crowd of spectators compressed, those at the back nudging others ahead in their eagerness for a better view.

"Ms. James! Ms. James!" they cried, vying for her attention. I moved closer to the display glass, shrinking myself, preparing to slip away. I spared a last glance, obscured as a man stepped in front of me, then moved on swiftly as he found an empty pocket ahead. As he shifted out of my way, I found myself caught in the steady, hard stare of the glamorous creature, her dark eyes locked on mine with clear hostility. The driver had been leaning in, whispering something only she could hear, and at length, turned his attention to me as well.

He'd told this woman who I was.

Disbelief furrowed my brows, and I ceased lingering on the walk, setting on my way with greater haste. If I could be sure of one thing, if I'd ever belonged here, I didn't now.

There was something wrong in Nightglass, something

unfamiliar and crooked. I yearned for my sister, wishing I could ask her about all that had happened to alter this town, turning it into a strange world that barely mimicked the home I'd once known, making it as foreign to me as the moon.

The crowd thinned the farther I ventured, and when I turned down the street along the western edge of the Nightglass estate, I became the only pedestrian. I paused at the corner, contemplating the town jewel in its muted winter colors: white stone and brown gardens dusted with snow, dormant for the season. These lawns extended to the rear of the house, where the banquet room was visible, its many windows reflecting the last rays of daylight. Gray smoke billowed from the chimneys high above, and below, a bevy of stone balustrades and terraces, vines clinging like spiderwebs, bare of their greenery. Although my view was limited, I noticed movement inside the glass-encased hall, the warm illumination of lights. It was no business of mine what went on in that house, wrapped in its veneer of virtue, and I turned away.

The estate cast a shadow over this street, making the temperature nearly unbearable. As I pulled the collar of my coat close to my cheeks, I continued down a lane lined with neglected municipal buildings overlooked during the town's renovation: a modest city hall and post office, along with a small library wedged between them as a mere afterthought, deserted. Past a narrow alley, partially obscured by the crooked trunk of an oak tree planted to create a sense of separation from sorrows, stood the Nightglass morgue.

I opened the modest door marked with simple gold lettering: "Farvem Funeral Home." It seemed Mr. Farvem, the undertaker, still owned the place. I recalled little of him, except that he had a grandson who'd thrown dirt in my eyes and called me a whore when I was eleven. My instincts urged me to flinch away, but I stepped resolutely inside, enveloped by dim light and dark wood paneling. A bell chimed, but the thick carpeting dampened the sound, leaving nothing but a faint echo of its ring in my ears. The stillness was absolute, and in it, I was free to imagine the cries of children, mothers, lovers, and friends seeping from walls that had so dutifully collected them. My vision narrowed, heartbeat hammering as though driving nails into a coffin.

"Ma'am? Are you alright?"

In the midst of my turmoil, an elderly man had materialized out of nowhere, or perhaps he'd been there all along and my panic had made me blind to him. He was sturdy, with a low center of gravity, standing barely an inch taller than I. There was a swath of thick silver hair at his temple, hardly thinning, and his face, softened by years and the wisdom his profession afforded him, was kindly, watery green eyes keen.

"Mr. Farvem?" I asked weakly, taken aback by how well the undertaker appeared for a man who must be in his ninth decade. A pointless thought penetrated my mental fog, helping ground me: perhaps I'd misremembered him to be older than he was, my child mind viewing adulthood as one long stretch of old age.

"You're pale, and I'm worried you're going to take a tumble. Please, have a seat." He motioned to an overstuffed armchair. Repulsion rose, strange and immediate, and I took a step away from it. The spongy cushions looked too ready to welcome grievers, too eager for them to sink deep in their misery. To distract myself from feeling woozy, I considered making a joke about how my pallid complexion was entirely natural, but my voice found a sticking place where tears gathered in my throat. Still, the shift in thoughts did the trick, and the gray haze of panic lifted its hand an inch. Fainting in the front hall of this funeral parlor wouldn't do me any favors.

"I've come…" The words finally formed, though they were

tattered at the edges, and I was forced to clear my throat. The genuine sympathy in Mr. Tarvem's expression was making this difficult. "I've come to change arrangements for my sister."

"Change arrangements?"

"Yes. I'm her only living family. Some decisions were made regarding her burial that would grieve her. I want to amend them."

The undertaker nodded, understanding, prepared to do whatever was needed for those left behind by the dead in his care.

"I'll do everything in my power to make sure your sister is laid to rest in a manner appropriate to the wishes of her family, but I apologize, I'm afraid I don't recognize you. As much as it pains me to admit, I can't recall who your sister might be."

My breath stalled in my throat, and Mr. Farvem waited, likely believing he understood why I paused before saying my sister's name.

"Fiona Blackwicket," I said at last.

The anticipated horror didn't materialize, though there was a slight jump in the muscle near his left eye.

"Blackwicket?" he repeated, slow, "Miss Fiona had no living family other than her father, I was told."

"You were misinformed."

"So," he said, intrigued, an unusual reaction, "A Blackwicket. Are you, perhaps, Eleanora?"

A lie quivered on my tongue, instincts still inclined to conceal my identity. Instead, I nodded in silent affirmation, not yet ready to come back to myself aloud.

"I know this is very difficult for you," he said, his approach delicate. "Please be assured everything is already taken care of. The details needn't worry you."

This was ground I could confidently tread, the reason I'd come.

"About that." I pressed a finger briefly to my temple as if to hold the thoughts in place. "I want Fiona buried on Blackwicket property."

"I can imagine it's important to you that your sister be buried next to your mother, somewhere safe." His gaze was steady, scrutinizing.

I tilted my head, perplexed. If there was a grave for my mother in the little cemetery at the bottom of the hill where the Blackwickets rested their bones, there was nothing in the casket. The Fiend would have spared nothing of Isolde Blackwicket, body or soul. "Unfortunately, it's quite impossible."

"Why?" I asked, meeting his gentleness with abrasion. I hadn't come all this way to be rebuffed by someone with no right to refuse me.

"The funeral arrangements for Fiona Blackwicket have already been generously paid for and set into motion."

The door from the street opened and closed, and Mr. Farvem straightened, glancing over my shoulder. I didn't budge. I wouldn't be dismissed. My ordeal with the Authority had taught me several lessons, among them how to dig in my heels.

"Certainly not by Darren Rose?" I said. Darren never had more than a few dollars to his name at any given time. I'd be shocked to learn he'd scrounged enough together to pay for a funeral or that he even cared enough to do it. Mr. Farvem glanced behind me again, frustrating me with his attempts to excuse himself from our exchange.

"Who paid for it?" I demanded.

A firm baritone replied, "I'm the benefactor."

"Mr. Nightglass." The undertaker acknowledged the gentleman with a polite nod, and my stomach clenched in dread.

Grigori Nightglass. I'd earnestly hoped to avoid encountering him during my stay here, but my luck and this day were both awful. I shouldn't have expected clemency from fate.

With no other option, I turned to face the shining light of this town and the eternal tormentor of my family.

But I didn't find the ancient, hardened Grigori studying me with mild interest; rather, a much younger man, a handful of years my senior. His pale eyes were piercing, though not as cruel as the man he'd inherited them from, and he wore his flaxen hair long, swept back from his sharply featured face, ends brushing the collar of his navy topcoat. Despite being no more than thirty, he leaned heavily on a familiar snakewood cane, its ornate brass handle curving like a scythe. The dip of his shoulder diminished his otherwise tall frame, indicating a man whose body had been grievously abused by either sickness or injury.

I knew which.

"William?" I asked, barely managing audible words.

William Nightglass was the eldest son of Grigori, the city Principe, appointed by the Authority to govern the township by proxy. In our youth, he'd been a gaunt, troubled boy with a devilish smile that had often caused Fiona to fall to pieces. Now he appeared robust, stronger than I'd ever seen him, regardless of the heavy reliance on his cane, similar to the one his father used.

"Yes." He studied my face. "Are you a friend of Fiona's, Miss...?"

"Blackwicket," Mr. Farvem interjected.

William's expression converted to astonishment.

"Not Eleanora," he said, taking a smooth step closer, cane tip thumping, the sound refusing to be swallowed by the space, unlike lesser noises. He regarded me with such razor-sharp attention I blushed, turned bare beneath his dissecting gaze. Aware of his intensity, he relaxed with some effort. "Forgive me, this is unexpected."

"I've been away for a long time," I conceded, still off-balance.

William shook his head, rejecting my acceptance of his reaction.

"Eleanora," he said, tone grave. "Fiona told us your mother took you into Dark Hall that night. As far as I'm concerned, you've returned from the dead."

CHAPTER EIGHT

I stood in the morgue, facing a man my sister had loved, hurt with the knowing she'd considered me good as dead.

"I'm glad to see you well, William," I said, uncertain of my standing in his graces.

"And I'm glad to see you *alive*, Eleanora," he replied, still scrutinizing me, before a slow smile curved his mouth, making him handsome enough I recognized what had drawn Fiona to him. "I never would've recognized you. You and your sister never did favor each other."

I appreciated his deliberate choice to accept my status among the living without question, and it was true what he'd said. Fiona was our father's doppelgänger, honey-spun hair and skin that browned in the sun, turning the dusting of the freckles across her nose all the more charming. I'd taken after our mother, hair like charred chestnut and a complexion that burned far too easily.

My relief over his lack of prodding was short-lived, his smile settling into something with a bite, a look his father often wore, one that suggested he knew all your secrets and would be pleased to use them against you. The sudden resemblance chilled me.

"Where have you been all this time?" he asked, more to himself than me.

The bell chimed as the door swung open again, sparing me the effort of constructing a response that included nothing I didn't want William to know. A young boy in oversized work trousers entered, holding a simple wooden box, the size and form of a miniature casket, tightly against him.

When he noticed me, he stopped dead still, resembling a wild animal caught in bright light. His eyes flicked uncertainly to William.

"Jack. Come, boy. You're letting the cold in, my bones can't bear it." William waved him forward.

Doing as he was told, the boy named Jack let the door close and wiped the fresh snow off his boots on the entry rug, glancing again in my direction, uncomfortable.

"Is he yours?" I asked.

William laughed; a powerful burst of noise that made me jump.

"Eleanora, the boy's twelve."

It was all he needed to say. When I'd last seen William, he'd been twenty and childless.

"As much as he's underfoot, he might as well be," William said good-naturedly. "But—no, Jack is the son of a house employee. He's taken up a position as my assistant."

William clapped the boy on the shoulder with some affection, but Jack remained stiff. He was a mop of a child, all lanky limbs he didn't quite seem to control, topped with a crop of auburn hair he'd tried, and failed, to shove beneath his flat cap.

"Miss," he greeted.

I managed to offer him a meager smile.

William nodded to Mr. Farvem. "Go with him, lad. Run your errand."

Jack did as he was asked, clutching the box, and making a wide berth around me to the old gentleman, who guided him through a door behind the reception desk.

"He doesn't know if he's coming or going," William said,

then redirected us to the matter at hand. "Eleanora, I regret this is the circumstance that brought you back here from…wherever you've been."

I pressed my lips into a tight line. I owed him no explanation.

"Fiona was a beloved member of this community." His expression was stricken. "I take full responsibility for what happened."

Here was the reason I was here in this town, in this morgue, and I took the opportunity to snatch at some scrap of truth.

"What did happen to her, William?" I asked, daring to reach for any familiar territory we shared.

He cast his gaze down to where the tip of his cane met the floor and the formality in his tone diminished.

"Your sister was a complicated woman. Secretive. She often mystified even me, and as you're aware, we—" He paused, rethinking his next words. I no longer needed to guess whether the love affair of their youth had continued. "In the past year, she became more reclusive. She roamed the cliffs but avoided visiting town. A few days prior to Yule, when she missed the fête, I sent someone to the house out of concern. They discovered her on the porch."

His voice grew quiet with the reverent hush belonging to death as he delivered the final blow. "It was a curse, Eleanora."

I raised a hand to stop him from saying anything more, from offering details he might feel obliged to provide. I was aware of the condition curse rot inflicted on a body. Unchecked, it infiltrated the bone and marrow, devouring the essential components of the human soul, reducing it to a husk, devoid of all that had made it a person. When the body ceased being a solid vessel, the curse would move on, preferably to the nearest entity with any spark of magic: an animal, another person, or a house made living by the hearts that had loved and died for it.

For those unaccustomed to handling tainted magic, the threshold for the number of curses it took to empty them was low, but a Curse Eater, particularly one as capable as my sister, could face an army and survive the experience. At least, that's what I'd once believed.

"I wish I could have done more for her," William said, "but she had a habit of taking on far more than she was able to handle alone."

He leveled his eyes on me, the emphasis of the last word a clear condemnation. The woman he'd once loved, regardless of how their story ended, was gone. And I, the sister who wasn't dead, was the altar to place blame upon.

It was my fortune Mr. Farvem and Jack returned, the former with a sheaf of papers, interrupting the tenseness poisoning the air.

"I've brought the documents, Ms. Blackwicket, outlining the service at the Nightglass estate and dates."

I could afford no more patience. I wanted nothing else to do with this mortuary or the people in it.

"That's what I'd like to change. There'll be—pardon me, William—no service at the Nightglass estate. I want her to be home, where she belongs."

The undertaker opened his mouth to object to the significant reorder of plans already set in motion, but I couldn't leave this wretched parlor until I'd asserted my will.

"Mr. Farvem." Venom was poised on my tongue. "This isn't a request. You have a legal obligation to me, and you will change the plans."

William's firm grip came to rest on my shoulder. In his palm, a current of energy pulsed, characteristic of the Nightglass family, adept practitioners of magic whose long-standing ties to the Authority granted them amnesty from the law.

Gooseflesh prickled along my skin, the lingering essence of

the Drudge growing excited. I tried to retreat from the touch without revealing my urgency, but his grip tightened, and the curse grasped hungrily at his power. William's expression darkened and he withdrew his touch, severing the connection.

My mother had taken pains to convince everyone Fiona and I were incapable of magic, that curse-eating wasn't in our blood. Whatever he'd known of Fiona, he'd suspected of me, and now he could be certain.

When he spoke again, his eyes remained fixed on the undertaker.

"I'll have a few boys from the house at your disposal, Farvem. They'll assist with whatever you need to make Ms. Blackwicket's wishes a reality." It was clear he'd broker no argument.

With a defeated sigh, Mr. Farvem replied, "If that's what's necessary, I understand. I'll need some time to prepare. Unfortunately, I have no appropriate area for you to view the body, Ms. Blackwicket, as all of our viewing rooms are in use."

"I'm sure Eleanora prefers not to wait," William said, the hardness of his voice suggesting this wasn't assistance but punishment.

"Very well," Mr. Farvem replied stiffly, aware his authority in his own business had been revoked. "Give me a moment."

With an air of being put out, he retreated to a door hidden by a wooden screen, disappearing through.

"Jack," William said, the warmth of affection now absent. "Go ahead to Thea. I'll meet you there."

The boy, who'd taken off his cap and been twisting it in his hands, hesitated. "Mr. Nightglass…"

"This is not a discussion," William interrupted.

With a last wary glance at me, Jack took his leave.

William and I were alone.

"Do you plan on staying at the house long, Eleanora?" he asked.

"No, I'll be leaving as soon as I've done right by Fiona."

"And do you happen to be the woman responsible for the recent chaos in Devin?"

He'd made the connection quickly--my sudden arrival, the curse he'd found skulking in my magic. I attempted to keep my response measured.

"It's not my intention to bring trouble to your doorstep, William."

He regarded me with the sharp attention of a man familiar with the shape of dishonesty.

"Trouble finds your family, whether you want it to or not. Does your father know you're here?"

Silence was my answer.

"Ah." William shook his head, disappointed. "I wish he'd been more forthcoming. I hate being ill-prepared."

"It will come as no surprise to you that my father is a liar."

William's eyebrows lifted in amusement, and he averted his gaze, looking at the frosted glass of the front window as though he could see out into the day.

"Our fathers have that in common," he said.

Physical discomfort bolted across his features, a small grunt of pain rising from his throat as he leaned slightly sideways.

"I'm afraid winter cold mistreats me," he said at length when he'd gained composure, his eyes meeting mine again, like a hand hovering at my throat. "The result of an unfortunate injury."

An unfortunate injury. Little Thomas, driven mad by curses, maiming his brother before being brought to Blackwicket House for healing. Dying instead.

My heart beat a ragged rhythm. Nothing was forgotten. Nothing forgiven.

"Well, Eleanora," William said, approaching the entry, a new stiffness in his gait. "Welcome back to Nightglass. You'll find things changed since you left, but as you know, old histories have a way of coming to call, no matter how much we hide from them."

I tried to read between the lines, but our muddy past hindered me. Out of caution, I assumed the worst.

"I am not a woman moved by threats, William," I warned.

"You misunderstand," he said, opening the door and inclining his head in farewell. "It's merely a caution. Only a stupid man would threaten a Blackwicket."

CHAPTER NINE

Moments after William departed, Mr. Farvem reappeared, hunched, his years more evident.

"This way, Ms. Blackwicket. Everything's prepared."

We walked through a wide wooden door, its stain so dark it appeared almost black in the dim light. The hallway beyond was papered in a rich blue, reminiscent of the sea at dusk. This color was for the fathomless feelings that a heart risked drowning in. We passed several doors, muffling movement and low voices. Mr. Farvem's revelation about the number of families he was attending entwined with my knowledge about the Authority investigating disappearances. This dreadful line of thinking was difficult to disengage from, but the dead were the dead. I would mind my own and leave others to mind theirs.

We ventured farther into the funeral home, along a narrow hall, unadorned with decorative paper and carpets, the windowless walls washed in lifeless white, the floor's wooden planks scored with long, wavering gouges—traces made by wheels ferrying the weight of loss. I was regretting my stubbornness. I'd welcome waiting for another date, the opportunity to confront what was inevitable in a viewing room, designed to mute grief in subdued shades and soft fabrics. But we'd already arrived at the end of the hallway, to the one remaining door.

Mr. Farvem paused here.

"This area is for receiving, please be comforted in knowing it's not where I perform my work."

His work of preserving the remains of the departed until their internment, of tending the shells of those who'd lost their personhood in the careless pass of a moment.

I couldn't reply.

"Would you prefer I accompany you, Ms. Blackwicket?" he offered. Despite our previous unpleasant interaction and the slight indignity he'd experienced, he remained compassionate, his well of empathy infinite. "In my years, I've learned no one should suffer this sort of thing alone."

Mr. Farvem's kindness was the courage I needed.

"Yet many people must." I said, thickly. With a nod, he opened the door.

Other than the silence, I noticed nothing of my surroundings but the metal table, and there upon it, my sister. She was covered for decency in a crisp white sheet up to her shoulders, only her face exposed. I didn't want to approach, to know without a doubt that it was my Fiona. If I took no closer look, I could continue to hope there'd been an incredible error. But even from where I stood, I saw the sweet shape of her nose, its slight upturn, her golden hair gleaming and well cared for. With regret and unrelenting love, I closed the space separating us, something I'd not been able to accomplish while she was alive.

I'd expected the ruin of her, the hollowing of the body, skin puckered and mummified by tainted magic run amok, but my expectations were not met. Though she appeared thin, empty, she still resembled the woman I'd spoke with a mere month ago. I'd anticipated a person made a thing by death but saw only my sister and everything that made her beautiful: the small scar at her temple where she'd lost her footing on the slick rocks and taken a tumble, the delicate freckles across her nose, the bow of her mouth, tinged blue, once so ready to smile.

I'd thought I wouldn't be strong enough, but now that she was so close, I touched her pale cheek with the gentlest of caresses. Cold.

"Fiona?" I whispered, as though I were standing over her bed in the deep middle of the night to wake her for company following a nightmare.

Something shifted beneath my fingertips, and I recoiled, sight fixed on the spot in horror. As I was convincing myself I'd imagined it, more movement near her collarbone disturbed the sheet, a vague rising and lowering. I grasped the edge and lifted it, startling a Drudge.

It scuttled around Fiona's clavicle, the size of a mouse and barely more than a mouth and four spindly limbs. With a strident whistle, it leaped at me. Driven by reflex, I caught it in hand, inches from my face, biting back a shout. The contact with this tainted magic triggered an instant reaction. The scrap of the Drudge in me wrenched, recognizing its brethren, diseased creatures calling to each other.

"Ms. Blackwicket?" Mr. Farvem inquired, voice muted. "Is everything all right?"

"Yes." My reply was strangled. The undertaker couldn't find the curse my sister's body had been harboring. He'd throw us both onto the street, regardless of the impropriety. Unlike the curse I'd handled a mere week ago, this Drudge had nothing to eat, no magic to grow on. I'd have no trouble smuggling it out, but it was the last thing I wanted to do.

I exhaled as the borders of my magic opened, preparing to draw the curse in. But the creature thrashed, slipping from my grasp and landing with a damp rustle, like a clump of decaying autumn leaves. It vanished below the cadaver table, merging with the shadows as the door opened and Mr. Farvem leaned in.

The buzz of the corrupt energy had already vanished as the curse fled, a thing it did only when bigger monsters lurked nearby—an unpleasant possibility. In my flailing, the sheet had been tossed up, half covering Fiona's face. This, combined with the way I'd clasped my hands to my breast, created a convincing picture.

"I apologize for the interruption," he said. "I thought I heard… I'll check on you in a moment."

"No." I looked back at Fiona's body, which lay still, vacant. "That's enough."

"I understand."

Mr. Farvem ushered me out and took his position between me and yet another room set to haunt my dreams for the rest of my life.

I struggled to maintain control of my turbulent emotions as we returned to the parlor, the piece of Ms. Rosley's curse eager to gorge itself on my horror and grief if I allowed it.

"Your sister," Mr. Farvem said, his voice a calming harbor in the storm. "She was special. She had the spark. Magic recognized her, responded to her call. There are so few like that anymore."

I focused on his voice, and the compliments paid to someone I cared for.

"When I was a boy, a century or so ago." He offered a self-deprecating chuckle. The sound should have been jarring, but it belonged here, as a reminder that laughter existed "magic wasn't so hard to come by, but it was fading. We did too many bad things, my generation, set too many awful things in motion."

"The war?"

A type of sadness forged from significant regret clouded his expression. I knew the look well.

"The war. If I were magic, I'd have abandoned us too. I was infantry, you know. Top rank, because I could conjure a spell or two." He paused. "What they did to humans and magic alike in the name of power, well, the Authority tried to make sure it would never happen again, but I fear they've lost their way."

The undertaker's ancient hand rested on my arm, a hand that had helped countless dead.

"Eleanora." He grew hushed, worried someone might overhear. "People are looking for ways to bring magic back here, somewhere it doesn't want to be. All it can do here is create monsters. Your sister, she got caught in the middle of this new, invisible war, and look what happened. If you linger in Nightglass, it'll come for you too."

My senses sharpened in alarm. The high, tart scent of formaldehyde invaded my nose, and I became conscious of every noise, every shuffle of feet and small groan of sorrow. When I looked into his green eyes, I noted something more than urgency. Fear.

"We're not a world for magic anymore," he said. "We should let it die. In pain or in peace, let it die."

The house was no less foreboding when I returned to it, walking the hill slowly, focusing on the whip of the breeze, the snowflakes' steady kisses on my cheeks. My visit to the morgue had solidified my plans. After Fiona's burial in three days, I would run, and neither the Brom nor Inspector Harrow could stop me. The Nightglass port no longer functioned, but surely at least one remained open somewhere. An opportunity to escape to another country, though I knew nothing about nations beyond the sea, only that we'd once been at war with them, and that trade had been abruptly cut off when I was a child. My mother had avoided discussing neighboring lands with us, and the Authority limited information and discouraged curiosity.

The Inspector's car was absent, the door still locked, but that meant little, and I remained vigilant. I needed to check for broken windows, worn latches, any other way the loathsome man might have weaseled his way inside. This practical plan gave me purpose. The house opened to me with no struggle. Of course. I was the only person left who could keep it alive.

My head ached.

When I entered, I noticed lights—a dull wash of yellow spilling from the parlor, illuminating the front hall. A flash of outrage fueled me with fresh energy, propelling me toward a place I never intended to enter again, because stronger than my desire to avoid it was the wrongness of the intrusion, of someone invading a space full of painful secrets. Blackwicket House inhaled my furor as I rushed past the stairs, the kitchen, down the hall and over the threshold of the family room.

It was deserted.

Two lamps glowed, their sickly light intensifying the surrounding darkness, transforming bookshelves and furniture into ominous figures. The first thing drawing my eye was the cupboard-sized space between the white bookcases and fireplace mantel, where my ancestors had carved with consistent use an invisible door to the endless nebular void of magic. Throughout her life, my mother moved freely to and from that forbidden place, one I'd often secretly visited myself.

I tried to keep my eyes here, but more horrors awaited than the memory of the night my mother entered Dark Hall and sealed the portal. My gaze slid to a sooty smudge partially concealed by the rug. This was the spot where Thomas Nightglass had breathed his last breath.

The trembling came, the world growing small until I was aware of only the streaked wood that had drank blood and bile and couldn't be cleaned.

The shrill ringing of the phone in the foyer broke the thrall like a pick on frozen water, and I gasped, sucking in air I'd stopped breathing. I bolted, grateful for a reason to withdraw that wasn't merely cowardice.

I reached the phone, its screeching bell echoing loud and long.

"Hello," I said, turmoil making the word terse.

"Hey, Cricket." Darren's voice was so unexpected, and a sob lifted, but I swallowed it down. "Listen, I'm staying at this hotel, the Vanderson, in town. It's a damn sight better than sleeping in that wreck. I know you're mad at me, but why don't you get a room here? I'll pay for it. You shouldn't be up there by yourself."

I longed to sink into the concern in my father's voice, the care I'd have once given anything to experience, but it had come too late. Besides, the Inspector would ferret me out, make a scene. If Darren learned the Authority was in town, he'd beat a hasty retreat, and as much as it pained me to admit, his presence at Fiona's funeral would be stabilizing.

"That's nice of you, but I'm already unpacked, and I need to go through Fiona's things. I went to the funeral home, changed the plans."

"Right," he said. "When you set your mind to something, you're a bull. When's the service?"

"No service. Just a burial here at the house. I'm going to put her next to Mom."

Next to an empty grave.

"A lot of people in Nightglass loved your sister, Eleanora. You should have given them a chance to grieve her."

"What people?"

"She had friends."

"Where were they when she died on the porch?"

"Eleanora." The weariness in his tone infuriated me anew.

"If people loved her, they would have helped her."

"Sometimes there just isn't anything you can do, Cricket," he replied, and the sadness in his voice was too aching, too real.

"I have a lot to do. Fiona's burial is in three days, at noon."

"I'll be there. If you change your mind…"

I brought the receiver away from my ear and rested it in its cradle, cutting him off. My breath shuddered once through me before I picked it up again, bashing it on the corner of the wood desk, blow after blow, gritting my teeth against the jarring impact that sent tremors of pain through my shoulder, peppering the ground with splinters. With the phone smashed into unrecognizable bits of machine, I threw what remained at the wall, where it bounced on its curled cord like a hanged man, destroyed. Breath coming ragged in my lungs, I stared at the gouges I'd created in the antique desk, permanent trenches made by my lack of self-control, the same flaw that had triggered all these terrible events. There were no words too brutal to describe who I was for accusing Darren of crimes I was guilty of. I muttered a curse to the house, and it rumbled in return, drinking in my wrath. The lights flickered, corners darkening, and I was sure every Drudge would rise to feast on my inconsolable hatred for those responsible for murdering my sister with their greed, their contempt, or their neglect. Including and especially me.

Tears were needles at the backs of my eyes, and I chose to flee.

I was wearing my coat, but I wanted the cold to numb me, so I rid myself of it, left it on the floor as I dashed into the blue winter evening. Increasing my pace, I sprinted across frozen land, defying the wind that mounted the cliffs, my hair whipping free from its pins, lashing my cheeks. I wasn't going to stop at the edge and prepared to let the air carry me over the water and into silence. But my feet slipped on the icy grass, and I collapsed a breath from the drop, rocks biting my knees and palms.

Looking over the expanse of dull gray water, I remembered the ships that sailed on the horizon before our borders closed. Fiona and I would name them, crafting tales of their destinations and the secret things they carried. Before our mother chose Dark

Hall, we'd dreamed of someday being passengers, carried away to lives we imagined were kinder than our own. Now, in this horrible future, my sister had left, but she'd gone alone.

The cry that had built in my chest since Devin spilled from my lips, first as a throaty whimper, followed by a wail.

I screamed until my throat turned raw, letting the sea swallow my grief.

CHAPTER TEN

I stayed on the cliff side as long as I dared until my teeth rattled together so forcefully I thought they might break. Emptied, I made my way back to Blackwicket House, the skin on my knees tight, feet aching, and the awful light of those lamps glowing weakly from the front windows. This place should have been beautiful, and maybe it had been when I looked at the world the way a child does, noticing the blossoms but never the thorns.

Everything was hushed when I entered, but not still, and this was all the comfort I could ask for. To whatever extent it would help, I locked the bolt. It gave me some satisfaction to imagine the Inspector forced to stand outside in the cold, filled with impotent rage and driven by the snow to search for a proper hotel in town.

Muscle memory guided me up two flights of stairs to the third floor, glass sparkling on the runners. I didn't bother to avoid the debris, crushing it underfoot as I approached the small suite that had been my family's haven, positioned across the hall from the room Inspector Harrow had chosen. I wondered if he'd somehow known when he picked the keys. The key. I'd forgotten again, too strange a thing to try and remember after years of never needing one. With fatigued desperation, I took the handle and begged mercy. The magic had barely gathered in my fingers when the lock turned, and I was granted access without dramatic consequence. I murmured my gratitude.

The anteroom was unchanged, a modest semicircle of three doors. The rightmost lead to our mother's room, the left, Fiona's and mine. The center door opened to a washroom shared by the three of us, the smallest but most private. The other four bathrooms, once intended for guests, had fallen into disrepair, their pipes frozen and rusted, with nobody willing to come and replace them. Blackwickets have never lacked money, yet generations of amassed wealth delivered a hollow promise of comfort. Money meant little if there was no one to help, no workers to hire, no local shop willing to sell their stock to the house on the hill where children went to die at the hands of Curse Eaters hungry for the innocent.

That was one rumor, anyway. The favorite of the town.

Exhausted, I entered the bathroom, its black and white tiles resembling a chessboard. Not content with just the floor, the tiling climbed the wall, reaching halfway to the ceiling before giving way to cream plaster. I'd expected stains, perhaps cracks in the tile, the porcelain worn to the iron in the tub. But here seemed untouched by the ravages of neglect, and I was grateful. I stripped out of my skirt, heavy from the slush and dirt of the cliff, the cuffs of my shirt blackened with the same. My underthings were the nicest I'd ever owned, a cream silk set purchased at employee discount at Galton's. I'd planned to wear them for Ben, but never had the opportunity.

I prodded at this wound of losing a companionship I'd begun to feel secure in. It didn't hurt as much as I thought it would. Ben hadn't been a great love of mine, merely a comfortable one, but for Curse Eaters in hiding, pickings were slim.

I prayed for hot water and received the answering knock of the pipes, with blessed steam rising from the basin in mere minutes. Sinking in up to my ears, I savored the soothing, muffled silence, my hair drifting around me like summer seaweed.

The rhythm of my heart and welcome warmth began to lull me to sleep, until a metallic clang reverberated, throbbing through my skull, as if the side of the tub had been struck with a mallet. I emerged, sending water sloshing, soaking my skirt, which lay in a jumble.

I scanned the ceiling, peering into the dim corners high overhead, but saw no movement. I was too tired, too broken, for whatever games the house was playing tonight. Still, I placed my hands on the rim and looked over, expecting to find a shape or shadow staring up at me from beneath the basin, but there was nothing.

Knowing there'd be no solace here after all, I submerged myself again and used the soaps and shampoos belonging to Fiona, all infused with the soft scent of honeysuckle, to wash away the horrors of the last few days. Despite my scrubbing, the memories clung to me, oily and uncomfortable, but at least feeling had returned to my limbs. My heart remained numb, but that was a blessing, and I hoped I'd feel no more in it for the rest of my life.

I refused to don my soiled clothes, but my bags were downstairs. I rejected the idea of that journey and removed a satin robe from its hook. Putting it on was like slipping into my sister's life, filling the void her absence created. I considered staying in my mother's old room, but Fiona had likely claimed it in the years since, and I couldn't bring myself to intrude.

I chose the leftmost instead, leaving the light switch untouched. The gloom was thick, the wood shutters closed tight to block the glow of the moon off the sea, but I could discern the shape of two beds—Fiona's near the high, far wall, and mine tucked neatly under the slanted dormer.

Bypassing my corner, I stumbled to Fiona's, collapsing onto

her coverlet, which rustled as I wrapped myself in it. I anticipated crying a bit more, but as I prepared myself for the deluge of emotion, I was waking, startled from the sleep that had borne me under without preamble. I'd dreamed of chasing Fiona through the halls, missing her with every turn.

Scuffling drew my attention, a deliberate movement along the floor as though something were crawling near. I strained to see, but the dark was absolute. I sat up.

The air pulsed with a vague energy, a confounding, befouled power humming with an undercurrent of organic magic. My sudden action resulted in an almost profane vibration that settled low in my body.

"Who is it?" I was wide awake now, the unusual sensation encouraging curiosity over fear.

Whatever lurked retreated at the sound of my voice, its sudden exit creating a vacuum, stealing my breath. I surged from bed, eager to discover the thing responsible for such strangeness. The door to the anteroom creaked, and I pursued the anomaly into the dim hallway, remembering the glass too late. I braced for the sting of slivers in the soft soles of my feet, but the carpet was clear of debris, every shard absent.

I stared down the long stretch of corridor, with nowhere for a person to hide unless they were the size of a child, and listened to the unsteady breathing of the foundation.

Making a tedious procession, I began testing doors. They were all locked. In my weariness, I'd let Blackwicket House get the best of me. When I reached the window at the end of the hall, I wilted against it, taking a moment to glance out at an expanse of bare branches, the blanket of hills rolling to the valley where Nightglass sparkled, even at this hour. It was both a foreboding and enchanting sight, a realm of fairies—beautiful, treacherous, and full of secrets. This strange tenderness urged me to lean my head against the windowpane, my inhibitions lessened by fatigue. I opened my magic, offering peace, but when I brushed the cool curve of darkness, it convulsed. Its convergence was swift as an unexpected wave, filling your nose and mouth with brine. I snapped my defenses shut, and the house moaned.

"I'm sorry," I whispered.

Forceful thuds reverberated within the wall like the desperate fists of prisoners, growing louder.

"I can't help you. You need Fiona, and she's gone."

The pounding came faster, overwhelming me. I covered my ears, opened my mouth to scream, but there was no need. Silence fell.

Tired of being bullied, I turned to beat a hasty retreat, only to collide with a solid figure. My shriek was stifled by a large palm pressed to my mouth, an arm encircling my waist, preventing me from falling as I struggled to break loose. I urged the curse within me to rise, but it was too weak to hurt anyone but me. With no other choice, I raised my hands to claw at the eyes of my attacker, only to recognize the moonlit face of Inspector Harrow.

He was disheveled, clothes rumbled, hair unkempt. I might have assumed it due to being abruptly awoken, except that his right cheek bore a fresh cut at the pinnacle of bone, skin mottled with fresh bruising.

"Don't wake the dead, Ms. Blackwicket," he intoned, voice silky in the dark.

I slapped his hand away.

"Lunatic!" My voice rang in the hush. "What are you doing wandering around in the middle of the night?"

"Heard something interesting," he replied.

He hadn't yet released his grip on my waist, and I pushed him back. Harrow retreated the barest of steps, but I remained cornered. There wasn't nearly enough space to slip by without bodily shoving past, and I was reluctant to make contact again.

"You told me this place was empty," he said. "But I doubted a single Curse Eater could make all that racket by herself, so I had a look around."

It's true he appeared to have dressed hastily, his trousers beltless, ever-present revolver in a shoulder holster he'd shrugged on over a white cotton undershirt.

I eyed the weapon with no modest amount of disdain.

"The things in these walls aren't afraid of your gun, Inspector."

It was a weak attempt at frightening him, but the narrowing of his eyes and the slight tilt of his head revealed it did the opposite.

"What things, Ms. Blackwicket?" The low rumble of his voice had an unsettling effect on me. I'd never been this close to Inspector Harrow before. Our previous interactions always involved a barrier, an interrogation table, or the bars of a public cell. The nearest he'd ever come was leaning over the table to look me in the eye when he'd been given orders to release me.

You're free to go, Ms. Knoles, but not in innocence. You and I both know you killed Brock Mofton. There's no hiding from that, and there's no hiding from me.

The Drudge I'd attempted to summon moments earlier lie low, creating space for my power to ascend, extending instinctively. I sensed no intrusion, no probing hand, just the eager surge of magic ready to share itself. The Inspector must have been up to something, searching in a manner I'd never encountered, employing a trick to entice me into a false sense of security, as the Brom woman attempted in the streets of Devin.

"Stop it," I said, much softer than intended.

"I saw you in town today," he replied, and the feeling abated. At the very least, I'd made it clear I was aware of myself enough to sense when I was being toyed with.

"I went to see Fiona's body. I didn't realize I was under house arrest."

I was anxious to be as far from him as possible.

"What did you do with the Drudge from Galtons?"

The question was abrupt. He was trying to knock me off balance and was doing a decent job. I hadn't bothered to plan a lie about this, and I hesitated.

"Don't forget, Ms. Blackwicket, I witnessed what happened." He didn't need to remind me, but he probably enjoyed doing it. "Are you harboring it?"

Capable of giving infuriating answers to infuriating questions, I replied, "You'd know if I was."

"Did you sell it?".

"Of course not!"

"So where is it?"

I had no choice but to weave truth through the tale I was going to spin; otherwise, I was at risk of giving myself away. As my father had pointed out, the number of curses in my bag downstairs was a felony. But there was more than that here. Far more.

"It's gone, Inspector." The lie tasted like blood.

A soft scoff. "Gone where?"

"Back to where it came from."

This had been our song and dance the first time we'd met. Pointed questions, half answers, appeals to ignorance.

"Dark Hall?" he asked, leaning in a bare fraction as though his next question were intimate. "Can you access Dark Hall, Ms. Blackwicket?"

Damn it. I tried to pivot, to focus on the contempt I harbored for this man.

"That's what you want, isn't it? You want me to tell you I regularly steal curses and smuggle them to Dark Hall, confess that I and other Curse Eaters feed the Fiend with stolen magic, bending it to our will."

I resisted the urge to cackle theatrically to emphasize the absurdity, but restrained myself, my dignity unable to take the blow. Panic was already making me lose my senses, but he was silent, patient. Waiting for the real answer.

"The Authority wants us to be leaders of the Brom, not victims of them," I continued, more subdued, abandoning sarcasm for dangerous honesty. "Because it would make their job of brutalizing us all the easier."

I met his eyes.

"But you've never had any qualms with doing that, have you, Inspector?"

"You should be able to recognize nasty rumors when you hear them."

He was playing the same game I was, and he was better at it.

"You're wrong about everything," I said, weary.

"Surely not everything," he countered, affecting a wounded tone as he produced two gold cufflinks from thin air.

They glinted in the silvery winter light as he moved them through his fingers with smooth, practiced ease. These were the cufflinks I'd given to Brock when he'd started offering me inappropriate interest, tucked in a box with a yellow satin ribbon, toxic with curses I'd placed there myself. They'd been empty when the Authority found him, face down in his own vomit, surrounded by bottles of whiskey. But there'd been the telltale sinking of his skin, and the inquest was alive, searching for the person responsible for driving this man, who'd never once indulged in liquor, to drink himself to death.

I watched them move across Inspector Harrow's knuckles.

"Do you have any idea what Curse Eaters are meant to do with curses, Inspector?"

He raised a brow, eyes glowing a peculiar shade, like cognac amber, his curiosity ignited.

"I've been told a few different stories, but why don't you tell me yours?"

"Set them free."

It was the most basic explanation of our core function, the directive that drove my family and others for hundreds of years, perhaps since time immemorial, when man and magic first touched and a spark ignited.

"That's what you're meant to do, is it?" He stopped spinning the cufflinks and leaned in so close I could smell the magic on his skin, reminiscent of frost before snow.

"Then why do you keep them in this house?" he murmured.

Though it brought my face closer to his, I lifted my chin in defiance, proof he couldn't intimidate me. He was twice my size, but I'd grown up with monsters at my bedside.

"Ask them yourself."

He smiled, slow and languid, inviting an inexplicable panic that gave me the courage to push past his bulk. Shoving him aside with my shoulder, I began a swift departure.

"Sleep tight, Ms. Blackwicket," Inspector Harrow called with mock tenderness. "Don't let the curses bite."

CHAPTER ELEVEN

The unfeeling sun, oblivious to my sorrows, pressed between the slats of closed shutters. I hoped I'd slept an entire day, planning to stay in bed until Fiona's funeral. But as my surroundings came into focus, I was encouraged to climb from the warm sheets and unfasten the shutters to squint in a bright wash of cold sunshine.

Photos lined the walls—rows of them, framed in gold, countless faces captured in time. Many featured people I didn't recognize, strangers who'd entered Fiona's life while I was gone. Everyone else appeared joyful, but Fiona's smile was thin in each, an effort made on behalf of her companions to appear happy. In some frames, a white petal had been pressed in the corner beneath the glass like a kiss. Blackberry flowers. I glimpsed at the land outside the window, where the garden fence still stood, crooked as a cemetery gate. Blackberries had been a favorite of ours. We'd grown them every summer, with our mother producing endless sweets and pastries for guests who never came.

Mingling among the others were the occasional photos of Fiona and me in various stages of growing up, from early years brimming with joyful mischief to later days when our bodies had grown long and unfamiliar, and life at Blackwicket House had become difficult to bear. Although our smiles diminished over time, our affection endured, a fierce love I believed unbreakable. I reached for the photo of us on the shore, bare feet in the waves, our hair—light and dark—tangling in the wind. Mother stood, awkward, with her arms around us as we tried to take a formal picture. This attempt had made Isolde Blackwicket laugh so hard she cried, hiccupping for half an hour afterward. She'd kept it by her bedside.

I ran my thumb gently over my sister's youthful face, comparing her features to those of the woman she'd become. She'd traded her long braids for coiffed styles that complemented her various hats, forsaking the A-line cotton dresses of her youth for impeccably tailored skirt suits and sweater sets. Judging by the pictures, her wardrobe was significant, though I found no evidence of it here, where there'd never been a closet or wardrobe, only the cedar dresser. I investigated the drawers. They were filled with clean sheets, slips, and stockings. Nothing more.

Little else in this space had changed. The wallpaper remained green striped, our beds dressed in handmade quilts, cream and yellow. Our mother had woven the blankets with magic that glowed like fireflies in the dark, encouraging our dreams to be sweet. This magic had long since faded.

A relic from my childhood rested on my pillow. A rag doll, with button eyes, a needlepoint nose, and a crooked smile. Its yarn hair, once the color of strawberries, had dulled to an elderly pink. The curse that had taken residence in this doll, turning it black and sodden with turmoil, had been the first I'd ever eaten.

My mother had guided me through every step, unlatching the parlor window so the sound of the sea enveloped us.

"When I was your age, I sat right here to work. The waves helped me concentrate," she'd said, tucking hair behind my ears, comforting me as only mothers who understand the fears and determinations of their children can. "This is a big job, Ellie. Don't you want me to help you? No? Well, alright. Here, hold the doll

tight. The curse is depending on you. Close your eyes, find the heart. Do you have it? Good. Breathe out slowly. Now breathe in."

It had rattled me. No amount of warning could have prepared me for the shock of thick, oily curse smoke invading my nose and mouth, filling my head and lungs with a suffocating pain that didn't belong to me. But the ache had been brief, and my tears had been wiped away, kisses given on cheeks. For the next two hours, we'd sat at the window together, and I unraveled the curse, picking it apart like a knot from a ball of thread. My mother relocated the freshly healed magic to the Narthex with as much care as she took when replanting a sprout.

In the coming years, I ate curses whenever I could, and though capable of working on my own, I was never allowed. The strictest rules in our house were the limits on when Fiona and I could handle magic—especially cursed magic.

I bent and scooped up the raggedy thing, holding it close and burying my face in the rough yarn. It smelled of old perfume and cotton. Sitting on the bed, I saw to the matter of the Drudge burrowed inside me. The curses I'd collected, festering with my things downstairs, had accumulated because I'd been avoiding this moment—the baring of my magic to hurt.

The curse remnant had buried itself deep, but as I plucked patiently at the raw layers, coaxing, it began to unwind. It surrendered its hold because the power I offered was bigger and promised, at last, a release from misery. I fed the strings of the curse through my magic, as though spinning wool, and when the final tainted fiber was cleansed, I tilted my chin and released it.

A translucent cloud, shimmering in the light, slipped from my lips. In it, I imagined the faces of Ms. Rosley and her children, together wherever the soul journeyed in the end. I had no Narthex to give it to. It would have to find its own way.

I made my sister's bed, replaced her robe on the hook, and dressed in my soiled clothes. A sense of duty had returned to me, and I was ready to take stock of what was left of our home. My resolve to leave after Fiona's funeral persisted, but my heart had softened to the idea of gathering a few items here and there to bring with me when I said goodbye to Nightglass forever.

I checked the hallway. The Inspector's door was closed, and I heard no movement. In the downstairs foyer, I pulled aside a curtain to check the front drive, finding it empty. I was alone. I rummaged in my bags, changing where I stood, unable to withstand the sensation of the filthy clothes for even a second more. Then I advanced to the board of keys, primed to scoop them all off their hook. I was done using magic.

I halted in my steps.

The parlor lights were on again, and the hallway drapes open, framing a vision of gray sky stretching over water until they met in a lover's embrace with no land between them. The house was baiting me, but I wouldn't fall for it.

"You're not clever," I said, risking the taunt.

The low reverberation of a single piano note rang, soft and muffled as a sigh against a pillow. I'd never known a Drudge to play the piano. They were creatures of dark energy, and while they could manifest vague physical forms, especially here in Blackwicket House, they rarely interacted with things that couldn't breathe.

My heart jumped, and I hurried to my bags, keeping an eye on the hall as I foraged. Catching the latch on the box where the curses languished, I snatched the first vessel my fingers touched—an old fountain pen, its lacquer discolored, the tip sharp. I'd swiped it from the desk of a bank manager interviewing me for a secretarial position when I'd gone by the name Joan Boldrade. By the conclusion of the interview, I'd known very well why it was cursed. I held the thing like a dagger, approaching as soft-footed as possible. The curse infecting this instrument was small and wouldn't do much damage, but the lethal point held promise, as the bank manager learned when his hand had ventured to acquaint itself with the buttons of my blouse. It was the last day I'd been Joan.

No more notes had been played, but as I neared the doorway, I could hear the crackling of a fire in the grate, the whisper of paper turning. I pressed my shoulder to the wall and peeked inside as far as I could without entering.

The visible portion of the parlor was awash in anemic winter sunlight and the glow of the two lamps, which I recalled I'd never turned off. But more than this, firelight flickered, the blaze glinting in the black sheen of the piano, its fallboard open, keys displayed white and wide as the grin of a Cheshire cat. From my current angle, the fireplace wasn't visible. It was a vast mahogany thing, boasting a towering overmantel inlaid with a gilded framed mirror that reflected the views and, in the summer, moonbeams.

Papers rustled, followed by the shifting of shadows, then that beastly voice.

"Ms. Blackwicket," Inspector Harrow drawled, turning the sound of my name in his mouth nearly obscene. "Good afternoon."

Leaning my forehead against the doorframe, I shut my eyes tight to ward off my temper and the blush venturing to develop. I'd stripped down to my underwear in the middle of the foyer while that man was mere yards away. I considered saying nothing, returning upstairs and leaving him speaking to thin air. But I didn't want him in this vault of my history. Aware that walking in with a weapon clutched like a threat in my fist wouldn't go over well, I tucked the pen deep in my pocket.

As I entered, I avoided looking at the old Narthex or the stain on the floor, and found the Inspector standing by the fire.

He held a worn copy of children's fairytales in his hand. This book had been my favorite as a girl, and I hated it had been discovered. The Inspector was clean-shaven, hair precisely in order, wearing his usual brown trousers and waistcoat over a crisp white shirt, starched and wrinkle-free, the ever-present revolver secured in its holster. I was satisfied he didn't feel comfortable enough here to go without it.

His gaze flicked from my face to my feet, perhaps sizing me up in case he needed to throw me in the trunk of his car, which was mysteriously absent.

"Your car isn't in the drive," I said, making it obvious I'd searched for it.

"I parked around back so as not to obstruct the view." The answer was dry, but he couldn't hide the sardonic bite.

"And what are you doing in here?" I demanded, unsettled by how pleasant it all appeared: the fire, the open curtains, the bookshelves lined with titles I'd read perhaps twice each. But both the room and the man were more than they seemed. Together, they brought to mind the yew berries thriving in the rambling overgrowth on the road to town. Beautiful and toxic.

I shocked myself with this thought, not because it was unjust, but because I'd unwittingly categorized Inspector Harrow as something beautiful.

"Getting my bearings," he replied blithely, closing the book with a snap and replacing it on its shelf.

"This room is off-limits."

"The most inviting room in this house is off-limits?" Though his tone was mild, the question had sharp edges. He tucked a hand into his pocket and advanced a few steps, stopping by the piano.

"There are family heirlooms here. I'd rather they continue to be untouched." I was proud of myself for not giving ground.

"Understandable." He brushed his fingers along the keys,

playing a single note, crystal clear, the same as before. I realized the instrument was tuned. When he regarded me again, there was an expression on his brow I'd come to recognize—a lock-jawed persistence to uncover the truth people kept hidden. "This house truly is a marvel, Ms. Blackwicket. The size of it alone, in such a beautiful location, would demand a fortune to build and maintain, and there are so many remarkable pieces here. This piano, for one, is extraordinary."

"Do you play?" I asked pointedly, knowing he didn't. A man like Victor Harrow didn't have hobbies aside from terrorizing his quarry.

He offered a controlled smile, a breath through his nose that mimicked the beginnings of a laugh, but ignored my question.

"Curse Eating must have been a lucrative business for your family to live in such luxury, despite the inn struggling for most of Isolde Blackwicket's ownership of it."

"We aren't a shop for black-market magic," I replied. "Curse Eating was a revered profession. People came to my family for healing, and they were grateful and generous. Many of the things here were gifts; the rest was paid for with the wealth accrued by my grandmother. She owned a port in town."

"Hm. It's such a pretty tale. Your family home, full of love and grateful people, warm and bright, and safe. A bit like something from one of those fairy stories on your shelf." He motioned to them.

"You can believe what you'd like."

"I prefer to believe what's true," he said. "So, where is this wealth now?"

"I don't know and have no interest in knowing."

"No interest in wealth?"

"No interest in staying long enough to go through my sister's accounting books to see how little our wealth benefited her."

His regard remained steady, and with a jolt, I noticed he was standing on the deplorable spot that often led me to panic.

"Do you bake, Ms. Blackwicket?" the Inspector asked. When my response was to stare at him, he nodded in the general direction of the kitchen. "The jars."

"Are you having a stroke, Inspector?" I replied, his abrupt change in subject unbalancing me.

A muscle tightened in his jaw, and I was pleased I'd annoyed him, but the movement came with a twitch of his lips. He was suppressing a smile.

"I take it you haven't been through the house." There was something in his voice, an amused tone he often adopted when he knew more than I did about something important.

"I haven't," I said flatly. "I keep getting interrupted by people who won't mind their own damn business. But I don't enjoy the kitchen and avoid it, so if you're mentioning it with hopes I'll cook something for you, you're out of luck. You'll have to go to town, you won't be able to call for anything."

"Yes, I noticed the phone," he said.

The phone. Damn. I wasn't painting a stable picture of myself, a necessity to survive this ordeal. My initial run in with the Authority had turned in my favor because they saw me as a plain woman, with plain hobbies, a boring but steady job, an uninteresting lover, and a small group of friends who had nothing to do with magic.

"Phone or not, no one will come here," I said.

"Pity. They're missing out on a gorgeous old place."

"Gorgeous." My echo sounded doubtful. I couldn't determine if the word was sincere. The Inspector had limited ability to inflect emotion, unless it was menace.

"To be clear, I don't need you to tend to me. I'm sure you're busy with other things."

He glanced to the ceiling, giving the impression he could

see through to the secrets hidden in the beams. In a terrible moment of coincidence, the house creaked as if it were planning to walk itself into the sea. I felt a twinge of unwelcome fellowship with it.

If I continued to demand he avoid this room, he'd have all the more reason to snoop, a dangerous gamble considering the scar of the Narthex so near. Though it lingered undetectable to anyone who wasn't looking for it, Inspector Harrow was someone who was always looking.

He started toward me and my hand twitched for the pocket where the pen was tucked. But he was coming nearer because I stood in the exit. I stepped aside to let him by.

"I'm going to see what I can dig up about all your sister was involved in these last few years." Rather than moving past me, he stopped, positioning himself in a way that reminded me I wouldn't have a snowflake's chance in hell if I dared go toe to toe with him. "People are on guard now that there's a Blackwicket back in Nightglass and that's already made my job harder, so stay here. That's not a request. Don't leave this house."

A swarm of fury gathered in my spine as he entered the hall. "You can't place me under house arrest."

Uninterested in my outrage, he ignored me and I was forced to follow him.

"You have *no* cause!" I said.

I'd no previous intention of going anywhere until he'd stripped me of the choice, and I couldn't tolerate it. The Inspector stopped abruptly, and I narrowly avoided an impact with him. He turned only enough to look at me, but I retreated a hasty step to keep our arms from brushing, knowing I looked like a startled cat.

"House arrest involves phone calls I can't make and paperwork I don't want to fill out," he said, as if he were explaining something complex to a simpleton. "If you're dead set on debating this and forcing me to suffer the trouble, I'd prefer making an official arrest and taking you back to Devin, Ms. Blackwicket."

Indignation inspired violent impulses I couldn't indulge in. Satisfied by my loss for words, he returned to retrieving his coat.

"You're a goddamn bully, Harrow," I grated.

"I use my faults to my advantage, something you're quite good at doing yourself." He snatched his overcoat from the rack and donned it with a sharp motion, the fabric snapping, betraying his calm exterior. He was irritated. Good. It was a small, meaningless victory, but a victory, nonetheless.

"I'll be gone all day, well into the night," he said. "Savor the privacy and rest easy knowing you're free to enjoy in as many spontaneous wardrobe changes as you'd like."

He'd seen me.

My flush was now muddled with something beyond rage as the Inspector left me to deal with my humiliation alone.

CHAPTER TWELVE

S till fuming, I marched to the kitchen, eager to find out what discovery the Inspector's snooping led to. I sensed it would cut deeply, but still approached the guillotine with a determined disregard for my own emotional well-being.

The kitchen was tucked near the stair landing, marked by a door that swung in both directions to allow coming and going when arms were full. In my furor, I pressed too hard, and the door flew inward, hitting a counter on the other side and clattering glassware. Immediately, I could see what inspired Inspector Harrow's question. It was impossible to miss.

Jars crowded every surface, filled to the brim with jam, black in the low glow of daylight bleeding through the single window's muslin curtains. I reached for the light switch without looking and flipped it on, the brass pendants coming to life overhead, uncovering the scope of the chaos. Pots and pans filled the deep copper sink, covered in a gelatinous goo, reminding me too well of Ms. Rosley. But instead of green, the mess shone with undertones of purpling red, deep as wine. Fiona had been making blackberry jam, just as our mother had done.

Isolde Blackwicket had become a zealous baker in the years following my shameful mistake. Using the spoils of our magic-fed garden, she'd gone through the motions of feeding guests we didn't have. Uneaten pies, cakes, and scones moldered on the counters, inviting flies and other unholy bugs to feast. But her favorite thing to make had been blackberry jam. Fiona and I had taken to bringing the jam jars and porcelain baking dishes to the cliffside, dumping the contents onto the water-bullied rocks below. We'd sneak them inside, wash and return them to the cabinets for our mother to use again. She'd never commented on the disappearance of food or the reappearance of bakeware.

Entering felt as though I'd walked into a wall of spiderwebs, thick with winged creatures struggling to free themselves. The buzzing energy snatched at my clothes and hair, an invisible swarm not yet compelled to take the forms that had plagued my childhood. Ones that had hidden beneath beds, in gloomy corners, and behind wardrobe doors. I knew the house had saved this particular display for me. If the Inspector had experienced this thrum of tainted power, he'd have already done what he was so well known for—torn the magic free one horrible strip at a time.

I investigated the sink, crowded with the work Fiona had been doing before she'd died. The sweet, festering fragrance of fruit was revolting and explained the smell upstairs. The scent must have permeated the pipes.

The story I'd been told of a reclusive woman my sister had become was at odds with this scene, unless she'd too begun a slow descent into madness. These fragments of my sister's life, the half-finished chores, the childhood confections arranged for some unknown purpose, weighed heavy on my heart.

I turned on the faucet, waited for steam to billow, then shoved my hands under the hot current. The biting pain grounded me, and I closed my eyes against it. When my senses adjusted, the sting decreasing, I scrubbed the pots clean with vicious intensity, rejecting my grief in favor of anger. I was mad at Fiona for letting things get this far, angry at her stubborn will to hold on to this house with both fists. Twice a year, I'd sent a letter with a set hour and destination, but she'd never shown.

Not until a month before her death when she'd arrived at my suggested meeting place, the cafe in Devin, and told me to leave her alone.

Fiona kept our room the same, displayed photos of us together. But she'd ignored me for years, then dismissed me as though I were an annoying dog yapping at her skirts for attention. Why was I here for a sister who hadn't wanted me?

I lifted the pot I was washing and slammed it violently into the basin, then grabbed hold of the sink's edge and screamed. I screamed until my stomach muscles cramped, the effort tearless, meant to unburden me of the building strain of this nightmare. The life I'd built for myself hadn't been perfect. In fact, it had been the barest of lives deprived of identity, honesty, and earnest love, but I'd been safe from all of this.

Inhaling raggedly, I watched the suds and berry residue wash away before shutting off the water. I pressed the back of my wet hand to my forehead, trying to calm my jack rabbiting heart, while admitting I was lying to myself.

I'd missed using my magic, detested hiding it, collecting curses only for them to suffer in perpetuity, me along with them. All the while, I'd feigned enthusiasm for a mind-numbing occupation, a lukewarm lover, and a future of straining under the burden of my lies. Fiona appeared to have lived her life just as she was.

And it killed her.

Sick of my thoughts, I made to abandon the kitchen, but was stopped in my tracks as I turned, my way blocked by a curse hanging inches from my face. It was a tumorous thing, floating suspended on the stringy lines of its shadow that trailed to the ceiling. Its miasma seeped outward, becoming scarlet mist. This Drudge was less formed than I'd expected something from Blackwicket House to be. Once, I wouldn't have been afraid, used to Drudge appearing with no apparent purpose other than to exist and to remind us to give to them. But I'd been gone such a long time. Familiarity was no longer my shield, and the house and I were not getting along.

The Drudge's countenance was underdeveloped, sagging pockets in place of features trying to form. The edges of its polluted magic rippled, the tendrils extending, patting my cheek, cold and fluttering. It didn't appear to be searching for a meal, driven more by curiosity than hunger.

"I'm not her," I whispered.

It reeled away, startled, grabbing hold of a thread of my magic as it went, plucking it away, resulting in more than physical pain. I yelped and the Drudge dissolved, racing across the ceiling to descend the wall where it merged with a much larger monster peeking in from around the kitchen door. Only a mere portion of it was visible—the top of a head, grim magic hanging lank as strands of hair around a humanoid . As I laid eyes on it, the thing retreated as quick as a gasp.

Auntie.

This was a familiar Drudge, the oldest of them, present even before my mother was brought to the house. It refused to leave, refused to be healed. I'd spent my childhood falling asleep with her standing by our beds, silent and watching, dipping in and out of view as the clouds obscured the moon. She'd never hurt us, just observed, waiting for something we weren't quite sure of. My mother began calling her *Auntie* when it became clear she was frightening us. The familiar moniker did its job, and while she remained unsettling, she was merely another strange aspect of our lives no other soul was aware of.

Except for Thomas.

Not needing both my sister's and Thomas's ghosts haunting me, I spurned the memories and sprinted after the creature, seeking to verify it was truly her.

The hall was dimly lit, the glow of the foyer chandelier

reduced in the presence of Auntie, and the vast energy it took for her to maintain form. I couldn't determine where she'd gone until a shift of light caught my eye, moving beneath the door of a storage room behind the check-in counter. This space had been a ladies' parlor, but its function was rejected by Blackwicket women who had no intention of squeezing themselves into such an isolated, quiet space. Instead, it served as a safer storage alternative to the crumbling tower. Another rotation of shadow encouraged me closer.

As I approached, I hummed a long-ago tune my mother had taught me. Her soft singing voice, far superior to mine, echoing in my ear with every step.

Oh, Moira, my love, I meant not to stray
But the sea it was calling that bright summer's day
And the sea, as you know it, takes lovers away
But call me back with your sorrows,
And in spirit, I'll stay.

She'd woven this ballad into our daily lives, asking me to sing as she did her curse eating work or whenever I was afraid of Auntie. During the times I was too scared to do it on my own, Fiona had chimed in, inserting my pet name.

'Oh, Ellie, my love…'

I opened the door to the storage closet, finding it had been transformed into an office, feminine and delicate, with pink damask paper and a simple white desk, its single lamp shining. The lamp's yellowed fringe swung delicately from the vibration of my footsteps, interrupting the daylight streaming through the window. The space was deserted.

I furrowed my brow, frustrated I'd let myself be led on a

wild goose chase. As I stood in the doorway, I wondered what Fiona had been doing with a space like this. What work had she been tending to? Needing a distraction, and with nothing else to occupy me, I took a seat and began rifling in the three desk drawers, none of them locked. I wasn't sure what I'd find or what I was looking for. Perhaps a ledger, something to help me comprehend what Fiona had done with her life. What friendships she'd formed, and hardships she'd faced, what had driven her to make such an absurd amount of blackberry jam.

The top drawers contained nothing of interest: newspaper clippings of town events, receipts for food and clothing. I pulled open the bottom, revealing several stacks of letters folded neatly and bound with twine. They were organized in a way indicating she cared for them, and I withdrew the top one.

The letter was romantic in nature, signed by William. I read no more than the first few lines, then returned it to its envelope. I wouldn't pry. My sister's romances were her own, and William was still alive and capable of being embarrassed by the contents. But curiosity drove me to pull the remaining stack free, and check the dates on each. All were over three years old, signaling an end to their romance. I'd never been fond of William, less because of his own faults and more due to his stealing my sister's attention from me when it had always been mine.

As I arranged them back in place, a second sheaf of letters caught my attention, the papers were mismatched, words written on bits of stationery from hotels and various postmasters. These were the letters I'd sent to Fiona over the years, all thoughtfully folded.

Here and there, I discovered half-written responses, never sent, full of affection and concern. Some begged me not to write anymore, to move on and live, others were filled with requests that I come home. These hurt the most. The last was dated a week before I'd sent my final plea for her to meet me in Devin.

Ellie, it's pained me all this time to keep secrets, but the bowels of hell offer more gentle hands than Nightglass and I'm grateful you are anywhere but here. This town is a wasteland of beautiful faces with terrible intentions, and I've never harbored such disgust for others, even during the worst times with Mother. For a while, I bore it, believing I could do something for this place.

The Drudge send their regards; they're peculiar as always but have been restless, making a nuisance of themselves. People are becoming wary of the house again, but it's for the best, though William isn't happy.

There are days I regret encouraging you to leave, and others, like today, when I'm grateful beyond measure you were never forced to live this imprisoned life. Are you still in the apartment with the view of the bakery? I'm happy knowing you think of me when you see it. Please, tell me where I can meet you and I'll be there. I promise.

Fiona

In the stillness of night, I thought I'd never cry another tear, but they came easily now, sliding down my chin and plinking onto the paper. I sat this way for so long that when I looked up again, the sunlight had turned to the faint golden yellow of late afternoon.

I collected the letters, deciding they'd be the only items I'd save from Blackwicket House. As I closed the drawer, hollow hearted, light caught the edge of a miniature golden frame, hidden at the bottom. The photo inside captured a candid moment on a lush green lawn. My sister, mouth open mid-laugh, sat on a picnic blanket in a pink linen dress between two people. William, whose cane rested close by, lounged to her left, his smile shy and genuine. To her right was a beautiful woman whose red lips curled in bemused affection. It was Ms. James, the Vapors headliner who'd glared at me with considerable hostility.

Fiona was touching them both, a hand on Ms. James' arm, another on William's knee, her joy seemingly genuine.

I turned the frame, removing the backing to reach the photo, when something tucked inside fluttered onto my lap: a small oval cut image, meant for a locket. It was of Fiona, her hair unpinned, her cotton dress plain. She stood barefoot on the rocky beach, a little boy in corduroy overalls clinging to her leg. The corner of this picture was marred by a spill of ink, a black stain spreading over the boy's pudgy toes. Without thinking, I touched it with my thumb, and the stain shifted.

It was a curse—small in its bare beginnings, growing like mold in the dark. The little effort it would take prompted me to bring the snapshot to my lips, as if placing a kiss on the faces there. The curse rose with little resistance, and I took a minute to unravel the pitiful thing and release it again, white as frozen breath.

I examined the photo, hoping for a date, finding an inscription.

My son, Roark, age four.

Son.

The word burned my eyes. Or perhaps it was the horrible shock of discovering how deep our bond had been severed that she'd hide even this from me. My sister had been a mother.

But where was her child?

I stood from the desk so forcibly the chair overturned. I left it and hastily pocketed the photos, forgetting the pen was there. It nicked my fingertip, and I yanked my hand out, a dome of red welling on my finger. The minor pain aided in clenching my decision. Damning the Inspector and his orders to hell, I hurried into the foyer and grabbed my coat.

I was going to town to hunt down Ms. James.

CHAPTER THIRTEEN

When I arrived on the main street of Nightglass, it was early evening, and already the town was alive. Tourists were filtering in and out of the restaurants and boutique shops filled with the high-end trappings and trimmings of the wealthy: luxury cosmetics, rare liquors, and expensive cigars. The glow of the shop window lights strained to present a cheery sight amidst the gloomy blue of winter dusk, but it looked jaundiced and feeble to my eyes.

The sidewalk in front of The Vapors lounge, where I'd first encountered the woman in Fiona's picture, was no less claustrophobic to me tonight. But my mission was compelling, and the thrill of disobeying the inspector quickened my step. A flashing marquis crowned the entry with the headlining names:

THEA JAMES AND THE BUTTON MEN

No doorman waited outside to welcome guests, and I wondered if they were closed. But when I tested the handle, the black lacquered entry swung open, inviting me into an intimate foyer, adorned in blue velvet and soft golden lights. A podium stood stationed by a cascade of lush indigo curtains, and muffled music echoed from beyond, peculiar and magnetic.

I ventured to the curtain, but as my hand reached to push it aside, a man emerged from them, and I retreated a respectful distance to let him pass. Instead, he followed my steps, eyes locked on mine until we were standing far too near for strangers in a dimly lit room. It was the man from the crosswalk.

"Look who's here," he said, his grin a lopsided affair that was not as charming as it was hostile.

"Excuse me," I replied, snappish, abashed by the gross overstep of personal space. I wondered if he was drunk.

"Can't, love. You won't be coming in here."

He was security. It explained the way he loomed, though I was hardly size enough to cause any trouble, and of all the tactics that might have worked on me, intimidation wasn't included among them. I set my jaw, and despite the rage clawing its way one bleeding inch at a time up my spine, I maintained an unbothered tone.

"I'm new to Nightglass. This lounge came highly recommended. Is it private?"

He chose this moment to try to feel me up again, the tendrils of his magic like tentacles, uncomfortable and disgusting. I gave them a yank, and he withdrew with a grunt like he'd caught a smart blow in his stomach.

"Thought so." He chuckled, the harsh, angry sound of a man ready to resort to violence. "You've got some kick to you. Blackwicket bitches usually do."

"I recommend you take a step back before I offer further demonstration." The words were a snarl, and he sucked a breath in through his teeth, pleased, as though I'd just attempted to seduce him.

"Big threats coming from such a small, breakable body."

He made as if to grab me, but the curtain was pulled roughly to the side and William Nightglass appeared, saving me from considering my worst options.

"Coppe," he said, tone hard as stone. "You'll keep your hands to yourself or you'll lose them."

I scrambled to squash the rise of my magic, hiding it away.

"Was just trying to keep out the riffraff."

"Miss Blackwicket is hardly that." William offered a nod to me, keeping the curtain open with the tip of his cane, onyx as the entry doors. "You're welcome here, Eleanora, and I look forward to showing you what Nightglass has to offer. Please, wait inside for me."

My instincts tingled, a sure sign the decision to enter would lead to trouble, but my pride wouldn't let me retreat, and the photos rested heavy in my pocket.

"Thank you, William," I said, gratified when Coppe's upper lip raised in a grimy sneer.

William let the heavy fabric fall behind me, muffling many of the words the two men exchanged, though I caught…hanging *by your dick on the town green* in Williams' steady baritone.

I didn't doubt such a spectacle would please the crowds, and none that William's threat was empty, though the vulgarity of it shocked me. In his youth, William had been intense but sensitive to the needs of a town he'd inherit, slow to anger. I was unhappy with this evidence that he might be following the path of his father, and I moved away so I wouldn't overhear anymore.

Another set of curtains ahead separated the corridor from the theater, but these were fully open, offering a glimpse into the dimly lit room beyond, and a sample of the slinking rhythm of the band. I approached them and took in the spectacle.

On stage, Thea James, dressed in a white gown accentuating every magnificent curve, shimmered in the spotlight that shined on her with the reverence of an acolyte at the feet of an angel. More than the smoky voice she poured into the microphone like warm honey was the magic infused in it, a shameless presentation of clear, bright energy that rolled over the crowd sitting rapt in their chairs, soaking it in. An audience member writhed, her partner pulling her close to savor the effects of the heady enchantments. If these people had focused on more than the gratification of imbibing someone else's magic, they'd have noticed the stunning prism of the music and the twinkling radiance of this woman's deepest self blooming around them.

Thea James possessed magic in spades, and she *used* it. It radiated, warm and alluring as her voice, softening parts of me I believed would never yield.

"Incredible, isn't she?" William murmured behind me, his voice near my ear. My back brushed against his chest as I turned toward him. He smelled of brandy and tobacco, and this sensory stimulation threw me off balance. I leaned too far, prompting his hand to press at my waist for support. The connection shattered the spell, and I sought sobriety, inhaling deeply, though the odd tingling lingered on my skin. "She's been with us for several years now. Haven't seen a slow night since."

"William, is this legal?"

The restrictions on magic were so extreme, and even the enchantments allowed during the Yule season paled in comparison. The amount of power here begged for Drudge.

"I find it amusing that the legality of all this concerns you." A charming grin lifted the corner of his lips. "But yes, it's completely legal. We have all the required licensing, including a special exemption raising the allowable cap by a significant margin."

"Your father's always known the right people to bribe," I said. There was no point in hiding my animosity toward the man. Besides, the magic had loosened my tongue.

William laughed, the sound pleasant.

"I did the bribing."

I scanned his face to determine whether this was a jest, he winked at me.

"Don't be too scandalized, Eleanora," he said. "There's no need to pretend you don't know what my family's involved in, and since our meeting yesterday, I'm up to speed on all the trouble you've been getting yourself into as well."

I prepared a rebuttal, but applause overwhelmed us as Thea's song completed, and the audience came to their senses. Above the roar, I could hear someone crying. The two who'd been in the thrall of ecstasy were gone, a glass tipped onto the tabletop, perhaps in their rush to leave, wine seeping across the white linen like the remnants of violence, not love. William, the ghost of his previous smile lingering, tapped a light touch on my elbow, then raised his chin in the direction he wanted me to go. Toward the private table where Thea James had taken residence after her graceful, victorious ascent from the stage.

"Come, I'll introduce you. Your sister and Thea were great friends, I imagine she'd like to make your acquaintance."

This was the entire purpose of my coming here, but a worthwhile conversation was impossible with William present. Still, I agreed, preferring not to incur suspicion. At the very least, I'd be able to get a feel for who I was up against.

The spotlight dimmed, leaving the theater aglow in a sparkling blue light, creating the impression of being submerged in water. With none of the earlier magic, The Button Men continued to play smooth music, guiding the place toward intermission. The audience returned to their conversations, drinking, and smoking, with many rising to head to the bar—a cherry wood counter stretching across an entire wall, boasting a mirror set in the carved swell of breaking waves. The glass reflected watery light onto the patrons, casting everyone in a ghostly pallor. People were watching our progress. Not interested in me, but in William. They regarded him with open admiration. To my knowledge, William possessed little magic. The power attracting their attention was another kind entirely.

Thea James didn't regard our approach, too busy speaking to a sleek, auburn-headed woman who'd descended on the table, a roster in hand. She gave the paper a harsh tap, dismissing the assistant, whose lovely face had twisted in frustration.

"Thea," William said, remaining close to me, as if he thought I might run. I couldn't hold that against him, it seemed to be what I was known for. "This is Eleanora, Fiona Blackwickets sister."

"The dead one?" Thea asked with a cool disinterest, taking a sip of ice water, without even bothering to glance at me. I bristled.

"Behave yourself."

It wasn't clear whether William's warning was a sincere reprimand or a good-natured gibe. She seemed unmoved in either case.

"I'm always on my best behavior, it's why we're booming." The mix of snappishness and friendly affection kept me from pinning their dynamic. "Come on, doll, sit. Have a drink."

William pulled out the seat next to her and when I sat as she offered, he took up the chair across from me.

"I'm afraid I don't drink," I said.

"Imagine that," she replied blithely, waving down a waiter, who stopped in his tracks, making a quick turn at the beckon of the star of the house. When he arrived, she ordered something for me anyway. "You'll enjoy it. It's tart."

She propped her chin on the back of her hand, elbow on the table, leaning toward me with a conspiratorial gleam in her beguiling eyes.

"Now, tell me all about yourself. I'm eager to talk to someone risen from the grave."

CHAPTER FOURTEEN

Sitting at that private table in The Vapors, a place I didn't belong, I realized I had no plan. I'd been shoved in Thea's orbit too abruptly and hadn't expected William's presence.

"Never dead," I said, response clipped.

"Clearly."

William cleared his throat and Thea clicked her tongue in response.

"This spoilsport never lets me tease anyone anymore, and it's one of my greatest talents."

"Your magic." I pulled the conversation in a direction that would lead somewhere. "I've never seen anyone with such remarkable control over it."

"Well, Fiona is who you can thank," Thea said, before remembering Fiona was gone. She stopped short, all hardness fleeing from her expression. "I barely knew how to handle it until she gave me a few lessons."

I found it in myself to offer a small smile.

"She was a great encourager."

"She was a great many things." Thea gave no smile in return. "What are your plans while you're here in Nightglass, Eleanora? I heard you cancelled the service."

I wouldn't let Thea throw me off course.

"Yes." I shared no further explanation. "It's so rare to meet a natural magic user. Does it run in your family?"

"Thea comes from a very prominent magical genealogy," William answered in her stead. "I'm lucky to have acquired her. It's hard to find someone whose magic hasn't gone to rot."

Discomfiture squirmed near my navel, and I resisted the urge to clench the tablecloth. Grigori Nightglass once spoke these exact words to my mother. It was becoming more and more difficult to hope that William hadn't chosen to stand in the shadow of his horrible lineage.

The server returned with three different drinks—something golden brown, lacking frills for William, a martini for Thea. When he presented mine, the color of the liquid inside put me off. It was pink, but not the dreamy hue of cotton candy or the taffy from Galton's, but the shade of diluted blood, the scent pungently sweet.

"What's this?"

I placed my fingers on the cool glass, wanting to prove I was game to at least try it, if not for any other reason than to avoid offending the woman who might know something about Fiona's child.

"Go on, doll, it's not strong. I had Phillip put in half the amount of vodka it calls for." Condescension poisoned this confession. As I brought the drink to my lips, I wondered how Fiona became friends with someone like this.

The drink bit into my tongue, its sweet notes demanding, the tartness of citrus overpowering. There was something else, something the overbearing flavors were trying to mask, and it spread in my throat. I coughed, pulling the glass away, yanking my head sideways as a jolt of panicked magic rose to eject the curse crawling from my drink. It was feeble, and slid from my mouth like a miniature squid, retreating into its pink haven, where it curled around the shadows of the ice cubes at the bottom. I gagged, coughed again.

"Not bad," Thea said, reluctant to compliment me, even for something as basic as avoiding the ingestion of a curse-laced drink.

"Not at all," William responded, a sultry edge in the reply as he watched me try to catch my breath, eyes watering.

"You're the first person outside Fiona who didn't just swallow that straight down." Thea took a sip of her own cocktail.

"I didn't come here to be drugged," I rasped.

"Just a little test," William said. "Not enough to do any actual harm, especially not to you."

I slammed the glass down, bright pink sloshing over the rim. "This is beneath you, William Nightglass. Leave those tactics to the Brom."

He chuckled, leaning back in his seat and raising his hands in a brief gesture of waiting, allowing me time to process my own words. My blood ran cold.

"You're lying."

"Come on, Ellie." William shook his head, impatient with my indignation. "There's no need for a disguise of righteousness. You've been running from the reach of the Authority for years. Beyond that incredible display in Devin, who knows what you've been up to."

The cadence of his tone suggested he knew exactly.

"Your shame doesn't serve you here. We *embrace* magic. People travel from everywhere for this freedom. They fill the hole in their souls the Authority left when they enacted their ridiculous ban. Look around you."

He swept his arm wide, indicating the theater, the crowd filling its tables. A sense of wellness and wholeness lingered here, unlike the streets beyond the doors, where the very air felt fractured.

"Magic begs to be used, Eleanora. We've made a business of doing just that. The Authority doesn't bother us; in fact, some of them are patrons. Frequent ones."

This moment revealed my position, the part that William saw me playing.

"What did my sister have to do with all of this?" I demanded.

William's composed presence altered, and he appeared pained for a moment. He observed the crowd, the tightness of his expression belying some inner battle.

"So much," he replied at length, reverence ringing with a sadness I felt more than heard. It wound from him, dark and dense. He pulled himself together, one man becoming another in the blink of an eye. When he met my gaze, the tenderness was gone, and he was once more William, Grigori Nightglass' heir. "But the world moves on and leaves us holding our grief alone. Whether we allow it to drown us is our own choice. People depend on me, on Thea, and we won't forsake them."

Thea remained silent throughout the entire conversation. Sipping her drink, she observed her band as they finished their set and prepared for the next, to the light applause of the crowd. At the mention of her name, a muscle near her ear twitched, as though she were clenching her teeth.

"We're missing something," William said, holding my gaze, the ghost of a grin on his handsome mouth. He resembled a man prepared to tell me a secret I didn't want to hear. "We're sorely lacking someone familiar with the ins and outs of the darker side of this beautiful project."

I had no reason to pretend I didn't know what he meant.

"You need a Curse Eater."

"Thea, unfortunately, never learned how to do it." Here, Thea finally engaged, beginning to protest the criticism. William held a finger up, halting her. "While I'm confident you're

123

capable, Eleanora is a stronger candidate, and you know it."

Thea James leveled an acrid look on me. She did know it, and she wasn't happy.

Discomfort and disgust crowded together too tight to stay in me any longer. Laughter seemed the safest way to express it, so I let out a chortle that mismatched the emotional weight of this meeting. "I'm not going to curse eat for the Brom."

I looked between them, my bravery gathering as rage simmered.

"You're insane believing you could tell me you'd been using my sister as your filtration system for all of this *bullshit* you've been shoveling in this godforsaken town, and expect me to jump in and fill her position as eager as a bitch in heat." My volume intensified, and several heads turned our direction. "You're a fool, William Nightglass. Whatever you were to Fiona, I know it ended, and now I can clearly see why."

"Hm." It was William's only reply to my pronouncement. He stood, using his cane for support, and I maintained my glare as he walked to my chair, lifting a hand as he approached. A slinking, luminous magic gathered on his fingers, growing from William in a way I'd never seen him capable of. The smoky edges of it formed the amorphous shape of a flower, solidifying into a bloom, silky white petals gleaming. Despite my rage, the action mesmerizing me. I'd deprived myself too long of the little pleasures of creating, of bending magic to build small, meaningless tokens. My mother had done it often, for no other purpose than to spread goodwill and joy. Resentment lived in my heart for the ways even such minor miracles were denied to Fiona and me by the changing landscape of magical law. I battled the awe attempting to upend my contempt, the draw of something that once meant everything. William caught sight of my weakness, ever observant.

"This is how it could be, Eleanora. We could all feel this

again," he said, twirling the blossom between his fingers before gingerly tucking it in the curl near my ear. The magnetism of his magic attracted even more attention to our table, a testament to how void human life had become. To my further surprise, he bent, pressing a tender kiss to my temple, murmuring, "Consider it, and please continue to visit and experience what good we do. You've been sorely missed."

He straightened, nodding to Thea his goodbyes.

"I'm sorry to leave you both so soon, but I have an important matter to see to. Enjoy your evening."

He departed in his steady, stiff gait, practically every eye in the place following him.

"What a mess you've walked into, Eleanora," Thea said softly, her thorny exterior melting a fraction. She massaged her forehead against an oncoming headache.

"You were Fiona's friend." I gave her no room to deny it.

"I was," she replied, taking up my abandoned drink. She knocked it back in three long pulls. I regarded her with a mix of horror and fascination as the shadowy curse slipped into the darkness of her mouth. She swallowed. The involuntary pull of breath came at last as the curse found its way. She held it, as though waiting for something ecstatic. After a heartbeat, her lips parted, and a white mist rose like glittering smoke. It dissipated, vapor rising from a stormy sea.

Thea James could curse eat.

"Apparently, William isn't aware you can do that," I said. The unraveling of the tainted magic had been smooth, uncomplicated, and well-practiced. Fiona had indeed been a good teacher.

"What William doesn't know can't hurt me." Her red lips twisted slightly. "This drink truly is disgusting."

As I was about to challenge why she'd so readily agreed to give it to me, she leaned close.

"Listen, it's important you're aware the Nightglass family is starving for adept Curse Eaters. I'm sure you're aware there aren't many left, and that makes you the most delicious thing to cross their path since Fiona. If I were you, I'd hop on the next train, and I'd do it right after you walk out the door of my club."

She'd already looked away, dismissive, when I took the photos from my pocket, sliding them across to her. She glanced at them, stiffened, her spine straightening as though a steel rod had been shoved through the top of her neck.

"My sister's son," I asked, low. "Where is he?"

"Fiona didn't have a son," Thea replied tersely, less composed, scanning the clientele in search of danger.

"Then whose child is this?" I tapped the photo, demanding.

Thea stood, the table rocking with the suddenness of the motion, and she smiled, the expression bright, unwavering, and perfectly painted. She ran a touch down the length of her beaded dress, as though smoothing it, but this motion signified more. It was a pose, body angled to accentuate the line of her waist. She hummed, not a song, but a single note of music. The minute pulse of magic that emanated from the sound encouraged the nearest tables, which had yet to fully lose interest since my outburst, to relax and return to their conversations and drinks.

"You're barking up the wrong tree," she said, false cheer in her voice to match her face. "Leave and stay gone. Your sister's dead. There's nothing left for you here."

When she waved to the band leader, signaling she'd return to the stage, her fingers trembled.

"Thea, please." I stood as well, touching her wrist lightly, ready to beg, then happened to glance over her shoulder.

There, watching from a shadow-dense corner of an already dim theater hall, was Inspector Harrow. He leaned casually against a nearby wall, half-empty glass in hand, glaring at me like a snake from beneath a rock. I snatched my touch from Thea, my sudden change in demeanor pulled her brows low, and she followed my gaze.

"Oh, honey," she said. "I really hope you don't know that guy."

"Do you?" I asked, breathy with the need to understand how the Inspector fit in here, in this awful, beautiful little world my sister had inhabited.

"He's a brute." Her reply was emphatic. "Bad news all around."

"He's Authority." As I said it, I grew stupefied with my naiveté. William said the Authority frequented this club.

"Is he on your tail?"

"I have to go," I said, unable to bear being stared at by a man who held portions of my future, my safety, in the palm of his hand. One who'd seen me waltz into the den of the Brom, sit at their table to drink, and be kissed by their shining prince.

Our roles reversed when Thea reached out to take my hand in hers, stepping close, her movements evocative. The tilt of her chin was sensual, and she brushed two fingers along my jaw. She smelled of jasmine, rose powder, and heady, moonlit magic.

"Come back tomorrow night," she crooned. "Wait until dark, take the alley to the staff door. Wear something sexy, they won't blink an eye at you. They'll assume you're here to meet a client."

"A *client?*"

She shook her head, a practically imperceptible movement, warning me to play my part.

"You're too deep in this to be worrying about your reputation. I'll meet you and tell you everything I can. Until then, you look out for yourself. There are too many people interested in you for all the wrong reasons." She tapped my chin playfully, but it was caution disguised as flirtation. She hummed again, the beginnings of a tune this time, slow and mournful, as she moved away from me, warming her magic for the performance ahead. The resulting energy of it pleased the audience and vibrated in my marrow.

I was wary of engaging in these games, but knew Thea was an expert in moving through this world. If I ever wanted to find out what had happened to my sister and the son she never had, I'd have to follow her lead.

Before I took my leave, shaken by the events of the evening, I looked for the Inspector, planning on giving him plenty of room, but he'd already gone.

CHAPTER FIFTEEN

I scanned the theater and scrutinized shadowy corners as I left. The man at the podium by the entrance wasn't Coppe. He wished me a good night as I dashed into the cold. The biting wind stung my cheeks and ears as I paused, unsure of my next move. The tides of tourists swirled around me, and for a moment, I didn't know which way was up. I willed myself to go in any direction, and at last, I took a step—toward the train station.

The ten-minute walk gave me room to ruminate, and when I reached the busy taxi posts, where arriving travelers were securing rides, I'd decided I wouldn't leave yet. I wanted closure, answers, but was in danger of getting caught in the machinations of the Brom. I'd ask for a departure schedule, prices, and make my plans to beat a hasty retreat when it became necessary.

This time of evening, no line waited at the Ticketmaster's window. A man about as old as Darren but much wider in the middle, and happier for it, smiled at me, his charming face red-cheeked beneath his white moustache.

"Evening, young lady," he said, loud and jolly. "Last train's run for the night. The first comes bright and early, 6 am."

"I'm here to browse the departure schedule, if you don't mind?"

"Of course!" He offered me the ledger listing the week's departures and arrivals. "That'll take you to three days after next.

Evening's cheapest. When were you planning on leaving us, Ms…" he asked, raising his white eyebrows high. It wasn't a sinister question, but I buckled, adopting old habits.

"Jonas," I replied with a warm smile of my own. "Elyse Jonas. I'm afraid my husband couldn't meet me for our winter holiday, so I need to decide when to return home. I'd rather not vacation alone." The candid, open expression I adopted was that of a woman with nothing to hide.

"That's a shame," the man commiserated. "The best time to depart is first thing in the morning. Few people are awake then, so you'll have plenty of peace. If your husband wouldn't miss you too much, I'd recommend two days from now, there are fewer seats booked than usual."

He was so pleasant it made my bones ache.

"If you buy a ticket today, I'll give you a discount," he said. "The railroad men don't want their train cars to be empty, and my life is easier when they're happy. If your plans change, ask for me. Christopher Thatcher. I'll get it switched for you, Ms. Jonas, no troubles."

I had the money—barely, and the safety net was too necessary, so I acquiesced.

"You've talked me into it, Mr. Thatcher," I replied.

"Good, good!" He said, slapping the wooden sill. He retrieved a beat-up clipboard and pulled a pair of spectacles from his pocket, placing them neatly on his large, rosy nose.

"Ms. Elyse Jonas," he repeated, jotting down my name. But when he looked at me, a smile lifting the ends of his moustache towards his eyes, there was a change in him, a sort of halting like a toy whose wind-up mechanism had stalled.

I kept my smile on, bright, leaning forward to see what he was writing.

"It's E-l-y-s-e." I said.

He continued to stare, his grey eyes magnified by the thick

lenses of his spectacles. He abandoned his clipboard, a sheen of sweat appearing on his brow as though it were suddenly summer.

"Mr. Thatcher?" I said, concerned he was having a heart attack.

"Eleanora Blackwicket?" He breathed at last. "God, you're the mirror image of Isolde."

I forced my comforting smile to remain steady. "You're mistaken, Mr. Thatcher. Are you well? Do you need me to call for someone?"

"I'm sorry," he mumbled, his jovial demeanor becoming anxious haste. "If you'd come any sooner, I… William Nightglass was just here."

To ensure my exit was caved in.

"Please," I said, quiet, hopeful.

"I wish I could help you," Mr. Thatcher said, tears bright in his eyes. "I can't go against a Nightglass."

The flimsy scaffolding of my alternate persona crumbled.

"You could." It was a condemnation.

"No. The cost is too high. I'm sorry."

Taking the glasses from his nose, he raised his arm to grab hold of the rolling panel at the window, snapping it shut.

I lingered, hoping Mr. Thatcher would reopen the window, gesture for me to come forward, and risk his life to sell me a ticket. As the station clock struck the hour, I left. No driver would take me to the next town with snow covering the cliffside roads, even if they didn't know who I was, and walking would be as reckless as trying to swim. My earlier plan to stay a few more days was no consolation to the new, persistent impulse to flee. But now, there was nowhere to go but home.

Home.

I rejected the word bitterly as I exited the station. This wasn't home. It was a cage, and I was trapped between the Brom and Authority, options of Annulment or a life of servitude as a whore to the Nightglass family's suspiciously saccharine ideologies.

I walked briskly, seeking to expel the nervous energy built up since my arrival, threatening to drive me screaming mad. As I reached the second block, heading to town, a man, dressed in an old brown overcoat a size too large, wool flat cap pulled low, stepped into my path.

"Miss your train, Ms. Blackwicket?" he asked. Though I couldn't see his face clearly in the dark, it hardly mattered; he'd the same dockman lilt as Coppe, the same nasty swagger.

"Tell William his message was clear. I want no more explanation or gangster theatrics. I'll seek him out when and if I'm ready," I replied with utmost contempt, attempting to bypass him, only to encounter another figure blocking my path. A second goon, similarly clad in faded brown, shorter by a head and much younger. He spat at my feet, prompting me to take a swift step back.

"We don't have nothin' to do with William Nightglass, miss. Our boss is a big fan of yours, though. Would love a chat. Sent us to escort you to him, safe and sound."

"Don't be stupid," I countered. "If you know anything about me, you know you can't make me go anywhere I don't want to go."

"Sure, we can." The taller of them flashed a trench knife pulled from his coat. He held it with a practiced casualness, used to the weight of the hilt in his palm. "Magic won't do you no good with a hole in your guts, girl. You'll get me, but I'd get you right back, right under the sternum. You really want to die on this sidewalk because you were too stubborn to accept a friendly invitation?"

For the first time, I regretted I didn't have a curse on me. Exhausted, angry, and thoroughly trapped, I gave up.

"Go ahead," I offered, weary. The knife wielder released a

bark of incredulous laughter as I unbuttoned my coat, pulling it open to expose the threadbare wool vest and linen shirt, inappropriate for the cold. The thin fabrics would allow a blade to slip through nicely. "There. Under my sternum, you said."

The second man broke first, casting an uneasy glance at his cohort. Clearly, I wasn't wanted dead. "Hey, Patrick, ya can't..."

"Shut it," my assailant barked, expression twisting. He was being bested, and he wasn't taking it well, complexion splotchy with rage, grip tight around the hilt.

"You've got one swing. Make it count, you sorry little shit," I growled, ready to court death with a recklessness I'd never entertained. Insulted and happy to oblige, the thug twitched the knife a hair lower in preparation for its inverted arch into my stomach.

"Eleanora." The voice thundered through the street, and my would-be murderer snapped his head up. He hastily concealed the blade with a motion that seemed magic. The firm touch at my waist was unexpected, and I tensed, but the voice had been familiar.

"You were supposed to wait for me at the lounge," Inspector Harrow admonished, pulling me into him until my side was pressed against his, possessive. "Who are these deadbeats?"

His voice was dangerous, tinged with a jealousy that posed an explicit threat in its own right. I could have moved out of his grasp and shattered the facade with my disgust, but Harrow's presence was making these men uneasy. His angle was foggy, but I was a beggar, and he was doing something for me. I briefly wondered how much it would cost.

"We didn't know the lady was unavailable," said the younger man, hands shoved deep in his pockets, almost like a child. I considered his face, noticing he barely wasn't one.

"I'm glad I could clear it up," Harrow drawled, dismissing them with a quick gesture of his head. "Now fuck off."

"Sure, Victor." The man who'd meant to stab me, raised his palms to show they were empty. "No problems here."

They slunk off, the youngest glancing back, resulting in his companion giving him a swift box to the back of his skull. Once they were out of earshot, Harrow's voice reverted to its emotionless cadence: logical and unbothered.

"It's in both of our best interests if you stop looking like you can't stand that I'm touching you," he muttered, steering me to turn to the street with the press of his palm against my lower back.

"I can't control my face that easily," I snapped, angry that I felt relieved to still be alive, that it had been Harrow who'd made sure I was.

"Then for the next few minutes," he said, walking me into the street, waving to stop oncoming traffic. "Think of your old beau. What's his name... Ben.

As we finished crossing and stepped onto the other walkway, I wondered if Ben would have been brave enough to step into the middle of that and concluded it unlikely. I spotted the Inspector's roadster parked nearby and realized where we were going.

"You expect me to get in a car with you?" I asked with some disdain.

"I'm returning you to the house. It'll be a good time. You can tell me all about your eventful evening," he replied flatly.

"Like hell."

I tried to twist free, but the arm around my waist tightened, and with minimal effort, he lifted me enough for my heels to leave the ground, forcing me to keep pace or be dragged. I stumbled the rest of the way to the passenger door, which he opened for me.

"Get in, Eleanora, or I'll get handsy. How many people do you think would stop me? They didn't blink an eye when a woman was being threatened with a knife. At least it's not a police car. Look, I'm letting you sit in the front."

He was annoyed, and the disruption in his smooth tone was gratifying.

"I thought the Authority at least pretended to be decent."

"And despite my other uncharitable beliefs about you," he replied, scanning our surroundings for any other trouble as he spoke. "I didn't think you were the type to spend your period of mourning, drinking and flirting in a Brom lounge. Sometimes we're wrong about people."

He was crowding me with his body, herding me into the car, and I jerked my elbow back, striking him in the ribcage. He absorbed the impact with hardly an exhale, which became a patronizing chuckle.

"Feel better?"

Knowing my other options were likely even more unpleasant, I climbed in, slamming the door shut. As he approached the driver's side, I exhaled shakily, my stomach knotting, limbs quivering, as the reality of what had almost happened took hold. I sniffed, briefly covering my mouth to hinder the tears threatening to overflow, turning my face to the window as Harrow settled in the driver's seat, his dominating presence filling the small space.

He swerved from the curb into traffic with an aggressive turn that nearly sent me careening into his lap. My hand landed on his knee, and the flower William had tucked in my hair was jarred from its place, disappearing into the floorboard by the Inspector's feet. I cringed away as if burned, wound so tight that a snowflake's weight more of panic would snap me in half.

"I didn't survive a knife attack so you could kill me in a car wreck, *Victor*." Scowling, I used his given name, echoing the thug who'd been familiar enough with him to do the same.

"What were you doing at The Vapors with William Nightglass and Thea James?" he asked, ignoring me.

"Why are you stalking me?"

"There was no stalking involved," he replied. "You just don't pay any goddamn attention. I was there the moment you walked in on William Nightglass' arm."

"I wasn't on William's arm, for godsake. And I have every reason to believe you're stalking me. You did it in Devin!"

"Person of interest," he said, tired of saying the same line.

"Exonerated!"

"It would do you a world of good to drop the act, Ms. Blackwicket. It's tiresome. We both know you killed that man, let's establish that and move on so we can focus on more pressing matters."

I glared at him. "Like who hurt my sister?"

He glanced at me, the bare turn of his head.

"Curse Eaters die by accident all the time."

I couldn't decipher the strange edge in his tone.

"No," I corrected. "They don't. Regular, inexperienced, people who are forced to eat curses die by accident. A trained curse eater who's been doing it since she was five years old doesn't die by curse rot, accident or not."

I stopped short of my full tirade.

"You already know that," I accused.

He didn't look at me, but a wry grin momentarily crossed his lips, unsettling me in a way I despised. We reached the end of the main strip, moving from the lights and onto the shadowy side street. The inside cab descended into a murky gloom, lit by the sporadic glow of the half-moon peeking behind snow-filled clouds.

"Why were you at The Vapors, Eleanora?" he said, doing what he did best, wresting control of the conversation.

"Why were *you* there if you weren't following me? Thea

James recognized you, and, by the way, there's no love lost there."

"Thea's got her own problems. I'm not one of them."

"Lucky woman."

The silence following was heavy with the billowing of my own emotions. The Inspector remained impassive, unimpressed with my sass. I wondered what good this was all doing, what I was achieving in my struggle towards gaining the upper hand. Tonight, for a short, dizzying minute, I'd been ready to forfeit my life. If I were so depraved, what did it matter to me if the Inspector had a piece of the truth?

The car pulled up the drive, gravel crunching beneath the tires. When he shifted it to park, I didn't immediately get out. He'd expected me to, his hand lifting as if to catch me. He rested it on the wheel and waited.

"William and I have known each other since we were children. I didn't know he would be there, that he was involved in… I went to…" I spoke softly, pausing, wary to offer honesty when it had never protected me. I retrieved the two photos I'd discovered in Fiona's drawer and offered them over. He took them with the barest of curiosity.

"I went to see Thea James," I said. "She was friends with my sister. I expected she'd know who the child in the photograph with Fiona is. I just wanted answers."

"Did you get them?" The words were a soft thrum in the darkness. It was the gentlest tone he'd ever used with me, and I risked a glance at him, observing his stark, angular profile and the proud, crooked curve of his nose.

"No, but you're investigating disappearances. It has something to do with the Brom, and if my sister's death is related, then it's your job to find out how."

The paleness of his scar shone in the dim light. A beat of

quiet passed before he looked up again, giving the photos back to me.

"Fiona Blackwicket was an illegal Curse Eater. As far as the Authority is concerned, her end was a logical result of her profession. The Brom had no reason to eliminate her. She was an ace in their hand."

I couldn't accept this, not after I'd debased myself with such vulnerable honesty.

"And what about as far as *you're* concerned? You can't sit there and say you don't care at all what happens to people. She didn't deserve this. She was trying to survive!"

As my desperation grew, Inspector Harrow's tone became increasingly detached.

"A lot of people are trying to survive, Ms. Blackwicket. Not many of them resort to black-market magic."

I was too exhausted to resist the tears collecting on my lashes from this rebuke. I recalled the face of one of the young men who'd accosted me, the softness of childhood still visible.

"The Brom wouldn't be such a thorn in your side if that were true, Inspector," I replied, raw.

"Speaking of aces," he said, my pain failing to move him. "The Brom just lost their leading lady, so you must look pretty enticing. Does that explain why you were at the Principes' private table tonight?"

"Grigori is Principe," I corrected harshly, the Inspector's lack of interest in the photos, in my sister's life and death, incensing me.

"Grigori Nightglass is dead."

This news stole in my breath. Why hadn't William mentioned that?

I did the bribing, he'd said.

I snorted with all the derisive loathing I could muster. "Past time he was in the ground. Grigori was a devil and a madman."

"He enjoyed a decorated military history, worked closely with the Authority to weed out Brom factions in several cities, Devin included, and was a much-lauded Principe, even after surviving such tragedy," Inspector Harrow remarked, as though he were reading a eulogy.

My heart kicked behind my ribs.

Thomas. Thomas. Thomas.

"It didn't make him good."

"From what I know, he kept your family out of trouble and legally employed for many years."

I rotated in my seat, the energy of my rage renewed.

"He blackmailed my mother!"

Harrow held my gaze.

"Is that why she murdered his son?"

Overcome by a jolt of fury, I aimed a slap at Inspector Harrow's face, but he captured my wrist, my fingers mere inches from the scar on his cheek.

"Thomas Nightglass's death was a terrible accident." The words were jagged and bitter, filling the car with my grief. A vibrant current of energy coursed between us. In my turmoil, I'd dropped my guard, giving the Inspector access, and magic moved toward him as naturally as a brook flowing downstream. The sensation lacked the greasy violations of Coppe's magic and the sterile precision of William's, but still sent a shiver down my spine. I tried to heave free, but Inspector Harrow's grip was a vice.

"Tell me what happened," the Inspector coaxed, low. "All I have are the rumors. A young boy makes friends with a Blackwicket girl, ends up filled to the throat with curses. Grigori takes him to your house, where people supposedly go to be healed, and the boy comes out dead."

"Thomas was dead before he came through that door," I whispered. "No child could survive curses like that."

His fingers tightened.

"You're lying to me again."

"I'm only returning the favor," I snarled, struggling like a trapped animal, "My mother never killed anyone!"

"How did she die, Eleanora?" He asked, calm as the eye of a storm even as he pulled me violently forward. I slid across the seat toward him. "Where is her body? It's not in the cemetery, the coroner confessed the casket was empty."

I was vaguely aware he was provoking me, pushing my boundaries, hoping I would reveal my power, but the panic was too overwhelming for me to resist.

"Let me go." I intended it as a command, but emerged as a plea.

Gaze set on the tear streaks making tracks to my chin, the Inspector murmured, "I'm going to peel back every rotting, soft layer of your life, Miss Blackwicket, and I'll uncover the truth."

In response, I finally did what he'd been goading me to do, releasing my magic as if pulling the trigger on a pistol. The bolt of it should have ricocheted through him, singeing his senses. This type of magic didn't kill but could be agonizing in large, unexpected doses. Yet instead of causing harm, it struck as if hitting warm tar. In reaction, his own power began to envelop mine, consuming my energy as effortlessly as a ravenous sea swallows a stone. His eyelids drooped, a deep rumble escaping him, reverberating through the charged air of the cab, and his grip slackened. I threw myself against the door, clambering to open it and escape. He didn't attempt to stop me.

"If you're so interested in the truth," I grated, standing in the driveway, chest heaving, cheeks hot as coals. "Find out what happened to my sister."

I turned my back on the Inspector's callousness, and the unwanted, terrible ache in me, branching from the place where our magic crossed, where his touch still stung my skin.

CHAPTER SIXTEEN

T he house hummed as I entered, responding enthusiastically to the caustic energy I was emitting. The sound mingled with the shifting gravel as the Inspector drove away from the house. I didn't need to run, but still vaulted every step, my magic, long suppressed, pulsing freely along with my heartbeat, entwining with adrenaline and fury.

As I arrived at the third floor, my vision rocked in and out of focus. I was too full of negative emotions, fueled by the maddening indifference of a man whose sole aim was to dig deep into the soft viscera of my past, extracting whatever he needed to justify his contempt for me, my sister, and all others like us who were struggling to survive in a world that used us as tools or as alters for blame.

Instead of seeking refuge in the bedroom of my childhood, I turned to the one my mother kept, which I assumed Fiona occupied in years past. I was desperate to be close to the memories of the women who'd loved me, two people who'd been intrinsically part of the only joy I'd ever felt in my life.

As I pushed the door open, Williams' words slithered through my burning thoughts—menacing yet provocative.

It could be like this again.

I stood in the doorway, shaky, unsure of what I'd find. On this side of the house, the moon never cast its insistent light, so there were no shutters, no heavy curtains obscuring the silvery light of night beyond the two dormer windows that gave shadowy shape to the sparse furniture: a bed and two wardrobes. I searched the wall for the light switch, snapped it on, and the two sconces by the bed buzzed to life, their light golden and soft, illuminating the space with a warm calm, in contrast to the storm I carried inside.

No pictures or paintings hung here, the grass cloth papered walls bare. A single circular rug spanned the center of the room, once as green as summer trees, faded into the dusky color of drying moss. The bedding was white cotton, not as comforting or whimsical as our old quilts. It appeared sterile, hospital-like in its austere setup. It smelled sweet here, the high tart redolence of summer fruit before it turned, and I covered my nose. But it must have been my heightened senses causing the overwhelming aroma, because as I stepped in, it dissipated, making space for the fainter scents of dust and old wood.

I'd wanted the riot of my sister's life to exist here, an unmade bed, clothes strewn across every surface, left in small piles as she'd done every day of our lives. I'd been eager for a moment spent in the comfort of her disorderly housekeeping, which had frustrated me. But nothing of my Fiona, nor my mother, remained here.

The house shuddered, alive with anticipation of what I'd do with my magic now it was free. I seethed as I approached the wardrobe by the windows, flinging open the heavy doors to reveal rows of impeccably arranged garments—luxurious fabrics like organdie and silk hanging neatly alongside moiré and velvet. This was where my sister stored her clothes, all those stunning outfits I'd seen in the pictures adorning the walls. They represented a life she'd chosen to live without me, filled with choices we'd sworn we'd never make, and in a sudden fit of anger, I reached in, seizing handfuls of fabric, pulling down countless dresses and skirts. I channeled my power to ignite each in an incinerating magical flame, tossing them to the floor to burn.

The room brightened, shadows retreating like innocents cowering from violence as an aspect of my sister's unknowable world disintegrated. I would have destroyed everything, but my magic twisted in grotesque response to my fury, and the silk gown I held slipped away, hovering as though draped over an unseen figure. As the enchanted flame engulfed it, the invisible form writhed and stumbled toward me as charred pieces fell away, seeping red smoke.

"No," I whispered to nothing, realizing what I'd done. "No, no."

The sleeve of the gown raised, an invisible arm reaching in desperation as the remnants of the dress collapsed, squirming as though in agony. When the flames subsided, there were only charred debris, the results of my loss of composure, and the ever-rising rust-colored smog of transforming magic.

I dropped to my knees, immersing my hands in the smoldering pile, attempting to fix the pitiless thing I'd done, to revoke my anger and my actions. The newly formed Drudge still rose through my fingers, ghastly and vaporous, retreating from me, its creator. It tumbled, stretched, and darted in frantic directions to escape. I crawled after it like a supplicant, begging for forgiveness, but it slipped into the narrow gap between the doors of the second wardrobe.

Grabbing the ornately carved handles, I pulled myself up and opened it, expecting to dig through more of Fiona's clothes to find where the poor thing had gone to hide, but there were no women's clothes inside. Instead, an array of children's toys and games lined several inlaid shelves. Among the paraphernalia of youth were a bag of marbles and jacks, a deck of cards, and a puppy whose velveteen ears were worn bare from petting. On the right, an assortment of children's trousers and shirts, all in varying sizes, were arranged from smallest to largest, creating a detailed map of their owner's growth. Below the clothes, a quilt similar to the ones my mother had made for my sister and me, was neatly folded, an uproar of colors and varying fabrics, ragged and worn practically to bits. In the corner, stitched in small letters by a careful hand, was a name.

Roark.

As I touched the name, heart leaden in my chest, the claw-like hand of something long dead darted from the darkness at the back of the wardrobe, seizing my elbow. The grip burned like a harsh frostbite, and I instinctively recoiled. The Drudge hiding in the gloomy corner released me with little resistance, emerging partly from amidst the clothes, hanging from the shadows like a primate from a tree branch. This creature was old; not as ancient as Auntie, but old enough to assume a vaguely humanlike form. It was a habit of most Drudge to adopt the appearance of those they tormented, or as my mother used to believe, those they sought help from.

This creature possessed only a suggestion of features: the vague contours of cheekbones and brow, the hollows where eyes might be, and the slash of a mouth, like a tattered rip in a curtain.

The tainted power I'd generated had flown to the nearest of its kin to be absorbed. There'd be no mending it, not unless I cared to take on this Drudge alone. Considering how I'd handled the much smaller one I'd stolen from Ms. Rosley, I didn't trust myself to try, especially with magic weakened by the act of forging a curse.

Sensing my reluctance to engage with it, the Drudge extended its rangy limbs, sloth-like, four fingerlike talons folding around the edges of the doors and pulling them shut. Its fingers disappeared last, like smoke from an open window.

Eyes still locked on the wardrobe, I retreated until my legs collided with the bed and gave out.

I remained still until sitting became unbearable for my weary body, and I lay down, resting my head on pillows that smelled of lye and honeysuckle. I stared into the dark, listening to the sounds of the house, which had returned to the natural noises of a lifeless structure, battered by winter. The horrible use of my magic appeared to have shocked it silent, and it was a silence I regretted deeply.

In my twenty-six years, I'd never misused my magic, never given it reason to distort and turn to something ugly and hurt. Pain made tangible. A piece of myself was irrevocably gone, and I felt hollow, not better.

I evaluated the damage, my magic moving sluggishly and thick, fatigued from the incident. To invigorate it, I positioned my right hand by my face, palm up, invoking my power—not to heal a curse or protect myself, but to create, to make beauty from nothing as I'd once done at every opportunity.

A frail thread of magic formed in my palm, stabilized with recollections of Fiona's sweet smile, her delicate mannerisms concealing a passion for curse work and music. I imagined her face as she played the chords of my mother's favorite song. Hearing the ghost melody, I sang the words to myself.

Oh, Moira, my love, I meant not to stray...

I had nothing in mind for what I was making, only sang to the emerging magic lacing itself together, tentative and delicate. I would let it form itself how it pleased, giving no more orders, releasing my will. But the shape it took didn't comfort me, the edges rounding into silky crimson petals, mimicking both the flower William had given me and those I'd tended as a child.

I brought the bloom to my nose and breathed in.

"Your garden is strange. The plants are all black, even the lilies. Are they dying?"

"No," I'd said, barely eight, so sure of myself as I packed more

rich dirt at the base of a vine I'd newly transplanted from the house. "They're not all black. They're red. Look, hold this one in the sun."

Thomas was a few years older than I, but was still all curls and boyish softness. His meek demeanor encouraged me to attempt friendship. I handed him a small clay pot with a dark blossom perfectly unfolded and he took it skeptically, holding it up.

"Oh, yeah," he said, amused at the novelty of it. "Are you feeding them magic to make them this color?"

"You're not supposed to know I use magic, remember?" Grouching, I scanned the cliffside ahead and the lawn behind for signs of my mother. I'd be in trouble if she discovered I'd told someone.

"It's just us here." He was unapologetic, putting the pot back. "And I use magic too. I don't get to do this stuff, you know, make things grow."

"What do you get to do?"

He never talked about his magic. I knew he had it from the way mine responded, like a wave buffeted by the wind. My question quieted him, and he pushed at the new pile of dirt I'd made, patting it.

"Nothing I like," he said at last. "So, can I help you?"

"No."

"Aw, why not Ellie?"

I hesitated. Thomas and I had been friends for a year, since his father, Grigori Nightglass, began coming to the house more frequently to do business. I hated Grigori and his greasy smile, but Thomas seemed pleasant, shy, and he'd shown me how to find pill-bugs and race them along the path to the garden.

Even when Grigori briefly stopped harassing us, Thomas continued to show unannounced. Mother never allowed him inside, but let me out to meet him. Fiona had played with us for a while as she was closer to Thomas' age, but she'd grown bored with our rowdiness, preferring her calmer creative activities to throwing rocks into the sea, scaling the porch trellis to the roof, and racing up and down the hill from gate to garden until we were flushed and breathless.

Aside from Fiona, Thomas was my only friend. And friends shared secrets with each other.

"You can't tell anyone, ever…"

"I never would! Cross my heart."

I believed him.

"It's not magic."

I grew shy myself, picking at the leaves of a nearby thistle.

"What do you use then?"

"Curses." I confessed timidly.

I half expected him to get mad. His father was Principe, in charge of making sure no one was using illegal magic in Nightglass. My mother's license had been sponsored, but that didn't include me. I was breaking the law. But he didn't recoil or laugh, didn't call me a liar. He looked over his shoulder at the bulk of Blackwicket House hulking behind us.

"Like the ones in your house?" he asked.

"How do you know about those?"

"Can feel 'em from here."

I panicked. "If you tell Grigori, I'll be arrested!"

"I never tell him anything," he said by way of reassuring me, but that wasn't enough.

"Just in case, tell me one of your secrets."

He eyed me, incredulous. "Why?"

"So, I can make sure you never tell mine," I replied with all the solemnity of someone demanding a blood oath.

"I don't got any."

"That's a lie. Everybody's got one!"

He smiled his self-conscious smile.

"Yeah, ok. I guess that's fair." He spent a moment thinking, *and I guessed he was trying to find a worthy trade. "Grigori's not my dad."*

"Who is?" I asked, the revelation not so shocking. I barely had a dad. Fathers were a mystery to me. I still hadn't figured out how they worked.

"Dunno," he said, shrugged like it didn't matter, but looked so sad. That afternoon, I made the first of several stupid decisions only children can make.

"Ok, I'll teach you to plant curses."

"How come you use curses and not regular magic?"

"Mom says it's a good way to store them, helps them heal," I replied, knowing no more.

The following two years had been an opening of my world. I'd snuck Thomas in the house when my mother was in town, even to Fiona's great delight, and we'd terrorized the smaller Drudge, catching them from their hiding spots in the shadows. I'd taught him how to inhale and hold them without it hurting too much. We'd woven them into our plants a little at a time, and our garden grew. Then, following my tenth birthday, Grigori's demands on my mother became more aggressive, and Thomas visited less and less. When he turned up, we played fewer games, and sometimes he'd only sit on our porch in a solemn state that worried Isolde Blackwicket. When I'd asked her about his change in behavior, she'd grown somber and warned me Thomas was likely going to stop coming soon but wouldn't explain why.

Terrified of losing my closest friend, I'd devised a plan to keep him interested in visiting, and did something that would haunt me for the rest of my life. I'd shown him Dark Hall.

The creaking of the wardrobe door pulled me from the bleak memory. In the gloom, I could discern the barest silhouette of a bowed head through the few inches of space. The Drudge didn't reach or move, simply watched, just as Auntie had watched all those years.

I enclosed the flower in my fingers, crushing it against my palm, pressing my fist to my chest as though I could hold on to everything I'd already lost.

CHAPTER SEVENTEEN

Morning came to spite me, and I awoke to a room that hadn't changed or cleaned itself up during the night, erasing the evidence of the cruel work I'd done. I opened my fingers to pinpricks of pain, blood rushing back to my hand, where angry indentations from my nails framed the crushed remains of the flower in my palm. I didn't know how to move on, surrounded by my grief, suffocating under the attention of the Brom who'd use me as a tool and the Authority, whose unchecked Inspector was digging too deep. But time wouldn't wait for me to catch my breath. It moved on with no remorse.

Maybe I could still escape this, return to a nameless existence that rolled on dull as dry hills, draped in the ill-suited skins of imaginary women, and shielded by a meager armor I'd forged in lies and abdication of power. But another option had been whispering to me since I'd stepped over the threshold of this house. I could settle into my own bones, painful as it was, and deal with the terrible consequences of being myself with dignity. No matter my choice, death would catch me. I was future nourishment for weeds and worms, regardless. My grandmother, my mother, my sister, they'd all died young and tired - but they'd died as themselves. Blackwickets. Curse Eaters.

But not murderers.

A knit cardigan had survived the massacre, and I plucked it

from the foot of the bed as I left the room, nothing but blind determination guiding my steps. I bathed, dressed in the last of my clean clothes, then donned my sister's sweater, the texture and color of a spring fawn's soft belly. When I glanced into the gold-framed mirror above the sink, I noticed my sister's features echoed in mine. I'd always believed we'd never favored each other, but we both possessed our mother's cheeks, the same bow of our lip.

I gathered my courage, using it to approach the Inspector's room. It had been late when he'd left me to reel from what passed between us, the clashing of passionate and stony animosity, undermined by the way he'd enticed my magic to burn bright and hot, only for his to swallow a piece of it. Inspector Harrow wanted to know my secrets, and I was becoming more and more interested in his. Appealing to his humanity hadn't worked, but perhaps a bargain would.

For a moment, I listened for familiar sounds—shuffling, breathing—but it was quiet. I rapped my knuckles against the door and waited, knocked again when there was no response. Pursing my lips, I chose to be Eleanora Blackwicket, grabbing the knob to pour in magical intention. The lock clicked.

I was unsure of how the Inspector kept himself in sleep, but his revolver was likely close, so I didn't enter, merely called out, voice firm.

"Inspector Harrow - I need to speak to you."

It remained quiet. Curious about the silence, I pushed the door open and was met with a sight I hadn't expected. I'd assumed the Inspector suffered in the squalor of a neglected room, bloated and warped by moisture and mold. Admittedly, those thoughts had given me grim satisfaction, and I'd often pictured his regret over bullying me into letting him remain at Blackwicket House. But the room I entered was tidy, entirely untouched by the ruin that had once characterized it.

There'd been renovations—broken glass panes, rotted wood beams, and misshapen floorboards were all replaced. The moldering bed dressings were gone, exchanged for fresh linens, plain but new. His bed was empty but slept in, sheets rumpled, pillows in a haphazard pile. A pair of trousers and a white towel hung over the bedpost, suggesting he'd discovered the guest bath and made use of it. The scene was so unexpectedly intimate, an unwanted flush crept into my cheeks. I tried to withdraw from the far too personal intrusion I'd committed in the name of bravery, but was halted by the sight of something unusual.

Gouges marred the wood along the doorframe and adjacent wall, taller than I could reach, even on my toes. The savage grooves were deep, carved by the repeated boring of something sharp, like the tines of a garden tool. Upon inspection, the panel of the door boasted the same, as though a large animal had been attempting to find its exit, though nothing else in the room appeared damaged. I fought the urge to touch the furrows, to feel them against my fingertips and judge their origin. Instead, I returned to the hall, closing and relocking the door, wiping my palms on my skirt, unsettled. Fionna's time here in Blackwicket House became ever murkier. I wondered what Inspector Harrow thought of the markings.

Regardless of the strange discovery, my unresolved conviction smoldered, and I ventured down the stairs to signs that the Inspector was in the house after all, exactly where I'd asked him not to go. The curtains at the end of the hall were open again, the lights of the parlor mingling with the sunlight.

I found the Inspector standing at the window, observing the vista: the slope of the cliffside, the meager wood fence acting as a barrier between life and the sheer drop into crashing water below. His severe presence was softened by the inviting surroundings and the lack of his typical uniform. He'd forgone the stiff waistcoat and wore only a white button-up, collar open, sleeves rolled to his elbows, revealing the powerful lines of his forearms. Though the revolver was present, the weapon was secured in a more discreet belt holster at his waist. I'd never seen him like this in the light of day, and I didn't appreciate it. He looked too much like a predator softening its snarl so prey would amble closer, and worse, it was effective.

"Miss Blackwicket." He greeted me before turning his gaze from the window. It flicked from my face to the ensemble I wore. "You look at home in yourself today. Near-death experiences suit you."

The impulse to retaliate with a volley of my own, or to demand why he was in the parlor when I'd asked him to stay away, was mitigated by an awareness that his influence was largely fed by my tendency to react. He needed me to remain unsteady, to lower my guard.

I lifted my chin, channeling whatever audacity my sister had wielded to survive in Nightglass.

"Inspector," I said, with every ounce of authority as the sole heir to Blackwicket House. "You need to see something."

Minutes later, we stood in my mother's old room, the Inspector eyeing the debris of my frenzy from the night before. His bulk was strange in the space, intrusive despite the invitation. I should have corrected the mess, worried the image didn't look good for my state of mind, but what I was going to reveal was far more damning a gamble.

I approached the wardrobe where my sister kept the gallery of children's things, where the hoary Drudge made its nest in the shadows. The Inspector should know what this house was built for, what it required of my family.

"Was this room your sister's?" Inspector Harrow asked, maintaining a respectful distance from me. Although he didn't seem wary, his shoulders were tense, and his hands tucked in his pockets, likely to give him close access to the revolver.

"I don't know for sure," I answered honestly. "I assume it was her son's."

He guessed where I was guiding him.

"You believe the little boy in the photo was Fiona's son?"

"If you'd bothered looking at it, you would have seen the inscription." Nerves had made my patience brittle.

"Fiona was on the Authority's radar for a long time. There was never any reason to suspect she had a child."

"Maybe because he's dead," I spoke the fear, the horror of it softening the edges of my tone.

"What makes you think so?" he replied, with an overly-gentle indulgence, making it clear he was humoring me.

Nettled by his continued hardheartedness, I flung open the wardrobe doors, revealing its contents.

"Why would Fiona keep toys? Clothes? They vary in size and abruptly stop. She's stored everything precisely. It's a goddamn memorial."

My tumultuous emotions were ascending to the surface, and I pressed my fingers into the hair at my temple, trying to restore my face to its mask of neutral assurance.

His interest finally engaged, the Inspector stepped forward, expression tight with what I hoped was embarrassment for not having taken my concerns more seriously. He scanned each shelf, every hanger, as though categorizing the contents. Evidence. This was evidence. He couldn't doubt what I was telling him. With this victory in my pocket, I prepared to bare the house's soul.

He extended a hand, ready to start a closer inspection of the shelves, but I moved to stop him, uncomfortable with the idea of someone else handling these items.

"Please, don't touch anything."

When my hand fell upon the bare skin of his forearm, a circuit closed, and the current of magic moved so swiftly that we both reacted. While I hastily pulled away, he merely shifted his focus to the place my hand had been, expression unreadable. The trail his gaze took back to my eyes idled, catching on my lips, which had parted in alarm, in *apology*. My eagerness to assure him I wasn't seeking to pilfer his magic sputtered, then died in brutal irritation. My magic being agitated and difficult to bring to heel was a result of his obtuse, willful goading. He was in my house, and I'd be damned if I apologized for any of this.

"Don't touch anything," I repeated. This time, the words were a command. The only crack in his usual impassive expression was the slight upward twitch of a brow.

"Well, Miss Blackwicket, you certainly have my attention," he said, his voice dulcet, like a murmur in a lover's ear. He was testing the limits of my newfound resolve, sensing it was fresh and unsettled, seeking soft junctures he could exploit. I was on the verge of losing my nerve, and he knew it. If I countered with calm instead of reacting, I could at least keep pace, even if I never quite could outmaneuver him.

"I know."

I'd attempted to match his lilting inflection, but the words emerged too rigid, resentful.

I prepared to unveil the Drudge, explain what I could while still safeguarding the most volatile secrets, creating the impression of transparency and perhaps tempt some understanding from a man who held my past and future in his indifferent hands.

So as not to startle the cursed creature nesting in the wardrobe, feeding off whatever sadness my sister had left behind in the artifacts of this lost childhood, I pulled the clothing aside.

The Drudge was gone.

Once again, the new reality of the house confused me. All the rules had changed. Growing up, Drudge of this size had settled in preferred locations to lurk, and there they'd remained, either scaring off smaller beasts for territory or consuming them, as this one had done to the poor, accidental curse I'd produced. They didn't migrate unless...

Abandoning caution, I dismantled the psychic gates that restrained my magic, casting my power out and giving little thought to Inspector Harrow's reactions. The vibration of it was palpable, much as Thea's had been on stage. Though dread had produced it, the result was strengthening, grounding me in the house, into the earth it was built upon. Inspector Harrow released a small breath, not fully immune to the effects. He yanked me around to face him, as the net I'd cast found what it searched for, the shape of a Drudge, not where it should be.

"What are you playing at, Miss Blackwicket?" he barked.

My gaze traveled to where my magic had tethered itself, high above the apex of the dormered windows, in the dark corner of the ceiling where the shadows had coalesced, thick and viscous. Inside them, clinging to the wall, was the reason the Drudge from the wardrobe was no longer in residence.

Auntie.

She'd always been more substantial than the other drudge. Power, consolidated by ages, had given her a shape unnervingly proportionate to a human woman's, though she remained too elongated, limbs spindle-like. She dripped with tarry magic, the effluence turning gaseous, rising to rejoin the dark gloaming where she'd been hiding, observing. I hadn't noticed her. I'd been too closed off, too guarded to detect the noxious force she radiated.

The small hollow of Auntie's eye sockets had been angled in my direction, but following my noticing of her, the truncated neck turned, clicking, toward the Inspector, stringy tendrils of hair wafting around her skinless face as if submerged in water.

Whether it was my expression or his own senses involuntarily activated by my magic, Inspector Harrow's attention snapped to where this matriarchal demon clung, and she sprang from her perch, wide mouth opening to emit a sound like train brakes, shrieking. I attempted to lunge in front of him, but was caught in the unyielding enclosure of his arms as he hurled us both to the ground, escaping the line of impact. The three of us hit the floor simultaneously. I landed on my back, Inspector Harrow on his side, hulking form hovering close, narrowly avoiding crushing the breath from my lungs. Auntie tumbled in a flurry of limbs, skittering, resembling a cat on a slick surface. She collided with the bed, which screeched across the floor in protest. Her struggle to find purchase continued, giving the Inspector enough time to draw his revolver and raise it.

Though it wouldn't have hurt the Drudge, my instinct to prevent the violence was immediate, and I grabbed hold of his arm as he fired the weapon, sending the bullet shy of its target, crashing into Fiona's clothing cabinet, splintering the door.

"She's scared!" I screamed, realizing I was talking as much about myself as Auntie. The house pitched, and it felt as though we were passengers on a ship at sea. I'd never experienced anything like this.

"*She!*" Inspector Harrow bellowed in response, as Auntie finally regained her balance and leaped to the top of the wardrobe, holding Fiona's sweetest memories inside. The collision caused the wardrobe to rock, and it began its slow tip, directly toward us. As it came smashing down, Inspector Harrow rolled onto his back, dragging me along, just as the heavy wood smashed inches away from my face, the force rattling my bones as violently as Blackwicket House's own shaking.

I was sprawled across Inspector Harrow's broad body, chest to chest, my right knee positioned between his legs, his arm draped over my shoulders. He still clutched the revolver in his free hand, raised to track Auntie's retreat from the room, moving like night chased by the break of day.

CHAPTER EIGHTEEN

"Why the hell did you shoot at her?" I yelled, unhinged by the adrenaline pumping liquid lightning through me. I pushed off him, making my best effort to strike his ribs with as much force as possible in lieu of landing a punch square in his face. I grabbed at my skirt to prevent it from riding up my thighs any further. In the haze of my animalistic panic, I was aware I would be humiliated later if I wasn't on my way to an Authority maximum security prison.

"The fact you keep calling it *her* begs an explanation, Blackwicket," Inspector Harrow growled, the fight in him activated. Shoving himself onto his feet, he jogged out into the hallway in pursuit. I followed him, livid with his inability to leave bad enough alone.

Hurrying after, knowing the danger of touching his skin, I took a fistful of the back of Inspector shirt. He was facing me before I could draw in the breath to demand he stop, his sleek hair mussed from the jostling of the confrontation, a new ferocity in his eyes which shone hard and gold. He looked bedeviled, obsessed with a hunt I'd interrupted for the very thing he'd spent his career eradicating with the methodical picking off of magic users. I'd effectively turned his attention from his quarry, but landed on me. As he stepped closer, the house rumbled in response, lights flickering, lengthening the dark.

Steps away in the alcove framing the attic door, a foul stench of overripe fruit and decay wafted on a phantom breeze, and rising with it where she'd been crouching in the gloom, Auntie. I had no alternatives, no weapon of my own besides what was embedded in me by my heritage. As she lunged toward the Inspector, I ducked around him, catching her against my chest. Air shot from my lungs, freezing in the cold orbit of the Drudge's body. The impact shoved me into the Inspector, whose attempt to catch hold of me only resulted in a tangle of our feet, sending me sideways. I crashed on top of Auntie, her form so solid it felt as though I were touching something once human, wasted away. She clawed at me, her fingers yanking my hair, her sharp joints jabbing, eager to reach beyond me to the man who'd threatened me, who threatened her and the existence of Blackwicket House.

Despite the clarity of her motives, I couldn't let an Authority Inspector be torn to shreds for his magic. I dug my fingers into the claylike bone of her face, opening myself to the invasion of her ancient grudges, her decades of grievances. If she didn't relent, this would be the end of us both.

"I'll feed you to Dark Hall." My warning emerged high and gasping as my lungs expanded. Auntie's curses were magnetic and my magic too eager, the sequence of power required for curse eating already in motion. And like a lounge girl drawing on a cigarette, the curses that made up this monster gorged my throat.

Inspector Harrow attempted to pull me free from the Drudge, who grappled at us both, desperate to keep hold of the curses I was unintentionally stripping away from her.

"Let them go!" The Inspector's voice roared in my ear, disturbing my thrall enough for the powerful Drudge to break free. The burning sensation retreated as fresh air rushed in to replace it. Whether out of rage or pain, Auntie clambered up the wall with her mouth open, wailing—a long, piercing noise—as she disappeared down the slope of the stairs.

In response, the remaining sconces repeated their dramatic

reaction to my arrival at Blackwicket House. A high electric whine vaulted to meet the pitch of the Drudge's cry, lights brightening. When the inevitable was obvious, the Inspector swore with violent enunciation and propelled me against a door, where he shielded me as the glass globes and their bulbs exploded, the sound eerily similar to the discharge of the Inspector's revolver. This was retaliation for continuing to hurt what I was meant to help, for siding with the enemy.

Glass shards rained on us, nicking my chin and arms, Harrow absorbing most of the impact with his continuous efforts to stave harm to my body. The man whose threats of Annulment had filled my sleep with vivid, brutal nightmares, who was notorious for shedding the blood of magic users, was continually ensuring my physical wellbeing.

When the hall ceased its chaotic explosions, the last of the electric lights making an angry, gritting sizzle, dying at last, I raised my head to find he was looking down at me, visage inscrutable.

"I've dealt with a lot of Drudge, Miss Blackwicket," he said, arms tensing on either side of me as he leaned closer, voice dipping into a rumble. "The behavior of that one was, if you don't mind the language, real *fucking peculiar*."

We were close, as close as we'd been in the hallway, the car, but something about this time frightened me more than those— my lack of revulsion. From this angle, with his collar unbuttoned, I could see where the livid scar continued, where it stopped below his collarbone in a horrible, jagged arch towards his sternum. His scent remained peppery, underscored with a frosty bite incapable of being replicated by humankind. My magic was a squall, denied the satisfaction of engaging in the purpose it was trained for. It searched for another way to release the pressure generated in the struggle. Without my instruction, it sought the edges of Inspector Harrow's magic, drawn to its like, but his protections were in place, the murmuration of his power barely perceptible. Still, he sensed the prodding and, for a white-hot moment, inclined closer, then pressed his palms into the wall and righted himself.

The distance gave me clarity, the befuddled fog lifting. My magic withdrew, but didn't settle, my jaw and collar burning where I'd suffered small nicks. I concentrated on this discomfort as I replied to his previous observation.

"Just because you've been in the field harassing Curse Eaters for the work they're made to do in secret doesn't mean you know a damn thing about any of this," I said, testing my minor injuries, searching for remnants of glass in my skin. I spoke to distract myself from the huge mess I'd made. "That Drudge is *old*. It's been here since I was a little girl, before my mother even arrived. It refuses to leave, but it hasn't done me or anyone else harm. This is the first time I've ever seen it do more than lurk! So many things have changed here, but I thought if I gave you some of the truth you're so desperate for, then you'd be a fucking decent human being and take my concerns seriously."

My monologue complete, I stood in the fallout, controlling my breathing so my chest wouldn't heave with the ferocity of this small confession.

"Miss Blackwicket." The Inspector watched as I pulled a glinting, bloody shard the size of an eyelash from my chin, wincing.

"What," I snapped, ready to bite if he goaded me.

He looked rumpled and abused, blood seeping through the white cotton of his shirt near his shoulder where he'd taken the brunt of the petty blow the house dealt.

"You said 'before' your mother arrived. She wasn't born in Nightglass?"

He'd been waiting for this, for my carelessness, and the mistake that would reveal more than I wanted.

"She was." I tried to stumble back on the correct path, the one I'd built with falsehoods.

"It was an interesting choice of words." He nailed me to the spot with this intense scrutiny, his unfeeling armor in place, as though nothing we'd survived had been any more upsetting than a walk to the post box. "Stories circulated for years among the riffraff that Brom could procure children with magical ability for those willing to pay a pretty price. Authority expected it was drivel, a scam. Magic gave up on this backwater world after the war. All that's left to the children born here are the festering remnants you happen to be eyeball deep in."

He gave me no time to rebut, and continued, "Then, by happy accident, I met a Bobbit woman."

This name drew me up short. The Bobbits had been a family of Curse Eaters out west, well known and much loved, eradicated by the Authority. Their downfall was the opening Grigori Nightglass had needed to corner my mother, to appeal to her fear and offer protection, all the while tightening the noose.

"The Bobbits are gone," I said, unsure now. "The Authority Annulled them."

"Oh, there's still a Bobbit or two around. And this one knew quite a bit about a curious practice Curse Eaters had adopted - stealing children from Dark Hall."

A new panic bounced in rhythm to my heartbeat, the resigned sort, a kind aware that no amount of fighting or fleeing would prevent the inevitable. Still, I laughed, the sound hollow and ugly.

"That's a far-fetched story to invest belief in even for you, Inspector Harrow," I replied, knowing he'd never understand the truth. "Nothing like that could be happening."

"Your confidence in that statement is a marvel."

"There aren't anymore Narthex, are there?" I couldn't

control the testiness. "The Authority made sure of it. There aren't any ways to get to Dark Hall."

"Unless you're an adept magic user."

"You said yourself magic is dying."

"Except I watched you inhale a Drudge like it was opium smoke." He was harsh, the veneer of his stoicism cracking, "Then scurry straight out of that department store only to pop up here a week later, fresh as a goddamn daisy. It takes considerable power to walk away from that. You're living proof there's magic enough somewhere."

"Does that make you feel like a failure, Inspector?"

He laughed then, running a hand over his mouth, likely talking himself out of shooting me. I noticed the hollowing of his cheeks as he bowed his head to refocus himself, the dark hue gathering beneath his eyes. He appeared unwell.

He pointed at me, the motion emphatic.

"You threatened the Drudge with a trip to Dark Hall. So I'll ask you again, Miss Blackwicket. Can you access it?"

I'd trapped myself, and there was no more safety in completely lying.

"Not anymore. That threat was empty."

"But you've been there before."

"When I was a child."

"Your mother took you there?"

"No. She forbade me from going. I snuck in."

"Did your sister?"

"She never showed any interest. She was always afraid of it."

"Because of the Fiend?" he asked. "But you weren't afraid?"

The Authority's ignorance continued to both astound and enrage me.

"The Fiend doesn't bother people who don't keep curses, Inspector. It feeds on broken magic. If there is none, it's harmless."

In truth, the Fiend was horrifying, a smoky horde of hellish faces and grasping ghostly limbs. When I'd first encountered it I'd been sure I was dead. I'd huddled and cried for my mother as it rolled over me like fog, chattering my name. I'd emerged unscathed and never saw it again, not until I'd taken Thomas.

"Eleanora, if you could access Dark Hall as a child, why should I believe you can't now?"

His use of my given name was always jarring, and I fumbled.

"There's not a Narthex anymore, Inspector. It was closed the night I left this house."

"The one in the parlor."

As usual, he showed his hand when it would do the most harm, overpowering my senses with a resentment so strong I could taste its bilious bitterness coating my throat.

"Yes," I grated. "If you already know the answers to your questions, why are you asking them?"

"I didn't ask you about the Narthex. You supplied that information yourself, and you expect me to assume there's not another Narthex somewhere in this house."

"If there were, there wouldn't be nearly so many curses here."

"I imagine it's less lucrative to feed them to the Fiend."

"We don't *sell* magic!"

"Yet, your and your sister's friendship with Nightglass…"

His words were severed by a spasm taking over his body, every muscle tightening, as if a seizure was pulling him inward, dragging his eyes shut amidst an onslaught of pain. It lasted for seconds, yet the torment lingered in the tension that kept his shoulders from straightening.

I made to approach. "Inspector?"

He raised a hand to prevent me from coming nearer.

"I'm fine, your sympathy isn't required," he said, the aftermath of the fit making his tone brittle.

"I was offering medical attention, not sympathy," I replied. I'd once been happy to imagine the Inspector suffering, but seeing it in person wasn't as pleasant as I'd dreamed. If I'd been a witness to the outcome of what I'd done to Brock, I wondered if I would have experienced the same concern.

The Inspector's chuckle was unexpected, breathy, and humorless. "Neither are needed."

"Did the Drudge…"

"I'm well." At last, he was capable of his previous intensity, shoulders leveling. "As much as this conversation has been eye-opening, I need to excuse myself to rest. Being in this soggy little town is a drain on my soul."

"I don't think you should stay," I said, hoping my warning wasn't received as a threat. "I can't guarantee this won't happen again."

He began his trudge to his room.

"Drudge don't scare me anymore than they scare you," he replied. "I was caught off guard today, I won't be next time."

I was going to let him go, but as he passed, the question burning inside me spilled.

"Do you really believe the Brom are stealing magical children from Dark Hall?" I asked, giving proper reverence to the weight of the question.

He paused, weary, his energy diminishing even as we stood there.

"Was Isolde Blackwicket born here?" he asked in return, and he wasn't inquiring if she'd been born in Nightglass, or in Blackwicket House as Fiona and I were.

This was my mother's secret, the shame of a family that didn't belong to her, given to me and my sister to keep. But she wasn't here, and the storm this would bring couldn't hurt her.

"No," I said, the word hushed.

He examined my face, eyes lingering once more on my lips as though looking for the trace of a lie there.

"Yes," he replied, then surprised me with a shift in his tone, made soft by his peculiar exhaustion. "Miss Blackwicket. I want you to consider the possibility that the clothes and toys in the wardrobe weren't meant for just one child."

Dread draped me in an oily shroud. I glanced at the open door leading to the suite of rooms, once a haven, now destroyed and soiled by the implication that my sister had turned Blackwicket House into more than a waystation for cursed Brom.

"She wouldn't." I said it with conviction, permitting myself to reject the possibility without being sure. I owed Fiona that much. The Inspector didn't refute me.

We went our separate ways in resigned silence, until Inspector Harrow's voice carried the short distance across the hall.

"Eleanora."

I glanced back from where I stood, staring into the room Fiona had made her own. The Inspector leaned against his door frame, preparing to close himself away.

"I'll find out what happened to Fiona," he said. "But you need to mind yourself and the company you keep. You should know better than anyone that there are monsters in Nightglass far bigger than those you harbor here."

CHAPTER NINETEEN

I sat in the threshold of that room, knees to my chest, staring in at the wreckage for so long that the afternoon began to fade. I imagined the many memories hiding in the cracks of the floorboards and seams of the wallpaper. A million rice-sized secrets undulating out of view like maggots. Once, nothing could have made this room feel unsafe. Now, all I could sense was the foul possibility that my sister had been helping the Brom kidnap children, just as Grandma Fora had taken my mother. It would have required traveling between the joints Dark Hall's magical corridors—quadrants I'd never been brave enough to venture into. The ones where reality grew insubstantial as a cloud, and magic moved in illuminated streaks through the vacuum of darkness.

Mother had never spoken an ill word of Fora Blackwicket, the only parent she'd ever known, but in truth she'd hardly spoken *any* word of her. Isolde's childhood was a mystery to me beyond the occasional story told by others. Even after she'd divulged her origins as a Dark Hall child, she'd never discussed with us the possibilities of where her home was, but I suspected she was searching for it during all of her trips to Dark Hall near the end.

We'd been taught the Fiend was a creature born of necessity, a monster made by magic to protect itself from those who'd enter its sacred home with curses clinging to them. And despite what I'd said to the Inspector, I believed the Authority's fear of it was well earned.

Fiona had never expressed interest in the strange byway built by generations of Curse Eaters, where magic could be shaped with ease into anything a heart could think up. Like living in a dream. The first time she'd chosen to join me on an illicit trek, she'd made it two steps in before beginning to sob so fiercely she'd given herself hiccups.

How could that same person have navigated Dark Hall to steal children for the Nightglass family?

At length, I grew brave enough to reenter the room, approaching the decimated wardrobe. The toy puppy rested on top of the quilt, which peeked from the beneath the ruins. I crouched and nudged it aside. The embroidered name wasn't visible, but it was clear in my mind's eye.

Roark.

If my sister kept so many children, there'd be no need to embroider a single name, no purpose to keep a sole photo of herself and a small boy. I glanced up, my eye catching what remained of Fiona's clothes in the half-empty wardrobe. A pale blue dress mirrored the meager light from the window, its beadwork shining.

Thea had instructed me to come to the lounge tonight.

I hadn't decided to go. I didn't trust the woman, not when she seemed so involved with William and so ready to put on a well-practiced facade. Not when she'd tried to taint me with a curse hidden in a sweet drink.

But if she had any information about what all of this meant, it was worth the risk.

At twenty 'til ten, I slipped away from Blackwicket House. I hadn't heard Inspector Harrow leave, but the car was gone. It didn't matter. He hadn't warned me to stay in the house again, hadn't made his threats. Whatever work he did in the dead of night was his business, and this was mine.

Along with the outfit I'd borrowed from Fiona's collection, I'd added a more sensible coat, one that would shield my bare shoulders and chest from the frost of the night. Snow was falling, and it took me longer than usual to traverse the distance in satin heels, feeling ridiculous. Why Fiona even owned a dress that covered so little of her shoulders confounded me. But I bet she'd been stunning in it, and not as awkward as I.

I didn't consider myself unattractive, merely uninteresting, a requirement of the life I'd chosen to lead. Flashy dresses, cosmetics, and elegant hairstyles were a unique risk I hadn't ever mustered the courage to explore.

The sidewalk was busy as ever in front of the Vapors, and it required some bossy maneuvering to reach the narrow passage between buildings which I'd spotted from the crosswalk. I wasted a moment peering down an alley so narrow a broad-shouldered man would struggle to navigate it, then walked nearly the full length of the theater before the wall bowed, forming an alcove for hind lot deliveries.

As I emerged into it, I discovered I wasn't alone.

Several men, some clad in waitstaff uniforms, leaned against the walls, puffing on cigarettes. Upon noticing me, a few stood straight, while others offered low whistles. The fact I was covered from head to toe didn't dissuade them. I reacted with disgust and strode towards the side door, which was ajar, held open by a brick.

"What's the hurry, gorgeous? Surely you got a minute to do something pro bono for us hard working fellas."

"Alright," I said, smiling wide, channeling the effortless charm my friend Magdaline possessed in spades, adding a sultry accent the dancehall girls in Devin favored. As much as I loathed to utter the words, it was my best bet of getting in without a scuffle.

"I'll just tell William Nightglass I was late because I was enjoying myself in the grimy alley with... say, what's your name?"

A scoff from the oldest of them, "The Principe don't mess with the girls that come 'round back, princess."

"You sure?"

As if sent from the heavens, the door creaked open wider, and Thea James leaned out to find me standing mere inches away. Her makeup was impeccable, the white feather nestled behind her ear, fluttering in the icy breeze. Her wrap dress was a deep shade of red, with such a daring neckline that even my gaze snagged. The men adjusted their postures, discarding their cigarettes and straightening their shirts and jackets.

"What took you so long? You were supposed to be here hours ago!" She grabbed hold of my arm and as she was pulling me in, I regarded the flabbergasted faces and winked.

"Bye," I said, sweet as spun sugar.

Thea paused inside the doorway and began yanking at the buttons of my coat.

"Get this off. God, I hope you didn't dress like a damn librarian."

I let her jostle the coat from my shoulders. After revealing the dress, she gave me a complete once-over, scrutinizing the blue silk sheath draped with a gathering of white chiffon, the hem ending at my ankles, generous slit climbing above the knee, offering both daring and ease of movement. The neckline exposed my shoulders and décolletage, which I'd left unscented in honor of self-preservation. Given the circumstances, I wasn't eager to attract any more notice than what was required.

"When Fiona wore that dress, she looked like a goddess," Thea said.

I flushed, touching the dip of the neck, self-conscious.

"If she could see you in it," Thea continued, shoving the coat into my arms, "she'd be one jealous woman."

The abrasive compliment hooked its teeth in the way Thea meant it to, with no softness or room for the recipient to question its sincerity.

"Follow me, we have to go through the theater."

"Why have me come in the back if..."

"Coppe's working the front tonight." She cut me off, making it clear the thought of him knowing I was here was unsavory.

We moved down a dim hallway, papered in gold stripes. Heavy doors lined the walls, leading to offices or dressing rooms, although none boasted plaques or names. As we neared the main hall, I finally heard the muffled music of Thea's band playing something low and languid, and above this, a more insistent noise emerging from a doorway on my right: the sounds of people enjoying themselves in ways unrelated to music. Separate from the warmth that crept up my neck was that sensation of loose magic flooding the hall ahead. Unlike Thea's magic, this didn't work slowly like wine on a tranquil night, but blitzed my senses like hard liquor poured too recklessly down a gullet. I stalled, swaying slightly, already woozy.

"Shit," Thea uttered, steadying me. "You're a lightweight. I didn't expect that. Make your guard air tight—no magic in, and none out. I don't want a single person to sense you. Hold your breath if you have to. Tonight isn't a night for a novice."

I took offense at her suggestion that I was a novice, considering my history, though I wasn't completely certain what skill she was discussing.

"Then why'd you invite me *tonight*?" I asked, lowering my voice to her level, bare whispers in the hall. A woman cackled.

"You have a right to see something. I'm going to show you what Fiona did for this town."

We arrived at a set of velvet curtains, identical to those at the entry, appearing black in the gloom. Thea parted them to peer out.

"You're ready now, or you're ready never. Stay close, don't let anyone touch you and if they try, you say you're William's."

I snorted, prepared to protest when Thea leveled a look on me so grave I balked, and considered the weight of this moment. I was walking into the arms of my sister's secrets, and as Thea said, I was either ready now or never.

"I'm William's," I replied in agreement to her terms.

The theater was awash in blue light, so dim that the guests appeared as mere impressions, silhouettes of shadow lounging on the chaises and couches that had replaced tables, huddled in unmistakably obscene configurations. Scattered throughout were low benches, adorned with flickering candles which occasionally illuminated a rouged cheek, a diamond earring, the flash of an expensive cufflink, and the stockinged toes of a woman whose leg draped over the shoulder of a kneeling man.

I looked away. Thea stood so close our hips brushed. I straightened my spine and pretended I belonged here as we made our slow trek along the side of the theater toward the bar. The air was hazy, filled with a white miasma, mimicking tobacco smoke, without the stench. Instead, it carried the vivid scent of magic, tinged with decay—the same scent that had overwhelmed me in the crowd on the street. I slowed, prompting Thea to clear her throat, a warning.

"Is this the magic people pay William Nightglass for?" I asked, my voice low, scandalized by this realization far more than the other goings-on. People were allowed to enjoy themselves, spending their time with the company they chose in whatever manner they wished. But this magic wasn't the sort formed by human souls.

"Some of it," Thea replied, irritated with the stalling of our movement, keeping watch for any signs that any mind was being paid to us.

I raised my hand, drawing my shield down a fraction to test the magic.

"It's weak," I said. "Barely untainted. If anyone tries to use it, it'll all revert to curses in a few days."

Thea grabbed my wrist and pulled my hand down.

"Stop it, you'll attract attention."

I pulled from her grasp, but with controlled force so as not to flail. She didn't hold on.

"They have to return, don't they? For the fix. You give them the poison and then the medicine over and over again."

"Don't pity these people, Eleanora," she said, shaking her head, regarding the sea of bodies with poorly concealed disgust.

"My sympathy is for the magic, Thea. It's a living thing and this?" I motioned to the lewd vista. "This is *torture*."

An arm snaked beneath my breasts, enveloping me in the harsh embrace of a man whose face was obscured in shadows, but whose voice wasn't difficult to identify.

"Look what we have here," Coppe muttered from around the cigar clenched between his teeth. His fingers dug into my hipbone as I attempted to sidestep him. "You didn't tell me she'd agreed to be the new one, Thea."

"Nightglass won't be happy with you putting your paws on her, Coppe." Thea's voice was cool, with a bite of animosity that was a warning for any man. But Coppe seemed a stupid sort.

"William ain't here. So what're you up to bringing an untested Blackwicket here on High Tide, hm?"

I was forced to lean quickly away as he turned his head, the ember tip of his foul cigar moving past my cheek, so close the heat of it stung. He chuckled at my reaction. I longed to shove my fingers into his eyes, but I was aware of my position.

"You're acting a little tepid," he said, pleased with himself for recognizing my resignation. "I guess Thea told you that you can't risk using your magic or you'll get torn to shreds by all the lovely people here wallowing in this filth."

"Come on, Coppe, you're making my job hard." Thea's coldness melted as easily as snowflakes on a tongue, and she was smooth as velvet, disentangling me from the loathsome man's grip, tucking herself in my place. Her tone grew placating, as syrupy as the one I'd used with the men in the alley.

While Coppe released me, his hand coming to rest on Thea, far lower than I could have lived with, his gaze remained steady, and I received the distinct impression he was imagining me as a corpse. It required some murmuring from Thea to get his full attention, but at last he gathered her against him, and she glared over his shoulder and pointed with her chin toward the bar, imploring me to go that direction.

Vulnerable in this unfamiliar, hazardous territory without Thea's guidance, I still preferred my odds a solid distance from William's henchman. No patrons lingered around the bar counter, so full of the intoxicating magic that liquor wasn't a consideration. I'd never witnessed freshly healed curses being used to fill the empty with a promise of power. I thought of the Drudge I'd encountered at the mortuary, a few blocks from here. With this type of magic in such abundance, any Drudge, big or small, would find reason to come sniffing, so how were they keeping them at bay? A Curse Eater like Fiona was capable of the job, standing guard and absorbing any approaching danger. This might have been her function, but it was just as easy to assume she'd been obliged to supply the faltering magic from the curses unraveled at the house.

My head was spinning, from my thoughts and the effort to seal myself tight enough that the magic, already infused with lust and greed, wouldn't find a way in. Thea was correct; I was a lightweight, having hidden from the harsher realities of my kind for too long. When I reached the long stretch of mahogany, I glimpsed my outline in the mirror behind it, which reflected the gloomy lighting.

I knew my name, my history. But Eleanora Blackwicket had never been asked to do anything harder than say goodbye and run.

I wanted a drink.

As though summoned by my thoughts, a familiar man appeared. Phillip, the waiter from the night before, who'd agreed to serve me a cursed beverage. He didn't ask for my drink order now, but motioned me to the end of the bar.

"You're the new girl? Good, you've got to get back there. The load's too heavy tonight, someone'll croak if you don't jump in."

"Excuse me?" Taken by surprise, and not willing to follow this man deeper into the belly of the Vapors, I glanced at Thea, to find her mouth pressed to Coppe's. Had it been a kiss, my interest wouldn't have lingered, but there was something about the arch of her back, the curl of his body over hers, and I saw it. A thin line of light extending from between her lips, to be inhaled by Coppe. Unwound curse magic.

"Woman," the bartender snapped, and my gaze returned to his alarmed face, the creases of his brow anxious. "I'm begging you here. They're really struggling, and I'm worried someone's going to void."

"Void?"

Realizing the full danger of what was happening in The Vapors. I left my coat on the bar and rushed to follow the stranger toward whatever horrific revelation awaited.

CHAPTER TWENTY

The bartender led me through a door tucked in a recess behind the bar, an area convenient for the staff to come and go. Even with my guard up, I could sense how dense yet uncertain the enchantments were here. This was the source of the magic that fed the people in the lounge, a pulsing tide of energy.

High Tide.

The hall was short, and we'd walked just a few steps before coming to a door that opened onto a scene I wasn't prepared for.

The space was a dressing room, with mirrors and lights lining the right wall, along with a stack of dressing screens that had been folded out of the way. A rack of dresses and staff uniforms was pushed to the side to make room for chairs, but only a few of the many individuals crammed in here—men and women alike—were seated. Most were collapsed on the floor, curled like children shielding themselves from nightmares. I heard neither a whisper nor a moan, not a grunt or loud breath; simply stillness and the silent release of unwoven curses from the lips of the human vessels they were being fed through.

"Oh my god," I breathed.

"Just do your job," Phillip grunted, uncomfortable, withdrawing into the hall as soon as he'd deposited me where he expected I belonged.

I scanned the faces I could see, noting the mixed expressions of focus and fatigue. It would be a miracle if even two of these people possessed the ability to handle this task. As weak as the magic wafting to the ceiling was, combined with the poor condition of everyone here, I imagined none of them did.

This is why Thea had invited me here. To help manage this heinous task.

These poor people were part of the slapdash machine fueling the depraved event, and I was eager to throw a wrench in it.

Giving little thought to the repercussions, I leaned near the man closest to me, elbows on his knees, his head cradled in his hands. When I tapped him, he didn't respond, so I delivered a sharp jab to his wrist, the hand slipping from his face. He rocked upright to avoid falling, and the white spirals of magic faded.

"How much is left?" I asked.

He stared at me, dazed. I snapped my fingers in his face.

"How much?"

Realizing I was talking about the curse he was picking apart, he searched himself, "Maybe a quarter?"

"Fine, get rid of it, then get out."

"But there're more, I can't dump the rest on everyone else. Mr. Nightglass…"

"Can go to hell," I barked.

Relief encouraged him to obey me, a total stranger, and with renewed focus, he returned to the curse, impatient to be free of it. I began rousing the others, each of them exhausted from the ordeal, but capable enough to complete their current task and get gone.

Halfway, I encountered a woman slumped against the clothing rack, a cascade of red hair framing her face, concealing it from view. There was no telltale white wisp hovering above her, and her body was unnaturally still.

"Hey, time to go," I said, leaning to touch her shoulder.

This motion shifted her weight, which she hadn't been supporting on her own. I caught her limp body as she fell, losing my balance and tumbling to the floor with her cradled in my arms.

The face was gaunt from the early effects of curse rot, yet her chest rose and fell as she continued to exhale faint breaths. This was the woman with the list who'd stalked away from Thea's private table the night before. I prepared to lower my defenses, but paused, considering the potential influence of the curse-born magic surrounding me. But the power here hadn't yet reached the theater for a chance to be corrupted.

I opened my battlements a bare fraction, finding the curse in less time than it took to blink. The hot, ashy shape contrasted starkly with the cool tendrils of unwoven curse magic in the air. It was already embedded deep in her chest. If I removed it all at once, she'd void—die from exhaustion and magic depletion.

Thea chose that moment to enter.

"What's going on here? Why are people leaving?" She demanded. As she saw the woman, her face collapsed with genuine concern. "Oh, Cora."

She rushed to my side, pushing the hair from the woman's face, calling her name with an affection that alerted me to a connection beyond someone handling their employee.

"It's not a powerful curse," I said, "But she's too depleted. If I try to remove it all at once, she's dead. I need you to help break it up, and when it loosens its hold, I'll take it."

"I don't know how to curse eat from a person," Thea said, her exterior calm and collected, despite the hint of panic in her voice.

"The same way you take curses from a non-living vessel," I instructed, attempting calm of my own, though I held a secret terror in my chest. The last time I'd attempted to take a curse from a living thing, it had ended horribly. "She has active magic, that's the only difference. You'll have to avoid it. If you get too close, you risk pulling a piece of it away, and she doesn't have any to spare. She shouldn't have been doing this."

Thea glanced up at me, almost angry, "I know."

We huddled close, two women in evening gowns, and Thea's magic brushed mine as we both took our places, searching for the edges of blighted magic inside this improvised Curse Eater named Cora.

The going was slow, Thea unsure and cautious, never venturing to unweave too much at once. The healed portions emerged from between her lips, barely the size of snowflakes. But the consisted effort yielded results and, like ice melting beneath the persistent warmth of spring, the curse lost its grip on Cora's fragile magic. I drew the remnants toward me, Cora's mouth opening in sync with mine, a distorted echo of Thea's gift to Coppe. The curse coiled its way inside, less powerful in the reservoir of my magic than it had been in the barren heath in hers.

It tasted of blood.

Gasping like a woman nearly drowned, Cora sat upright, her ribs expanding until the force of her inhalation arched her back. She released the stale air, inhaling deeply, drawing in several more breaths of the delicate magic surrounding us as if it were oxygen. Gradually, her cheeks lost their gauntness.

Thea uttered a relieved oath, and Cora focused on her. The two women embraced, with Thea's fingers weaving through Cora's red hair.

"You weren't supposed to work tonight," Thea admonished. "I told you to find someone else."

"There wasn't anyone else." Cora's reply was muffled in Thea's neck.

As Cora recovered, I roused the others from whatever trance they'd entered to do this work they weren't built for, trained for, or even capable of. These were people the Brom coerced into standing in for a woman who was no longer here.

As people regained consciousness, exclamations of concern arose over Cora, with a small gathering hovering nearby as she acclimated to her body. Thea waved them away, helping Cora to her feet. The redhead was short, barely reaching Thea's chin, and she met my gaze with eyes green as fairytale meadows.

"You're the Blackwicket sister, aren't you?" She said.

There was no reason to deny it.

"Eleanora," I replied, to a hum of both curiosity and relief from the bystanders.

"Thank you, Eleanora."

I offered an awkward half-nod.

"High Tide's done tonight. Go home." Thea instructed everyone, and they moved from the room, quiet as ghosts. She followed them, Cora's hand clasped in hers, until the woman assured her she was fine. She placed a kiss on Thea's cheek and murmured something too low to hear and departed. Thea watched her leave with something akin to regret.

"Cora worked last High Tide, too," she said at length, answering a question I hadn't asked. "We have a strict rule against back-to-back shifts like that."

"You tricked me into coming here tonight." I pointed to the room, rage emerging from the shock that kept me numb throughout the harrowing experience. "You wanted me to see all of this, so I'd do what William wants and take Fiona's old position."

But Thea shook her head, and the feather behind her ear shifted, brushed her temple. She wrenched it out and discarded it on the floor.

"Yes, I needed you to see this. You don't understand what we're going through here, Eleanora."

"You're forcing people to eat curses!"

"We don't force anyone to do anything; they're here by choice."

"What were their other options?" I snapped.

"Don't play righteous with me, Eleanora Blackwicket." Thea took a step towards me, her own fury darkening her cheeks. "You have no idea what I know about you."

I intended to clarify that she knew nothing, but that was a pointless argument. We stared each other down instead, each of us trying to find traction. At length, Thea straightened her shoulders, proud.

"You're right," she said.

The concession was unexpected.

"Those people are desperate," she continued. "Most of the Brom here in Nightglass are. When the Authority axed the ports, they lost their way to make ends meet, and most of them couldn't leave. Fiona poured her heart and soul into this town after that, all the money she had."

So that's where the fortune had gone: toward renovations that turned a crumbling tomb back into a functioning Inn, and to a dying town my sister loved despite everything.

Thea was struggling not to deflate, the pressure heavy.

"She opened Blackwicket House, took the curses the Brom collected, and gave them back the magic we used for this sickening circus. She never attended. By the time I got here, Nightglass was prospering because of her. She was always standing with arms and heart open for whoever needed her, never a complaint, never a waver of fortitude."

Thea's voice was thick with something—frustration, grief, I couldn't determine. My sister's dress suddenly felt overtight on my body, constricting me with the responsibilities she'd shouldered because her heart had been too big for her own good.

"But things started to go wrong, people went missing: clients, customers, and a few of our own guys. Gone. It was getting more and more dangerous to do the devil's work, but the devil didn't care." Thea raised a shoulder, as if she could shrug off the horror of everything she must have been living. "Grigori was an old bastard, but he was putty in your sister's hands. Fiona knew how to handle the Nightglass men, how to sweet-talk them."

Just like my mother.

"Then Grigori got himself murdered."

Murdered. The Inspector hadn't been forthcoming with this information.

"Throat cut like a fucking holiday turkey. Like that poor Ticketmaster at the station."

"Mr. Thatcher?" I asked, shocked.

Thea nodded. "Happened last night."

Her revulsion and regret matched mine. Grigori had done everything to justify his bloody exit, but Christopher Thatcher had merely seemed scared.

"Grigori deserved worse," I said, and Thea's dark gaze found mine.

"Damn right he did," she whispered, taking in a shaky breath. "William had always been strange, but he was kinder than his father, and he loved the hell out of Fiona. We thought he was going to step up, change everything, but..." She paused here, stuck on information she didn't want to give me. "When he and Fiona fell apart, he went strange, spent a lot more time with that crazy geezer. Then Grigori died and locked himself away for weeks. When he finally showed face again, it was with new plans for the Brom, goals for a long and prosperous future. He was meaner, unpredictable. That's the time Fiona began acting wrong, too. She withdrew, closed the house, and wouldn't talk to anyone."

I wanted to ask about Fiona's son, or the son she'd believed she had, but wondered how much she'd tell me, how deeply she was involved in what led my sister toward the spiral that ended her life. Thea appeared genuinely disturbed by the world she lived in, but if there was one thing I'd learned in the handful of hours we'd spent together, this gorgeous musician was also an incredible actress.

But I had little to lose, so I took a page from the Inspector's book and attempted to throw her off guard by a quick change of subject.

"When we talked last, you told me my sister didn't have a child."

"She didn't," Thea replied without missing a beat, but there was a hardness in her tone, a warning that this was territory she wouldn't cede easily.

Either I wasn't good at asking unexpected questions, or Thea was always on her toes. It was possibly both.

"So whose boy was in the picture, Thea? Who's Roark?"

"I don't know everything about your sister. We were close, but she never let anyone into her inner world. I've never even been to that house of yours. What I'll tell you is that the only way women like us survive in a place like this is to go along, Eleanora. It's what Fiona did, what she had to do. Then she changed her mind and started bucking. It exploded in her face."

A heavy silence fell between us. This night had been far worse than I expected, and there was nothing to show for it but a deeper loathing for the Nightglass family and a fresh curse to replace what I'd just gotten rid of.

"I'm going home," I said, before regretting the word I'd used. Too late to take it back, it hung in the air, heavy with unintended meaning.

"Wait, Eleanora," Thea stopped me with a graze of her fingers on my arm. "It isn't safe for you to walk. I'll get my driver to take you home."

"No, thank you. I don't know where I'd end up," I replied bitterly.

"I swear to you we'll take you to Blackwicket House. All the way to the front door." Her earnestness, which she realized wasn't worth much given the situation, was punctuated by a small grin that transformed her face, which became something beyond beautiful—the face of a woman who was only that and nothing more.

"Honestly, I've never been that close. I'm a little curious."

"I'm sure," I replied, not bending to the friendly smile.

"Or you can be a stubborn mule and walk yourself, alone." She leaned against the door frame, a hand on her hip, confident that she was making a good argument. "In the snow, with a whole crowd of magic-intoxicated lunatics who are going to be looking for any way to keep the high going after being cut off earlier than expected."

My laugh was a short expulsion of breath. Somehow she'd made this absurd reality sound like a joke. My magic was still active, jittering around the curse I'd taken from Cora, and with the battle of the cold facing me, I might not be able to keep the barriers up to protect me from detection.

"I'll accept the ride," I said, "But Thea, I'm not opening the house. I'm not going to help William keep doing this."

She regarded me as though she were tracing all the lines and features where my sister and I collided.

"Eleanora, honey," she replied, "I'm not sure William's going to give you a choice."

CHAPTER TWENTY-ONE

We made a hasty exit through the Theater, the cloud of magic dissipating, low conversations rising above the music being diligently played by the Button Men on stage, who were starting to droop in their chairs. She left me at the alley door.

"Stay here, I'll get Ramsey to pull the car around. Don't talk to anyone." She demanded, her stony exterior repositioned, the friendliness dissipated. As she hurried away, I realized I'd forgotten my coat, but a mission to retrieve it would be ludicrous.

From outside, I heard a scuffling, muffled moans, voices cut off in protest, then the sound of a heavy weight hitting the ground. These weren't the salacious noises of attendees to High Tide. I wanted to mind my own business, let Nightglass handle itself, but the recollection of my earlier run-in with some of the overeager staff compelled me to intervene.

Despite being inappropriately dressed for the weather, I jerked the door open, prepared to do whatever I had to, and found two men crumpled on the alley floor—one unmoving, the other struggling to roll onto his shoulder, finding it impossible. This man's face was a pulp of swelling, a river of blood pouring from his nose and the cut above his right eye. Two of his fingers were broken, resting crooked at their joint. The snow-dusted stone was dappled with vivid red.

But there was still activity, out of view in the stretch that lead to the lot where Thea's driver would be waiting. Less concerned about the fight since it was among Brom rabble, I nearly stepped inside. However, the crack of knuckles against bone, coupled with a chillingly familiar low laughter, urged me to lean forward and glance around the corner.

Inspector Harrow had a third Brom by his throat, pinned to the ground, delivering ceaseless blows, as the weak hands of his victim raised uselessly to fend off the onslaught. From my vantage point, the Inspector's profile was fully visible, hard and expressionless as he grabbed the pitiful creature by his shirt and pull him to his feet.

It was Patrick, the man who'd ventured to spill my entrails on the street outside the train station. If he were here, it seemed he worked for William after all, and was paying for it.

Inspector Harrow's bulk was significant compared to the Brom, and although Patrick had wanted to stab me to death, the clear imbalance sat wrong in my stomach. The Inspector was the obvious winner of this fight. There was nothing more to do unless death was the purpose.

Why shouldn't it be?

This nasty thought sat with me for longer than it should, but Inspector Harrow didn't raise his fist, didn't draw his gun. He muttered something indecipherable, and the Brom made a noise, a gurgling as he tried to push the Inspector away with the strength of a lamb.

The bowing of Inspector Harrow's head came with a pang in my chest, a lurching as magic rolled from Patrick's bruised throat, emerging as a cloud of crimson steam. Inspector Harrow inhaled it, deep and complete, like anyone who'd been curse eating for a lifetime, but even as the dark smog of the polluted enchantment faded, the confiscation wasn't complete.

The wretched undertaking grew grotesque as Brom's body

began to collapse in on itself, the muscles in the Inspectors neck straining as his head tilted back, jaw opening wider than should be possible without tearing his skin. Yet he remained whole, flesh and bone contorting to accommodate the monstrous feeding, as a wisp of pure magic, bright and white as a falling star, trailed the dark tendrils of the curse. It was the threads of the Brom's soul being pulled free.

Annulment.

I should have let him drain the man dry, kept my mouth shut and slunk into the lounge. Ran home. Prayed Harrow never knew I was there. But this atrocity was more than even I could stand.

"Inspector!" I cried, voice hoarse from horror, stumbling forward a step.

The consequence of my intervention was immediate. The Inspector's bearing transitioned, the withdrawal of magic tapering as his muscles relaxed, his face rearranging to its natural state. He released his grip on the Brom, not in startled guilt, but in the deliberate act of discarding something no longer useful.

The man slid down the brick, his legs failing to hold him. When he landed, he toppled into a small bank of snow swept to the wall by the gusts of wind blowing through the alleyway.

"Blackwicket," Inspector Harrow rumbled, his tone and posture newly relaxed, satiated. "You're always in the middle of every trouble I come across."

He wiped his mouth with the back of his hand, finally turning his eyes to me. I didn't take his languorous posture at face value. The power he'd imbibed was seething beneath the surface, hungry for more, and I was in his sights, trembling from the cold and writhing adrenaline. I couldn't run. The alley was too long. I hoped saving Patrick's life was worth whatever I'd condemned myself to.

"You know," he remarked, expression impassive as he took

a menacing step in my direction, "I had a feeling you'd be coming out tonight."

I broke, turning to lunge towards the staff entry, grasping the handle. But he caught me, turning me to face him as he pinned my body to the freezing brick wall with far less power than he was capable of.

Once again, I found myself trapped in the cage of his arms, but this time, it was he who posed the threat, and no one would shield me from the fallout.

Refusing to mewl and cower, I met his power with rage, fighting to free myself.

"You killed him!"

I reached to scratch his face, pulled my knee up to catch him anywhere I could, but I was restrained by the tight dress, whose slit tore with my effort. Harrow took hold of my arms, binding them to my side. My body was useless, and so was my magic. In his current state, anything I gave the Inspector, curse or otherwise, would make it worse.

"No, no, no," he murmured like a wolf to a rabbit it was about to bite. There was blood on his collar, a fresh bruise on his jaw where one of his victims managed a shot. "Patrick's going to wish he were dead, but the rat's breathing. Go on, take a look."

I turned my head, finding the man shifting, grunting as he tried to sit up.

"Feeling sympathy for him? He was going to murder you, Eleanora." Harrow's lips were so near my ear I felt the warmth of his breath on my neck, the heat sending goosebumps rising on my cold skin. My magic turned molten, pressing at the walls of my defenses, eager to be swallowed by the gravity of Harrow's power, which I was only just beginning to fathom.

"Does the Authority know you're a Curse Eater?" I spat, pushing against his chest. He relented, but only gave me enough space to meet his gaze, bright as gold glinting in sun-drenched water.

He smirked, the malice deliberate. "Oh, I'm something much worse."

The timbre of his voice stole into the cracks of my shield, pressing them further open to expose the magic marrow.

There was a transformation, a physical shadow that emerged absent a shift of light, briefly distorting the planes of this face. Leaning close, he breathed me in, and new unwelcome heat mingled with my temper.

"You broke into my room. I could smell your magic everywhere. Too sweet for its own good." His voice vibrated at my temple, "You enjoy snooping where you shouldn't. Is that why you were here on High Tide? Looking for answers? Or for another experience entirely."

"I'd never use magic that way," I protested, and although it was true, my delivery was less emphatic, softened by the strange reaction I was experiencing to the Inspector's feral magic, powered by energy that wasn't his own.

"Just like you'd never murder a man," he crooned.

Voices rose from the staff exit as people approached and the door rattled, but instead of drawing away, the Inspector yanked me to him, hand snaking beneath the torn slit of my gown, bruising the soft flesh of my thigh as he crushed his mouth against mine in a fierce, punishing kiss.

My hands were caught between us, leaving me with nothing to do but grasp his coat. I tried to hold on to my will to resist, but it evaporated in the inferno my magic had created, and my lips parted. Harrow deepened the embrace. He tasted of the earthy peat of whiskey mingled with sugar. I no longer noticed the bite of cold; a furnace of something unwanted yet unstoppable roaring to life, fueled by sensations never present when kissing lovers past.

There was a brief silence as whoever stumbled upon us processed the scene, followed by a click of the tongue.

"Wow." A woman's voice, tinkling and melodic, slurred from liquor or magic.

"Easy, killer," a man said, footsteps passing us. "They've got laws against that kind of thing in public."

"Gosh, would you beat up any scum who went after me, Jimmy?" The woman warbled.

"Sure, honey," her beau replied, as easy as saying he'd wash dishes, the sight of this violence commonplace. Their voices receded. "Tell you what, the bastard's got some guts. Wouldn't catch me messin' with William's girl."

The last words prompted an intensification of the Inspector's tactics, leaving me near senseless. As I prepared to humiliate myself further by easing into him, he loosened his hold and ended the kiss, remaining disrespectfully close.

"What the hell was that?" I demanded, attempting to infuse the words with disdain and deep offense, but they emerged with a trembling vibrato encouraged by the rapid beating of my heart.

"So, you're William's girl, are you?" The Inspector replied, and the question was spoken with a note of something I detested, as though he'd discovered an answer he'd been searching for.

A wave of shame gave me the strength to wrest myself from him, and he released me, but my humiliation was just beginning, because standing at the mouth of the alleyway, having come from the car waiting in the distance to ferry me to Blackwicket house was Thea, my coat draped in her arm.

"Well, Inspector Harrow, I see you're making a nuisance of yourself as always," she said, but she was glaring at me, dark eyes accusing.

"Just enjoying High Tide, like any other decent member of the Authority," he replied, and as with all of Harrow's words, the careless delivery had a hidden sharpness that sought the softest point of its mark and pierced.

Thea's nostrils flared with insult.

"Get the fuck out of my alley, Victor," Thea barked.

"Oh, I think I'll hang around a little longer. The night is young," he rejoined, wasting an indifferent glance at me before taking himself to the staff door, unabashed by the blood speckling his coat. He disappeared inside.

Thea stalked to me and threw the coat in my arms, taking a moment to observe the wreckage Harrow created. All three men were groaning, more aware of their surroundings. Tonight, Harrow had crossed every line imaginable, but at least no one was dead.

"You definitely have your sister's passion for men with the power to reduce you to two dates and a dash," she said callously.

"Harrow and I..."

"I don't care. Get in the car. I'm tired of tonight."

I wasn't surprised to find Thea's driver to be the same man who'd resentfully driven my father and me, then pointed me out to Thea that same day. He caught my eye in the mirror.

"You get around," I said, tone corrosive.

"It's my job," he grunted in response as Thea climbed in and directed him to Blackwicket House.

The ride was quiet, Thea and I both angry with each other. I at her for trying to manipulate my conscience into doing all the wrong things for reasons she framed as justified, and she at me for refusing to help when I was able. Also, likely, for catching me in the arms of a possibly corrupt Authority inspector who I now suspected had spent the past few evenings beating the Brom to near death and stealing their magic on her doorstep.

The monstrous image of Inspector Harrow's unnatural face, as he drew in magic that didn't belong to him, chilled me. I'd only ever witnessed one other person's body alter itself to accommodate a glut of power: my mother. But she hadn't been stealing magic. She'd been vomiting Drudge into the house, all the horrible things she'd taken from Grigori Nightglass in the name of keeping us safe.

"If you're using make-shift Curse Eaters to provide your black-market magic - how are you dealing with the Drudge?" I asked at last, interrupting the silence, knowing there must be some method or means of keeping the creatures at bay with what was going on here in this town.

"There aren't any."

"What?"

"No Drudge. Haven't been for years. Least, not that I've noticed. William and Fiona kept the place pretty clean, never let the curses get out of hand."

"But Fiona hadn't been Curse Eating," I repeated the information she'd given me, wondering if I'd caught her in a lie.

"Like I said, when Grigori died, she withdrew."

I didn't push further. Thea wouldn't give me what I needed, and I didn't blame her. But when healed magic was being abused, as the Brom was abusing it, Drudge were undoubtably close by.

"You'd be safer giving in to William than aligning with the Authority," Thea said suddenly.

"I refuse to align with *either*. There's nothing they can do to twist my arm. My life's all I have to lose, and I'm not sure how attached I am to it."

"Look death in the eye, you'll change your mind."

"One of William's men in the alley tonight, Patrick, he tried to gut me in the street."

"You mean the man Harrow almost turned inside out? Patrick isn't Brom," Thea said, measured, unsure of the waters she was wading into. "He's always causing trouble for us. Hates us much as his grandfather does."

"Grandfather?"

"God, you're as clueless as a newborn. Horatio Farvem," Thea replied testily. "The undertaker."

We pulled to a stop. I hadn't noticed we'd passed the gate, let alone the top of the hill.

"If he's not Brom, why would Mr. Farvem's grandson be harboring a curse?"

"With the amount of loathing that family carries in their souls, I imagine it's natural." This image of Farvem didn't match with my experience of him. "If Patrick's being a menace, he thinks you've joined our ranks, which means William's already talking you up. You're good as got, Blackwicket."

"Not if I don't want to be." I rejected her prediction, my vehemence making her laugh.

"The power of apathy must be nice, but some of us like to be alive, Eleanora," she said. "We still have people we love, lives we want, futures we hope for, and all of it can be taken away, as slowly and horribly as watching your own skin being baked off the bone."

She was right, I'd said something stupid and unfeeling, and Thea's admonishment humbled me.

"I'm sorry," I replied at length. "I'm sorry you're trapped here."

"And so are you. I guess it remains to be seen what you'll make of it."

I exited but couldn't stand to end our exchange here.

"Fiona's funeral is tomorrow at noon. Despite everything, I believe you were a genuine friend to her, Thea, and I'd welcome you."

Thea's smile lacked showmanship and looked only unbearably sad.

"No," Thea said. "I can't bring myself to say goodbye. I'd rather keep pretending she finally got out."

"She did," I replied, gently.

Thea's eyes filled with tears, which spilled over her cheek as I closed the car door.

CHAPTER TWENTY-TWO

Morning came, gray and dismal. The day of my sister's funeral had finally dragged itself by its fingernails to the front door of Blackwicket House. I'd slept terribly, waking with a cold, empty stomach, and a heaviness on my chest. It was the weight of dread at what I'd soon face—the final separation from my sister. Six feet under.

I emerged from the bedroom and noticed Inspector Harrow's door ajar. Closer inspection revealed the room cleared and the bed neatly made. Skeptical of his departure, I checked the parlor, but it was dark. The car was missing, parked neither in the front nor back.

It appeared Harrow had left Blackwicket House for good.

Snow had fallen in the night, blanketing the ground in soft white, likely hindering the gravediggers as they prepared Fiona's final resting place in the family plot.

I found myself eager for my father to arrive, but hadn't talked to him since he'd invited to pay for my room in town. I wondered whether he was still around. It would be typical of him to have second thoughts, hop on a train, and vanish, too cowardly to confront something this difficult head-on. I attempted to convince myself I was being unfair. Darren had, until now, done more for me than he'd ever done in his life, and I'd rebuffed him at every opportunity. Maybe today was when I'd reach across the chasm he'd created and take his hand. He was right. We were all we had. It wasn't treasure, but was preferable to emptiness.

The house felt strangely inactive, listless, its steady hum a bare whisper. I sat in the foyer, the space I'd often occupied as a child, allowing myself to be vulnerable and encouraging the house to connect with me. Even Auntie lurking beneath the stairs would have been welcome, but there was nothing.

I was alone.

Wishing for the puddle of sunlight from so long ago, I lay on the floor and cried.

No one came to fetch me. An ancient car pulled to the gate and stopped, Mr. Farvem climbing from it. He was too weak to walk the hill, so I suspected he'd wait at the cemetery.

Darren hadn't yet arrived, and it was already noon.

I dressed in a skirt of my own, but wore a vest of Fiona's, spritzed her honeysuckle perfume in my hair, then wrapped myself in my old coat, proceeding to her graveside. The hole was open, the coffin already lowered in.

"Afternoon, Ms. Eleanora."

Mr. Farvem greeted me with his usual gentleness. If Patrick were this man's grandson, he had to be a black sheep. As I reached the bottom of the hill, Farvem took my hands in his, and this human contact was almost too much.

"Steady on," he said with affection, offering a comforting squeeze and a tight smile. "I'm afraid I have unfortunate news."

"At this point, Mr. Farvem, I'm immune to unfortunate news," I replied, the words clotted in my throat.

"Well." He paused, the wind bustling his white hair, the furrows of his age-worn skin deepening further as he frowned. "Only one man showed up to dig this morning. I'm old, you know, and can't do such things anymore. Once it was done, he took off. Couldn't convince him to stay."

He sighed and glanced at the hill of dirt, two shovels stuck in, trowel first, like markers for the dead. There was no one to fill the hole, to pile the earth on my sister's casket.

"I'll see to it." My reply was swallowed by the sudden gale. The undertaker and I braced ourselves, and when the air was calmer, he shook his head.

"No, Eleanora. The Brom aren't trustworthy, but my people are, and I have someone who'll come first thing tomorrow and tuck your sister in. Don't worry yourself. We could do the service then, if you prefer."

Spending another day waiting for the end of this ordeal was too excruciating to consider.

"Thank you, but I'd prefer it be done with."

Mr. Farvem nodded, forever understanding. "Are you ready?"

I regarded the gate, the emptiness of the street. My father wasn't coming.

"Yes," I said.

The service was short, a reading of the typical rites, the spreading of herbs and dried flowers to dress the dead in peace and honor their transition from this world to the next, though I wasn't sure such a place existed. All I knew for certain was that wherever Fiona was now, it wasn't here.

I stepped to the graveside to drop a handful of dirt onto the casket, finding it black and shining, engraved with her name in burnished gold lettering and a flurry of embellished roses. I hated it. Fiona belonged settled upon a bed of real flowers, set to sea on a cloudless summer day with a lily in her hand, not tucked in this cold winter earth inside a ludicrous box her tormentor had commissioned. I let the dirt fall from my gloved fingers, mixing with the frost.

"Thank you," I said in the end. "I hope you don't mind if I'm not present for her covering tomorrow."

"Of course not. I'm sorry it's all worked out like this." He wasn't talking about the grave digging. He hesitated, adding, "I've heard through the grapevine you've decided to stay and re-open Blackwicket House."

William was making efforts to ensure everyone believed I was here of my own free will.

"The grapevine is poisoned," I responded. "I'm not opening Blackwicket House."

"Ah, I apologize. I was informed a man from the Inn stopped by to assist in the digging. I shouldn't have assumed he was a guest."

My eyes lit upon the two shovels standing erect in the dirt. Two men working rather than one.

Inspector Harrow had helped dig my sister's grave.

"An unwanted one," I said, struggling to find this new information believable. "But he's gone now."

The sound of a car turning onto the street distracted us, and we watched as a long black sedan pulled through the gate. I didn't recognize the man behind the wheel. My father must have bribed someone to bring him, so he wouldn't have to brave a walk in the snow.

At least he was here, even if he was too late.

But Darren Rose didn't climb out of the passenger seat. The gold tip of a snakewood cane emerged first, and William Nightglass followed stiffly, his golden hair in stark contrast against the black collar of his coat.

Mr. Farvem looked uneasy, knowing this violated my wishes, having no power to stop the Principe from doing whatever he decided pleased him.

I met William halfway, hoping my expression remained neutral.

"William, you weren't invited. Let me bury my sister in peace."

"This is the woman I loved." His response was matter-of-fact, as though that were enough to excuse his part in whatever had put Fiona in the ground. "I'm here to pay my respects. Please don't deny me my last chance to say goodbye to her."

"Did you have Mr. Thatcher murdered because I tried to buy a ticket?" I asked sharply, choosing not to respond to his appeal to my sympathy.

William placed both hands, one over the other, on the arch of his cane handle, pale blue eyes settled on mine with a long-suffering patience.

"Thatcher's death was a tragedy. I admit I instructed him not to sell you passage out of Nightglass, but nothing more. Whoever killed Thatcher remains, unfortunately, at large." He sensed my doubt, adding, "Why would I kill one of my own for doing exactly what I instructed them to do?"

It was a logical argument. Thatcher had denied me a ticket, as he'd been told to. The glint of Patrick's knife in the street gleamed in the corner of my memory, and the temperature of my blood dipped to match the winter sea.

Already tired and preferring to move on as quickly as possible from this meeting, I indicated the graveside and let him pass. He moved with proud, rigid grace. I didn't follow. Mr. Farvem approached, and we both stood a healthy distance from William.

"I hate to go, but I have to return to the funeral home. My work feels never-ending these days."

"Are so many people really dying here, Mr. Farvem?"

The old man urged me to stroll with him to his car so our conversation wouldn't be easily overheard.

"Curse rot," he said, keeping so quiet that I had to turn my head to hear him above the breeze as we walked. "Victims are mostly Brom, but I have a few tourists in my care whose families are going to be asking questions. I expect the Authority will turn on William's little experiment. It's all we can hope for. You can't give in to him, Eleanora. If you open the house, you're giving them the freedom to keep this game going."

"I've been warned that if I don't help, people will die."

"I'm afraid that's true, but if enough of them die, maybe that's when this insanity ends."

Mr. Farvem bid his farewells, and when I returned attention to my family's modest cemetery, William was still at Fiona's graveside. I couldn't be sure from this distance, but he seemed to be wiping away tears.

I neither approached nor abandoned him, only waited for his departure. My nose was numb by the time he finished paying his respects, but instead of approaching his car, he walked in my direction. I regretted not going inside. If he wanted to talk to me, I'd lead the conversation.

"I want to leave Nightglass, William," I said, ignoring the redness around the rim of his eyes. "You can't keep me trapped here in this town. Eventually, I'll find a way out."

"And where will you go?" He sounded genuinely curious.

"It doesn't matter. I demand the freedom."

"That Inspector staying here, Harrow, I doubt he'd take kindly to you slipping through his fingers, after what happened in Devin."

"That's my concern, not yours."

"But it *is* my concern." His eyes narrowed. "When the Inspector's not happy, he makes damn sure I'm not happy. He's an Authority strongman. They send him here from time to time to prevent me from thinking I have them in my pocket, to show me they can still bite."

He clacked his teeth together for emphasis, then scrutinized me.

"The good Inspector likes to rough people up, put everyone on edge. Ultimately, he's a weak threat. The Authority's too curious to discover what comes of all of my hard work to put a stop to it." As he spoke, he shifted his weight, revealing his annoyance by the way he dug his cane into the rocky drive. "But admittedly, the man's been pulling on his leash lately."

I stared at him, searching for any signs of the William I'd known. The young man who fell in love with my sister, even though her family had been involved in the loss of his precious brother. He'd walked the cliffs with us, explored the beaches, stolen kisses from Fiona on the porch. And when he brought flowers, he'd always taken some aside for me. He'd once understood our isolation and loneliness, and had commiserated with us over the villainy of his father.

"You used to talk of becoming a better man than Grigori, of taking care of people," I said, examining his face, looking for any signs that the old William was still there. "You promised Fiona you'd make her life better."

"I did all of those things."

"You did none of them."

This hit a nerve, the hidden underbelly of William's ego. His anger was immediate, but not violent—it didn't distort his features or raise color to his face. Instead, it turned his words hard as the broadside of a steel blade, the sneer implied.

"And what have you done, little girl? Run away from home. Hidden like a mouse in the dirty corners of cities, pretending you're safe while you scrounge for the scraps of a life, forgoing true pleasure and peace, letting yourself be rutted by weak men, betrayed by unloyal friends. All the while collecting curses, never healing them, never using them, just abandoning them to languish in a dark box that you've filled with your useless guilt. Until at last you did the glorious thing you were created for only to send a man to his death."

William's cadence of speech had altered, his words so coarse and unpleasant that if I hadn't been looking at him, I'd have been convinced a different man was talking. My mouth twisted into a disgusted snarl.

"You don't know anything."

"No secrets among friends, Eleanora." His tone remained serrated, antagonizing, "I know you better than you think. We've been keeping track of you for quite a while. Whose idea do you expect it was to have Darren fetch you to Nightglass?"

If he'd backhanded me, it would have hurt less than this revelation did. Of course, my father had ulterior motives. He'd never come to retrieve me out of sentiment, grief, or guilt. He'd been there on an errand, to act as a courier, whisking me back to this hellhole for a price.

"How long?" The words were razors in my mouth.

"Long enough to know you'd jump at the chance to help that poor Rosley woman if we positioned her right."

The bracelet. Still tucked with the other cursed items in my unpacked bags inside Blackwicket House.

Some good friends gave it to me. The jewels... one for each of my children.

"She and her husband were fairly well known by the Brom in Devin for being some of our neediest clients. Always looking for more magic. Always willing to pay the highest price. Her poor children, being exposed to all of that cursed magic."

He shook his head, but the sympathy was too polished to be honest.

"In the end, her loss was our gain."

"You *killed* her."

"I believe you did, Ellie." His use of my childhood nickname nauseated me, and my rage finally became action.

Giving in to an inescapable urge, I kicked his cane out from under him. I'd intended for him to fall, to tumble to the ground and give me room to run to the house, but although the tip slipped across the frozen dirt, he remained upright, steady on his feet. A laugh preceded the rage, which broke across his visage like a storm crashing to shore. He brought the tip of his cane down between my ankles and, in a single smooth motion, twisted it so it caught my left heel. With a solid shove of the hard wood against my thigh, he knocked my feet from beneath me, and I hit the ground on my hip.

William pinned the layers of my skirt to the frozen earth between my calves, forcing me to remain in an awkward sprawl. To free myself, I'd have to roll onto my stomach and crawl away. A thing I would never do for William.

He towered above me, the monster Thea and Mr. Farvem were afraid of, the one Fiona had eventually seen and recoiled from.

"Now there's a pretty view," he intoned, the edges of his voice regaining their charming, harmless shape. "I won't make you apologize this time, but let's remain civil in the future."

He crouched close, running his gaze purposefully along the curve of my hip. Had I not been twisted in such an awkward position, I would have leaned in to bite the nose off his face.

"This is all so unnecessary," he said. "I'll tell you everything, Eleanora. You just have to cooperate with me. Let me show you what power tastes like. No more fear, no more running. Do what I ask of you, and I'll be at your mercy. You'll be the most powerful woman ever to walk this earth."

"Is that what you promised my sister?" I growled, then spat in his face.

He barely flinched. I expected him to raise his hand, to further attempt to degrade me, but he only wiped the spit from his cheek, a smirk pulling at the corners of his mouth.

"What can I say? A Nightglass man can't resist a Blackwicket," he replied, even and jovial, rising to his feet. He released my skirt, and I adjusted myself, hastily standing, soaked with snowmelt, as he watched on. I rejected the urge to throw a punch. William was more than he seemed, and I was already in plenty of danger.

"Leave," I commanded, and my voice quavered, frightened and brittle.

"Of course." He pressed a hand to his chest, offering a slight bow, a gentleman again. "Thank you for accommodating my request to bid farewell to Fiona. I'm sure you have things to tend to."

He began his trek to the waiting car, and I watched him go, clutching the collar of my coat closed just to have something to hold onto, shivering from more than the cold.

"I'll be in touch, Eleanora," he called back. "And we'll continue this chat. Perhaps at the next High Tide."

CHAPTER TWENTY-THREE

O nce William was out of sight, I bundled my rage close and set into town, not bothering to change my wet clothes. I was so distraught that even as I pounded on Darren's hotel room door, I couldn't remember arriving or asking for a room number.

I raged against the barrier between me and the object of my fury, bruising the soft edge of my hand on the wood, the glaring gold number 15 rattling from the force. My magic was turbulent, and it snapped under the sleeves of my blouse like static electricity, small sparks flying as I continued to beat the door. Just when I thought the skin of my pinky knuckle might split, the door was yanked in, and there stood my father, in grey trousers and a rumpled undershirt, dark circles beneath his eyes.

"How much did he pay you?" I demanded.

"What?"

"You sold me to William Nightglass!" I was shouting with the wrath of a hurricane fallen to shore. "How much was your *own daughter* worth?"

"Woah, woah!" He reached to pull me inside. "You can't be out here screaming stuff like that."

He checked the hallway for anyone sticking their head out to investigate what was going on before he shut us away. The room was a damn sight better than where he'd hidden me in Devin, clean and more modest than other Nightglass accommodations likely had on offer, but I knew what money had paid for it and couldn't appreciate his frugality.

"But it's true, isn't it? William arranged everything in Devin, the disaster at Galton's. He's the reason that woman and all her children are dead, and you played along to get to me. So I want to know how much money he dangled in your face to make you stoop so low."

"You've got it all wrong!"

When I opened my mouth to interrupt, he did something he'd never done in my life. He shouted in return.

"Would you shut up for just a second!"

I pressed my mouth into a thin line. Darren ran a hand through his hair, unbrushed, several day's worth of beard on his chin. He looked as though he hadn't been sleeping, and I could smell the tang of old brandy on him.

"I knew nothing about that dame with the curse until after the fact," he said. "Fiona was dead, and yeah, William offered me a pretty decent sum to convince you to come back here."

He witnessed my preparation to resume my rampage and held up a hand. "But I was already going to Devin to let you know about your sister! It seemed like easy money."

"You didn't think to ask him why he wanted me here?"

"I'm not stupid, girl. I knew exactly why he did." It was Darren's turn to be angry, but it wasn't with me. He swiped a half-smoked cigarette from an ashtray on the round breakfast table and shoved it between his lips, taking the matches next as he talked, lighting it, trying to calm his nerves. "He needed someone to fill Fiona's shoes. There's no one else in the world who knows how to handle that house and what's in it. You were a perfect fit."

"You were after a quick payday."

"I wanted you to be *safe!*" he roared, yanking the newly lit cigarette from his mouth, jamming it down into the sooty pile of the others without even taking a drag. He grabbed hold of the breakfast table, steadying himself, then shook it violently to dispel some of his anger. The crash of the legs on the floor echoed. Someone would call the Authority at this rate, but the worst that could happen was being taken into custody. Preferable at this point.

In a final act of frustration, my father slapped the ashtray from the tabletop, and it hit the wall, scattering ash on the golden-striped wallpaper; the smudge of black it left behind was reminiscent of a bruise. "You think I didn't check on you? Didn't track you while you wandered all over the east cities, barely living under the radar? I'm the one who cleaned up your mess in Harpridge after you stabbed that bank manager in the crotch!"

"He deserved it!" I battled the urge to grab anything of my own to shake, wishing it could be Darren.

"Of course he did! And I was damn proud of you for it! But you were never in good hands alone, and it was only a matter of time before you fucked up in a way I couldn't even help you with. This world isn't for people made like you, kid." He'd calmed, his energy for this battle depleted, and his tone softened. "But Nightglass is. At least, that's what I thought."

Silence fell, heavy with my hurt and his irritation that I couldn't understand him, his intentions and methods, his distance.

"I didn't need your shadow." I let the tears make their tracks on my face. I hadn't cried in front of my father since I was little. "I needed *you*, Darren."

His eyes grew red-rimmed, and he lifted his hands, palms up, offering me all he had. "And I was there for you, Cricket…in the only way I'm good at."

I needed us to keep arguing, to continue yelling at each other, reignite the emotional squall. It was the sincerest my father had ever been with me, but the fight was out of him. I considered demanding why he hadn't attended Fiona's burial, but I knew the answer. Finally, I recognized the cowardly habit he had of insulating himself from the grief that came with loving people, how he slunk from difficult moments because he'd never learned how to sit with hurt.

I reached into my coat pocket where the photograph of Fiona and the young boy remained, crumpled and wrinkled from all my handling of it. I thrust it toward him.

"You're going to answer my questions. You owe me at least that much. Who is this boy?"

He eyed the picture, but didn't approach to take it, knowing exactly who it depicted. He went to retrieve the ashtray instead.

"I met him once." He scooped the thing up from the floor, threw it haphazardly onto the tabletop where it rattled, then approached the unmade bed, and sat heavily on the edge, elbows resting on his knees. "Roark. He was six. She told me he was the child of a friend she was helping care for, but that boy called her mama."

The sadness in his voice was so potent I wanted to leave, to walk out of Nightglass and into the woods until I froze to death in the wilderness.

"I asked around," he said. "Heard a few different stories—Fiona couldn't have kids, or William couldn't, you know, with his injury. But I've been doing my job for a long time, tracking curses, judging the magic on people, and this kid felt like walking too near a live wire. Buzzing."

Darren finally returned his gaze to mine.

"He was a Dark Hall kid, Cricket. And I have a hunch Fiona retrieved him for Grigori."

I didn't refute his claim, didn't argue my sister's morality. I'd learned some things. Knew better.

"Was he the only one?" I asked.

My father sighed, "Wish I could say. She wouldn't have let me in the house even if I'd wanted to go, so I never saw anything. There wasn't ever a bizarre number of kids wandering around that didn't belong to anyone, but, then again, I guess I wasn't ever here long enough to tell the difference."

It was all I cared to know or bear asking. I returned the picture to its place in my coat, touching its soft edges for a moment to ground myself.

"I need you to leave Nightglass," I said. "And stay gone."

"Eleanora…" Darren was going to protest, to attempt to charm his way out of discomfort and consequence, but I'd already started to go.

"Wait." He stood hastily, bounding after me and grabbing hold of my coat sleeve instead of my arm. Outside of my better judgment, I lingered. Unable to look him in the face, I turned my head to indicate I was listening. He let me go, didn't force himself into my line of view, didn't offer regrets or apologies.

"There's something moving in this town," he said. "Something I've never felt before. It's bigger than I think even Isolde could have handled. I don't know if William's using it or if it's wild, but I think it's responsible for what happened to Fiona. If I'd known, I swear I never would have brought you, Cricket."

I understood what he was offering, but it was far too little, too late, and I wouldn't accept.

"I never want to see you again," I replied, cold as the deep earth my sister rested in.

Stepping into the hall, I closed myself off from my father for what I'd decided would be forever. I'd made it to the glass elevator, the lobby, and to the rotating entryway, when I slipped my hand into my pocket and discovered the photo missing. My anger was renewed. Darren had picked my pocket, had stolen from me, a thing that didn't and would never belong to him.

I'd stopped, blocking the door, and a woman tapped me on the shoulder, hoping to get around. Her expression when I acknowledged her suggested I wasn't hiding my temper. She apologized and retreated to the lobby. I stood fuming, hating that I was forced to decide between eating my words and seeing Darren again or abandoning the photograph.

All the way back to room 15, I steeped in resentment, working myself into another firestorm. The door was partially open, cracked several inches. I didn't bother knocking, only shoved it in, prepared to spit venom.

The room smelled of iron and decay, vivid red mottling on the white curtains drawing my eye first, crimson droplets on the windowpane so fresh they still traveled in a drunken slink towards the latch, as though racing to escape the carnage that had been visited upon the room in the few minutes I'd been gone. The spatter continued across the bed and onto the floor where Darren lay on his back in a halo of blood, fed by the streams still flowing from the gaping slash of flesh in his throat.

Anger evaporating, I screamed for help, hurrying to my father's prone body, falling to my knees and pressing a hand to his throat to staunch the pulsing flow of blood. The pressure of my palm only forced more from his veins. The cut was too deep, too wide.

Darren was still alive. Two tears slipped from his eyes, mirror images of each other as he looked at me.

"Help!" The word escaped long and wretched. Doors began opening, voices raising in the hall, fast approaching.

Darren laid a hand on my shoulder as he gathered the strength to touch my face, his fingers finally grazing my cheek. Blood bubbled from his lips as the corners curled into a frail smile.

His hand fell to my collarbone, his body, which had been convulsing from the effort to draw in breath, stilled, and the white, gossamer threads of his magic rose from the wound as his body released it, no use for it any longer.

My vision grew grey, head woolly and light, as I grasped his hand in mine for what would never be long enough, even as strangers pulled at my arms, dragging me from my father's body and the horrible sight of my careless wish come true.

I sat in the hallway covered in my father's blood. Bodies moved around me, passing feet, rushing one way and another as time marched ever forward, leaving me floating in a strange, lonely world, trying to understand what had happened. A woman spoke to me, her soft hands brushing the hair from my brow, rubbing the gore from my fingers with a damp cloth, but I couldn't hear anything beyond the pounding of my heart in my ears. Every beat brought to mind the torrent of life that had slipped through my fingers.

I was lost in all the moments of my childhood I'd long forgotten or ignored. The rosy days when Darren had shown, unannounced, with flowers for my mother and more sweets than Fiona and I could ever hope to eat. He'd come inside the house back then, when Isolde Blackwicket was in control of her mind. Sometimes he'd lingered for weeks, and in those sunny stretches, my life resembled one that was normal and easy. He'd disappeared for the longest stretch when Isolde had started deteriorating, staying locked in her room for days, leaving Fiona and me alone to fend for ourselves more and more, barely registering our presence when we were right in front of her.

I love the sea. She'd said the last night she was alive, sitting at her favorite window in the parlor. *It sounds like home. I want to go home.*

"Eleanora." My name reached me from a world away. A

firm touch lifted my chin. My vision focused, hazy colors bleeding together to form solid shapes, at last registering the eyes looking into mine, searching for a sign I was still there.

Inspector Harrow.

Though there was no concern etched on his brow, there was something softer about him, less feral and strained. Harrow was not a vision of comfort, but he'd become a familiar presence, and of all the people who'd ever threatened me, so far, he'd been the one who hadn't followed through.

I sniffed, moved from the touch, not with disgust or petty disdain, but because he'd returned me to my body, where heartache dug its sharp edges. He couldn't be my guide in this storm.

He redirected his attention to a young man who'd approached to ask about transport for the body. Harrow answered, but I wasn't listening anymore. As a high-ranking member of the Authority, of course, he'd been called to the scene. I expected the next steps would be interrogation. My father and I had fought, loudly, and I'd been the last to see him alive. I was covered in his blood. I was the most obvious suspect, and with my prior history, it seemed likely this would be the thing that got me out of Nightglass and straight into an Authority prison where I'd be annulled.

"Get up." Inspector Harrow's voice was sturdy, giving me something to hold on to. "I'm taking you home."

Surprised, I searched his face for signs of a trick, manipulation, or cruelty. There was only his steady attention, stoic and unflappable.

"You're not taking me into custody?"

"Should I?"

I sat there, staring at him, blood drying on my coat, my hands, my cheek where my father's fingers had touched.

"No," I replied, my sincere plea of innocence.

"Then let's go." He didn't reach for me, didn't offer his hand to help me stand, perhaps knowing I wouldn't, *couldn't*, take it. As I stood, he divested himself of his suit jacket.

"Take off your coat," he said. "Leave it here, I can't walk you down the halls looking like the goddess of death."

I numbly attempted to unfasten the buttons, fingers fumbling, Harrow made a motion, and the woman who'd consoled me earlier appeared. It was Cora. She looked tired, but much improved from her ordeal, the gauntness of her face reduced, her green eyes keen.

"You…" I began, but she shushed me gently as she helped me with the buttons.

"It's alright, Ms. Blackwicket," she said, her way of telling me she was well. She took the coat from me, and it looked like the grisly skin of a beast. "You're in safe hands. But, look, don't tell Thea you saw me here. She doesn't know yet."

"That you're Authority?" I said flatly.

The woman offered a self deprecating smile, shrugged one shoulder.

"A girl's gotta make a living."

The Inspector draped his jacket across my shoulders, instructing me to keep my red-stained sleeves out of view. I drew the lapel tight, fingers tucked inside. It smelled of Inspector Harrow.

"Cora, when the undertaker arrives, tell him the Authority will be demanding a full inquest, then make yourself scarce."

"Yes, sir," she said, whisking herself and the bloodstained coat away.

With a firm hand at my back, Inspector Harrow guided me from the scene of my father's death and towards the place I'd never thought I'd be eager to return to. Blackwicket House.

CHAPTER TWENTY-FOUR

The ride to Blackwicket House was mercifully silent, and I spent it trying to determine how deep the pain had rooted. My father had always been the absent kind, and my dependence on him had eventually become nonexistent. When I'd told him I never wanted to see him again, I'd meant it. Yet now I was forced to face the uncomfortable fact that while Darren was alive, I'd been able to pretend someone out there cared about me, at least a little. Not in the right way, but in some way.

I was aware of Inspector Harrow next to me. When we'd last sat here, he'd pulled my magic free and swallowed a piece of it whole. It felt like a lifetime ago, a thousand years between that moment and this one. I couldn't look at him.

I didn't wait for him to open my door when we arrived, exiting right away, still wrapped in his suit jacket. Blackwicket House welcomed us both, the state of me sending a buzz through the foundation. For a fraction of a moment, I wasn't completely lost. The house needed me.

"I'll check around," Inspector Harrow said, closing the door behind us. The lock clicked on its own, giving him pause. I awaited a reaction, but he chose to say nothing.

"No. You have questions, and I want to answer them." I removed the jacket from my shoulders and handed it back to him.

He took it, his regard trailing from the sleeves of my blouse to my neck and cheek. All the places where blood remained, drying.

"You should clean up," he said.

"We talk now. I don't want this conversation hanging over my head. I'll never sleep."

To indicate my will, I rooted myself to the spot, my insides trembling with resurfacing emotion.

"Very well." Inspector Harrow donned his jacket, abandoning his attempts at feigning care. "Did you murder Darren Rose?"

"I didn't," I replied, in the same stiff tone I'd used the first time he'd asked me if I'd killed Brock Mofton. Only now, I wasn't lying.

"But you fought with him before he died." It wasn't a question. He was already aware of what others had heard.

"Yes."

"About?"

"Are you honestly here to bring the Brom to justice, Inspector?" I threw off the balance by asking my own question, a prerequisite to my answer. If I were going to divulge everything, I wanted some assurance it wouldn't be brushed aside.

"Justice." He repeated the word with some curiosity, as though he'd never felt the shape of it in his mouth, "There's no justice for what the Brom are doing. What they've done. There's only retribution, and yes, that's what keeps me in this godforsaken town."

Retribution was enough of a promise to encourage my decision to give to the monster that would bring down William, the Brom, even if it meant feeding it my hand, perhaps much more besides.

"William Nightglass paid a visit to me this afternoon."

Inspector Harrow became perfectly still. "He came under the pretense of saying goodbye to Fiona but stayed to threaten me and promise me the world."

I briefly detailed the fraught exchange, excluding his leering to save myself the shame.

"William paid my father to entice me to Nightglass," I said, when I'd finished the whole terrible, foolish tale. "That's why we were arguing. He said he'd done it for my well-being. Apparently, I was never good at hiding from anyone but myself."

The Inspector was silent, studying the parquet tiles as he absorbed the information, filing it away in whatever perfect system he kept in his mind for tracking the wrongdoings of the Brom. When his gaze found mine, as cold as it had ever been during interrogations past, he asked, "Was Darren really your father?"

My breath collapsed from my lungs. I couldn't take offense. I knew why he was asking.

"He was."

"You sound more sure than most people would be."

"Fiona and I aren't Dark Hall children, if that's what you want to know, Inspector." This was the moment I chose which secrets weren't worth the cost of keeping. "My mother was the last Dark Hall child the Blackwickets procured."

"Are you certain?" he asked pointedly.

I resisted the memory of Thomas's face, weeping with the red smoke of curses as he died.

"Yes."

Thomas hadn't belonged to our family. He'd been a Nightglass. "My mother wanted to break tradition, and couldn't stand the idea of stealing children, but she believed it was important to carry on the family legacy, so she chose Darren."

"You make it seem like a transaction."

"It might as well have been. I can't imagine what she saw in him other than an opportunity."

"You assume she wasn't in love with him."

"It doesn't matter," I answered, bitter. The same anger that took me to Darren's hotel room door clawed through the shock of his loss and reminded me of the pain he'd brought to my life before finally leaving it. "Maybe she was. She was always so glad when he showed, and her heart broke each time he left. The truth is, he couldn't handle being here."

"This is a difficult house."

Inspector Harrow's words were too close to excusing a man who'd been given every opportunity to choose us and never had.

"We were his *daughters*," I said, and the word was broken glass, shattered by the hurling of a stone Darren Rose had thrown again and again. The force of my anger propelled me a step closer, and the Inspector squared his shoulders, standing his full height, prepared to respond if I chose violence. "I loved my father until I hated him. He wasn't a good man, and nothing he ever did, no small amount of decency, ever made up for it. But I didn't want him dead."

"Then who would have?"

"The easier question is, who wouldn't have? He swindled and hurt a lot of people." My train of thought stuttered, skipped. I considered Mr. Thatcher, William's insistence that he'd had nothing to do with it, Thea's assurance Patrick hated the Nightglass family and everyone involved with them. "That man you nearly murdered in the alley."

"Patrick Farvem," he said, not denying it.

"Yes."

"Patrick was found dead this morning on the village green. I was at the scene when I got word about the murder at the Vanderson."

My palms grew clammy. Patrick had been in bad shape when I'd left the lounge. "Did you…"

"Like your father, Patrick's throat had been cut clean." His response was measured, but with no gentler an edge than usual. Inspector Harrow knew the sort of world I'd lived in, knew there was no use in softening the blows. "Rough business. And here's the thing—your father worked for the Brom. Thatcher and Patrick didn't. Thatcher was a regular Nightglass resident doing his best to get by, and to my knowledge, Patrick Farvem was a thorn in Brom's side. None of these men had anything in common, but you, Eleanora."

Mr. Thatcher hadn't let me leave Nightglass, Patrick had tried to stab me, and my father, well, his list was too long.

"You're insinuating I'm a serial killer?"

"It's a coherent line of reasoning. But knowing what I do, I don't see you being so direct. It's not your style."

He'd circled to the thing that had brought our paths together, still lock-jawed on proving he was right, and I'd slipped through the cracks of the system. His system.

"Is it yours?" I asked, stooping to his level.

"If I'm not mistaken," he replied, low, conspiratorial. "You've already witnessed mine."

He was discussing Annulment, the way he'd been separating Patrick's magic from his soul. But it wasn't that image that flickered in my mind, briefly illuminating unwanted memories. Instead, it was Inspector Harrow's body, the warmth of his mouth. These thoughts were disgraceful after everything that had happened, and my anger grew in the fertile soil of shame. I reminded myself that the Inspector's behavior hadn't been sincere. He'd intended it as a smokescreen. Still, my belly warmed, and a shift in his body language brought him a bare fraction closer to me. I wouldn't have noticed had my magic not expanded, gathering beneath my breasts, pressing.

"Whatever's going on, it has something to do with William Nightglass." I managed the moment by changing direction. "He wants me for the Brom. That puts me in a special position to figure out what his endgame is, whether he's behind all of this. I'm willing to do it if you'll tell me what you're looking for, what you're trying to find."

Inspector Harrow's lips twitched, but the smile was more mocking than amused. "He does want you. So you're saying you'd be happy to waltz into his arms and use your charms to get me answers?"

"I'm saying," I replied sharply, "I'm involved in this as much as anyone, and I want to help you if you'd stop being so egotistical."

"No offense meant, Ms. Blackwicket, but I don't trust you." He tilted his head, falsely apologetic. "I'm sure you understand."

His dismissal of my help, when it had cost me to offer it, was the ultimate affront.

"Don't trust *me?* I'm gambling my life on the longshot bet that you're not just hanging around to shed blood and lap up feeble magic like the rest of the dogs."

"Careful."

"You're the one who should be careful."

My magic was riled, begging to be released following so much turmoil, so many moments of fear and anger. It was trapped, churning into darkness that threatened to solidify. Already, the edges were turning tarry. This is what my family had been forced to endure: a thousand injustices and wounds coiling and tightening like a noose.

"What are you going to do, little Curse Eater?" Inspector Harrow intoned, sensing the rise of my power, his own responding, hungry, vampiric. "What terrible mistake are you about to make?"

After witnessing his behavior at the Vapors, I understood why his magic pulled at mine, and I wanted to use it to my advantage, to prove to him I had bite.

"You treat me like I'm untrustworthy, but look at all the vile things you've done in the name of the Authority, of your ideals," I said.

My magic met his, the curses in him easy to find, their shadowy shapes clear in the warm current of power, far more than could belong to a typical man. I dug in, catching a solid hold. In return, he mirrored the threat, but with his hands on my body, fingers encircling my upper arms with a force that would leave my flesh bruised. In a vicious tug, he maneuvered me towards him, my feet dragging. I wound his curses tight. They were my only leverage.

"You want vile things?" Depravity glinted in his eyes, lit by a fire inclined to blaze unbridled. "If you knew what I was thinking, you'd never sleep again. Unhook your little claws, or I'll do it for you."

A disturbed hive, the house reacted to the rise in energy, lured into motion by the unprotected magic pouring from us both as we remained locked in a battle of wills. I was determined to win, driven by a need to punish someone other than myself for everything. For all that I'd missed, and for my many mistakes.

I wrenched the curse forward, and as it rose, it unfolded. It had been the tip of a crag hidden by deep, murky water. It eclipsed the Inspector's magic and infiltrated mine like a plague. Alarm plucked at my senses, but my instincts had already taken charge. Ready to let me reap what I'd sown, Inspector Harrow shifted his tight grip from my arm to my chin, turning my face to his, where wisps of curse were emerging, the taste of it slipping across my tongue, my lungs preparing to expand. But just as I began to panic, he retracted his magic, and the curse followed, much preferring where it had come from to whatever I could offer it. The power that was required to control tainted magic in the middle of an exodus was extraordinary.

There was no longer any danger of transference, but Inspector Harrow continued to entice my magic to mingle with his, turning the tables. Our mouths were nearly touching, and he inhaled deeply, a misty cloud of natural power rising from my lips. He took it from me. It should have felt as if something important had been ripped away. Instead, a languid heat spread where emptiness was meant to be.

Shaken, I grabbed hold of Inspector Harrow's arms, gasping at the peculiar sensation of equal loss and gain.

"Maybe," he murmured, still close enough to kiss me if he leaned in an inch more. "I should teach you a lesson about rash decisions, give you a taste of exactly what William Nightglass would do to you if you agreed to his terms."

He was threatening to empty me, turn me inside out for my magic, draining me of everything that made me who I was. I should have flinched away. Paying no heed to his warning, I raised my chin. His hold on me loosened to allow it.

As our lips met, there was pounding at the door.

"Ms. Blackwicket! Are you there?"

The Inspector released me, and my head cleared, senses returning. I could blame him for what had happened, for befuddling me, for using magic to turn my common sense upside down. But he'd done nothing but rise to meet me.

I was glad to open the door, to put space between me and my stupidity.

Mr. Farvem stood on the porch, harried and distraught, stooped with his age more than usual.

"There you are, I've been so worried, I thought…my god look at you."

I brought a hand to my face, to the crust of lifeblood there, remembering the state of myself.

"I'm alright, Mr. Farvem. It's not mine."

This failed to put the old man at ease.

Inspector Harrow appeared behind me, and the undertaker seemed ever more taken aback.

"Inspector, you're here?" he said, surprised. "That's your vehicle there?"

He looked over his shoulder at the roadster in the drive, strangely anxious. I remembered then. Mr. Farvem had a car. Why had he walked?

"I came to deliver Ms. Blackwicket home," Inspector Harrow said.

"That's good." Mr. Farvem wrung his hands. "I heard what happened. Well, I expect we should discuss your father's arrangements."

I wasn't ready to consider my father's burial.

"I'll leave you to your preparations, Ms. Blackwicket. My condolences once more for your loss," Harrow said, and there remained something simmering, a warning that none of this was over. He nodded goodbye to Mr. Farvem, who stepped well out of his path. I watched the Inspector go, a glut of discomfort making my skin feel stretched too tight. The house was restless, but retreated as the tap of magic closed.

"I'm so sorry to intrude," Mr. Farvem said, tired. "But could I trouble you for a glass of water, my dear? I walked here rather quickly, and at my age, well."

I was shocked by the man's interest in coming inside, but opened the door wider.

"Of course," I replied. "You're welcome at Blackwicket House, Mr. Farvem. Come in."

Inspector Harrow's car roared to life as the old mortician

hobbled over my threshold, the first guest I'd invited across since Thomas.

I hoped the house's sudden silence was a good sign, but I very much doubted it.

CHAPTER TWENTY-FIVE

"You can wait in the parlor, Mr. Farvem," I said.

While I was still uneasy about the room, I had no alternative. The kitchen was still filled with Fiona's blackberry jam.

"You'll be comfortable there. I'll bring you some water."

He touched my wrist to delay me.

"My Patrick's dead, you know."

The hush of his voice was heartbreaking, and my tender response was for Mr. Farvem's sake, not Patrick's, although I wondered if he'd been aware of the type of person his grandson had been. Either way, it was irrelevant now.

"I heard. I'm so sorry. It's too much tragedy for one town."

"During the war, that's how we killed the Curse Eaters." He confessed, as if I hadn't spoken. "We slit their throats, let their corrupted magic flow out with their blood."

A ripple of alarm swept down my spine.

"I'm not sure I understand."

"I was part of a special unit. The Veil. It was our job to eliminate the most formidable magic users, prevent them from spreading their curses across borders. Our men were so tired, filled up to the gills with tainted sludge. So many died. When the war ended, I vowed I'd do everything in my power to make sure nothing like that ever happened again."

He hadn't been looking at me before, choosing a distant

spot beyond my shoulder, but now he caught my gaze in his, and he sighed.

"Then the Brom began to grow."

A shout erupted from outside, followed by a thunderous explosion that rattled the house, windowpanes shaking, flakes of ceiling plaster falling on us from overhead. The chandelier rocked back and forth, the crystals clinking, and a deep moan, like a steel boat hull adjusting under pressure, resonated through the house as the Drudge inside it moved.

"What was that?" My voice warbled. "What's happened?"

I made to run for the door, but Mr. Farvem halted my momentum by seizing my hand.

"Don't look, my dear." He pulled me back. "You don't want to see. It's a shame. The Inspector made successful strides in eradicating the Brom, but men like him no longer fit here. We need to learn to take care of our own problems. No magic, just utility."

I withdrew my hand from his, adrenaline spiking through my limbs.

"You should've been in that car, Eleanora. It would have made this easier."

Farvem produced a scalpel from his sleeve. It slid into his palm in a sleight of hand that mimicked Patrick's disappearing trick with the trench knife. My eye was distracted long enough for him to bring the weapon in a close arc towards my throat. I reeled backwards just in time, nearly tripping, and the instrument glanced the underside of my chin.

I screamed in pain and horror, and the undertaker reached for me, gripping the collar of my shirt, which tore as I jerked aside, the top buttons popping free. He swung at me again as I fled, and I felt the blade in my hair.

"Fiona was supposed to make everything better," Mr. Farvem roared. "We had an agreement!"

The nearest refuge was the kitchen. Although its doors swung both directions, Mother had installed a latch when her compulsive baking peaked, and she didn't want to be disturbed by the outside world.

I made it, grabbing the door and pushing it too hard. It swung out first, and I was forced to lunge, grab hold of it again, as Mr. Farvem raced to stop me. He aimed a swipe at my fingers, missing barely, as the door found its casing, and I slammed the metal lock home. It wasn't a strong thing. It hadn't been meant to keep out insane old men with sharp objects, only curious, lonely teenage girls who missed their mother.

The force exerted against the wooden panels was remarkable for a man in his nineties, each impact exceeding the last, rattling the pans on the wall and unsettling the spices on the shelves.

"I knew better than to work with a Curse Eater," Farvem yelled. "But decided to have faith! I helped her!"

Bang.

"I *trusted* her!"

Bang.

The door was splintering. I stood straight, trying to find a controlled breath in my panic, as blood dripped from my chin onto my arms. I hurried to the wooden block table, where all the jams sat wrapped in their satin ribbons for gifting. I attempted to push it, but it budged only an inch.

Please. Please.

I pleaded with the house, lowering my defenses, reaching for any help it could offer, no matter what I'd be asked to give in return, and it came alive. Like curls of smoke from a snuffed candle, drudge materialized in corners, behind pantry doors, beneath the table. Something grazed my ankle—a leathery, cursed creature clawing its way from beneath the sink. The wood holding the latch in place cracked and splintered, sending the metal flying, crashing onto the table in an explosion of glass and pulpy blackberry jam.

Mr. Farvem entered, eyes wide, his frail body no worse for wear from all the turmoil he'd put it through. Immediately, the Drudge converged, scrabbling up his figure from the floor and dropping from above to engulf him. I braced for his screams, anticipating the garbled choking sounds as they invaded his body, but all I heard was a chilling stillness. Then Mr. Farvem, obscured by the gaseous ashes of the Drudge, began to walk toward the table.

"They can't penetrate my defenses, Eleanora," he said, lifting his arms as though showing me a trick. The scalpel caught the fading light of day filtering in from the tiny window, which offered no prospect of escape. "I run a tight ship. Learned that in the infantry. To survive, you can't let the curses in. I've encountered more impressive monsters than these paltry bags of dust. Humans and Drudge joined in terrible union."

Despite the confidence in his voice, he became agitated by the swarm, swinging the scalpel in wild punctuation to his final remarks. The Drudge, bewildered and uncertain, retreated, creeping to their corners to observe the events as they developed, waiting.

By calling on the Drudge, I'd unwittingly put myself at a disadvantage. If I invited one in to bolster my magic, they would all come. I leaned into the power I already had, hoping it wasn't so under-used it wouldn't respond the way I needed it to. What I was preparing to do would be painful, and risked dangerously depleting my energy, but it would give me the opportunity to put some distance between us. Mr. Farvem's strength was unnatural, driven by magic, but I thought I might still have a chance of outrunning him.

"What are you doing, girl?"

I thrust the table, power erupting in a panicked, desperate

burst, sending the heavy piece of furniture flying several feet forward. Jars crashed, breaking one by one, the corner rocketing toward Mr. Farvem. But instead of being knocked down, he slammed his hands on the tabletop, heedless of the glass, and vaulted over it, as nimble as a boy, sliding through the remnants of sticky jelly. He seized a handful of pinned curls near my temple, and I slipped on the mess I'd created in my useless efforts.

"Don't take it to heart, young lady," he said, kicking my feet so that I slipped further down in the glass, weakening my ability to stave him off. "I bent the rules a little bit, took on a bit of nasty cursed magic to regain some of the vitality I've lost over the past twenty years. Disgusting but necessary."

"Mr. Farvem, don't do this. I only wanted to help." I gasped, both hands wrapped around the wrist holding the blade, barely keeping it from coming any closer to my neck. At the angle he was holding me, I had very little leverage, and if I slipped any further, my arms would buckle.

"So did Fiona. She was supposed to stop the Brom, set it on fire from the inside. Instead, she created a living hell for us all. So many dead. My Patrick, murdered."

The scalpel came ever closer, and I sobbed. The Drudge were moving, sneaking in like carrion birds waiting for their chance to feed.

"Magic abandoned us." Spittle dripped from his mouth as he yelled. "The Fiend is our punishment if we keep trying to bring it back. Your sister became a monster, and I'm going to make sure it doesn't happen to you. Let me save you, Eleanora!"

The sound of gunfire shattered the air. Two shots.

Mr. Farvem fell against the table, an awful gurgling rising from his missing throat, blown away by two well-aimed bullets from the gun Inspector Harrow held steady in his hand at the threshold of the decimated kitchen door.

Seeing their opportunity, the patient Drudge converged, burrowing into Mr. Farvem's red mouth with such feral vigor that his jawbone snapped. As he slid to the floor, the flesh between his jaw and neck tore, making room for more Drudge to settle in, feasting on whatever magic remained. But not just the Drudge moved towards this source of sustenance. From the debris of jam, rose furls of red. Breaths of curses tucked in each jar.

Inspector Harrow holstered his gun, and in a few strides, he was leaning over me, tucking an arm under mine and another behind my knees, scooping me off the floor. He smelled of gasoline and smoke; his clothes filthy with dirty snow and soot, skin smudged with the same, blood seeping from a gash above his eye.

I held onto him, burying my face in his neck, anguish twisting my features while I struggled to suppress tears of relief rooted in the reality that neither of us were dead.

Wordlessly, he carried me up two flights of stairs, and slipped into my family suite. He kicked open the bathroom door with the toe of his shoe, and deposited me on the vanity stool with a care I hadn't believed him capable of.

"How are you alive?" My trembling made the words a shaky vibrato.

"Halfway to the gate, the front driver's side wheel started to smoke. I worked two car bombings in Devin, and the acrid smell was familiar." His voice was strained. He was stifling emotions that had gathered like ants under his skin, whether it was anger or panic, or concern, I couldn't tell. "These bastards barely knew what they were doing; the spring-loaded trigger wasn't balanced, the fuse was too long. Gave me enough time."

He stood at the sink, gruffly grabbing a cloth and soaking it in water to tend to my face. Small bits of glass fell from my clothes, and I considered every part of my body with care, looking for pain. My arms ached from shoving the table, my temples were tender, and my chin, which Inspector Harrow was examining, stung viciously.

"You need a stitch," he muttered.

"I'm not leaving this house."

"Well, then, do you have a sewing kit?" he asked, with a significant amount of sarcasm. We both became aware he'd made a joke. He didn't seem happy about it.

"I can try to use magic," I said. My mother had treated our minor injuries this way. Cuts, sprains, and contusions were all magically nursed, despite the difficulty of bending the material of the human body. Magic was stubborn and unpredictable when it met with human biology, and even before magic use had been restricted, hospitals had banned the inclusion in medicine. Blackwickets, as far back as anyone could remember, had despised hospitals. Our mother especially was worried someone would recognize what her children were and take us. We were lucky we'd never needed one.

I tried to stand, but the Inspector placed a hand on my shoulder, guiding me to sit again.

"I'll do it," he said, returning to the sink to rinse the cloth and wash his hands in the scalding water.

"You know how?"

"You pick up some things working with the Authority."

Kneeling before me, he pressed his fingers to my cheek in a silent request for me to tilt my head. I lowered my eyelids to peer at him as his fingers brushed from my cheek to the wound, blood still trickling down my neck. Suddenly, there was quiet in him, something very near serenity, and the world turned soft and pillowy before a pinch jolted me back.

"And you can soothe as well."

"Stay still."

I followed his instructions, pondering his gentleness.

"How long until the Drudge are done?" He asked when he was finished, handing me the washrag to press on the magically cauterized wound as he stood.

He meant with their work of feeding from Mr. Farvem.

"They're done now, is my guess," I replied softly, dabbing my chin to distract from the memory of the old man's throat. "What are we going to do about…"

"I'll handle it. Wash. Rest."

As he turned to leave, I noticed a tear in the shoulder of his jacket, to the right of his shoulder blade, blood staining the gray fabric in a broad patch. I didn't call after him. Instead, I remained in the quiet bathroom, grappling with the knowledge that Inspector Harrow had tended to my wound first, even when his injuries were far greater than my own.

CHAPTER TWENTY-SIX

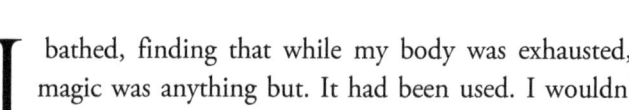

I bathed, finding that while my body was exhausted, my magic was anything but. It had been used. I wouldn't be able to produce another surge of considerable power anytime soon, but the bright, cool energy stretched inside me, liberated.

I refrained from lingering, worried about what the Inspector was doing and eager to know how he was handling Mr. Farvem's remains. For a moment, I let myself mourn a world that diligently chose to move toward its bleakest future. Patrick hadn't been so different from his grandfather after all, and there must be others with the same ideology. With this grim thought in mind, I gathered myself from the embrace of the hot water and prepared to face the fallout downstairs.

The kitchen door hung crooked on its hinges, and I walked just close enough to ensure the body was gone, although the terrible mess was not. Through the front foyer window, I spotted the remnants of the car, still smoldering, billowing its noxious black smoke in the winter sky. The bomb had detonated by the gate, reducing the left portion to a pile of charred bricks, with the once sturdy iron gatepost lying across the road.

There were people milling around—half a dozen. Inspector Harrow was easy to spot among them, the tallest of a small group who were gesticulating wildly, calling to others on their way up the road, some dressed in evening finery, tourists and townspeople both crossing the border of the Blackwicket property. A few yards from the wreckage, a figure lay on the ground, someone's long coat draped over it in a makeshift shroud. I expected the scene would eventually make sense.

Something plucked at my senses, a presence reaching for my magic, like tiny hands searching for sweets. I averted my attention to the source, a figure lurking at the top of the stairs. A Drudge clung to the banister with primate-like fingers, observing me, its face long and doughy as soft wax.

"Would you have eaten me?" I asked.

In response, it released the railing and slunk away, unhurried.

Of course, it would have. Drudge didn't mourn, nor form attachments. They existed to look for ways to return to the state they deserved to be in, free of the horrors handed to them. They preferred me in my living condition because it offered a consistent source of magic, no matter how weak. But if I were to die, they wouldn't waste me. I couldn't fault them for it.

Needing to make use of myself, I shed the squeamishness and returned to the kitchen to clean the foul muck of jam, blood, and glass. The blood was plentiful, and the room smelled of iron and sweet syrup, inducing me to gag. I saved myself the ghastly trouble of touching the offal of Mr. Farvem's brutal end and called on my magic. Long ago, Isolde Blackwicket had used hers to soak up the blood and bile from a young boy who I'd loved dearly.

Instead of burying the thought of him, I held Thomas' memory close as I cleaned, wondering if he would have grown to be like his brother, become a man who manipulated and intimidated all to maintain power for the Brom. A man who'd do anything for the empire his father built on the backs of townspeople cut off from their livelihoods. These thoughts troubled me more than gathering the blood into a puddle and coaxing it in an unnatural direction, up the iron legs of the kitchen basin, and into the drain, where the house drank it hungrily down. I did the rest by hand until I heard the front door creak.

Inspector Harrow returned haggard, with the weary look of a man who'd survived many ordeals and was no longer surprised by them.

"Mr. Farvem was the unfortunate victim of the car bomb," he said. "While he was on his way to the house, he got caught in the blast that I barely escaped. The story was corroborated by a few witnesses who'd seen him walking this direction earlier. His assistant from the funeral home has already collected his body."

"Who were all the people at the gate?"

"They heard the explosion. Came to help."

"I'm shocked."

Inspector Harrow, by now, was well aware of how the citizens of Nightglass viewed my family and our house on the cliffs.

"You shouldn't be. People always discover a great deal of goodwill in themselves when violence is no longer politely ignorable," he said, starting toward the stairs, an unspoken signal he was planning to stay. I couldn't admit out loud that this was a comfort.

"Do you need anything?" I asked, unsure how to repay the unexpected kindness he'd shown me by saving my life and tending to my injuries.

He paused, foot on the first step, holding my gaze for so long, an unknown feeling twisted in my chest. At length, he continued his ascent, saying low as he went, "Yes, Ms. Blackwicket. I need the hand of god to drown this whole goddamn town in the sea."

Late in the evening, when I'd finally corrected the kitchen and there was no more cleaning to occupy my mind, I went to bed.

But as I passed the Inspector's room, there came a muffled grunt, a sound of pain. I'd intended to leave him be, but then there was another rumble of agony.

Worried, I knocked.

"Inspector?"

"I'm well, Ms. Blackwicket." His reply was curt.

"I noticed…" I shouldn't be hesitant. The man was hurt, and the location of the wound made parts of it inaccessible to treatment if he were mending it alone. "I noticed you were injured. I'm not a nurse, but I'm probably a better option than whatever you're trying to do in there."

"Your concern is noted. Goodnight."

Dismissed, I retired to my room, but couldn't sleep. I tossed in the dark, formulating nonsensical plans and half-formed ideas regarding the secret politics of Nightglass before finally throwing off the blankets. Dropping to my knees, I reached beneath the bed to pull forth the carpet bags I still hadn't unpacked. I maintained no further illusions about the possibility of escaping from this house, so I might as well settle in.

In the dull glow of the nightstand lamp, I emptied the bags and tidied things away. At last, I came to the wooden box with its cursed treasures. It was time to let go of my former lives.

I opened the box, the curses vibrating with anticipation, and noticed right away that something very important was missing. The bracelet.

I rummaged through, moving aside the vessels I'd collected: coins, hair ribbons, a small hand mirror, a figurine of a ballerina with her feet missing. It wasn't there. The only people who'd handled my bags had been Thea's driver Ramsey, briefly upon delivering me to Blackwicket House, and Darren. The most likely candidate was obvious.

Sitting in silence, I waited for the tears to come, but there weren't any left for Darren Rose. I'd cried them all while he was alive. I came to terms with the fact that my father would never take anything from me again, then, one by one, I unraveled the curses.

The grounding work encouraged my newly invigorated power to confirm itself, and I forged on, returning each empty vessel to the box as the gossamer strands of healed magic gathered above me. It remained unsure, unprepared to dissipate into the ether. It was a shame there wasn't a Narthex.

I reached into the cool, ephemeral clouds of energy as an idea took hold. A highly illegal one, dangerous with the Inspector so near, but I had little left to lose, and the untangled magic would find peace in returning home. Unlike myself.

It seemed a fair way to balance things.

It had been a decade since my last attempt to open a portal, and it would be challenging work, like bailing water from a sinking boat. A doorway not etched by years and constant use tended to snap shut and was difficult to open any wider than a porthole.

The truth was, this world didn't want to touch Dark Hall anymore. Or perhaps it was the other way around.

I crawled across the floor to the space of wall between my bed and Fiona's. I pressed my fingers to the wallpaper, scraped and peeling by the baseboard, letting my magic do the searching, brushing the contours, seeking weak spots between the borderline of here and there. The wall was solid, nothing more than plaster and lath. But then a point gave way and my fingers sank in. Elated, I parted space and substance, the effort making my chest burn, and cycled magic to and fro, shoveling bits of reality away to create an opening large enough for my hand.

The air chilled, and my grip slipped as the portal breathed, uncomfortable with its own existence. I yearned to look inside, to glimpse a place I once cherished, but I was already losing my hold. Knowing home was close, the lingering magic brushed past me, retreating to a realm that would never harm it. Even after it faded, and despite the strenuous effort, I tried to hold the portal open, to feel Dark Hall. But I wasn't strong enough, and the portal snapped shut with the sound of a bulb filament popping. My magic quivered, mournful, conscious of the loss of connection.

More restless than ever, and with sleep too distant to even attempt, I donned my sister's only remaining wool coat over my nightdress, shoes hanging from my fingers. My momentary connection with Dark Hall had encouraged nostalgia, and I wanted to be near the sea.

My stockinged feet produced no noise on the stairs. The winter moonlight was pleasant, and the house uncharacteristically idle, satiated by its earlier banquet of magic.

By mid-stair, I could see the parlor lights were on, and had no doubt about who was responsible. My plans to walk along the cliffside and watch the winter sky change as the sun rose were derailed by my curiosity. As expected, I found Inspector Harrow. He'd opened the parlor windows to invite in the scent of salt and snow and stood awash in the night and the calming lullaby of waves. His shirt and trousers were rumpled, collar unbuttoned, and for the first time since I'd known him, his gun was absent.

"My mother used to say the song of the sea soothed the curses," I said, letting him know I was there, maintaining a respectful distance, "because it sounds like the place magic was born."

His gaze migrated from the moon-bright water to settle on me. He seemed human in this setting, in the late hours before night tipped into dawn. His presence was an assurance, if not exactly a comfort, and my interest in solitude waned. He monitored my approach, taking in my coat, the shoes still clasped loosely in my hands.

"Going somewhere?" he asked.

"To walk the cliffs."

"It's freezing."

I eyed the windows, the frigid air bracing, fighting with the heat of the fire he'd tempted to life in the fireplace. He didn't backtrack or elaborate.

"I couldn't sleep." I deposited my shoes on the windowsill, signaling my decision to linger and enjoy the same view. "Neither could you, I see. I bet this isn't how you imagined things to turn out when you followed me here."

"Actually, it's right on par with how I expected things to go."

"And now I'm sure you wish you were still in Devin."

It was a friendly jest, but I regretted it. I no longer knew what the Inspector and I were, but it certainly wasn't friends.

He trained his eyes on the sparkle of the water and said dryly, "I'm where I'm meant to be."

I was bad at this. We'd never encountered each other as anything more than mutual enemies. The new ground I was attempting to walk, with no logic of why, was not just unfamiliar, it was unreciprocated. I grabbed my shoes.

"I hope you can get some rest," I said in parting, flustered by briefly feeling less alone, only for the moment to cave in at my touch.

"It's not a smart idea for you to leave the house, Ms. Blackwicket."

"Talking about house arrest again? Well, if you or anyone else wants to keep me in here, you'll have to…" My impertinent rebuttal tapered as I caught sight of the spot of red at the horizon of his shoulder.

"Do continue. I'm very interested in your next words." Inspector Harrow's tone implied he wasn't in the mood to be patient with me.

"Are you bleeding?"

I marched to him, taking hold of his upper arm, urging him to turn enough that I could inspect his back. He permitted it.

There was a bloom of red spreading from his injury, with no other signs of smoke or oil, and no tear in the fabric. This wasn't the shirt he'd been wearing earlier. The blood was fresh.

"Bang-up job patching your own wounds, Inspector." I said.

"Are you scolding me?" There was an air of disbelief in his tone, like a storm surprised by the admonishments of a thistle.

"You're being stubborn by rejecting help when you honestly need it."

With some annoyance, he turned to face me, and I retreated a step to save myself from having to tilt my head quite so far to see his face.

"I find some irony in you daring to call someone else stubborn."

"You'd honestly choose an infection over allowing me to tend to you, Inspector?" I asked, pointing out his obstinacy.

There was a tense beat of silence before Inspector Harrow began to unbutton his shirt, gaze steady on me. The action took me by surprise, and I glanced aside.

"Shy?" He untucked the hem, making discomfort my punishment for chiding. "How do you expect to *tend to me* if you can't even get to the wound?"

He wore no undershirt, avoiding fabric that would chafe against the raw edges of the laceration, and the olive-toned skin of his chest was exposed, showcasing the well-defined contours of his abdomen, marked by scars of varying sizes and colors, resembling notches in driftwood. But more than these, the prominent token of violence on his cheek trailed beyond his collarbone, to the center of his sternum.

"Just sit," I said, agitated, motioning to the piano bench as I made to leave. "I'll be back with a bandage."

CHAPTER TWENTY-SEVEN

The brief walk to the despicable kitchen for a raid on the cabinets, where my mother had once kept first aid, offered a much-needed moment to gather my wits. I was reacting foolishly. I'd seen men half dressed, in much more intimate circumstances than this, yet had never blushed like a bashful virgin, even when I'd been one.

In the small corner cupboard behind the door, I discovered my sister had continued Isolde Blackwicket's habit of overstocking medical supplies. Balm, iodine, rubbing alcohol, aspirin, adhesive bandages of varying sizes, and rolls of cotton gauze filled the shelves, enough to supply a small hospital. I didn't want to think about why she needed so much.

When I returned to the parlor, Inspector Harrow was sitting on the piano bench, arms resting on his knees. He reminded me of the boxers who'd exhibited in Devin, an event that Ben had taken me to for reasons beyond my comprehension. But I'd attended, smiled, clapped, and cheered, all the while longing to be home.

He said nothing as I approached to stand behind him, my heart skipping unpleasantly at the sight awaiting me. Mirroring his chest and stomach, his back was a map of brutality.

Scars marred his flesh, accompanied by multiple bruises at varying stages of healing. But none was more vicious than the blue and purple discoloration that spanned his left shoulder. The gash in its center continued to weep blood. As I suspected, the Inspector had been unable to reach it, and it remained only partially cauterized.

There was something about manipulating living flesh that made magic recoil, rendering even minor repairs to the body highly complicated and requiring a focus that was impossible to achieve when pain was meddling. That Harrow had managed to seal the cut on my chin while enduring this wound was a testament to the concealed virility of his power. As I examined the other marks, I pondered their origins and whether anyone had ever been there to help him mend.

"I'll have to do this slowly. I'm not practiced in this kind of magic, but a bandage won't be sufficient on its own," I said, preparing him for the process.

"You can't hurt me, Ms. Blackwicket."

"Yes, I can." I gently rejected his assurances that he was an inhuman creature who couldn't feel the ache in his own body.

His head turned a fraction.

I'd never attempted to soothe with magic, and I doubted the Inspector would lower his guard and allow me to try. Keeping my touch as tender as possible, I disinfected the opening with alcohol, hovering my touch above the last two inches of flayed skin. I ushered my magic to act, fusing skin like metal met with a soldering iron. The demand of the effort caused my hand to tremble. The results wouldn't be pretty.

He remained deathly still, but here and there, he winced, the swell of muscle in his arm twitching. I tried to distract him, opting for questions that might draw his ire, the best of pain medicines.

"You helped dig my sister's grave. Why?" I asked.

"It cost me nothing."

"She was Brom." It was the first time I'd admitted this, accepting it as true.

"She belonged to you. While I don't believe you're innocent, I've seen enough to conclude you're not a Brom woman."

A clenched jaw followed this proclamation as my fingertips swept along the jagged tear, his teeth grinding. Driven by empathy, I rested my free hand upon his right shoulder blade, allowing a small portion of magical energy to flow warm and free. Its purity would serve as an analgesic, softening the misery of this process.

He sucked in a sharp breath as his power responded radically, entwining with mine with a starving urgency.

"Eleanora." The murmuring of my name was a warning, and I withdrew.

"I'm sorry, I was trying to help with the pain."

He grunted in response.

When I'd finished wiping the last of the blood, I pressed the gauze into place and began to wrap it. The method required me to stand at the Inspector's side and tuck my hand beneath his arm, knuckles brushing his ribs. My face was close to his, the smell of his hair still smoky under the clean scent of soap.

He watched me, eyes half-lidded, as I fastened the gauze. We lingered like this, so near one another, and at last I gave in to the deranged urge to graze my thumb across the scar on his cheek.

He caught my hand, neither encouraging me closer nor pushing me away.

"You said a Brom did this to you." I spoke quietly, confounded by the compassion I'd found in myself.

"He was fighting for his life," he answered with poorly concealed contempt for the memory. "He lost."

"You killed him?"

I needed to know, even though I hadn't been fully honest myself.

"Yes."

"Have you killed many people, Victor?"

His grip on me contracted ever so slightly, and my pulse picked up pace for too many reasons to name.

"Have you?" he replied.

"Why would you choose this life?" I evaded his question, desperate to understand what had made him into the shape of the man he was, violence a mantle on his broad shoulders.

Rather than letting go, he pressed my palm to his chest. His heartbeat was sure, steady.

"Take a look. You have my permission."

I hesitated, but he'd dropped his guard. His magic entreated, and I surrendered. The unsettling thought that this might be a trap—that I would lay my magic in his hands merely for him to seize it—was ignored.

Unlike before, Inspector Harrow didn't dampen the tide of his power, and it swept mine under. There was no taking, no wrenching it from me, only an unspoken invitation to sink into a magic this world couldn't fathom.

He observed my face as I explored this vastness.

"You're a Dark Hall child."

I needed no confirmation beyond the experience of our energies weaving themselves together, the moment becoming suddenly more intimate as this secret was revealed. Yet as I drifted further, I came upon something else welded into the essence of the magic that made Inspector Harrow a commodity, and upon contact, it rose.

Inspector Harrow's eyes closed briefly, exhilaration coursing through him, and thus through me. He brought my knuckles to his lips and inhaled, the change in his demeanor unmistakable.

"It's time for you to go to bed now, Eleanora," he said against my skin.

I should have agreed, should have retreated to my room, allowed the Inspector to find peace in solitude. But I was hungry for the connection, a force that stirred my magic in a way I'd never believed possible.

"You don't need to hide from me," I replied. "I'm not afraid."

He sat up, his free hand cupping the back of my neck, dragging me to him. The crush of his lips was unforgiving, devouring, and he released my hand at his chest to hoist me onto his lap, coat and nightgown rising as my legs parted around him.

The layers of fabric were infuriating, preventing me from experiencing the full firmness of his body. I pushed my hands into his hair, parting my lips to invite his tongue, which delved to taste me in the same way it had in the alley, when this fire had first begun to smolder. I pressed into him, the sensation of his hard length against my sensitive heat making me ferocious.

He began undoing my coat, his hands sure, and soon he was yanking it from my shoulders, exposing the slip, cotton and simple. Some distant part of me, not addled by lust, lamented that I hadn't worn the silk set of underthings. As it stood, I wore no brassiere at all, and the frisson of ardor had hardened my nipples, which rose prominently beneath the fabric.

"An interesting choice of wardrobe for a winter walk," he grated, all the while tucking his finger into the strap of the garment, sliding it down my shoulder, tugging the front panel from my breast to expose me to the frigid air.

He braced an arm between my shoulder blades, twisting a handful of my hair in his grasp, pulling so that I was forced to arch nearer him. He didn't lower his head to torment me as I hoped he would, but ran his mouth along my jawline.

"Were you hoping to run into someone?"

I wasn't sure if it was teasing or an insinuation.

"A girl's allowed her amusements," I replied, irritation and want creating a heady mix.

"And tell me what you were going to do if you'd found no one to play with you,"

I wasn't well-versed in this sort of banter, though it heightened my arousal. My experiences had all been mostly silent, punctuated by grunts and nonsensical exclamations from lovers.

"Victor, I've never done this," I said, breathless, hesitant to admit my lack of experience in this field. In response, he inclined me further, angling my hips, my nightdress pooling in the aching juncture of my thighs.

"Touch yourself, Eleanora," he growled.

My magic heaved, warming me from the inside so that a flush rose to my skin in contempt of the cold.

As any woman, pleasing myself was a thing I knew how to do well. I slipped a hand along my thigh, and Victor aided me by gathering the fabric, tugging it further up to expose the cream linen underwear and soft curve of my abdomen.

I guided my fingers over the fabric, damp with need, and across the crest of my desire, shuddering at the sensation, enhanced by having a witness.

"Finally doing as you're told," he said, bringing his mouth to my breast as I stroked myself, catching the hardened crown of my nipple between his teeth and tongue.

My core grew molten, and I rose to him. I worked knowingly at the taut nerves, the ministrations of his tongue nearly more stimulation than I could withstand. He unhanded my nightdress, utilizing this freedom to fondle my other breast, still clad in cotton, rolling the delicate flesh in his fingers, as my climax began to build. But as my muscles grew tense, Victor seized hold of my wrist, denying me.

I protested, the nonverbal noise of frustration encouraging a laugh from Inspector Harrow, rich and resonant.

"I prefer that gratification be mine to give." His tone was

rough with his own desire, and he caught me against him, standing as though I weighed no more than sea foam. My legs encompassed his waist as he carried me to the piano, setting me down on the closed top, and reaching beneath my gown to slide the underthings from my hips. I aided him by lifting myself, allowing the panties to fall down my calves and onto the floor. When they were disposed of, Victor's bruising fingers seized me behind the knees, raising them. I reclined, elbows on the mahogany wood top, pressing my heels onto the edge of the piano. His half-lidded eyes, the color of honeyed mead, remained on mine as he coaxed my thighs apart, opening me to his view. His gaze drifted languidly from my face to my mouth, dipping down the line of my body to the dewy pink swell of my sex. He muttered a low oath, widening me further.

"You're a fucking sight to behold, Eleanora Blackwicket," he said, finally stroking his thumb over the throbbing swell, just to make me tremble.

"Victor, I've evaded death twice since coming to this hellhole, don't let this be what kills me. Please." I was begging, longing for release, for more of him. He stroked more evenly, circling the pad of his thumb in aching arches.

"Eager to be violated by an Inspector of the Authority, Curse Eater?" Slipping his hand behind my head, he tilted it forward so that I could watch the slow, purposeful motion.

"I'm already tainted." I panted, fingernails raking against unforgiving wood. "You can't make it worse."

He leaned forward, taking in the scent of my hair, lowering his guard so that his magic could slip into me with obscene intensity. With it came the diabolic shape of his affliction, but I wasn't horrified; the coiling wrongness of it brushed closed, promising.

"You're mistaken," the Inspector replied, taking my ankles and raising them to his shoulders, where they slipped around his neck. Aware of what he was about to do, I balked, overwhelmed by the idea of it. My desires had always been many, but my demands of lovers incredibly few. I'd never known how to ask.

Lifting my hips, he drew me nearer, his mouth a prayer away from enveloping me. He caressed my naked side and lower belly, snaking his fingers over my mound and into the dark curls, before slipping between swollen lips, parting them to expose me to his intentions.

"Victor." I moaned, teetering on the precipice of an irredeemable action.

"Say my name again."

I could do nothing but give in.

"Victor."

His name was profane magic, wickedness whispered with impiety in the pitch-black hold of night, when no innocent thing dared move.

His warm tongue ran across the hill of my pleasure, teased stiff with both mine and his attention. The sound that rose from my throat was grating, a groan and a cry, strangled by the overwhelming sensation I'd craved. It encouraged another foul word from him, and he drew me into his mouth, sucking at the sensitive flesh.

My breath came heavy, the vision of him framed by my thighs sending currents of want so strong, my head grew light on my shoulders. Victor Harrow could have asked me anything, could have ordered me to swallow hot coals, and as long as his tongue continued its languorous strokes, I would have opened my mouth to take them.

"You're unbelievable," he groaned, the vibration of his words driving me toward a place I'd been many times, but never in this way, never so desperate.

I cried out, a warning throb tightening. I lifted myself to him for more, but he slid my legs from his shoulders, replacing my heels on the piano top. Then, leaning over me, his stomach brushing against my slick cleft, he kissed me, letting me taste myself on his tongue.

"Victor, please," I pleaded when the kiss traveled to my neck.

"Begging doesn't sway me," he said, pressing his body close to increase the friction, "But it's such a pretty sound."

He allowed space for his hand to move between us.

"Look at me," he ordered, and when our eyes met, he slid two fingers into my silky heat.

I arched, grabbing onto his arm as he withdrew and buried them in deeper, caressing my clit with his thumb as he found a rhythm of stroking that was robbing me of thought, of my ability to be anything but a pillar of sensation.

I needed more. I lowered my foot, rising to reach a hand to his groin, drawing my palm along the hard length of him. My fondling elicited a surge of power that overtook me, washing me in a white-hot tremor of ecstasy that was not all mine.

"Careful, Curse Eater. There's very little decency remaining in me; if I lose it, I'll do something neither of us could forgive."

"Nothing you've done to me has been decent."

Emboldened by eagerness, I unfastened his belt as he continued to pet me, catching my mouth in a fervent kiss. In my enthusiasm, I nipped his bottom lip and lost my position of control. With a harsh, guttural rumble, he removed his hand, grip digging into the muscle of my backside, as he dragged me forward, until I was again wrapped around his waist, my nakedness pressed against his concealed cock. Utilizing his strength, he raised and lowered me against him, grinding into my cunt. I lost my sense of presence, aware only of the barreling approach of my climax. In two more fierce motions, I came, shuddering, suspended in a realm of ecstasy.

But at the height of my delirium, Inspector Harrow's

unholy magic rose, not to tease, but to overtake in a violence that intensified my orgasm. Victor had become a maelstrom, carrying me into vicious waters. The lights dimmed, the ocean waves deafening as the house quaked.

"Eleanora." The rumbling of my name was inhuman. Victor's magic twisted within mine, igniting the same mix of rapture and profound ache. I exhaled, lightheaded, as my euphoria ebbed, and his teeth caught my shoulder, biting, encouraging a brief electric jolt of pain that stoked fires still blazing.

I was prepared to give in to him again, as many times as he wanted, but he loosened his hold, lowering me to the ground, the hem of the gown falling to my calves. He stepped away from me, and I replaced the strap of the nightgown onto my shoulder, covering myself, suddenly cold.

"Victor, what's happening?"

He couldn't answer, his face contorting into something monstrous, the elongating of his neck stretching muscle and dislocating bone, skin darkening like the cruel bruise upon his back, red tinged. He lurched forward to catch hold of me, but was halted by a tremor of pain that wracked his body, mirroring his peculiar seizure in the hall the day Auntie had attacked. All of his muscles tightened in tandem, agony deforming him into an unbelievable shape. When the episode passed, Victor was himself again. The ordeal had left him sweating, huffing as though his lungs had lost their ability to hold air.

I pushed aside my panic, the instinct to flee, choosing to reach out to him. But as I stepped closer, he retreated.

"This was a regrettable circumstance," he grated. "We both nearly died today, our common sense is blown to hell."

"You don't have to hide from me. I can…"

"Ms. Blackwicket," he snapped, his formal use of my name a slap after everything that had just occurred. "I've given you your pleasure, now leave me in peace."

Raking his fingers through his hair, he moved past me, snatching his bloodstained shirt from the piano as he went. I stood staring after him, shaken, humiliated, wondering how deep Inspector Victor Harrow's monstrousness went, disgusted that despite it, I hadn't wanted him to stop.

Chapter Twenty-Eight

I had no sense of the time, knowing only that I'd slept so long my limbs didn't feel like my own. Mind muddled, I roused, throwing open the shutters to a dreary afternoon. I didn't want to see Inspector Harrow, not while I was still piecing together what had occurred in the early hours, when he'd introduced me to desire I'd never experienced.

I reminded myself, again and again, that we'd both been reeling from the traumatic events of the day, eager to occupy ourselves with something other than dark thoughts. Still, the Inspector's admission of being a stolen child, his face becoming monstrous in the golden glow of the lamps, haunted me. As did the ghost of his hands on my thighs.

Pinching the bridge of my nose, I leaned on the dresser, crowded with all the powders and perfumes my sister had collected. I imagined turning the clock back to the night I'd left, choosing to stay instead, choosing my sister over freedom. Maybe we could have been safe together. Maybe she'd be alive, and I'd be an asset of the Brom, helping her operate an illegal boarding house.

I touched several bottles, assessing the extensive array of fragrances, many of which I'd sold to customers at Galton's. One bottle caught my attention, emptier than the rest. I brought it to my nose, savoring the scent of summer jasmine, before recognizing who it brought to mind: the smoky-voiced Thea who ran High Tide for William, thorny and puzzling.

I returned the bottle and hugged my arms to my chest for comfort while I contemplated the photos on the walls. They needed to be taken down and stored. It pained me to see all the people who may have exploited my sister for her abilities, her position of influence over William. I considered the blackberry flowers pressed inside the frames, displayed in no particular order.

Goosebumps rose on my flesh, spine straightening as I made the horrible connection.

I quickly dressed, still tucking my blouse as I hurried into the hall to the Inspector's room. Without calling his name, I banged on the door with the flat of my hand, never relenting. He wouldn't be able to ignore me, no matter how badly he wanted to.

The door opened abruptly, and there he stood, dressed and shaved, his hair precise, with not a strand out of place. He'd returned to being the cold, authoritative man he'd always been, the crack in his armor repaired.

"What's going on?" he barked.

I looked him dead in the eye, "Fiona was poisoning people."

Moments later, we stood side by side in my girlhood room. The Inspector filled the space, the slant of the ceiling making him seem taller than ever. He took stock of the photos, his countenance growing ever more stern.

"The Blackberry jam. Fiona put a curse in each jar." I tapped the glass of a picture frame where white flower petals had been pressed. "Blackberry flowers."

"And what makes you think these photos and the cursed jam are related?" The tone of his voice suggested he was humoring me, sparking my irritation.

"When I first visited the Vapors, William and Thea spiked my drink with a curse."

His eyes cut to me, the slight twitch of jaw muscle indicating he didn't appreciate I'd never mentioned this.

"It didn't work," I said. "I recognized it, but many people wouldn't. In my case, it was a test, but Fiona may have been using the same tactic to infect unsuspecting people, and I don't think she was doing it for the Brom."

"Then who?"

"Mr. Farvem said he trusted Fiona, helped her, and believed she would improve things here in Nightglass. From what I know, Farvem and his family hated the Brom. Fiona was in a special position to cause them damage."

"A compelling theory with little evidence."

"What do you know about the Veil, Inspector?" I pivoted, still unraveling my line of thought, hoping it would reveal something that made sense.

The silence that followed my question was a touch too heavy, betraying that I'd struck close to something.

"The old war unit?" Inspector Harrow asked.

I nodded.

"The Authority prefers people stay pretty tight-lipped about that part of history. How did you hear about it?" he asked.

"Farvem mentioned it while he was trying to murder me. I figured it was pertinent." My flat delivery encouraged a blunt exhale of amusement from the Inspector, who appreciated the morbid humor. When our eyes met, he adjusted his attention back to the photos, tucking the hand closest to me into his pocket.

"Well," he said, choosing to tell me. "The powers that be back then discovered a way to use stronger magic wielders as vessels for Drudge. When it started benefiting them, they made more Drudge, enlisted more capable magical folk, and then lost control of them. If a magic user didn't die from consuming too many curses, they went mad."

Like mother. Like Thomas.

I shivered, and perhaps it was my imagination, but the Inspector seemed to move a fraction closer.

"Then the Veil was formed and tasked to take care of the problem they'd created for themselves. But members became fanatical and didn't stop with the magic users who carried Drudge. They began going for anyone who could so much as light a spark on their fingertips. Between the Veil and the Military making monsters, this world became a lost cause for magic."

"My mother never taught us much about life before the war. She thought it was irrelevant to our daily lives. Do you know who we were fighting?"

The Inspector regarded me with a look I'd have mistaken for regret if I believed him capable of it.

"No. Only that they thought what people here were doing with magic was an abomination and needed to be stopped."

I examined his face. This wasn't Inspector Harrow's history. It belonged to a world that didn't belong to him, one he'd been whisked to before he was old enough to remember anywhere else. And when he arrived, he was handed suffering, molding him into the brutal man he was, with tainted magic woven so deep it was likely irremovable.

"Maybe there are still people who feel that way," I concluded. "Maybe my sister did."

"That would take rather extreme self-loathing."

"Or enough hatred toward those hurting her that she'd join another side just to escape them."

"You're very perceptive, Eleanora," he said, and the comment wasn't laced with dry sarcasm or condescension. "In the last several years, there's been a rise in violence directed at magic users."

Bitterness climbed my backbone, and I resisted a quip that the Authority needed no help with that. It wasn't the time.

"It's linked to a growing faction of anti-magic ideologists. They function under the name of that special unit from the war seventy years ago. They're the antithesis of the Brom in all ways but violence. The ends justify the means, and they believe they're doing something good. So, you may be on to something," he motioned to the photos. "Each of those people marked with a blackberry bloom is on the Authority list of missing persons."

"Are you sure?"

"I know the faces. They're a smaller part of the reason the Authority established a presence here in Nightglass."

I rubbed my arms, the static of my magic tingling as my anxiety rose. Since letting my power free, it was formed to the shape of my emotions, and such a thing took some getting used to.

"What was my sister doing?" I wondered out loud.

Of course, Inspector Harrow didn't answer. If either of us had known the truth, we wouldn't be standing here, staring at dozens of photos of missing people, all with my sister smiling warmly next to them. The silence allowed me to notice how close I was standing to Harrow. I wanted to move past this moment, find an excuse to rush him from my bedroom, but every option would betray my discomfort, not of having him near, but of wanting him to be. The silence stretched, and I realized he must still be studying the pictures, letting his mind work and make connections. But when I glanced at him, he wasn't examining the wall of photographs. He was looking at me.

"Eleanora…" he said.

A raucous pounding resounded from downstairs, someone banging at the door, followed by unintelligible shouting. My pulse had already jumped in response to the Inspector speaking my name, but the new shock drove it further.

"Not more trouble," I pleaded, trailing behind Inspector Harrow as he hurried to glance out his room's window into the driveway below.

"I know that car. Brom," he said, striding angrily toward the stairs, grabbing his shoulder holster and gun from the desk as he went. There was an alarming change in his brow, a tightening of his broad mouth.

"Maybe we should ignore it," I suggested, struggling to keep up with his strides. He halted, and I almost collided with him.

"Do you expect the house to protect you from someone trying to get in?" His question was unnecessarily pointed, because I'd already realized how ridiculous it was to consider hiding when Blackwicket House had allowed entry to Farvem and, for argument's sake, Inspector Harrow. Any defenses it possessed were compromised. "Either way, we shouldn't lie low. There's a child with them."

A fresh wave of alarm propelled me into motion alongside him, and I barely registered the stairs under my feet. When we reached the bottom, the Inspector extended a hand to belay me as he positioned himself in a blind spot to the left of the door and drew his gun. He nodded, giving me the signal to confront whatever new nightmare awaited us on the porch of Blackwicket House.

I opened the door to Ramsey, the grizzled chauffeur, and Coppe, who held the body of a listless boy in his arms.

Jack.

The detestable man seemed unnerved and didn't wait for an invitation, barreling inside, proving Inspector Harrow's point. Ramsey stayed outside, hands folded, eyes cast to the wood boards.

"William told me to bring the boy here, said you could fix him up," Coppe said gruffly, and I clocked his anger, perhaps at being forced to come to this house and ask for help.

"What's the matter with him?" I said, reaching to touch Jack's face, turning his head towards me. Tears of red ash were trickling from the corners of his eyes. I froze as memories engulfed me.

"Do something, woman!" Coppe yelled, and Victor stepped into his view, gun raised, the barrel level with the Brom's head.

"Victor," Coppe spat. "The hell are you playing at?"

"Give the boy to Eleanora," Inspector Harrow instructed.

I reached for Jack while struggling with the hysteria ripping at the fragile membrane of my mind. Coppe hesitated, then handed him over to me. The exchange brought me closer than I ever wanted to be to this man, who smelled of cigars and sour whiskey. Although Jack was tall, he felt remarkably light, and I cradled him to me as if he were a much smaller child.

"Get out," the Inspector ordered, using the revolver to indicate the door.

The rim of Coppe's eyes had gone red, the same color as the rest of his face, as a violent rage bloomed.

"Don't you hurt this kid," he started, but Victor was on him, grabbing his collar, yanking him off balance so he could toss him out the door like a stray dog. He landed on his ass near Ramsey's feet. The driver stepped away from Coppe's prone form as though he were filthy water thrown from a window. He then raised his head, locking eyes with me meaningfully.

"Ramsey," Jack said, the name falling dry from his cracked lips, and the man made an assuring face as Inspector Harrow slammed the door and turned the lock. Holstering the weapon, he came to collect Jack from my arms.

"Curses. I don't know how many," I said, as Jack was gathered from me. The inspector made a direct course to the parlor.

"No!" The word a high shriek, and I mindlessly clutched the fabric of the blouse near my heart. I couldn't help

Jack in that room, where another child, infested with polluted magic, had breathed his last breath, all because of me.

When the Inspector stopped, I gestured to the stairs, attempting to regain my composure.

"Up. The first room. Take him there," I led the way, giving the Inspector no room to argue. I was grateful that he asked no questions.

The doors were still locked, but I didn't need keys, not anymore. My magic coursed, the lock snapping, the door flinging in with such force it crashed against the wall as though blown by a gale. Inspector Harrow was right at my shoulder. He took Jack to the bed, neatly made in crisp white linens, and lay him down with all the gentleness of a father.

Attempting to mimic Victor's unearthly calm, I sat on the edge of the mattress and pressed the child's hair from his temple. "Jack, look at me."

The child's head rolled in my direction, wisps of curses rising from his mouth.

"How many curses did you eat?"

"Dunno," he rasped, "One? Don't remember."

I took his hand in mine as his eyes closed, his breath coming in deep, uneven pulls. His fingers were icy despite the fever in his cheeks. I began my search for the blight, fearful of what I might uncover. His affliction wasn't hard to locate; it churned in an oily cloud, eclipsing Jack's natural power, trying to suffocate it.

This wasn't a single curse.

"Victor, it's a Drudge," I said.

"Help him," Inspector Harrow replied, low.

Tears sprang to my eyes as memory after memory of Thomas Nightglass's face flickered in my thoughts: his bright smile, gradually becoming solemn resignation, the way he'd held my hand so tightly the night we walked Dark Hall, and the tears that left tracks on his temples from fighting then as Jack was fighting now. And I'd done everything wrong, hadn't been able to help. I'd killed my best friend.

"It's going to hurt him."

"Better hurt than dead."

I took hold of the shattered pieces of my life and my history and pulled them together, knowing I would have to be whole to help the boy whom the Brom had used as bait, a trap to keep unwanted Drudge at bay. The Drudge was so entwined, I couldn't coax it free. Even when presented with an offering of my stronger magic, it had no interest in coming willingly, happy with its current quarry. So I began the tedious work of plucking at the Drudge, like pulling threads from a knot, searching for whatever was left of Jack's magic. It was a process that might take more time than we had.

Jack opened his eyes, whimpering, not from the pain of the corruption gnawing at his insides, but from fear. His gaze fixed on the ceiling, where a Drudge had emerged from the shadows of the beams, slinking in a ghostly crawl, its neck disproportionately long, its head small and concave. It twisted its face as it moved to keep the boy in sight, eyes billowing with the same smoky red as Jack's. Another was forming on the underside of the desk, limbs tangling with the chair legs. They would keep coming, sensing death nearby and preparing for their next meal.

Jack was panicking, and the Drudge he'd consumed fed off this turmoil, growing stronger and pushing me further aside. I'd been so close, but the tainted power was more determined than ever to consume what remained of the boy, and I could no longer sense the thread of his natural power.

I was going to fail—kill another child, the same way I'd killed Thomas, through my ineptitude, my lack of strength.

"Hey, kid," Victor's voice startled me, stern. Jack's eyes turned to him, wide, the whites yellowed. "You think they'd get past me?"

The boy shook his head slow, delirious. Inspector Harrow raised his hand to block the view of the creature hanging above us, trembling with anticipation.

"Not a chance in hell, but if I'm being honest, it's not me they're scared of," he said in a conspiratorial tone, nodding in my direction. "As long as she's here, no harm's coming to you. Understand?"

This unexpected vote of confidence fueled my determination, and I continued my work with renewed focus, promising myself I would reflect on the strangeness of this moment when it was all over and Jack was safe.

"Like Fiona," Jack said, his exhaustion overcoming him. I lifted my head, exchanging a brief look with Inspector Harrow.

"Yeah," Harrow said at length, and I knew he wasn't sure it was true.

"I'm really tired," Jack said, and I shook my head in a small, quick motion, signaling to the Inspector that the boy shouldn't sleep. I was too afraid he would never wake again. A little at a time, I tore pieces of the Drudge away, the corrupt fragments drowning in my more mature magic. But I'd made limited headway, the boy's terror and belief he'd never survive strengthening the curse even as I weakened it.

"I got myself in a pretty bad scrape like this too," the Inspector said, and Jack's heavy eyelids flicked up. Mine almost did as well. "Used to make a nuisance of myself in Devin when I was your age. Caused a lot of trouble. There was this Authority man, Chief Barrick Harrow. Mean."

He sucked a sharp draw of air between his teeth to emphasize the last statement. I marveled at how different Inspector Harrow sounded while talking to this frightened child.

"I was scared to death of him, knew what the Authority did to kids like me. I knew everything back then." There was a smile in his voice. "I was pretty crafty, good at getting out of scrapes, and it took him a whole year to catch me."

The story did its job and when Inspector Harrow grew silent, Jack gasped in a lungful of air, gathering his energy to rasp, "How'd he get you?"

The Inspector obliged.

"See, I got into a row with these older boys. They wouldn't pay me for some magic I scalped for them. I was angry and stupid and started a fight. Almost didn't make it. Chief Harrow broke it up, took me to the hospital. He thought I was a goner. I did too."

"Were you scared?" Jack asked, his strength continuing to fade, the light of his magic growing ever dimmer.

"Sure, I was," the Inspector replied, "Anyone who says they aren't scared to die is a liar. But you know what Chief Harrow, the scariest man in all of Devin, did when I woke up?"

"Huh?" Jack was locked onto this tale, and I believed with my whole soul it was the only thing keeping him alive while I searched with increasing desperation for a path to the heart of the magic.

"He cried."

"Yeah?"

"Like a baby. Nurses told me later he'd sat by my bedside for three days, barking orders, praying prayers, willing me to pull through. That's why I'm alive. Someone was there to walk the hardest road with me, believing I was strong enough. You've got the same here, kid."

Inspector Harrow abandoned shielding the boy from the sight of the monster and instead took Jack's other hand, encapsulating it between his palms. The effect was immediate: Jack's magic surged, breaching the horrible miasma. I grabbed hold as quickly as I could, like reaching for the hand of someone drowning in dark waves, intertwining my power with his.

I laughed in disbelief and utter relief as the Drudge came apart, dissolving piece by piece in the warm current. Gradually, the white vapor rose, not only from my lips but from Jack's as well. Tendrils of mended and tainted magic merging to become pink, diaphanous clouds before fading, running clean.

Jack was curse eating.

At length, his breathing grew even, his magic calm, and he fell asleep, just as the last of the Drudge passed from him. His feverish skin cooled, though there remained a purple cast below his eyes, a gauntness to his cheeks that would be relieved with rest. Pale helixes of restored magic circled our heads, finding their way into cracks and crevices, sinking into gaps in boards, searching for sanctuary, a place to hide until it was well and could move on. Surprising me, the Drudge remaining in the room didn't rush to these strands of power, letting them pass with scant curiosity, attention firmly on the boy. They no longer seemed to be waiting for something to consume, instead, they watched him as they'd once watched me.

"They want to be near you," mother had said one night when Fiona and I had run to her bed in fear, cuddling close.

"Why?" I'd asked, pressing my cheek against her chest, comforted by her powdery scent. There were Drudge in this room too, but they kept their distance, never stood at the foot of the bed.

"Because you two are special. You remind them of their home."

"But you said we didn't come from Dark Hall," Fiona's words had been teary. She'd always been the most sensitive, the sister most likely to cry.

"You came from me. Dark Hall's in your blood."

"Inspector," I whispered, careful not to wake the boy.

He heeded me, hands still clasped around Jack's.

"That Drudge would have killed another child in minutes."

Once I said the words, my greatest fear would become a reality. But there was nowhere to hide from it.

"He's from Dark Hall," I said.

CHAPTER TWENTY-NINE

I trudged upstairs to the linen closet to fetch a blanket for Jack, burdened by the grim realization that William and the Brom were exploiting him and possibly other children to create a refuge for the wealthy to gorge on magic free from the threat of Drudge. Perhaps their plan involved cultivating a young army of guardians, using them until their magic ran dry. Of course, it'd be practical for Nightglass to keep a Curse Eater to mitigate the side effects of this disgusting ambition, but it was unlikely William was focusing on me as a nurse for those who'd taken on more than they could handle. He was after something else. I was beginning to believe he wanted me to uphold my sister's legacy of abducting children.

In my ten-year absence, Fiona had evolved into someone I couldn't recognize, and I was finding it increasingly difficult to justify what she'd become.

A wave of static tingled at the back of my neck as I shut the closet door, the cloying odor of overripe fruit disturbing me. With the blackberry jam in the kitchen gone, I was confused by its presence. Hinges creaked, and I turned to look the length of the hallway, toward the attic door, slightly ajar, revealing the monstrous face of Auntie peering at me.

So this was where she'd been hiding, locked where I couldn't reach her without significant danger to myself. She'd grown much more unpredictable and elusive than I remembered. Once, she'd been an oft-present, almost docile entity who visited more and more as Isolde Blackwicket deteriorated, like a nanny stepping in to keep an eye on neglected children. The dark angel of Blackwicket House.

She'd transformed into a source of comfort, a reassurance. I'd fallen for the fables and romantic hues my mother had painted this house and its legacy in, an effort to make our childhood here seem easier, something special rather than the terrible thing it was.

I slammed the closet door, causing Auntie to retreat, bypassing the unsafe stairs to scuttle along the wall.

She was as much a monster as the others, with no heart beyond hurt, existing here because the alternative was worse—Dark Hall, where a shadowy leviathan that devoured curses roamed—curses that could never hope to be healed, trapped in an eternal hell.

I worried about Jack and any other children Fiona had brought here.

As I returned, quilt draped over my arm, I heard talking. Jack was awake, his voice strained and angry.

"I don't want to eat curses anymore! It hurts, it makes my insides burn. I want to go home."

"Where's home?" Inspector Harrow asked, meeting Jack's anger with assured calm, allowing the storm to rage while offering a safe harbor. I speculated he'd learned the technique from Barrick Harrow, a man who'd adopted a broken Brom child from the street.

"Nowhere," Jack spat, and the tears constricted his vocal cords. He snuffled. "I hate crying!"

There was a faint breath from the Inspector, a laugh. "Why?"

"Crying never did nothing for nobody," Jack said. "Just let's people know you're soft."

"Who told you that?"

"Coppe."

My hatred for the man increased tenfold.

"Don't let them take the tears from you, boy," Inspector Harrow said. "They're yours, something you need."

"For what?"

"You're a Curse Eater, aren't you?"

"I guess. Don't want to be."

"Sometimes we don't get to choose who we are, but a Curse Eater's a fine thing if you're a good one." The cadence of the Inspector's voice was almost narcotic, a low-pitched rumble of words that never grew too loud, never varied too much in tone, encouraging you to remain still and listen closely to catch every syllable. "To be a good one, you can't keep the bad feelings bottled up. That's what creates the curses in the first place. It's the magic gone wrong with all the anger and fear you hold tight. That's what the tears are for."

"What do tears do?"

"I don't know exactly how they work, but my best guess is they give somewhere for all the hurt to go."

"I bet you don't cry," Jack grumbled, before breaking down, his soft sobs drifting to meet me in the hall. My vision blurred, and I leaned forward enough to see that Jack had curled into a trembling ball, his knees tucked near to his face, while the Inspector sat close by in the chair he'd taken from the desk.

"No," Inspector Harrow said, placing a hand on the child's head. "But I'm a weak man, Jack. You don't want to be like me."

I waited a moment longer in the corridor so it wouldn't appear I'd been listening. When I entered, Inspector Harrow sat back, giving me room to drape the blanket over Jack, a modest bit of shelter from the world. The boy stirred from his position, gazing at me with puffy eyes, his auburn hair a chaotic mess, sticking straight up at the crown of his head.

"When I was little." I took a seat again on the edge of the

bed, far enough so he wouldn't feel crowded by a stranger. "My mother would weave her magic into my quilt to help me sleep. If you'd like, I'll do the same for you."

When Isolde had stopped being aware of us, I'd attempted to replace her magical comfort with my own, enchanting fibers of my quilt, only for the magic to escape. I'd become so disheartened, I'd stopped trying. I hoped I wouldn't fail now.

"Guess so," he said, wiping his face vigorously with his hands as though he could erase his sorrow with enough force.

I explained the importance of intention, giving direction to power so it knew what form to take, what task to perform. I repeated my mother's words about how vital practicing magic to create beautiful, useful, comforting things was.

"Why?" Came Jack's question, echoing the one I'd asked many years ago.

"If we show magic how important it is," I said. "How much it means to us, maybe it'll come back."

I'd believed these things until my mother's death, when my grip loosened on the hopes of childhood. But for Jack's sake, he needed to feel they were true. It would give him a shield against the troubles awaiting him as a child of Dark Hall. A flimsy one, perhaps, but far better than none. My power was pliant from use, no longer rigid and difficult to control, and unlike in my youth, what I wove into the fabric, between each weave and weft of thread, remained secure, glinting like a field of fireflies in summer.

The joy on Jack's face would be a lasting memory, but short-lived, quickly becoming forlorn.

"Fiona did this for me, too. I guess you both learned it from your mom." Fresh tears filled his eyes.

"Did you spend a lot of time with Fiona?" I asked, struggling not to sound too desperate for the answer.

Jack nodded, "Are all the toys still upstairs?"

"They are." I stopped, cleared my throat, "It's a mess right now, but they are."

"I liked coming here, but Mr. Nightglass stopped letting me."

"Why?" I inquired, tucking the blanket around his shoulders to soften the difficult question.

"Fiona was sick, he didn't want me to get sick too. Then she died."

Instinctively, I rubbed his back, wishing I could ease the pain in his voice, knowing it would remain for a long time.

"Were there other kids, Jack?" Inspector Harrow asked, "Other children like you here at Blackwicket House?"

The question put him on his guard, his face growing slack, two spots of red forming on his cheeks. "Don't know."

A lie.

"Why don't you try to sleep?" I replied before Inspector Harrow could ask anything else.

He didn't reply as he tucked himself deep beneath the enchanted blanket, his eyes trained on the wall.

"Do you want someone to stay here?" I asked.

"No." Came the sullen response.

We'd pushed too far.

"If you need anything…"

Before either of us could move, Jack spoke, words muffled by the sheet.

"I changed my mind. Stay 'til I'm asleep? Both of you?"

We remained there in silence as the afternoon sun cast the room in a flaxen glow, punctuated by the twinkling of the magic, bright enough to shine even in daylight.

At last, Jack's breaths grew long and even, and we left him to rest from his ordeal.

"I'm not returning him to William," I told the Inspector as soon as the door was half shut.

"I didn't expect you'd want to," he replied, "But how do you plan to care for him here? William Nightglass controls this town, and if he can make sure you don't get a train ticket out, he'll make sure you can't get necessities."

"I know. Grigori did that to us."

"He tried to starve you?"

"He couldn't. My mother was too smart. We had little gardens and grew everything we needed."

Admittedly, I'd become tired of potatoes.

"And in the winter?"

I smiled at him, the upturn of my lips carrying both a fondness for the memory and a curdling resentment.

"Magic isn't just good for sweet dreams."

"Sounds like a lonely life." The statement came with no sympathy. He'd simply acknowledged of the true shape of things.

"It was good for a while. My mother worked hard to make it seem we were the luckiest children in the world. I only realized later that the things that made it special here were actually hardships." We were treading perilously close to memories I didn't want to consider, so I deliberately changed focus. "You were a Brom boy?

Inspector Harrow glanced at the partially closed door, checking for young boys who snuck from of bed.

"I was," he replied after a breath. "Until Chief Harrow."

"Your name," I said, and it wasn't a question, more an acknowledgment. Victor Harrow only existed because a grizzled Authority chief took pity.

"Interested in my history suddenly?"

"Not suddenly," I replied, "Besides, you know everything about me."

"Not everything," he murmured.

All at once, the hallway was too narrow, and the internal panic I'd grown used to experiencing around the Inspector kindled, making it all the more difficult for me not to bare my soul.

"It's just that the gentleness you experienced surprises me. The Authority has always been cruel," I said, no affection lost for an administration that vilified the vulnerable, who'd pushed my mother to confess to a crime she hadn't committed all to protect me from the horrible consequences they'd impose for my actions.

"You think the Brom would fear us if we weren't?"

"Being what you are, how could you support what they do to people like you, like me? What they would do to Jack."

"What would I do to him, Eleanora?" Inspector Harrow asked softly. "He's innocent. He didn't choose this."

Neither had I, but I stowed the defense. I'd been a full-grown woman when I'd made my decisions regarding Brock Mofton, who hadn't been Brom, only an awful man.

"I was the first kid Barrick took into his home." The Inspector surprised me by continuing to divulge some of his history. "He knew I wouldn't last anywhere else. I was too impulsive, bad tempered. But I wasn't the first Dark Hall child he'd rescued. He'd made it his mission to ferret us from hiding and out of the clutches of people who were misusing us. Do you honestly believe Curse Eaters were keeping the children they kidnapped safe?"

I wanted to answer, to refute his prejudices, but I knew nothing of other Curse Eaters. I knew only what my mother had told me. But Isolde herself believed the practice of procuring children from Dark Hall was barbaric, had broken tradition instead. I wondered what sort of person Granny Fora had been.

Had she been a Dark Hall child herself? Sadly, there was no one left to clarify my family's sordid history.

"I can't say," I confessed. "But I suppose you believe the Authority did."

"Barrick Harrow did," the Inspector said. "He found places for them to go, people who'd care for them. For as long as he was alive, he kept track of every single kid he'd recovered. His work was the entire reason I followed in his footsteps, joined the Authority. What he was doing wasn't sanctioned; nobody knew what was going on, only that he was good at keeping Brom and their Curse Eaters under control. They probably assumed he was murdering them, but he never invited anyone to think different."

The Inspector was describing a man who pretended to be a monster so he could do good. I wondered for the first time how much of the Inspector's monstrousness was for show. But I was in no danger of convincing myself Victor Harrow wasn't who he claimed to be. I'd been a witness to his violence.

"Why isn't he here doing this work with you?" I asked, noting the Inspector spoke of Chief Harrow in the past tense.

A beat of weighty silence followed.

"Barrick Harrow was murdered by a Brom agent connected to Grigori Nightglass, two years ago," the Inspector replied at length.

The picture of the Inspector's recent life became clear. The Brom he'd killed, the vicious scar, his loathing for Nightglass and all the people in it, and his contempt for William and those associated—all connecting back to what he'd lost. There was no softening of his eyes or tightening of muscles in his jaw revealing the pain of this confession, but the thread of wayward magic that broke free of its shackles, reaching across to me on instinct, contained his anguish.

He deliberately moved away to avoid psychic contact, but

it was already too late; his power had summoned mine, and I'd involuntarily responded. It was bewildering to be near someone from whom you couldn't shield yourself, who perceived and touched your deepest person, even against their own wishes. And because it was equal parts perplexing and unwelcome, we both strained to ignore it, determined to show no sign that we sensed the pull.

"I'm going to protect Jack," I said. "I'll die trying. I can't keep looking on while William terrorizes the people of this town who can't escape. Inspector, I have a unique set of abilities, and there's no reason for you to reject my help with bringing the Nightglass dynasty to its end. William thinks he's cornered me. All I have to do is pretend to give in."

A darkness crossed the Inspector's face, the tinge of gold in his eye more prominent. He grew icy, magic retreating, creating a void where it had once been.

"It's a pretty offer, Ms. Blackwicket, but your seduction of William Nightglass isn't required."

Frustration and no small amount of offense sparked like a flint.

"Don't twist my words. I don't know what else to do to prove to you I'm trustworthy, that I'm not involved in any of this. I've lost family, was nearly murdered *twice*, I've shown you the secrets of this house and bared my shame to you."

I'd worked myself up, wanted to raise my voice, but lowered it instead, the words a vicious whisper.

His ire responded in kind, and he took a menacing step, pinning me with his next accusation, a true one.

"But you're still lying to me," he growled in return.

"What do you *want* from me?" I demanded, the crack in my voice humiliating.

"Everything, Eleanora," he replied. "And that's the trouble."

With no other warning, he reached for me, his hand catching my hair, tangling in the pins I'd haphazardly arranged as I'd rushed to dress that morning. His initial touch was rough, a loss of control, but when our mouths met, he didn't devour, didn't bruise my body with demanding hands. He merely held me, inviting me to respond, to mold my body to his.

I had every reason to resist and cared for none of them.

I fit against him as though we'd been made together, forged by the same hand in heartache and turmoil. It was true I was lying, but so was he, holding the truth behind his affliction close.

I didn't care.

He was reminding me I was still capable of something other than rage and grief, and I wanted to explore what it meant to meet magic that felt like home the way his did.

It wasn't the rising of the sinister part of him that broke the kiss, but his own regret, clear in his eyes, which lingered on my face as if to memorize me before he let go forever.

"I'm here to ensure that William Nightglass and everyone who enables him burns, Eleanora. You don't need to be part of this. You simply need to stand a safe distance away and watch."

He brushed the hair from my forehead with his thumb, tracing the trail of his finger across my temple with his gaze. He released me, my heels finding ground.

"You can't do it alone, Victor. No matter how vicious you are, you're one man. They'll kill you."

He smiled, such a rare thing to see, but even more uncommon was the resignation in it.

"Don't waste gentle sentiments on me, Curse Eater," he murmured. "Save them for the boy, and spend your time figuring out how you're going to handle the Authority when they finally draw the connection between Nightglass and the Blackwickets. My suggestion would be to make damn sure they never find either of you."

CHAPTER THIRTY

I'd expected hell to return to Blackwicket House with haste, but it chose to wait in deadly silence, always just a breath away. Inspector Harrow departed following our discussion in the hall, warning me he wouldn't be present during the day, never explaining where he was going. He returned each night before sunset, weary and evasive. He'd ask tersely about the boy, then disappear into his room. So, for three strange, peaceful days, my world revolved around Jack.

The boy remained weak, but on the third day, had enough energy for boredom. Although he'd asked, I couldn't show him my sister's room upstairs, with the curse-burned rug and splintered wardrobe. Instead, I took him to the parlor. The room, with all its grim history, felt brighter with Jack in it, and I enjoyed his enthusiasm for the books lining the cases flanking the fireplace.

"Oh, this one," he said, reaching to grab a cherished edition. Its spine had loosened from the binding from all my childhood readings of it. I was pleased he'd chosen it.

"That was my favorite when I was your age."

"I like it too." With the ease of a boy moving within his own home, he settled in the high-backed chair near the fireplace, which I'd brought to life, and leafed through the pages, his touch respectful of their delicate state.

"You've read it?" I asked, sitting in the chair opposite, so as not to hover.

"Lots." His reply was distant, his attention already on the pages in front of him.

We sat in silence, and I watched the flames dancing behind the bronze grate, marveling at how this moment reduced me to a ten-year-old girl again, sitting in this same chair next to my sister while our mother unwove curses at the window.

Jack began to hum absentmindedly, disjointed fragments of parting songs and ballads he'd encountered here and there. At last he assembled one I recognized. I waited, expecting him to move on from it as he had with the others, but it lingered, and he kept repeating the first few seconds of the tune, drawing my childhood in too close.

"I know that song."

The boy brightened, his book forgotten.

"Want to hear it? I've been practicing."

I laughed, appreciating his exuberance, turning my palm up in invitation.

He closed the book, tucking it by his leg, sitting straight in preparation for his performance. Then, he sang, clear and confident, the high tenor of his boyish tone not yet robbed of him by age.

'Oh, Moira, my love, I meant not to stray
But the sea it was calling that clear summer's day

I didn't have the heart to stop him, though my chest squeezed tight.

And the sea, as you know, it takes lovers away
But call me back with your sorrows,
And in spirit, I'll stay.

I'll stay, I'll stay, 'till you meet me across
And discover in death that our love wasn't lost
It was fickle time only that kept us apart
Until then, I'll be near
In both dreams and your heart.

I hadn't known there was a second verse, always singing the one in repetition like a prayer. When the song ended, his face was full of youthful pride, bright eyes, and a crooked smile, over a job he'd known he'd done well.

"Did Fiona teach you that?" I asked. Regardless of what she'd done, the deep well of love for my sister spilled over, and I was overcome with the agony of missing her.

"Yeah. She loved that song." He collapsed onto the cushions, picking the book up again without opening it. "Eleanora, what's a Narthex?"

The sudden change in topic startled me out of my grief, and I grew suspicious.

"What makes you interested in Narthex?"

"I just want to know what it is."

"Well, there aren't anymore. They've all been closed by the Authority."

Understanding I wasn't eager to talk about it, he quieted, but not for long.

"I think Mr. Nightglass wants one."

I made a heroic effort to keep my expression neutral.

Of course, William was involved. His father, Grigori, had been urging my mother to build him a Narthex for most of my life, yet she'd rebuffed him repeatedly, arguing she didn't know how. He knew, or at least suspected, there was one in Blackwicket House, but he could never get inside. Back then, the house was wary of everyone my mother invited across the threshold, protecting itself and its inhabitants. We'd never needed to lock windows or doors like I'd been compelled to do last night. I'd checked each latch and lock before going to sleep, a room away from Jack.

I found no reason to lie.

"A Narthex is a portal between here and Dark Hall, a sort of doorway only certain people have a key to."

"Curse Eaters?"

"Yes."

"What'd they do there?"

Steal children.

"A lot of things." I avoided details because I was woefully uninformed. By the time I'd been old enough to know about them, the halls were empty, doorways shut tight. Curse Eating families no longer moved freely, and the original purpose of the hallways was lost, leaving me to experience it only through my mother and my lonely solo jaunts. "Mostly, they used it to gain access to powerful magic. It helped repair the curses people brought to them."

"How hard is it to make one?"

"Very," I replied, cautious, knowing if I asked why he was so curious, he'd likely shut down, just as he did whenever I brought up the subject of other children in Blackwicket House. "It takes years, and a single person couldn't do it alone."

"Could you let Mr. Nightglass know that?" Jack asked, pretending to be half absorbed in the book. "When he comes to get me?"

"Why?" I couldn't avoid being direct any longer.

"Cause I overheard him telling Coppe he wants me and Thea to build one. That's why he's been making me eat so many curses. Says it'll make me stronger, so it's easier for me. But maybe if you tell him how hard it is, how long it takes, he'll change his mind."

"Jack..."

"Please? It's like when I wanted to have a funeral for my bird, Pips. Mr. Nightglass was mad at me and didn't want to do it, but he got convinced when Thea talked to him. He apologized and everything, and was nice for a while."

I recalled the small box Jack had brought with him to the funeral home, how afraid he'd looked.

"Why was Mr. Nightglass angry with you?"

Jack's fingers fanned the page corners of the book in his lap.

"He wanted me to practice pulling magic off something. You know, not curses but the fizzy stuff that's inside everything. He told me to use Pips, but I was scared it would hurt him." His eyes grew teary. "Mr. Nightglass said if I didn't do it, he'd kill Pips anyway. So, I did."

"And Pips died," I said gently, and Jack dissolved into fresh tears. Inspector Harrow's advice had done its job, because Jack didn't resist them. I hurried to his side, kneeling to pull him against my shoulder, where he collapsed.

"I'm so sorry, Jack. It wasn't your fault." I rested my chin on his head.

I paid no mind to how long we remained like that, allowing myself to imagine how satisfying it would be to remove William's eyes and shove them down his throat.

"Eleanora."

I lifted my head to find Inspector Harrow in the parlor doorway, still wearing his coat, his quick nod toward the hall a signal that I should join him.

Jack had sat up to see who'd arrived, sniffing and drying his eyes.

"Be right back," I assured him, but he rose with me.

"Actually, can I go to my room?" He asked.

"Of course."

We walked together to where the Inspector waited, his expression somber as ever. An unsettling static energy radiated from him, tension permeating the hall. Jack noticed it too and slowed.

"Alright, Jack?" Inspector Harrow asked.

"Tired is all," he replied, glancing at me and moving past the Inspector with a new trepidation, as though seeing the man clearly for the first time. We both watched his departure.

"Something's gone sideways," Inspector Harrow said when the boy was out of sight. He kept his voice quiet, an attempt to keep the news from carrying, "Cora's dead."

Cora. A double agent with reassuring words and a self-deprecating smile, who'd been so willing to step in and help others handle undue burdens at the risk of herself. Thea had touched her with gentleness, worried over her when she thought she'd been in danger.

"Did she void?" It seemed the most likely event, given the strain William was putting on the Brom.

The Inspector didn't appear eager to tell me.

"Her throat was cut," he replied. Bile climbed in my throat. "They found her at the Vapors this morning, behind the bar. I expect she'd been there since last night."

"Thea?"

"I haven't seen her, but I imagine she's not in a good way. Her and Cora's involvement was a poorly kept secret." There was an unexpected tinge of sympathy in his tone.

"Since throat cutting is a tactic of the Veil, is there a chance they're the ones responsible?" I asked.

"Or someone pretending to be the Veil. The victim pool is too varied. Patrick Farvem wasn't their enemy, and Cora breaks the streak of murders tied to those who've done you wrong. But beyond that, people have been going noticeably missing after visiting the Vapors. It's causing panic. Tourists are trying to leave in droves, but the station can't accommodate everyone. The cliff road out of town is frozen; passing is impossible."

"Maybe William's involved."

"He wouldn't shoot himself in the mouth by scaring off his base. He had some kind of showcase scheduled at the Vapors in place of High Tide on next month's full moon. Dramatic fuck," Victor muttered, glancing toward the stairs. "He moved it to tonight, and has Thea working double to calm everyone and entice people to stay."

Poor Thea, shocked and grieving and forced to continue doing public relations for the Brom.

The delivery of the news triggered an eerie wave of energy from the house, which had been silent since Jack's recovery. Now it moaned anew, and the Inspector's curses responded. He winced in pain, leaning forward as if struck in the stomach. I considered offering comfort, but knew the consequences of physical contact. After a breath, he steadied himself, flexing his hand as if he had touched something charged with electricity.

I observed the amber of his eyes, the color filling in otherwise dark irises, and considered the possibility this was the result of Inspector Harrow clearing the blast zone before he lit the fuse.

"Do you have anything to do with this?" I asked, keeping my tone hushed.

He caught me in that chimeric gaze, which dipped briefly to my mouth, followed by a throaty noise that might have been a laugh or a scoff.

"Suspicion looks good on you, Ms. Blackwicket," he said, raising his attention to the ceiling where the red stain of curses coiled like wood smoke from the cornices, towards the Inspector. "Despite my blissful time here, I'm still not familiar with the way the house works. Is this a typical experience?"

"No," I said, staring down the hall where the daylight had gone gloomy and blue as dusk, which was still hours away. "Something's wrong."

A scream, frantic and piercing, shattered the air, already thick with dread.

"Jack," I choked, sprinting with all the speed I could manage, realizing halfway up the stairs that the boy's screams weren't coming from his room on the second floor but from somewhere on the third. Inspector Harrow followed closely as we scaled the second flight. Upon reaching the landing, I noticed the attic door stood wide open, but the earsplitting howling wasn't coming from there; it peeled from Fiona's bedroom.

We found Jack huddled in a corner, something clutched tightly between his hands, pressed to his face to shield him from what perched vulture-like on the back of the demolished wardrobe. Auntie wrenched towards us, her mouth open, scarlet smog billowing forth alongside a high, grating wail.

On hands and feet, Auntie climbed down, prowling, her lower jaw popping as it shifted side to side, gnawing on air. The house had become a reverse beacon, pulling in light until everything around appeared to be collapsing, growing smaller. Finally, I recognized the creature for what it was, what it was capable of. My mother had labeled it our protector, but as with the other twisted things in Blackwicket House, its only purpose was to relieve its own damnation.

I carefully approached Jack, who'd stopped screaming and was releasing shaky gasps in quick bursts. The Drudge mirrored my movements, seeking an opening to attack, but Victor intervened, his broad frame shielding me. The creature halted, snapping its maw in fury, yet didn't advance. Inspector Harrow was close enough to me that even in the unnatural gloom I saw the darkness pulse through him, poison spreading along his flesh, corrupt magic thick and noxious. It snagged at me but didn't take full hold, preferring the prize of more fetid power it would find in Auntie.

"Victor," I whispered, the sound overtaken by the snapping

of bone and cartilage as it rearranged itself under Inspector Harrows skin, stretching and pulling at his shape in gut-wrenching contractions.

"Get the boy," he ordered, his words a chasmic wreckage of hemorrhaged vocal cords, guttural and inhuman.

Sure of his ability to protect me, I took the last hasty steps to Jack, tucking my hands beneath his arms, murmuring words of comfort all the way.

"Don't look," I encouraged him, as he stood shakily, clinging still to the item in his hands—the small toy dog, ears rubbed smooth. Air lurched from my lungs, further contorted by the scrap of fabric Auntie had dropped from her clawed hand when she'd turned her attention to us.

Despite being torn, the lettering was recognizable.

Roark.

"Keep your eyes on the floor," I instructed, even as I was trying to get oxygen. "Walk quickly, we're going to the hall, then to the stairs. Move."

He followed my instructions, but as we took our first step, the dark angel of Blackwicket House sprang towards us.

"Run!" I yelled as she slammed into the solid barrier of Victor. The bellowing that rang out behind us reminded me of when two mountain lions had brawled for territory in the woods at the edge of Blackwicket property, the noise unholy and vicious.

We emerged into the hall, but didn't get far. Jack was yanked from my arms, his legs pulled from beneath him by the crushing grip of the Drudge. He fell face-first onto the hard floor, his forehead cracking against the wood. His screaming renewed as Auntie dragged him towards the open attic door. He clawed at the floor, his nails scratching and catching, his head flung back, wild eyes on me as blood poured from his nose from the impact it had made with the ground.

Auntie mounted the broken stairs, Jack's hands clasping the doorframe, and I bounded after, lunging not for the boy, but Auntie, throwing my arms around her as if to embrace. She was solid and carried the scent of dust and peat, the toxic mist emanating from her filling my nose and mouth. My body prepared for consumption, but that had never been my intention. Instead, I unleashed my magic outwards, the powerful tide draining my energy and breaking the Drudge's hold. But this wasn't a simple transfer. The blast had misplaced Auntie's curses, and they sought a place in the emptiness my attack had left behind. Even as I inhaled, breathing them deep, Auntie thrashed backward, pulling me with her as we crashed into the staircase, the rotten boards splitting, shards and splinters stabbing my skin. The Drudge released me, scrambling aside, only to collide with another monster head-on, the largest I'd ever encountered. Its humanoid form was as twisted as a vine-entangled oak, built of ashes, the soul of a fire-scorched forest made tangible. They clashed ferociously on the narrow staircase, the walls trembling with their forceful blows, while I pulled Jack to his feet.

The attic door swung shut on its own, almost hitting us, the impact echoing. The ceiling above trembled, the battle thundering for a few moments more before ceasing. In the span of one of Jack's sobs, it became eerily quiet, shadows retreating in favor of the afternoon light, which resumed shining through the latticed windows.

I spared a moment we didn't have to assess Jack's nose, already bruised, the bridge split, two rivulets of blood running down either side. My next words were meant to be a balm, to calm him with the safety of knowing he no longer had to lie, that he was with someone trustworthy.

"It's over, Roark," I whispered, taking his face in my hands, our eyes meeting. "I know everything, and it's going to be alright."

"I'm not Roark!" He screamed, yanking at my hands, "I'm Jack! Roark is dead! He's dead! I don't want to be dead too, leave me alone!"

He struggled, then all at once, became still, calling, "Thea!"

I assumed this was hysterics, crying for someone familiar, but with a last shove he broke away, running into the outstretched arms of Thea James, who stood a step behind William Nightglass at the top of the stairs.

Horror rooted me to the spot. The house had let them in.

"That," William said, with a manic gleam in his eye, his smile broad and satisfied, "was quite the display."

CHAPTER THIRTY-ONE

"William." When I found my voice, it was sticky, dry, clinging in my throat like a bur.

"I can tell you've taken care of Jack well, aside from this *unfortunate* injury," the man's mouth pressed into a thin line as he regarded the boy's broken nose. "At least he's hale and hearty on the inside, and that's what matters. Bodily wounds heal."

The snake grinned at me again. "Most of them. Take him downstairs, Thea."

I turned to Thea, alarmed and pleading. Dressed in a black crepe shirtdress, she held Jack to her as a mother who'd thought her son to be dead might, shining eyes conveying everything. Her impeccable makeup couldn't hide the bruising on her cheek, the cut on her bottom lip, both a few days old and angry. Whatever her connection to the boy, she had him back, and she wasn't about to let him go, even if it meant cooperating with William Nightglass.

She turned to help Jack down the stairs, a fresh red stain from the boy's blood on her collar. My magic was drained, but I would use my hands If necessary.

"I'm not giving him to you, William." I seethed, approaching, but he lifted his cane, pointing the tip at me, no longer a blunt gold cap, but sharp as a bayonet. I recalled how skillfully he could use it and froze, a storm of hatred brewing in me.

"If you harm that boy, I'll find you when you least expect it, and I will rip your throat out." I meant every word, already imagining the feel of his cartilage in my teeth, the crunch, the tangy iron taste of blood. My magic heaved.

"Like Fiona did to my father?" He asked, eyes narrowing in amused interest, watching as understanding dawned on me. He was enjoying himself. "You Blackwicket women love to go for the throat, don't you? Is it a kink? I bet you have some unimaginable ones."

His crudeness did nothing but encourage my loathing.

"Fiona's not a murderer." I knew this wasn't true, but the reality was too difficult to accept.

"I was there," he hissed in a flare of animosity, not inspired by Fiona's act but by my rejection of the truth. "Your precious sister was responsible for Grigori's death. She thought no one would ever suspect her if she used the Veil's favorite method, and she knew I'd keep her secret, because I'd encouraged her violent habits. They benefited me. I knew what she was capable of. The things I could tell you about her. Oh, it would curdle your stomach. She was so *delicious*."

He was goading me, hoping to slip his fingers into the seam of my anger and tear.

"What are you planning to do with Jack?"

"I want to give him a life worth living." The lethal tip of his cane brushed my chin. I flinched back, my retreat satisfying him. "Thea's quite attached to Jack, I'd never take him away."

"But you took Roark from Fiona." It was a wild guess.

"I didn't take Roark," he sighed. "I've no idea what happened to him. Here, then gone. Frankly, I thought Fiona had something to do with it. She was already rather bloodthirsty by then."

"Shut up," I spat, wishing I could raise my hands to my ears.

"You know what I'd like to see, Eleanora," he remarked,

bringing the cane to the floor in a smooth arc, leaning until it made a gouge in the wood. "You taking a bit of an interest in everything I've worked hard to achieve. You're about to be a very significant part of it. So, I invite you to come to my soiree tonight. It's a special High Tide at my estate, don't worry, there'll be no rutting around. It's a banquet for all those who've believed in my vision, and I want you to be my guest of honor."

"I'd rather die."

A laugh, as though I'd said something charming.

"I'm sure you'll change your mind when I tell you that Jack's well-being hinges on your presence."

He didn't wait for my response, but began his crooked descent from the third-floor landing.

I took a step, aiming to shove, but a jolt of noxious magic seared its way along my spine, entirely different from the raw void of Inspector Harrow's affliction.

"Don't be stupid," he said, casting a brief backward glance before continuing on his way. "Show up. Ramsey will be here to retrieve you at 9pm on the dot. We can't have you walking through the winter night, you'll catch your death."

Time was a slow crawl toward my own grave until the front door finally slammed shut. I rushed to Inspector Harrow's room, barreling to the window, just as Thea loaded Jack in the car's backseat, followed by William, who lowered himself in after her. Ramsey stared up at me from the driver's side window, as if disappointed in everything I'd done, everything I'd become. I whirled from the window, and the room came into full view.

Digs and grooves devastated nearly every surface. Wallpaper had been shredded, beams and floorboards bearing countless indentations carved by a sharp edge. The sheets lay in tatters, the feathers of the pillow scattered in a mimicry of the winter drifts outside. One might have thought a wild bear had been trapped inside—or perhaps a Drudge with knotted limbs like oak branches.

I lifted my gaze to the ceiling, the tower a floor above, long unused and unsafe to tread. But that's where Auntie and Victor had gone. The time had come for me to go too.

The bottom steps had collapsed during the scuffle. My lower ribs ached at the memory. The trim that had secured them to the wall remained intact, and I tested its narrow ledge. It held. Using the opposite wall for leverage, I hoisted myself onto this small outcropping and worked my way to the next stair.

About halfway through the excruciatingly slow journey, I detected a change in the air, like standing on the shore after years of being choked by the smog of a city, never realizing you were suffocating until that moment. In the crisp purity, there was also silence, complete and undisturbed. This is what Dark Hall felt like.

At last, I reached the door, left ajar, and inched onto the floor, stripped to its plank boards, the small gaps between becoming darkness that eventually became the ceiling of the rooms below. I remained on my knees, astounded.

Plants and flowers flourished in every corner, growing to the rafters of the ceiling high above, sprawling in all directions, vying for more territory. The leaves and vines were a rich green, punctuated by the petals of lilies, poppies, and bellflowers, along with clumps of frenzied wisteria—all scarlet red, resembling the exposed organs of a felled forest beast. The densest of all the flora twined throughout the others, twisting and choking, its sharp thorns serving as a warning, while the supple fruit it produced hung in bunches, ripe and black as death.

Blackberries.

This had been the smell haunting me throughout the house, the intense tartness of summer fruit beginning to rot. Fiona had cultivated a cursed garden of her own, trying to relieve some of the pressure from her shoulders.

I touched a berry, the drupelets distended, and it burst, staining my fingers with its juice that, in the dim tower light, reminded me of gore, a slim tendril of cursed magic wreathing my fingertips. Fiona had used these berries to make her jam, for a purpose I still hadn't determined.

I searched for signs of Drudge, Auntie, or Victor. They could have been hiding in the brush, but everything remained so still, and I was muddled by the gravity of the Narthex, which lured my magic closer with tempting caresses. I hoped, for Victor's sake, they hadn't gone inside.

Worried about falling through the floor, held together in some places by roots alone, I crawled. As I maneuvered around a cluster of hollyhocks, I spotted a wicker chest that had once rested at the foot of my mother's bed.

Its brass handle and hinges gleamed, and a vivid memory of my childhood surfaced. I'd emptied the chest to pretend it was a boat, and while playing, a Drudge had ventured too close, knocking the lid shut. It struck the top of my head, and I'd lurched forward, the latch catching, leaving me folded inside. An eternity passed before my mother discovered me, rescuing me from my makeshift casket, drenched in sweat and tears. It had disappeared after, and now I could see where it had gone—this last remaining artifact of a room once filled with the bric-à-brac of our lives. I picked my way towards the hope chest, then sat next to it, lifting the latch.

Inside were neatly folded clothes, men's and women's jackets, shirts, a bevy of pins, and ties. I rummaged among them, discovering they were of varying sizes, some still smelling of perfume and cigar smoke.

Also present was a single pair of earrings in the shape of peacock feathers, gold and jewel-toned. None of these items had belonged to Darren or Mother. Perhaps they were William's or my sister's unwanted items, but there was such an array, I didn't understand the point of it. Something rustled nearby, and I stood, scanning the plant-choked tower for any indication I wasn't alone.

"Inspector?"

When there was no answer, I nearly called for Auntie. My tendency to view her as more than a dangerous wretch would be a hard habit to break.

There was an eager tug at my magic, the shimmer of space undulating, turning the wall before me hazy and insubstantial. This was the portal to Dark Hall.

Driven by the need for answers, I didn't hesitate. I pressed my hands against the soft texture of the wall, and it yielded. The magic I'd used to repel Auntie was still regenerating, yet what remained basked in the proximity of this realm, mingling with the hoary power of the portal. As easily as diving beneath the crest of a wave, I sank in.

I was afloat, suspended in a weightless, liminal realm, before emerging on the other side, still enveloped in darkness. It would take several minutes for the magic to adjust to me, to piece itself together into a picture I could fathom. Threads began to knit themselves together, forming the murky aspect of an interior hallway from the top down. The gypsum corbel molding appeared first, coils of free magic drifting alongside them as though following a road. My magic fluttered, fed by the endless well of power flowing through these corridors.

I entered further, footfall muffled by the nothingness that still existed under me, holding my weight by hope alone. As a child, I'd taken advantage of expanding my magical ability, enjoying how easily things came, creating toys that moved on their own, paper butterflies that took to the air. My favorite pastime had been smuggling my beloved book, still tucked in the parlor's bookcase, and reading a story aloud to a pretend audience, bringing the scenes to life in a misty, miraculous world of shapes, much like a puppet master. It had been lonely, and I'd often attempted to convince Fiona to accompany me, longing to share it with her. But she'd been afraid of the Fiend, and no matter how I worked to convince her it only bothered people who kept curses inside of them, she'd never risk it.

"What if I have a curse I don't know about?" she'd argued.

"Don't you know when you eat them?" I'd groused, disappointed that she wouldn't try to find the courage to keep me company.

"You don't have to eat a curse to have one, Ellie. You can make them on your own, by accident. What if I made one and didn't know?"

She'd remained anxious about creating something terrible for the remainder of our life together, never enjoying the freedom and delights of Dark Hall. Yet here was a portal I hadn't known about. One I'd never seen in all the voyages Fiona and I had made to the tower to play. She'd made it herself, and she'd done it to do terrible things.

As my surroundings improved, I navigated forward, the tops of doors appearing in succession, steps from each other. All were inactive, each Narthex systematically destroyed by the Authority. I'd tested each, all either locked or opening to blank walls. The hallways branched in various directions, and I'd likely explored them all, eventually reaching the end of what Curse Eaters had built, where the architecture of Dark Hall faded to pitch black, punctuated by sparks of untethered magic mirroring bioluminescent life.

At some point, the architects of the hallways had become creative, and soon I would see the decorative paper, stripes of emerald green and ivy, and petaled arms of sconces holding dewdrop globes. Beneath my feet would stretch blue carpet runners, speckled with stars that mirrored the night sky over the sea. The world-building magic used to fashion these things had been called upon so often that Dark Hall remembered them.

The first new thing I noticed, alerting me to the possibility the hall had changed since I'd last set foot there, were the tips of green, leafy creepers that emerged clinging to doorframes, strung across sconces like string, the stalks bearing couplings of red bell flowers. They rang as they formed the tinkling music charming. I smiled despite myself, wondering if Fiona had given in to sentiment and made them grow. I stroked one, its petals silky, and it chimed.

Aware of the sliver of Drudge I'd torn from Auntie during our tussle, I kept a tight hold on my magic, so as not to give the Fiend anything to sense, though it seemed nowhere near. I stepped on something unyielding, and it rolled underfoot, producing a sharp crack as I tumbled into the blackness that still pooled below my waist, landing heavily on one knee with a slight twinge in my ankle. My hand rested on another peculiar thing, long and smooth against my palm.

My burgeoning curiosity about what these shapes were was waylaid by a tremble of power, like the flutter of butterfly wings, rippling to meet me, distinct from the portal tingling behind me, but familiar enough. Another Narthex existed nearby. I sat back on my heels to stand, keen to follow this thread, when the hallway bled the darkness away, completing its transformation and leaving me nestled in a copse of bones. Human bones. Dozens of skeletons sat either propped along the walls or sprawled over the ground, bringing to mind a looted catacomb. Each exhibited different stages of decay, dressed in evening finery and wrapped in dense, climbing plants, the trumpet flowers sprouting from eye sockets and open collarbones. The thing I'd stepped on had been a leg, its anklebone fracturing under my weight. The body it belonged to had long been stripped of its flesh and appeared nearly artificial, unreal. But the cadaver I'd touched wasn't clean. Remains of gray flesh still clung in clumps to its joints, wispy blonde hair hanging in small sprays from its skull. And pinned to the breast of its black cap-sleeve evening gown was a peacock feather brooch.

Blessedly, there was no smell, magic censoring the horror of death. Still, I gagged, gathering myself, stumbling as my stomach heaved, knowing beyond a doubt these were the bodies of the missing in Nightglass, whose articles of clothing now lay carefully folded in a chest in the tower. Dread caused my psychic ramparts to buckle, and the curse remnant shivered.

Then came that terrible sound. The sound I'd heard the night Thomas had been attacked, when I'd barely dragged him free of Dark Hall as the fiend sought to take him. I hadn't known Thomas Nightglass was full of curses. He'd hidden it so well, and I'd never bothered to look.

I retreated shakily, panic toying with my senses. I needed to exit the portal and pull my magic free, removing the key. The door had closed, and when I yanked it open, there was only bare, lime-washed wall. I slapped my hand against it, running along to locate the seams, but the portal that had existed here had been closed for a long time. The hallway had moved.

I sprinted to the neighboring door, locked, unyielding, even as I sent a course of magic into it, begging for entry.

I glanced over my shoulder as the noise echoed again, a ship's hull creaking before its collapse. Red fog filled the space in a rush, a swirling wave of diabolical magic that set to work unweaving the hallway that had just materialized. The surrounding darkness swelled as I tried a door, another, finding no escape from my terror. I only needed to close my eyes to sense the wavering portal outline, but fear held me captive, and the monster approached, eager to rip me apart for daring to bring fetid power into its domain.

I stumbled sideways, grasping one last handle. It gave, and I plunged in. I was upside down, discombobulated by the lack of gravity and light, and I reached frantically for the other side, sure that just touching it would mean safety. Cold slipped around my ankles, even as someone grabbed hold of my fingers and pulled. I was wrenched out of the Narthex, back into Blackwicket House, and I wrested my magic from the portal. The wall solidified, bowing with the strain of the creature struggling to enter.

My rescuer hauled me forcefully around a vice grip upon my waist, and I found Inspector Harrow. He was shirtless, hair a disheveled commotion, eyes golden embers, half-lidded.

"I was sure you told me you couldn't access Dark Hall, Ms. Blackwicket," he murmured.

CHAPTER THIRTY-TWO

I pressed my hands to his chest, his skin hot against my palms, magic pulsing unrestrained, confounding my senses.

"There are bones. There's never been bones," I said, shaking my eyes wide, pleading with him to understand what I couldn't say. He didn't release me.

"You were adamant that people with no curses shouldn't be afraid. So why were you running?"

"I took one from Auntie when she attacked Jack! I…". My breath stuck. The Fiend would devour a curse carrier with no discrimination or pity. All Fiona had to do was feed her victims the curse and introduce them to Dark Hall.

"The clothes." I twisted to look at the array of items scattered on the floor, hanging upon the lip of the wicker chest. "They belonged to the people my sister murdered."

Fury over this new blow, over still being restrained, drove me to pound a fist against the Inspector's chest, "Let me go, I need to think!"

He pulled me closer, his heady, faunish magic merging with my adrenaline, turning my body into a pyre.

"Was it really Fiona?" he asked.

"What?"

"Your sister's dead, but people keep disappearing, and here I am finding you in Dark Hall. All of this chaos coincides with your arrival in town."

"Think what you want, Victor." I snarled, ready to bite, embracing my volatile emotions, tired of being stalked and accused by someone who'd done things as terrible as I had.

"How did it feel to kill that man?" He lowered his head, and I turned my face away, not trusting myself, emotions fluctuating too rapidly to identify. "Did it excite you? Make you feel powerful?"

"Don't." I didn't want to disturb this truth, the piece of my soul scorched black.

"How many people have you murdered with your magic? Go on, tell me every dirty secret. What's it matter now? Get it off your chest before we both die with lies hanging between us."

"No more than you." I aimed a sharp stab of energy toward the familiar connection already forming, our power churning together, the same terrible magic of two broken monstrous people colliding in a struggle for the upper hand. I dug deep, the sensation exhilarating, like diving naked into cold water, and when I found the dark ruins of his Drudge, I took hold.

He sucked in a breath, then exhaled, the vibration turning to a lurid groan.

"That's the way. Do you feel safe when you hold someone's life in your hands? Call the curses up, devour me, leave my husk behind in this rotting house."

My power retreated as though it had been scalded, anger losing its harsh shape and turning to shame. The sound the Inspector made was a mingling of relief and disappointment, and he finally loosened his hold on me.

"I don't *do* that," I said, wresting away, creating space enough to notice the blackberry vines had stirred closer, growing toward the maelstrom of power we'd created.

They strangled their host plants, snapping the stems and branches supporting them, gorged with our anger and resentment, the suppressed desire to consume each other, no matter how depraved the need was.

"Your mother did. Your sister."

"My mother never hurt anyone." My head pounded.

"A child was murdered. Right downstairs in your parlor."

I wanted to refute it as a lie, but it wasn't. My hesitation was all he needed.

"The Blackwickets are murderers." The accusation boomed through the tower, the thundering of a gavel. "You're a killer, Eleanora."

"I know!"

I screamed the confession, the edges of my magic decaying, building a curse. Inspector Harrow had finally broken me open, spilling out the most depraved parts of me for his amusement.

"I didn't mean for him to die," I shouted. There were no secrets worth defending anymore. "But I'm glad he did, and I would give that disgusting pig those cufflinks again!"

I laughed, hot tears on my cheeks, hoping the Inspector was getting everything he wanted out of me.

"I'm only sorry I didn't get to watch him choke." The admission was poisoned honey, and I savored every drop. "When I heard he'd died, I raised a glass and toasted the bastard's departure."

I had nothing to grab onto, to break, or throw to expend the remaining anger beating behind my sternum. So I bent double and screamed, and from my mouth boiled the red tinges of the curse I'd been plaiting with my fury. The house quaked as though beset by vicious winds, vines snapped, and Blackberry fruit burst, adding their tainted magic to the rest. Victor stood in the chaos, a creature carved in stone, having done the job he set out to do, no longer needing to provoke and manipulate me with magic, fear, or lust.

When the hungry, haunted flora had devoured the last echoes of my wail, I pressed a palm to my breast.

"Something else you should know, Inspector. My mother didn't kill Thomas Nightglass. I did."

"You?" Harrow narrowed his eyes.

"You wanted all my dirty secrets," I said. "I murdered him."

This confession affected the Inspector strangely, and he was suddenly annoyed, vexation plain in his tone.

"What did you have to do with it?"

"I showed him Dark Hall." I stood straight, facing history as much as Inspector Harrow.

"For what purpose?"

"Because I was lonely, Inspector," I said, impatient. "I ran around Dark Hall like it was a carnival ground, but I was alone. Thomas was my friend. He wanted to go, and I wanted to share it. The Fiend had never bothered me, I'd only encountered it once. It ignored me because I didn't have any curses to feed it. But it noticed Thomas. We'd nearly gotten through the Narthex when it got hold of him, but I closed the portal, severed a portion of the Fiend in the process. I didn't see him again until Grigori brought him."

Do something, Isolde. Look at the boy. He's dying!

"I knew what had happened. The Fiend had infected him with its curses. I panicked. I was afraid for him and ashamed of myself, so when my mother left to get help from Fiona, I stuck my nose where it didn't belong. I tried to take the curses off him myself, to fix my mistakes. I was ignorant and egotistical."

I pulled my hair in frustration, driven by all the regret still lodged in my heart.

"There were too many curses, and they were stronger than me and started to hoard my magic. I couldn't handle them all.

When they started picking pieces of me apart, I reacted. I tried to curse eat, but I'd never consumed curses directly from another person, and I did something worse than take his curses, Inspector. I took his magic."

"You annulled him?" Disbelief replaced annoyance, as though he'd never imagined such depravity to be executed by a child.

"He was dead when my mother came back, and she told everyone it had been her mistake, her wrongdoing to bear. She was protecting me, but we all carried the weight of my stupidity."

"You were a child." The Inspector's statement was terse, rejecting my confession.

"I was, am, and will always be a Curse Eater, Victor Harrow," I bit off each word, punctuating them with a step forward, the foul misery of loss garroting me. Loss of family, of my identity, dignity, and home—even though it was one I hadn't wanted. There was no way to continue from here alone. "So, annul me.. Deliver your justice. Do what you've been burning to since you arrested me in Devin. I've nothing left to guard, and maybe when I'm gone, the plague of this house and my family will die with me."

My new proximity was intentional, allowing him to sense the curses I'd forged, and as I expected, tempted the Drudge in him to answer, and ensnare my power in its claws.

He regarded me with the interest of a hunter whose game has laid itself down at their feet.

"It's all there, Victor," I whispered. "My magic, my curses, take them."

"Given the freedom, Ms. Blackwicket," he intoned, leaning in with the promising menace I'd hoped to excite, "there are numerous things I'd like to do to you. Killing isn't one of them."

He took me by the throat, long fingers squeezing enough that my shocked intake of breath was cut short.

"You've told me the truth. I think it's fair that I return the favor. But in case this is the last time I get to take you up on such a tempting offer, I'll indulge."

He nipped my bottom lip, then kissed me, the pain vivid and rousing, and I met his intensity with my own as his tongue delved into my mouth. I remembered his taste from the night he'd laid me across the piano, and when lust ignited, I let it blaze, my despair burning away.

But this was more than a kiss. The Inspector was taking from me exactly what I'd offered him, teasing the curses that sullied my magic free, urging them to rise. I anticipated the torturous tearing of a curse extracted, but it never came. It slid from me like velvet gliding across delicate skin. If Victor had caressed me between my thighs, it wouldn't have induced such euphoria. I arched into him.

I didn't need to wonder if he'd experienced the same stab of ecstasy, as he turned rigid against my belly. When he inhaled, the remaining curse ascended along with a thread of my magic, which he imbibed with the reverberation of a moan in his throat.

Instead of emptiness where magic had once been, my power replenished, no less like a handful of water being taken from the ocean. I'd never encountered this kind of Curse Eating. An exchange that elicited longing, not pain, fulfilling instead of taking. I exhaled a shaky breath.

"I don't understand what's happening."

"I could take it all," he replied, running kisses along my jaw, digging his fingers into the soft flesh of my backside. "I've been aching to feed from you, feel your magic in my veins. You've become a vice of mine, and I'm finding it hard to let go."

"Then don't."

He breathed me in, his roaming magic discovering a part of me that had never been stirred, and I almost whimpered.

"Are you asking me to fuck you, Curse Eater?"

The agony of my desire grew. I'd never grow tired of it.

"Yes." It was a demand, a low growl as undone as the rest of me, and I caught his bottom lip in my teeth just enough to sting.

The result was immediate, his monstrous magic lunging to claim mine. I trembled as it held, throbbing with an energy that traveled to the damp horizon between my legs. In another vicious move, he tucked his hand into the collar of my blouse, popping the buttons to my sternum, exposing the cream silk brassiere. He wasted no time freeing my breast from it, running his thumb over the crest of my nipple, hardening it. Any sounds I might have made were caught in his mouth, as he encouraged another thread of magic from me.

He continued this rhythm, caressing and pinching, supping on me until I no longer knew where my magic ended and his began. I was at his mercy, quivering, my pleasure cresting, a wave ready to break upon the cliffs.

The waist of his trousers was already loose, the button missing from the violence of his transformation, and there was nothing to impede me when I trailed my fingers down the hard plane of his stomach, surveying a battlefield of scars, slipping beneath to take hold of his rigid erection. His groan encouraged me, and I freed it, running my palm along the magnificent length of him, wrapping my fingers around the girth while imagining the obscene, burning stretch I'd enjoy if he were sheathed in me.

"You're courting trouble," he warned, his limitations abused, strung too tight.

"I'm a Blackwicket," I said, enjoying my temporary power. "Trouble and I know each other well."

In response, his large hand enveloped mine, guiding the rhythm.

"But have you ever knelt for it," he murmured, continuing the strokes, running my hand from head to the thicket of black curls at the base and back. The eroticism of touching Inspector Harrow, a man who I'd believed was out for my blood, shattered me in innumerable ways.

His question was whiskey poured on an open flame. The intensity of my yearning became reckless, bewildering hunger.

With my eyes raised to his challenging, unwavering gaze, I lowered myself to my knees amidst the rootstocks and vines that had grown ever further near us in answer to the outpouring of magic, blackberry vines rustling as they reached toward us, plump fruit heavy on their stems.

The Inspector released his hold of my hand, allowing me freedom to touch him as I pleased, and though he curled my hair around his fingers, he didn't force my movement, but held me as I drew my lips along the silky head of his shaft. His skin was hot, and I laved my tongue across the engorged tip, and his magic sank further into mine, caressing otherwise unreachable, intimate places. With no patience left for teasing, I took his cock in my mouth, sliding him as deep as I dared. I couldn't accommodate all of him, so I kept my fingers curled around the thick plinth, glorifying in the texture of him sliding along my tongue. When I reached the end, I closed my lips.

"My fucking god, Eleanora." The near-reverent exclamation was a reward, worship, and he divested himself of his initial gentleness, hand tightening as he drove in. Despite his intensity, he abstained from choking me, though I'd have been eager for it. There was nothing Victor could do that would temper this growing, brutal need.

As I pleasured him, his manipulation of my magic turned me liquid, and I reached under my skirt, tucking my finger into silk, stroking frantically.

Victor had positioned his other hand beneath my chin, keeping my head angled at the perfect pitch as he took my mouth in measured, controlled thrusts. I stroked myself in time, awareness of the physical world growing hazy, and released his length to grab hold of the muscular flesh of his thigh, moaning in the onslaught.

The vibration of noise ruptured something in Victor, and on his next thrust, he disposed of caution and buried himself in me to the hilt. My throat opened for him, and though for a moment I couldn't breathe, my body didn't reject the invasion. He didn't remain, pulling himself free of my mouth before scooping me up, and flipping me roughly even as I protested the interruption.

"So impatient." The depth of his voice had dipped into a thunderous reverberation of erotic appetite, and he lifted me so I was on my toes, losing balance, forced to lean forward and place my palms on the bare wall, so near the portal which hummed and convulsed with the capricious energy we were feeding it. He ground himself against my backside, my skirt still an agonizing barrier. He freed the breast still encased in the brassiere, so my chest was bare in the cool of the room, and rolled the summit between his fingers.

"This is torture," I cried, trying to gain traction to press closer, my toes barely reaching the ground.

"Minutes ago, you were asking me to kill you," he crooned. "What's a bit of torture?"

But at long last he showed mercy, abandoning my breasts to lift the front of my skirt. Making no efforts to tease, he glided two fingers into my wet heat, pressing his thumb across the aching swell of my clit. His caressing of me, inside and out, remained consistent, coaxing me to the precipice. He didn't venture to please himself further, keeping me at a well-controlled angle so I couldn't do it for him. Panting, I raised my head, attempting to look over my shoulder at him, longing to watch his face as he claimed me with his hand.

"Eyes down," he barked, and the timbre of his voice was

unusual, guttural. I was too lost in the building power of my oncoming climax to be disobedient. The blackberries had flourished, drawing high and close like a cage, blocking the last of the sun from the window, trembling, the curses in each of them begging to be washed in the electric power of our passion. The house was holding its breath as I did, lungs pleading for oxygen, which I denied them in favor of at last tumbling from the zenith.

"Fracture for me," he enticed, drawing his fingers up to bear acute focus on the taut hill of my clitoris. "You beautiful, wicked creature."

I pitched into orgasm, the cry I elicited nearly a sob. Unlike the wail of anguish, this cry was jolting in its release. The rapture unexpectedly triggered my base instincts, and I parted my lips, inhaling, calling to the curses swarming among blackberry vines. The fruits began to burst, their sullied magic sweeping into the gravitational pull of mine, made inescapable by passion. The curses dissolved, emerging as misty white scrolls.

For the second time, Victor had brought me to climax and denied himself. As I was descending from the highest point of my ecstasy, I became aware of the sordid weight of Victor's magic, obscured by the Drudge infixed within him.

He removed his hand, touch slick with my lust falling between my still exposed breasts, rising to my throat as he gathered my body against his without lowering my feet completely to the ground, the still turgid pillar of his desire pressing into the center of my back. But it wasn't Victor's muscle-corded arm holding my waist, nor his steady, capable fingers at my neck, holding my head against his chest.

"That was very good," he grated, and his voice rumbled too low, overtones of whispers lingering like wind in the trees.

The curses I'd called forth from the baneful Blackberry vines continued to rise, wringing the plant dry of life, until one by one they collapsed in twisted, brown husks. The same force that pulled them in enticed my magic as well.

The new soughing lilt of the Inspector's voice encouraged gooseflesh to rise across my skin.

"Now it's my turn to give you the truth, Curse Eater," he said.

CHAPTER THIRTY-THREE

H e loosened his grip, allowing me down, and I turned to find myself eye level with the chest of a Drudge, long-bodied and arboreal, his torso as thick as oak core, burled limbs and skin knotted by brawny muscle. Unlike Drudge I knew, this creature possessed no spectral quality, no ghostly lack of substance; only a monstrous presence, with cursed magic rising from it like spindrift. I lifted my gaze to meet a face both hardened and fiendish, marked by a brutish jaw and an enduring scar, stark against the charred tone of its skin.

I clutched my shirt closed, shielding my naked chest, as I looked up into his face, ochre eyes burning, alight with chaotic magic.

"Victor?"

The creature leaned toward me, the skeletal points of its fingers scraping the wall above my head. "Regretting your lust, Eleanora?"

"You're a Drudge."

"Drudge, human, a profane version of both welded together by a man's hunger for power." A clicking growl emanated from him as he breathed.

"Someone did this to you?" The implication was chilling. To hear of the horrors of human made monsters during the War was one thing, but seeing the result of it, curses made flesh and blood, was another.

"Grigori Nightglass," he breathed. "When I was a boy."

Victor was a few years older than I. We would have been children at the same time, living in Nightglass together.

A wraithlike hand rose to my cheek, the touch cold as he traced trails countless tears had followed.

"That merger should have ended my life, but a little girl in the house on the cliffs took pity on me and fed me the magic that kept me alive."

The asphyxiating pressure of memories crowded the air from my lungs, recollections of events that had ruined everything and buried me in fear.

"You're frightened," the Drudge rumbled. "I'm not ashamed to admit I like it."

"Stop." The words were too quiet.

"This part of me enjoyed the terror you radiated across that table in Devin, as though you expected me to cross it and devour you whole."

His abominable power yawned wide, and my magic responded to it intuitively. It took effort to pull my guard into place as tightly as I was able.

"No longer eager to have a Nightglass man between your legs?" The laugh was primordial, like nature forming in fire. "Shame."

"You're not Thomas."

"You're right, Curse Eater. Thomas is dead, consumed by vile magic. Victor is the monster who replaced him, the one you tremble against now, who has tasted you, made you keen in the dark. This soul is rooted in blood and stolen magic."

He paused, shifting, standing to his full height.

"But you had nothing to do with that." The burr of his voice couldn't sound gentle, but the threat had lessened. "When your mother received me she knew what Grigori had done, believed it was better that I die. She walked away to let me, not to find your sister. She saw my future, what Nightglass had planned for me, and thought death would be a mercy."

Tired of fighting tears, I let them come. The memory of my mother, gentle and caring, giving and sacrificing everything for everyone, was forever altered. Just like Fiona, Isolde carried a darkness in her that I'd never seen, because she'd protected me from it.

"You took nothing from me when you stepped in to do your mother's work. You severed a piece of yourself, offered it, and it's lived in me always, tormenting me as the Drudge torments me."

My memories rearranged themselves as I exhaled, reshaping into a past where I hadn't killed Thomas, my mother was capable of cruelty disguised as mercy, and Victor and I were inexorably linked by a decision I'd made so many years ago, in the desperation of saving a friend I'd loved.

"Are you behind the recent disappearances?" I asked.

"Some of them," he responded, unaffected by the admission, standing like an infernal god answering to the feeble moral questioning of mortals who were incapable of following their own principles.

"Darren?" I asked

"No."

I was surprised by how much relief this denial offered me.

"Are you the reason there are no other Drudges here in Nightglass?" I thought back on the small Drudge that had attacked me in the morgue, the utter lack of them at the Vapors, and throughout the rest of the town, despite the vast amount of magic available to seize. I'd believed William had been using Jack, but this explanation was more likely.

"Someone like me. It seems Grigori made more." The possibility was nauseating, cruel. "It lurks in the skin of someone you may already know. I've been trying to lure it out."

"You shouldn't have kept this from me," I said, though instead of my heart hardening towards this man, condemned to live in damnation alongside a monster forced upon him, it softened, a burden lifting.

"And why not?" He asked, his voice a thunderclap.

"It was my right to know I didn't kill you!" I replied, matching his intensity, rising to meet him with anger of my own. I took a step closer, less timid. "That you weren't just Authority stalking me to my grave. What good did it do to hide it?"

My aggressive approach provoked the curses comprising this grisly component of Victor Harrow. He loomed, seething, reaching to take hold of me, possessive. I raised a hand to stop him, but his gnarled, tapered fingers encircled mine, pulling me in. He pressed my palm to his chest, and the insistent prodding of tainted energy retreated slightly at my touch. Though the Drudge remained, its energy settled into something less primeval.

"Until I saw you with your sister in Devin, I knew you as the woman who'd killed Brock Mofton. Even after I'd discovered you to be Eleanora, I assumed you'd chosen the path of the Brom. I felt betrayed. I wanted to punish you." These truths were yielded with an earnestness I'd never expected from Inspector Harrow, delivered from the mouth of a curse, blurring the lines between the two. "But you ignite me, soothe the ache of this affliction. Being near you is like feeling spring after endless winter."

I was a weak woman—weak and foolish. Inspired by the urge to preserve the infuriating, essential bond we'd created, I tentatively lowered my guard, allowing my power to rise to him, giving in. There was no greed, no unrestrained indulgence, only the caress of his magic.

"Can the Drudge be unraveled?" I asked.

"Neither aspect of me can exist without the other." He drew closer. "It's for this reason I should be destroyed, Eleanora, and William Nightglass must fall with me."

"That's absurd, Victor," I said, and his name sounded right. Thomas was someone he'd once been, lost forever, the moment etched into this house and our joined histories. "William deserves whatever's coming to him, and I understand wanting to be the harbinger of that justice, but it doesn't require sacrificing yourself. I'll help you. We'll figure out a better way of freeing Jack and other children like him from the Brom."

I recalled the way he'd cared for Jack, how he'd offered protection and security, enough to allow the boy's magic to believe in its chances. He'd known exactly what to say, how to hold on to hope for the child that couldn't.

"They need people like you on their side," I said.

His touch was light on my cheek.

"Idealism doesn't suit you, Curse Eater."

When the Drudge lifted my chin, lowering its face to mine, I didn't recoil. Its broad mouth was rough, electric against my lips, but it was meant to be. As he'd done in the moments before the tide of desire had swept us from our senses, he drew magic from me, but this time, there was simply the pleasing warmth of mutual connection.

In the catastrophic storm we'd unexpectedly found ourselves navigating together, we'd become each other's mooring. I accepted my role gladly, closing my eyes to savor it.

His mouth softened, skin and cartilage rippling beneath my hand, as his form slowly yielded to its human side, bringing Victor's scarred body back to me. The discomfort of the transformation remained clear in the tension of his muscles, the way his breath hitched. I touched his face, running the pads of my fingers along the scar on his cheek, brushing the hair from his forehead as he'd once done for me, seeing him anew.

For the first time since I'd known him as Victor, his expression was unguarded, revealing a tenderness that might have been the death of me on its own.

"William's High Tide is tonight. We should make a plan," he said, taking my hand to place a kiss on my palm. "But I'd rather be dressed for that discussion."

Relieved, I managed a breathy laugh, and we descended from the tower together, Victor assisting me down the broken stairs. There would never be a reason to return. My sister's crimes had been uncovered, but she was dead, the garden she'd grown to deliver her justice drained of life. The Narthex to Dark Hall was closed and was better off staying that way. A renewed sense of purpose had unfurled, and I was prepared to work with Victor on a plan to rescue Jack. He placed a hand, painfully gentle, at the back of my neck and pulled me close to press a kiss on my forehead.

"Stay here, Ellie," he said, and there was something strange in his voice, a thickness as his throat constricted with sorrow. Pinpricks of warning traveled across my skin, but my reaction was too slow. He seized me, lifting me from my feet and taking three swift steps to the door of the suite I'd shared with my family. I resisted his manhandling, but I was in no position, physically or magically, to counter his will. He tossed me into the anteroom with enough force that I stumbled nearly into the bathroom. I couldn't make it to the door in time to stop him from closing it.

"Let me out!" I shouted, clutching the handle, rattling it. Enraged and helpless, I watched as the door melded to its frame, soldered shut by magic.

I pounded frantically, calling his name, cursing him. But there was no answer.

I lost track of the time I spent channeling my magic into fused wood, fracturing it bit by bit, never enough to breach it. Even when I summoned all my strength for a fierce strike, the door only cracked in the middle without giving way. Unlike with Victor, my magic didn't replenish itself easily, and I wasn't accustomed to this level of psychic exertion. Fatigue was setting in.

My last option was the dormered window. At three stories, it was an unlikely escape, but I marched to it, flinging open the shutters to gaze at a darksome landscape, illuminated by the waning moon. From the third floor, the mansard roof slanted below the window, with its decorative cornice edge running along the incline, encircling the entire house.

I tore off my tattered blouse and wrestled out of my skirt, charging to Fiona's wrecked room to rummage through her clothes again. I was determined to get to High Tide, to stop Victor from enacting whatever self-destructive plan he'd engineered, even if I had to jump out of the damn window to make it there. Hurriedly, I put on the remaining formal dress in the wardrobe, its A-line shape softened by the gold chiffon pooling around the skirt, pleated sleeves draping loose over my shoulders, then spared an impatient moment to arrange my hair. I swept it into a severe chignon and swiped my lips with a violent red lipstick I found on the vanity. I could see why Thea wore this color so often. It was like wearing armor.

I tossed the gold tube onto the vanity counter, where it clattered and dropped to the floor, then stared at my reflection in the mirror. Anger suited me.

Soon, I was leaning precariously into the night, enduring the biting cold with no coat. I climbed over the windowsill and sat, adrenaline rocketing through my veins. If I fell, magic would cushion my landing, but it wouldn't prevent broken bones.

As I was about to slide to the ledge, the roar of a car engine approached. I waited, watching as the headlights climbed the hill. Ramsey, come to retrieve me. Taking a chance, I stood on the ledge, gripping the window frame, leaning further so he could spot me. The sedan disappeared, parking in front of the house where I would remain hidden. I shouted.

"Ramsey!" My cry was high and loud, but the crash of the waves swallowed it. "Ramsey!"

With luck, the driver heard me and appeared around the corner, but he had company. Thea was next to him, wrapped in fur.

"What the hell are you doing?" she yelled.

"I'm trapped," I called. "Third floor. You'll know which door."

I had no concerns about the house refusing them entry; it had been eerily silent as of late. I searched for curses, but encountered emptiness.

Minutes later, Ramsey's voice called through the door.

"Ms. Blackwicket!"

"Please get the door open!"

A bone-jarring crack echoed, shaking the door. Ramsey was striking it with something. With one final crash, the casing splintered and the door gave way, allowing Ramsey to open it with a harsh shove of his shoulder.

I stalked past the chauffer, who stood grouchy and red-faced, a tire iron in hand.

"You look full of angry bees," he gruffed. "How'd this happen?"

"Victor," I growled, storming to the stairs.

CHAPTER THIRTY-FOUR

T hea stood in the foyer, the door left open so she could escape at any moment, draped in a black fur stole offering limited warmth over her thin satin gown, simple save for the ruching below her bust. Upon noticing my expression, she raised her defenses in anticipation of the snap of angry magic I aimed at her.

"How could you lead Jack back to William?" I seethed.

"Is he safer in this house with your pet Drudge? Those creatures nearly killed him!" She echoed my fury.

My skin tingled with the electricity of her temper, equal to mine. The house ought to have reveled in this display, yet it remained motionless as a dead rabbit.

"Who is he, Thea?" I demanded.

"Not Roark." In so many words, she was telling me that not only was I wrong, but it was none of my business.

"Because Roark is dead, isn't he?" It was better my magic hadn't fully recovered from the ordeal with the door; otherwise, I might have been tempted to misuse it.

"I don't know." Each word was a staccato insistence.

"Was he my sister's son?" I urged, eager to extract at least one honest answer.

"No more than Jack is mine!" Her voice rose, sorrow flickering in her dark eyes, "She loved that boy, but he wasn't hers. She stole him."

Thea wilted, her determination to stay proud and unbending crumbling as her shoulders drooped. She raised a manicured hand to her face, pressing her fingers above her brows to stifle her tears. I wanted more from her, the urgency for it burning, but in the presence of a woman overwhelmed by the same forces that had devastated Fiona, I reluctantly softened and allowed her a moment to breathe. When she finally looked up, her gaze drifted around the foyer.

"I lied to you," she confessed, "About ever being in the house."

"You've come here?"

Thea smiled, and it was the shape of a beloved memory. She swiped at her tears. "We practically lived here. Jack and me. Before Roark's disappearance, before Fiona started blaming Grigori, and William began blaming her."

A horde of questions crowded my mouth.

"Is Roark's disappearance the reason Fiona killed Grigori?"

"Who knows why she did anything." Thea took a deep breath, her sense of fragility lingering. "I stopped knowing her that day. She turned her back on us, on the people who cared about her."

"She gave you her life," I contended, Fiona and my Mother blurring into a single person, both having sacrificed everything to meet the relentless demands of being a Curse Eater for Nightglass—a woman who continually cracked herself open to sew everyone else together with her own sinew.

"And I gave her mine." Thea pulled her stole closer, shielding herself from memories. "She needed me, and I stayed. Jack and I could have run, we had opportunities, but we'd built a life. Maybe not a life anyone else would want, but it was ours."

I understood—the picture of my sister, hand on Thea's knee, laughing in a moment of pure joy, the bottle of jasmine perfume on the dresser, half empty despite my sister favoring honeysuckle, the red lipstick on the vanity, the same shade Thea wore, and the children's clothes and toys for more than a single child.

She'd been more than a friend to Fiona.

"Oh, Thea," I said gently, heart aching, suddenly wanting to know her—this woman my sister had loved. But it was all far too late for that. Our paths hadn't converged in a manner that made trust or friendship possible. I distanced myself from these regretful new emotions by asking, "Did my sister steal Jack from Dark Hall?"

Thea cast a glance behind me, where Ramsey had been standing quiet as death, some ways away, leaving room for our animosity. He nodded to Thea, encouraging her.

"Jack belongs to the Authority," she explained, voice dropping low as though not wanting to be overheard, "They traded him to William Nightglass."

"For what?" I cried, voice pitching high in shock, the antithesis of secrecy.

"For access to curses."

The idea seemed almost too ridiculous to believe. The authority had built their platform on making the world safe, protecting it from the Fiend, from Drudge, by eradicating curses and rogue magic users capable of manipulating them.

"It's the very thing they're against," I argued, though it was feeble logic.

"If you haven't noticed," Thea's contempt for my ignorance was on full display, "The Authority is interested in power. They want to make sure they're the ones in control of it. It's why they snuffed out Curse Eaters, banned Narthex. But when the power dynamic shifted, and the Brom became strong, they grew interested in playing nice."

I remained silent, fearing a misstep would jeopardize Thea's willingness to share the crucial insights I needed to navigate the hornet's nest I'd stepped on, filled with warring factions I'd been, until now, ignorant of.

"So the people in charge gave in here and there, made concessions, let the Brom open clubs like the Vapors, rubbed elbows with powerful men like Grigori. Their elite got first access to all the vile magic we were pumping into the veins of our clients, got hooked, every last one, and when Grigori Nightglass asked for Dark Hall children to help support the whole disgusting scheme, they agreed. It benefited them."

"What was my sister's part in all of this, Thea?"

Again, Thea cut her eyes to Ramsey, and I caught the lead, following it to face the stocky man dressed in a driver's uniform, who was no more a chauffeur than a shark in a bow was a little girl.

Forgetting the regret I'd once felt for crossing a boundary I hadn't been invited over, I viciously snatched at the edges of his magic. This time, he didn't hide from me, and our power struck head-on. His unexpected strength fueled my ferocity.

"Easy there, Blackwicket," he cautioned, voice strained with the effort of holding me at bay.

"Is this magic yours?" I snarled.

"It is, girl, stand down." With effort he hadn't expected to spend, he shook me off and raised his defenses. It was an unnecessary precaution as I'd depleted myself well below any ability to attack further. The sensation in my head was airy and vast.

Ramsey noted my wooziness.

"A warning for you, Ms. Blackwicket. It takes stamina and control to wield magic that forcefully, and you have neither. You keep exploding like that and you're going to burn yourself out permanently." He shook his head. "It's a damn waste no one taught you to control all that power you have."

"I'm more than capable of keeping it under control. I've done it my whole life."

"Repressing it isn't control. It's fear."

I didn't want advice from this strange man.

"Why does Thea keep silently asking your permission to speak?" I challenged.

"She doesn't think you're safe," he replied, raising his hands as though he were calming a wild animal. "She's checking in with me because I'm good at determining that sort of thing. It's part of my job."

"As a *driver*?"

"There's something far bigger going on here than you know, Eleanora."

"Don't patronize me, Ramsey." I spat, wondering if they knew Victor was once a boy fed curses by Grigori until his soul couldn't remember a time before it wasn't half made of them.

"I know Fiona Blackwicket is responsible for the disappearances," he said, his curt voice like sandpaper on the hull of an old boat. "I know the Veil tried to use her to bring the Nightglass family to its knees, then delivered their wrath over her failure to your door. Now, I'll ask that you appreciate my honesty by keeping your magic to yourself."

"Who are you affiliated with?" I demanded, shivering from the cold sweeping through the open front entry. After expending so much energy clashing with Ramsey, the chill seeped deeper.

"Barrick Harrow," he replied simply.

"Inspector Harrow's father?" The words stuck slightly.

"A good friend of mine. We went to academy together," Ramsey's voice was rough with an emotion I recognized as grief. "He was assigned by the Authority to monitor the strongest magic users, keep them out of the Brom toolbox, so to speak. He was also tasked with uncovering Dark Hall children."

I knew a bit of this story already.

"But he didn't turn any of them in," I ventured. "He hid them away."

Ramsey studied my face briefly.

"Yes. You can't do that kind of job without eventually realizing what it's for," the man acknowledged. "And when Barrick figured it out … that's when he started doing his job too well. Suddenly, he was bringing down the boom so hard few magic users remained for either the Brom or the Authority, and all the children were disappearing. He was happy with everyone thinking he was annulling them, it kept the scrutiny off, gave him more room to organize safe places for kids like Thea."

Ramsey indicated Thea James with a tip of his chin.

"I was a child when the Authority began collecting unlicensed Curse Eaters," she explained, clutching the stole tight. "I'd been acquired by the Bobbit family."

I met a Bobbit woman, Inspector Harrow had said.

"He realized what I was, lost my paperwork, then sent me to live with a sympathetic couple on a farm far west with a new name: Theadora James."

"You and Victor know each other."

"I came to Nightglass because Barrick needed someone less volatile than his son to keep an eye on things," she confirmed. "I'd never met the Inspector, but rumors travel fast. I knew he was a wild card, zealous about his father's work. He was different then, not much cuddlier, but he had life in his eyes. Now he's frozen over. Sometimes I worry the only warm thing left in him is hatred."

The involuntary blush pinking my cheeks caught Thea's sharp attention, but I interrupted her comment as it formed.

"So you're an Authority informant, like Cora?"

Hearing Cora's name shook Thea profoundly, a visual quake of shock jostling her. Her reaction was genuine, and I regretted my callousness.

"I'm so sorry, Thea, I wasn't completely sure whether…"

"We weren't," Thea cut me off stiffly. "Not officially. Cora lied to me, I didn't know she was Authority. But I'm not. I was here for Barrick, to help him undermine the Authority's plans, but they caught on. Couldn't do much, because on paper he was doing it all right."

"But they found a way," I said, knowing the end.

Ramsey cast his eyes to the ground, the delivery of his next words difficult.

"Grigori took care of the problem for them," he said.

"What they didn't account for was Victor," Thea's tone carried no affection, but was free of the fear and revulsion I'd previously sensed regarding the Inspector. "He ripped through the Brom enclave in Devin. Scattered them to the four winds, then continued to come to Nightglass under the charade of being there for a good time, but he was out of control. The Authority attempted to rein him in, give him some work to do outside of busting heads."

"He mentioned he was here to investigate the disappearances," I replied. Victor was likely aware of the Authority's attempts to handle him and, true to form, had turned this to his advantage, agreeing to stay in the very location he already wanted to be in.

"We're both concerned he's involved," Ramsey remarked, the gentleness in his wording revealing his awareness that Victor meant something to me. Why else would I have known these details about his life if he hadn't confided them? And a man such as Victor didn't confide easily.

"He is," I said bluntly. There was no point in concealing information.

Thea narrowed her eyes, "How do you know?"

"Victor isn't here to bully the Brom, and I'd wager my life that he doesn't give a rat's ass about the people who disappeared." He hadn't cared that I'd found their clothes, their bones. It occurred to me he'd always known and was merely waiting to verify I hadn't been connected. "He knows what Grigori was doing, knows William is on the same power trip, and he intends to put an end to it tonight."

"He wants to avenge Barrick?" This alarmed Ramsey.

"That's been done," I said, taking the initiative to walk into the night toward the car, which remained running, its tailpipe steaming. "This is retribution for what he was forced to endure, and insurance that it'll never happen to anyone else."

Thea was working to keep up, her heels sticking in the gravel.

"What are you saying? Slow down, Eleanora!"

I didn't heed her, continuing my clip, heart pounding. I was going to share Victor's deepest tragedy, but it was necessary.

"Victor is Thomas Nightglass. Grigori used him to perfect the practice of soldering a Drudge to a human soul."

"That's impossible," Ramsey exclaimed, his barking voice enraged, horrified at the implications. "It would have killed him! Not a single known person survived that joining for more than a few weeks at best, and all of them went mad!"

I wasn't ready to confess Thomas had assistance, that I'd unwittingly become the final link in the alchemical equation that allowed the merger to succeed and endure. I was in a precarious position as it was.

I reached the car, grasping the handle to yank the door wide, but I didn't enter, not yet. "The Drudge you saw today, Thea. One of them was Victor. He was protecting Jack."

"*Which one?*" The question was shrill.

I was preparing to answer when a new, horrible thought bloomed.

"Where's Jack?" I blurted.

"He's with my wife," Ramsey puffed, out of breath from the brisk pace we'd taken across the drive.

"Far from High Tide," Thea assured, still flustered by the information I'd shared.

"Well," I said, bitter. "That's one person we don't have to worry about Victor taking with him to death."

I tried to enter the car, but Thea took hold of me, fingers tight on my arm, pleading.

"If Victor's agenda is to decimate Nightglass, we should let him do it," she implored.

"Didn't you hear me? He's not planning on making it out alive, Thea."

"A man should die if he wants to die."

"*I* don't want him to," I shouted, pulling from her grasp. "He's choosing this because he's angry, he thinks this is the only choice. Like Fiona."

The appeal spoke to Thea's love for my sister and, truthfully, to mine as well. Regardless of Fiona's past decisions, I chose to believe they stemmed from despair, an attempt to regain some control and shield her loved ones from enduring the same pain she'd faced. She'd chosen to protect those she loved by doing horrible things. Victor was no different. Neither was I.

After a stretch of silence in which Ramsey stood with his head bowed, knowing this exchange required privacy he couldn't give, Thea spoke, her tone nearly tender.

"You're too old to be a silly romantic, Eleanora."

Her delivery of this declaration was subdued, making it sound more impatient than rebuking. Like a sister admonishing a naïve younger sibling, whose rosy view of the world was irritating but precious.

"We're grown women," she said. "And I know that look. Victor got under your skirt, and now you're letting him get under your skin too. You're a goddamn fool."

Despite her arguments, she walked around to the opposite door and climbed inside the car, the veneer of a pragmatic woman restored. She glared at Ramsey and me, waiting in the cold.

"Why are you just standing there? We're late for High Tide," she snapped.

CHAPTER THIRTY-FIVE

The streets were hauntingly quiet as we made our way toward Nightglass Estate, a place I'd never once set foot in, and never expected to. Just as Victor had said, the remaining tourists were fearful, barely a handful daring to be out, walking in small clusters, their faces grim.

We were silent, each of us unsettled by the uncertainty of the night ahead. I glanced at Thea, who sat huddled on her side of the car, bracing herself for the impending impact of High Tide. I examined the bruised skin beneath her eye as the light from the street lamps passed by.

"Who hit you?" I asked, delicate with my tone.

"If I tell you, will you murder them like you did that man in Devin?"

"I never meant for that to happen."

"Are you sure?"

In truth, I seldom thought about my motivations for what I'd done to Brock. When I'd presented the cursed cufflinks to him with a flirtatious smile, he'd spent the next few minutes listing all the lewd things he intended to do to me behind Wendy's back, even while the marks of his violence on her body were healing. I hadn't worried about him dying. I hadn't cared if he did.

Though I often reassured myself I'd never intended to cause his death, I'd been aware of the possibility from the beginning.

To make it worse, I'd celebrated the results even as Wendy pointed the authority in my direction.

Thea sighed as though she'd thought as much.

"I don't need that kind of courtesy, Eleanora," she said. Chastened, I grew silent, aware of the person I was, acknowledging I lacked the remorse to regret my decision. We were nearing the estate when Thea added, with a touch of emotion, "Thank you for offering."

We pulled up to Nightglass Estate, its circle drive paved with smooth stone, crowded with vehicles, signifying that despite the threat of something lurking in the dark, this High Tide was not one to miss.

Ramsey made a low oath, directing our attention to a woman who waited in the cold, waving for Ramsey to stop. I recognized her by her silver hair and snowdrop earrings. She wore the same icy blue dress she had on the day we'd met on the street outside Galton's, where she'd offered to take the curse and warned me not to let the Brom have their way.

"Who is that?" I exclaimed, leaning forward in alarm.

"My wife," Ramsey replied as he parked the car and hurried to meet the woman, whose face was contorted in panic.

"But Jack's meant to be with her," Thea leaped from the car. As I followed, an urgent exchange began, arms flailing, and Thea dashed down the walkway to the house. Ramsey's wife regarded me tearfully, making no explanation concerning who she was.

"William has Jack inside," she said. "He tracked the child's magic."

She dissolved into tears, her husband gathering her to him and urging me with a flick of his eyes to follow Thea.

Hundreds of candles in brass candelabras lined the cobbled path leading to the front door. No one waited outside to greet guests, and there was no life inside the foyer, my heels on the marble tile echoing in the deserted space. Here, the candles continued, illuminating every surface, including each step of the gallery staircase rising to the dim second floor. Tonight, the absence of electric lights created a hushed atmosphere, blurring the grand interior in shadow, inviting the eye to follow the glow down the leftmost side hall.

Muffled string music hinted at activity somewhere in the house, but there were no signs of it otherwise. I followed the flickering candlelight trail into the corridor lined with countless doors, set between gilded, framed portraits and intricate ivory sconces, their lights dark. In this stillness, a hum of familiar, blighted magic vibrated, and I was overcome by the sensation of walking through my nightmares, running the twisting, endless halls of Blackwicket House, a devil always nipping at my heels.

I had to make two more turns, passing a wall of Palladian windows facing a night that felt too complete. I could see only my silhouette passing over the panes. At last, I heard voices.

"Shouldn't have tried to hide him." A man snarled.

"Coppe," was the reply, a plea, stunted with lack of oxygen.

My hesitancy evaporated, and I quickened my step until I reached a cross hall—one leading further into the house, the other flanked by candles. In the lightless hall stood Thea, pinned to the wall by a belligerent Coppe, his arm pressing across her throat, her fingers tearing at his sleeve.

I no longer needed to guess who'd put their hands on her.

My magic was still gathering strength, but I didn't need it. The intensity of my anger was sufficient.

"Coppe!" I yelled as I approached, encouraging him to twist his head toward my voice as I drove the heel of my hand into his nose. The crunch was satisfying, a small spray of blood spattering onto my skin from the impact. He roared, clasping his face.

Recovering more quickly than I expected, he lunged for me, but I'd done this before. I caught him between the legs, crushing his flaccid manhood in a grip as tight as I could manage, twisting. Thea acted as he grabbed hold of my hair in his agony, and drove the sharp tip of her thumbnail into his left eye, digging deep.

The pain and disorientation brought Coppe to his hands and knees, howling profanities, shattering the otherworldly silence. Thea clutched me, her breath labored with adrenaline, and I put an arm around her, steadying us both. As Coppe writhed on the floor, blind in one eye, Thea spat on him, then raised her heel, and aimed a blow to the back of his head, dropping him to the floor where he moaned. We left him there, returning to the path of lights, united in our mutual hatred.

"He deserves worse," she rasped as we went, finally finding a steady footing, no longer needing to lean on me.

"He does," I replied, wishing I could make sure he got it, acknowledging for the first time that I was missing a piece of my moral compass.

The music grew steadily louder as we trekked the last steps to an arching double door.

"That's the banquet hall," Thea whispered. "It's where William is hosting High Tide."

"Why is this one special?" I asked, quiet in return.

"It must be related to the Authority breathing down William's neck to show results for his project with Dark Hall children. We need to find Jack."

"No need." The smooth voice spoke from behind, startling us, our arms entwining in shock. William had approached from the shadows, standing a few steps away, dressed in a black dinner suit, a white rose pinned to his lapel.

"He's in his room, Thea. Waiting for you."

As Thea made to go, William stepped in front of her, and she was forced to stand nearly chest to chest with him, head lowered.

"I'm disappointed I had to go on the hunt for him, you know how much this night means to me."

"Don't do anything to him, William. He's just a boy." The cautious pleading in Thea's voice was devastating.

"And I was just a boy," William replied, "When my father showed me the power we could hold in the palm of our hand if we had enough gall. That's what I'm doing for Jack."

He leaned out of her way, "Go tend to him, then bring yourselves to the banquet as planned. Sing your song. I need our guests pliable."

Thea barely glanced at me as she disappeared down the opposite hall we'd emerged from.

"Regarding you," William remarked, stepping closer. I flinched, and he halted his pursuit, choosing to hold a hand to me, beckoning, "Don't be afraid, darling, I won't hurt you."

William Nightglass wanted to be in control and intended for me to surrender to the inevitability of his owning me as his father had owned the other women in my family. Thea had admired my sister for her ability to handle the Nightglass men, and while the thought sickened me, complying seemed the most logical path toward creating an escape route for us all.

I couldn't simply charm him, not after our confrontations. He wouldn't be taken in by it. But I could pretend to be afraid.

I placed my hand in his, and he began leading me from the dining hall, relying on his cane, though his gait was much smoother than I recalled.

"We've had our differences since you arrived," he soothed, "but it's all been a misunderstanding. It's time to put it to rest."

William opened a door for me, motioning me to step into relentless darkness. I couldn't know what was waiting for me.

"Eleanora."

A disagreeable shiver crept over my skin at his ominous tone, which he used to emphasize my lack of choice.

I entered, standing in the darkness for several moments until a lamp flickered to life, its green glass reminiscent of seaweed-choked waters. We stood in a compact, windowless study, the herringbone floors giving way to walnut paneling that stretched to the coffered ceiling. The rear wall was lined with bookshelves, filled to capacity with neatly arranged rows of leather-bound law books and medical volumes. A cold fireplace had been built in as an afterthought, small and unused, and a partner's desk hulked in the center, the only furniture. The space offered little in the way of comfort.

"Did you know this is the very room where I lost my ability to walk without this bastard?" As he neared the desk, he threw his cane into the air, catching it and eyeing the gleaming wood, the gold curve of the handle. My heart skipped a beat.

"Grigori was fashioning Thomas into something great - but it was a difficult transformation. My little brother always kept a stiff upper lip, but I couldn't handle it. One night the codger plied him with so many curses, I heard his ribs snap."

I didn't have to feign being shaken; my hands clenched at my side.

"I came here to his office, begged him to take Tommy to your mother, and he beat me senseless with this very cane. For good measure, he brought his heel down, right here."

He tapped his hip.

"You remember what a big man my father was, don't you, Eleanora?" He chuckled as though it were an amusing memory. "Acetabular fracture. He swore to his death I'd dreamed it up, that it was Thomas who'd done it."

I held no sympathy for this lunatic, but I was sorry for the child William had once been, the boy who'd tried to help and paid so dearly for it.

"I know you think I'm a beast," he said as he reached for the crystal decanter on the desktop, poured the tan liquid into two glasses. "But I'm afraid you're missing some vital information, and I want to clear the air."

He offered a glass.

"No, thank you," I said stiffly.

"Drink it." There was no command in his tone, but it was one. "No hidden curses."

I took the cold crystal in hand, and in a pointless show of annoyance, which benefited William more than myself, I knocked the liquor back in a quick tilt of my head. It burned, and I resisted a cough. I didn't drink, it made it too difficult to keep the shield protecting my magic in position, which William likely knew.

He raised his glass in approval and then followed suit, releasing a hiss of appreciation for the astringent flavor, before trailing his eyes over my features, searching for something familiar. When he touched my face, I resisted the urge to lurch aside, allowing him to trace his thumb along my chin.

"Why do I have a feeling this blood isn't yours?"

I had Coppe's blood on me. The frequency with which I'd worn someone else's gore on my skin was beginning to disturb even me.

"Because it isn't."

My flat response pleased him, and he fought his smile, though there was a twinkle of merriment in his eye.

"You're a dangerous little thing. There was the same fire in Fiona, but she never quite let it free. In the end, I think her restraint destroyed her."

I almost laughed. Instead, I moved to wipe any remaining blood away, revolted by it, but William caught my hand, intertwining his fingers with mine as if I'd been his lover since our youth rather than my sister.

"Don't do that," he said, "It looks too good on you."

"What do you want?" I asked, adding the right amount of tremble to avoid sounding combative.

"What does any man want?" He said, raising my knuckles to his mouth, brushing his lips across them. There was a tingling pressure, magic seeking magic, and I pulled my defenses tight, so he felt nothing when he reached into the void between us. He released my hand, annoyed, and took my glass, setting it on the desk with a hard clink. "A family, someone to love, someone to stand by his side in the trying times. Grief divided, joy multiplied."

As he spoke, he became more aggravated, at last slamming his hand upon the table, the crystal clattering. I jumped slightly.

"Someone who *understands*," he emphasized, leaning on his cane with both hands momentarily, gazing into some far distance I couldn't see. "My father was a lonely man, I watched him struggle with being the only one who recognized the collapse of our society under the weight of arbitrary morality. We feared the Fiend, feared the shadowy magic we were creating when we should have been embracing it. We were so close to breaking free in the war when the anxiety of weak men hobbled our efforts."

There was a manic light in his blue eyes that unsettled me.

"What are you talking about, William," I asked, afraid I already knew.

"Curses, Eleanora," he barked, striking his cane forcefully, the point splitting the wood plank beneath it. After his outburst, he smiled, broad and indulgent, approaching me again with his hand outstretched. "Your family knew better than anyone the strength of magic fueled by suffering, fed by our most volatile emotions."

His fingers traced my hairline, feathering along my jaw.

"The Authority is afraid of all of it, terrified someone will take hold of this incredible resource, dethrone them. Magic didn't flee from us, Eleanora, it was locked out, and the only way to break through is to harness what we've been left with. That's what tonight is for: showing the weakest of our people that change requires discomfort, safety requires sacrifice, and greatness a piece of our souls."

He kissed me then, his lips cold, corpse-like. His scent was overpowering, a combination of damp earth, with a sweetness suggestive of formaldehyde. Layered below it, the disturbingly familiar hints of natural decay, like the forest floor in autumn. Like Victor. To my everlasting gratitude, he didn't decide to taste me further, didn't attempt to part my lips. His magic pulsed, sickly and ravenous, but I held my defenses firm. Eventually, he drew his mouth from mine, but kept close.

"You smell like Fiona," he muttered against my hair, and the corners of my mouth tugged down.

"Tell me what to expect tonight, please," I asked, hoping my efforts to show willingness had softened him.

"You and I are going to show them how curses connect us to inimitable power, how stupid they've been for turning a blind eye to it all this time. Jack's the key."

I went rigid. William was going to attempt what his father had all those years ago, the efforts he'd made that had succeeded because I hadn't wanted my friend to die.

"William, you can't."

He shushed me, wrapped his arm around my waist, pulling me against him. Despite his injury, his closeness made it clear he wasn't impotent. "It's going to be a beautiful night, and later, when we have more privacy, we'll celebrate our victory."

My stomach curdled with the alcohol, bile rising in my throat as he pressed his lips to my neck. My insides screamed, and I released a breath to relieve the repulsion. William was as mad as Grigori ever had been, wearing the shadow of a man he'd hated well.

"Yes," he murmured. "We're going to do amazing things together."

The impulse to bite off his ear was significant, but I was saved from having to restrain myself by the arrival of someone unexpected.

Victor's hulk filled the doorway. He wore a double-breasted topcoat as dark as the midnight sea, lined with red silk, with a matching cravat neatly tucked in his breast pocket. He looked devastating, destructive, and furious as he watched William kiss my throat. My startled gasp was sincere, and Nightglass raised his head.

"Ah, Harrow. Is everything ready?" he asked, unbothered by the intrusion.

"It has been," Victor replied sharply, his golden eyes fixed on me, the muscle in his jaw clenched tight. I wanted to explain why I was there, explain why William was so close, why his hands and mouth were on me. "Thea's out there now, getting them loose. You have one last opportunity to impress the Authority, Nightglass, before they shut everything down, so don't choke on your own cock."

I ached to run to him, to warn him Jack was here, but he'd already gone.

"Hm," William rumbled, "I sensed a bit of tension there. I admit an Authority inspector fucking a Curse Eater seems extensively unprincipled, even for me."

"William," I grated, finally unable to control my disgust, quailing away only to be caught at the back of my neck, held, William taking so much pleasure in my discomfort that he grinned.

"I don't mind if you take lovers," he said with a hint of menace. "As long as you come when I call, there'll be no shackles required. And if your proclivities keep an Authority strongman pacified, I won't pretend I'm bothered by it."

"Was that your arrangement with Fiona?" I wondered how she'd been able to stand it, realizing it was Thea who'd made it bearable.

"It was, and she played her role very well until Roark disappeared. I miss her."

His face twisted, expression unsettling, a battle of genuine emotion so deep it was unfathomable, warring with a kind of disgust, as if he were appalled by his own feelings. He winced as he had at the funeral home, releasing me and leaning in the direction of his injury, pain momentarily racking his body.

"Wait on the mezzanine, in the banquet hall, up the foyer stairs and straight ahead," he huffed, his voice tight and peculiar. He kept his back to me, slightly hunched. "You'll do what you have to do, or Jack will die, and if you play your part well, I'll even consider changing my mind about gutting Thea for trying to keep the boy from me."

I understood my sister's decision to murder Grigori. I longed for a weapon—something I could use to ensure William would never harm anyone again. But I'd come unprepared.

I didn't hesitate to leave.

CHAPTER THIRTY-SIX

Thea's dulcet voice and sensual magic were already rippling through the corridors as I dashed through murky halls in search of someone—anyone—who could help me prevent this before it began. But the house was abandoned, residents and guests already in place for the banquet. Unable to gauge how much longer I had until William expected me to be present, I went to assume my station with reluctance.

After ascending the grand staircase, I followed a faint light into a vestibule, where I found the person I'd fervently prayed to any god who would listen to see again.

Inspector Harrow was positioned in the narrow space, gazing through a cracked door, the entrance to the mezzanine. He resembled a specter, observing the living from the shadows.

"Victor." His name was an invocation.

He caught me as I rushed toward him, but not to embrace. Instead, he grasped my bare arms, holding me away from his body as though the idea of feeling me against him was repugnant.

Despite my fury, I debased myself by opening my magic to his with no hesitation, tenderly searching for the connection it yearned for. Still, he remained hidden, unresponsive, devastating me.

"You couldn't resist, could you?" he said, demeanor icy.

"What do you think William would have done if I hadn't shown up?" I'd gone hoarse with anger. "Victor, he's insane.

He's going to attempt replicating Grigori's experiment, with Jack as the vessel, and me as the fucking battery. Somehow, he worked out that I was the one who gave you that magic."

"Because I told him," he replied, low. "Grigori had me locked in a fucking *closet* in an old third-floor guest room, so no one would realize I was still alive. But William would come to the door in the middle of the night and talk to me. He'd asked me what I'd done to make it through. Our father's eye was on him to become the next vessel, and he was afraid, wanted to learn how to survive it. He was my brother, so I told him the truth."

I was ashamed of the sense of betrayal I felt when there was no reason for it.

"And he told Grigori."

"He didn't," Victor said, and there was a mournful affection in his voice; love that lingered for someone who'd become unrecognizable. "He kept it a secret. There'd have been no stopping Grigori Nightglass if he'd known. But it appears William was just waiting to use it to his advantage."

I put my hand over his.

"We can walk away from this. Don't you have your gun? We can kill William, we can…"

"Half of the people attending are high-ranking officials of the Authority, Eleanora. Even if William is dead, this will continue to go on, more children like Jack will be yanked from their beds and brought to this wasteland to become cursed weapons. That was Grigori's dream — an army of Drudge with physical bodies to deliver the most effective destruction. There will always be a Grigori or a William waiting in the wings, and the only way to stop the spread of this is to burn the field."

"But you don't have to be kindling."

"I want to be," he said roughly, shaking me once, his cool composure rupturing. "I'm a *creature*, Eleanora. Half of me is a monster that feeds off human depravity, and I have less and less interest in restraining it. There has to be an end to it."

I selfishly rejected his desire to be free of the lot he'd been assigned. Instead of wrenching from his grasp, I placed my hands on his chest, but he didn't allow me to move any closer than this.

"You're not a monster, Victor. You're the inevitable, glorious outcome of survival. If you do this, maybe the Authority will be destroyed, but the Veil won't be, and your sacrifice will only prove them right. They'll toast your death, pat themselves on the back and tell everyone they knew magic was evil, and then move on to wipe out every person like us. You'll hand them that victory if you dig your own grave."

I'd kept my volume low, not wanting to attract attention and shorten the last minutes I had to persuade Victor to choose a different path.

"I see," he growled, the menace of the sound amplified by the lack of light, the circumstance of our standing so close at the threshold of a battle neither of us wanted to fight. "I should live so that I might be a looming consequence, a weapon for whichever ideology sounds prettiest?"

"That is the most witless thing that's ever come out of your mouth," I hissed, incensed, pounding a fist into his sternum to relieve the fury his willful obtusity inspired. At last he pulled me closer, but it was only to prevent me from striking him again. We glared at each other, my eyes welling.

"You should live because you deserve to," I said, refusing to look away, venting my remaining anger through my words. "You shouldn't die here surrounded by people who don't give a damn about you. Don't force me to suffer your loss a second time, because you can't be bothered to acknowledge what's in front of you."

The dull light from the banquet hall illuminated half of his face, casting the rest in deep shadow. For a moment, both of his aspects merged, and he stood before me, whole.

"What's in front of me, Eleanora?" he asked, meeting my ferocity with calm, his voice a murmur.

I was poised to tell him it was me, but I had nothing to offer Victor. We were no longer children racing bugs through a garden, or competing to locate the smoothest stone to throw into the sea. We weren't sitting shoulder to shoulder, hopelessly nurturing untamed flowers filled with curses—a useless idea dreamt up by my mother to distract us from the fact that we were drowning, and that help was never coming. In truth, our futures were bleak. Victor was right; even if William was gone, the Authority wouldn't be. Everything awaiting us involved a fight. Yet for the first time, I *wanted*, with all the life-affirming hunger a soul is meant to feel. I wanted Victor near, wanted the scent to linger, to penetrate my skin. I craved the warmth and shock of him, the surge of magic that rose in me when he leaned close. I'd experienced desire in both my body and beyond it, a desire that compelled me to remember I was more than just blood and bones, destined to be swallowed by the earth.

"I want some bit of happiness before I hand myself over to the fate I've been dealt. Even a moment of that is worth fighting the tide for. Let life be our revenge, Victor. Please."

He didn't touch me again, but his magic, which until now had been restrained, reached for me, but Thea's song was over, and she introduced, with warbling flair, William Nightglass.

Victor withdrew.

"When the Drudge come, keep your guard tight and get out," he said. As he stepped around me, his fingers brushed mine so softly it might have been an accident. "There'll only be one window open; everything else is sealed. Follow Thea and Jack, they know the way. Then find the thing that makes the fight worth it, Ellie."

"Victor." My voice trembled, but he moved on.

Thea slipped through the door, strung tight.

"Get out there," she hissed. "He's coming up."

I surrendered to inevitability, hoping the resulting numbness would protect me from whatever came next. Thea entwined her hand with mine, but instead of the softness of her skin, there was the cold, hard touch of metal—a pairing knife she must have swiped from a table.

"If there were ever a time to commit murder, I suppose it's now. I only wish I'd had the strength."

"You had the strength not to," I said. With both tenderness and regret for the moments I'd missed, for the chance I'd once had to be Thea's family, I kissed her cheek.

"She loved you so much, Eleanora," Thea whispered.

"I know," I replied, then entered the hall, holding a knife against my hip, obscured by the chiffon pleats.

The balcony where I stood encircled a two-story room of white marble and mahogany. Twin crystal chandeliers, splendid marvels of gold and glass, sparkled with candlelight, their electric bulbs dim. In the center of the mezzanine, a staircase ascended, flanked on each side by three-armed candelabras on each step. Victor hadn't been overstating when he'd said William had a penchant for the dramatic. Nonetheless, the gloomy ambiance served a dual purpose, hiding the identities of the High Tide attendees below. Adorned in lavish attire, they sat at banquet tables spanning the gleaming alabaster floor, its sheen reflecting a golden glow beneath them, like hellfire. Their faces were additionally veiled by black silk masks, obscuring their eyes and noses from anyone who'd report on those present.

The hall's only windows, five arranged along the rightmost wall, were veiled by heavy velvet curtains in the shade of absinthe, shielding the covert society formed among the Brom and Authority from the outside world. Those present, immersed in their own corruption, showed regard for neither the people nor the magic they viewed as chaff for their fires.

William stood at the base of the steps with Jack by his side. The boy was dressed in a fashion mirroring William's suit, unruly hair neatly combed in a style better suited to a grown man. As I came into view, all heads pivoted in my direction, and William beamed up at me, as if I were his bride, raising an arm to present me to the guests.

"Ms. Blackwicket comes to us as an angel in our hour of need. She's agreed to be here tonight because she believes in this mission we've chosen to undertake. One that will improve the lives of all in this room, including young Jack." He placed his hand fondly on the boy's shoulder. "Each of you here has already given a piece of yourselves to this worthy project. Your trust. And it's with my deepest gratitude that I deliver to you tonight, with the help of my two assistants, the product of my father's vision and many years of your most gracious support. Jack, the vessel."

Jack pulled a jewelry box from his pocket and offered it to William. Inside lay a bracelet featuring familiar, multicolored facets. This had been the vehicle of Ms. Rosley's doom, stolen from my bags by Darren, who subsequently returned it to its original owner.

"Many of you doubt the value of curses, concerned about their instability. Yet with determination and practice, they can be wielded for good and are, as I'll demonstrate, the most potent form of magic." William lifted the bracelet to catch the flickering light, and with the poise of a seasoned Curse Eater, he summoned the curse lingering within. It emerged as a vaporous red cloud, and with a deep inhale, like a gasp for fresh air after a century of suffocation, William absorbed it. I clutched the low banister, steadying myself.

A gasp of alarm arose from the crowd, calming when

William handed his cane to Jack and turned to the stairs, which his injury would make it difficult to climb without assistance. Nevertheless, he mounted them with the ease of a man whose hip had never been crushed by his abusive father.

The guests erupted in awe and applause as William Nightglass ascended to the second-floor balcony, with Jack following obediently behind. Upon reaching the top, he beckoned me to meet him, triumphant. Keeping the knife concealed in the folds of my dress, I approached, facing the crowd in a mimic of unity.

It was then that I saw Victor entering the hall through the double doors on the first floor. He paused, looking up at me with an unreadable expression. Then he went to work, unnoticed, sealing the door shut in the same manner he'd locked me inside Blackwicket House, stitching together the seams by encouraging long-dead wood to revive and grow together. If William noticed him, he either didn't care or this had been part of the event. I glanced at Jack, the boy standing stiff as a board, his hands clenched into fists.

"Curses, when handled by a body trained in resilience, create strength. My father's methods were long misunderstood, and his intentions had always been to create a society undeterred by hardship, free of fragility and fear. And here I stand as an example of his success. But I'm sure you aren't yet convinced. Before we continue, there's a small matter I must see to."

William faced me. I thought he sought to take both of my hands, compromising my hidden weapon, but he took only one as though he'd ask me to dance.

"I'm afraid I brought Ms. Blackwicket here under false pretenses tonight. She's very private, but this moment is too precious to keep to ourselves. It is my greatest hope to be bound eternally with this woman, sharing a soul, as well as a devotion that will sustain us for this lifetime, and all the lifetimes to come."

CHAPTER THIRTY-SEVEN

Complete shock rooted me to the spot, and I searched for any sign of jest on William's face, but all I found was a besotted softness that sat unnatural on his expression, combined with the horrific sight of his irises, gone white, creating the illusion that his pupils floated in the milky void of his eyes. The audience erupted with delight, along with a small murmur of surprise.

"William, you can't be serious," I said, but he was undeterred.

"Present your magic to me, my love."

I glanced at Jack, who watched with wide eyes, his uncertainty making him look his age, despite the costume of maturity he'd been dressed in. If I gave in to William, did as he asked, I'd be showing this child the only thing to do when standing before tyranny was crumble.

"No." My refusal echoed.

William raised a brow, and I thrust the knife toward the soft underside of his chin. Predicting the attack, he caught my wrist, his magic igniting like embers and burning my skin until I dropped the knife in agony, crying out.

"Oh, but I'm sure you mean yes."

His features became a rile of contortions, the telltale sign of something other moving beneath his flesh. As I'd seen in Victor, the very shape of his bones began to change, transforming his face into a monstrous vision, jaw unlocking, stretching. From his mouth emerged the hands of a Drudge. It rose, its face nothing beyond its squashed skull and two lipless mouths, teeth gnashing as it plunged toward me.

My defenses were raised, but the onslaught of this malevolent power was far stronger than any I'd encountered. It tore at me until at last it touched a tender spot, and my magic welled. Grabbing hold, it triggered my response to consume, to welcome it into my body. The screaming of guests was followed by the clattering of chairs, shattering of glassware as people attempted to flee from the atrocity unfolding in front of their eyes.

William held me as my knees buckled, the Drudge clambering, the violation of it oily and alive. It had a voice, which chittered as it burrowed.

Mine. Ours. Forever.

Feelings not belonging to me took root: hatred, lust, vile visions of dismembering every soft human body here, swallowing their screams. I was aware of Jack yelling, beating William with his fists, hysteria filling every corner of the hall, and I lost myself, my soul making room for this thing to inhabit me.

The deep, eldritch echoes of Dark Hall penetrated the chaos, freezing everything in place. Jolted from his trance, William's assault came to an abrupt end, his connection to me dissected. He dropped me in favor of the new, riotous view in the hall. I collapsed into a near-senseless heap, struggling to maintain consciousness, resisting the abyss of corruption whispering and pulsing in me. Dominating the center of the pandemonium was another Drudge, Victor's, towering over the guests, unleashing from itself a torrent of curses, flooding the room wave after wave. They rose in a dense fog, fluctuating with ancient power, taking on shapes reminiscent of creatures emerging from a primordial swamp.

The curses from Blackwicket House.

This is where they had gone, swallowed by Victor to be deposited here, where they had nothing to placate them, no access to Dark Hall's calming hum, and no hope of a Curse Eater coming to free them. Their natural instincts to feed on magic had consumed them, and they crawled their way up the guests. Candles had been knocked from their tables, catching tablecloths aflame. One rolled to a curtain, which ignited with eagerness, begging to burn.

William gazed in exaltation at the unfolding chaos.

"Look, Fiona," he cried, but it was not just my sister's name he called. In voices of varying tone representing the creature he harbored in his bones, rose the discordant vocalization of each name of the Blackwicket women. *Fora, Isolde, Fiona, Eleanora.*

The knife lay nearby, and I reached for it as Victor's Drudge turned towards the stairs, wading among the devastation. As my fingers closed around the weapon, Thea's voice called, panic-stricken and urgent.

"Jack!"

The spell of shock broken, the boy jerked his head up to find Thea waiting in the doorway, a handkerchief covering her mouth and nose, smoke separate from the inferno below billowing from the hallway. Other parts of the Nightglass estate were ablaze. He ran to her, and as they fled, she spared a sorrowful glance in my direction. She wouldn't help me. To her, I was already gone.

Using the banister, I dragged myself to my feet. Victor caught sight of me, slowed, waiting to see what I would do. Every nerve fired, muscles seizing with the agony of the curse I'd been forced fed. I didn't expect to survive this, but I was going to try. The next part of my plan wasn't difficult. The beast in me wanted it, wanted to drink blood like wine. With renewed strength, I lunged at William, plunging the knife into his neck, below his ear. There was a vile popping noise as the point penetrated flesh and muscle, a spout of warm blood as I used my weight to drag the blade down past his Adam's apple, until it stuck firm in his collarbone. He grasped the handle of the knife as I let go, trying to pull it free, his mouth opening to shout, gurgling instead.

I shoved him.

He tumbled down the stairs, head over heels, his body breaking as he went. His spine was crooked by the time he reached the bottom, disappearing as he was enveloped by the red smog, which had caught fire and churned together, a sea of flames. Victor stood in the middle, watching me, the tongues of fire lapping at his legs.

Despite the desire of the thing I harbored to watch the horror continue to unfold, I didn't want to, couldn't, witness Victor burning to death. I stumbled from the mezzanine into the smoke-filled hall, the strangling veil of it mimicking the foul miasma within my body. I crashed against a hall table, the vase atop it shattering as it fell from its perch. I called on my magic, but the Drudge William had given me a portion of constricted, smothering it.

Broken. Used. Nothing. Rotten Nothing.

Whatever this was—this thing William had made—it was sentient and cruel, urging me to submit to my dismal thoughts so my magic would spoil. It didn't want magic. It wanted more curses. My awareness of this was of little use; the pain in my wrist, the skin shining and red where William had seared the flesh, mingled with the ghastly whispers in my head, recounting every horrible memory—everyone who'd ever hurt me, everything I'd ever done to hurt someone else. Its voice was mine.

Lie down and die.

The thing keeping me on my feet was the vague knowledge that this thing wanting me to die was reason enough not to.

Oxygen was sparse, and I was sightless in the deadly smoke, searching for doors. At last I found a handle, the door opening, allowing me to stumble into an empty bedroom. There was a balcony door here, glass, and I staggered to it. It was unlocked, the handle moving freely, but still it didn't budge. Magic held it closed.

Coughs and sobs warred in my throat as I slid to the floor, inches away from fresh air and escape.

I wanted my mother. My sister. Someone to comfort me in the last moments of my life. But Blackwicket women were fated to die alone.

As awareness slipped away, I was jostled, sat upright. Cool hands passed along my skin, misty and soothing amidst the haze of smoke. I lacked the strength to respond, but managed to open my eyes a sliver to the hazy silhouette of a woman. Like water on parched lips, strands of foreign magic wove through the wailing cyclone of Drudge, plucking at fragments as they flowed—one strand, then another. The tainted power trembled, seeking to free itself, remaining ensnared. But this power wasn't merely binding the Drudge, it was restoring what had been drained, revitalizing me as I'd once done for Victor.

The giver began to undo the Drudge from me. It was painful going. The stranger didn't take it all, but relieved the horrible trilling of voices. More aware, I strained my eyes, attempting to focus on the face of my savior.

Auntie stared back, the muscle of her jaw working her exposed teeth back and forth, as though she would speak, but only a trembling whistle emitted, high and sad as a ghost keening for the lost.

A further noise, heavy footsteps, startled Auntie away, sending her fleeing just before a new figure entered, arms encircling me, lifting me to a broad bare chest, topcoat and shirt in charred ribbons. Victor. The jarring of movement rocked me towards unconsciousness, before the sudden frigid bite of fresh air shocked me awake. We'd arrived in another room, its balcony door standing wide—Thea and Jack's exit.

Victor jumped from the balcony onto a sloping canopy, sliding, and falling the single story to the ground, with me clutched to him. His body altered, changing partially into the inhuman thing that allowed him to land with little impact. I drew endless breaths of winter air, coughing and retching, and still he kept running, putting space between us and the house, now a pyre in the night.

Victor's face was gaunt, nearly skeletal in the aftermath of what he'd released, all the magic he'd parted with to deliver retribution to the Authority. He'd been planning on giving it all, but hadn't.

Voices raised, growing louder.

"Holy mother, Victor!" Ramsey's voice. "Did you do this?"

"Not the fire," he replied.

"Oh, Eleanora," Hannah's hands fluttered around my face.

"We can't find Thea and Jack, are they out?" Ramsey demanded.

"I saw them running across the back lawn when I was searching for Eleanora," Victor said.

"We need to get you both somewhere safe."

"Not Blackwicket House. Please." I croaked, never wanting to set eyes on the house again, to set foot in the place I'd once so loved that held secrets and horrors far beyond the curses of my childhood.

"But we can't go into town, and the train isn't running. Ramsey, we have to take them through right now," Hannah argued, though it made no sense.

"Not in their state, woman, they'd never make it."

"I know somewhere," Victor said. "Come, before someone notices us."

"I don't think there's anyone left to," Hannah replied solemnly.

Hurting from my injuries, both magical and otherwise, but far too glad to be alive for a woman who didn't deserve to be, I laid my head against Victor's chest and stopped fighting the dark.

CHAPTER THIRTY-EIGHT

I floated in the meadow of gray gloaming between life and death, with the pull of both suspending me in stasis. I could see nothing in the murky haze of this realm, either real or imagined, but I wasn't alone. Voices spoke in tongues I didn't know, murmuring in the middle distance, swirling like eddies in tide pools. And there was the smooth brush of the Drudge, a serpent winding through water. When it grew too bold, slithering over my stomach, a warm light, reminiscent of those that flashed in the immense vastness of Dark Hall, startled it away. And so I waited, for a lifetime, two, wrapped in the cycle of curses and magic, neither of them staking claim.

When I could sense my body — the smoky rawness in my throat, muscles sore from being tightly wound, the tingling in my wrist where magic had burned flesh — I knew I was being released.

I opened my eyes to a rough-hewn beech-wood ceiling, abused by the elements. The nip in the air was kept at bay by the fire roaring in the iron fireplace nearby. I'd been placed on an old sailor's cot, tucked under blankets smelling mildly of mildew and wood smoke. The sound of the sea was persistent, a white, even wash of waves hitting rocky shores. It sang a song that felt like home, even when I didn't have one anymore.

The ruined dress had been removed and lay discarded in the corner of the small room, and I wore my silk slip, skin washed clean of soot. Someone had unpinned my hair, rinsed the foulness from it with seawater, and left it to dry, coiling at my shoulders.

The traumatized skin of my wrist was smooth, scarred, and shining from the magical cauterization of the flesh, the outline of my fingers obscuring once-visible branches of veins. It should have been agony, but the wound appeared to have already healed, a mark I would bear forever in memory of William Nightglass.

As for the Drudge I'd been strong-armed into accommodating, Auntie had taken most of it, which was a mystery I'd consider another day when my emotional energy wasn't so depleted that I felt like a shell. What was left of the Drudge lay curled like a viper in its den, interested more in maintaining its residence than taking ground. For now.

The rest of the space was simple: a single room with no electric lights, a small copper sink, and a heavy wooden table. I was in a dock house, part of a row of bare quarters built for the sailors who had worked the ships. Although it had contradicted our mother's rules, Fiona and I had played in these houses, imagining someday having safe, humble homes of our own, our dreams small and impossible.

Near an open window overlooking the pebbled shore, Victor leaned, arms crossed, dressed in a worn cotton undershirt and a pair of battered corduroy work pants, favored by dockworkers from times gone by. His hair was untamed, curling at his temples, brushing the top of his scarred cheek. He gazed at the waves, golden light from either sunrise or sunset illuminating him with a divine glow, wisps of white escaping his mouth like smoke from an absent cigarette.

He was curse eating.

When I sat up, Victor's trance was broken, and he turned his head my way.

We stared at each other; the silence punctuated by the creak of the house's stilted foundation in the winter wind.

"Ramsey and Hannah are searching for Thea and the boy," he said. "They'll be back at sunrise, and we'll discuss what to do."

The comment was pragmatic, logical, making me aware the golden glow indicated nightfall rather than dawn.

"How long have I been asleep?"

"A full day," he replied, "less than you need. Get more rest. I'll keep watch."

Instead of lying back as instructed, I stood, pulling the blanket with me to offer some cover for my near-nakedness. Victor uncrossed his arms, preparing to catch me if I took a tumble.

"My injuries?" The words were accusatory, as if I were angry someone had stolen the proof of what I'd survived.

"Hannah's an adept healer. She was capable of things I've never seen." His gaze dipped to my wrist, and I raised it, placing my hand upon the melted flesh, smooth to the touch. "She tended to you, and pretty aggressively denied me entry until you were tucked in the cot."

I was trying to regain my bearings, accept that Victor was alive, that I was alive, that we were here together while William was dead, and the Authority was in shambles.

"You didn't die," I managed, tears overtaking me.

In two swift steps, Victor was cradling my face in his powerful hands—hands so often used to force compliance, to wound, now gentle, his thumbs moving to wipe my cheeks with a fondness that further wrecked me.

"I saw what was in front of me," he said, echoing my words, though his tone remained emotionless, his demeanor as grave as usual. "A fierce woman in gold chiffon stabbing a vile man in the neck with a dinner knife. Only a lunatic would give that up."

Relief and affection alloyed with lingering panic and fury. Still fed by a curse I feared might be permanent, anger won, and I knocked his hand away, the blanket dropping from my shoulders.

"I'd like to stab you too for putting me through that, you selfish…."

He enfolded me in his arms, the embrace ardent, his mouth claiming my rage as much as quieting it. Tired of repressing my needs, I lowered my defenses, permitting him to plunder my magic, if it meant I could feel him alive. He responded with little restraint, his power delving deep into the essence of me, causing the curse to tremble and retreat. We fed from each other, giving and taking until I was nothing more than molten need.

He ended the kiss in an effort to anchor himself.

"I am selfish," he said, voice jagged. "I deserve to be dust, but as long as you still breathe, there's something in this life I want, and I'm going to choose it always."

"Choose it now, Victor," I said, fingers clutching his undershirt, my flush of anger giving way to something much more demanding.

He led a hand down my back, coming to rest at the base of my spine.

"What are you asking for, Eleanora?" He murmured.

I'd done so many things I'd never thought myself capable of, yet in the face of genuine desire, there was a halting I couldn't overcome.

Victor's laugh was thunder deep in his chest.

"You're still struggling to tell me what you want. But if you can kill a man, you can ask me to fuck you."

I sucked in a sharp breath, annoyed at being found out, but he gripped my backside, bruising, pinning me close and inviting me to appreciate the hardened length of him against my belly.

"I've imagined you saying it since catching you chasing noises in the hall. It was a trial to be in that house at night."

The scratching in the night, the long marks on the wooden door frame, like a prisoner clawing at a cell wall.

"Restraint was hard to come by with you mere feet away." His voice was husky, lips lingering at my cheek, lowering to press along my jaw. "Protected by nothing but a flimsy wooden door. I wanted to taste you."

He ran his tongue along my neck, constricting the muscles in my core, encouraging the pooling wet heat.

"We've both wanted to taste you," he rasped, fluctuating from his familiar timbre to the register I'd heard once in the tower, the rustling din of every destructive force in nature.

I surrendered.

"Then please do it. Fuck me, finally," I begged, foregoing pride for necessity.

The words hadn't fully formed when he seized my thighs, lifting me so my legs parted around his waist, pivoting to deposit me on the kitchen table. For a chaotic moment, we were only our hands, grasping at fabric. Victor removed his shirt as I unclasped the belt at his waist, and when his beautiful, battered chest was in view, I leaned into him, running a hand along the notched skin, darting my tongue across a dark nipple, nipping it brazenly.

Victor swore, taking my slip and yanking it roughly over my head, my arms forced to raise and reveal to him the line of my body, bare breasts forming goosebumps, crests growing hard with both eagerness and the cold. Taking my wrists in one hand, he kept them hoisted above my head, leaning over me to return the favor, pinching a pink crown in his lips, the exquisite pain wilding me. My magic was writhing as I watched, lust-addled, as Victor continued to torture my breast with his attention, fondling the sensitive skin, circling the pink areola with his tongue, flicking the tight peak, deliberately provoking me to imagine other parts he could be worshiping.

Unable to use my hands, I tried to slide further forward, toward him, but he was too far from me.

"I need to feel you Victor, don't tease me," I grated, and he had mercy, releasing my wrists.

"Very well," he invited, removing the unfastened belt from its loops in a harsh pull before unfastening the button. "Feel me, Curse Eater."

He towered, broad and destructive, the firm plane of his stomach narrowing, framing the trail of black hair disappearing into the loosened waist, where his stiff length remained confined. I pushed the trousers from his hips, liberating him.

I led my hand up his shaft, beginning at the thick base.

As with the first time I'd held his rigid cock in my hand, I was daunted by his size, aware he'd restrained himself when I'd tantalized him with my mouth. This memory turned me liquid, and I dipped my head to take the swollen tip, sucking.

His groan was low, and he dragged my lips open with his thumb, though he didn't encourage me to accept him further. I taunted the head, licking along the ridge as I handled him. He kept his hold light, giving me freedom to acquaint myself with the shape and taste of him without taking claim of my throat, raw from our ordeal. I reveled in pleasuring him, the catch of his breath punctuated by an obscene instruction I obediently followed. At length, his grip on me grew tighter, but before his composure fractured, he withdrew.

"Let me look at you," he said, his tone coarse, guiding me to recline. I rested my weight on my hands, chest arching. He brushed his knuckles down the side of my ribs, instructing me to raise my hips so he could divest me of the last remaining item of fabric separating us, my linen underwear. When I was bare, his gaze brushed like feathers across every soft slope, drinking me in.

As I'd already determined he appreciated, I brought one heel to the table, opening myself to his view, running my fingers from my abdomen, through the curls of my mound, shuddering as they slipped along the hill of nerves, already screaming for release. He captured my hand in his, bending to replace my fingers with his mouth.

I cried out, the transition so sudden, I hadn't anticipated the sensation. As his tongue worked competently, the muscles and bones of his back shifted, shoulder blades momentarily jutting as his more ruinous soul rose. He grasped my hips, pulling me further forward as he skillfully devastated me. Tightening my fingers in his dark hair, I pressed him ever closer, entreating him to continue with greedy, insistent pleas. Just as my end began to build, he ceased his ministrations, surging up to besiege my mouth, the taste of me on his lips. But there was no room for complaint, because his insistent length rested against the tender flesh of my sex. He purposefully avoided my wet slit, sliding his cock over the sensitive bud of my sex in slow, torturous strokes.

I couldn't protest, my mouth too occupied with his, his magic coursing in punishing, rhythmic waves, like the pulse of bodies moving together.

At last, he positioned himself at my entrance. I grabbed hold of his sturdy shoulders, half in unhinged hunger and half in anxiety of what I was about to experience.

His body tremored, form oscillating. The divine pressure of him, so close to claiming me, receded.

"No! Don't stop," I implored.

"I can feel your uncertainty, Eleanora," he murmured.

"It's not uncertainty, Victor, for god's sake." I couldn't explain my trepidation without seeming like a virginal twit.

"I need to be sure you understand what you're risking," he cautioned. "If you give yourself-it will be to all of me."

He was talking about the Drudge, the monstrous side of him surfacing, driven by lust. I'd already been held by that body. Yet as I looked into Victor's face, I bore no apprehension.

"I give willingly," I insisted. "Please don't pull away. Not after everything that's happened."

"I could hurt you."

"I don't care," I said recklessly, body throbbing, aching for him.

"Is this what you want?" In his voice, husky and strained, was anguish, a loathing for himself that I couldn't bear. "To be defiled by a Drudge?"

My heart split open.

"There's only you, Victor." I passed my fingers along the scar on his cheek. "In whatever form, I crave you more than life."

He lifted a hand to my face, brought his lips to mine.

"Then I yield to you, Eleanora," he said, and in one smooth shift of his hips, he broke the barrier, thrusting into me. In the gorgeous, blinding moment of shock, I moaned, clenching, strung so tight even this was almost enough. My body spread to form to him, and he filled me so completely that there was barely room for breath in my body.

He unsheathed himself to the tip, driving forward again, setting a rhythm of harsh, shattering strokes. My legs ached beautifully where he held me open to him, the vicious impacts rocking the sturdy table beneath me. In the fire's glow, a primal magic flickered across our skin, summoned by our fierce will to exist in a world where neither of us was welcome.

I gazed down to witness the shadowy merger of our bodies, and the sight sustained my ascent to an incredible height. The angle of my hips allowed him to stroke where I needed, the size of him promising the elusive place couldn't be missed.

"Be a good girl, Eleanora," he growled, sensing in our connection that my desire was coming to a crescendo. I was desperate for release while simultaneously yearning for the bliss to continue escalating forever.

"No," I panted. "Not yet."

He released a harsh breath, a laugh, never easing the rhythm.

"There'll be another," he promised darkly, and the corrupted magic that had remained latent emerged, its intensity snapped my will along with the purposeful circling of Victor's thumb across my clit. Overcome by the onslaught, and with his name on my lips, I broke apart, the climax a salvation.

I arched, and Victor pulled me close, slowing his onslaught to savor the quake of my body while I clung to him, enduring the waves of euphoria. His heartbeat drummed vigorously, and I pressed my face into his warm neck, kissing his throat. He maneuvered me twice more along his shaft, lengthening my fading rapture, enjoying the final pulses of my orgasm around his arousal, which he hadn't relieved.

This left me with a foggy sense of frustration.

"Victor, you didn't..."

"We're not done."

Raising me off him, he changed our positions, flipping me so his length, still hard as steel, was pressed into my back. He directed his hand between my breasts, fingers climbing to my throat, rocking me forward onto his arm until I bent at the waist, raising me from my feet to perch me backwards on his lap.

He sat me firmly onto him, sheathing deep. The noise I made was cut short, not from the pressure upon my throat, but from the eruption of new desire. Inspiring my enthusiasm was Victor's terrible power, risen to gorge on my magic, the pain of this tugging no less erotic than that of Victor's teeth on my breast.

I leaned forward to brace myself on his legs, and found them corded with muscle that undulated, growing. He was changing, his body elongating beneath mine, the snap and cracking of bones deviating into new positions, startling me. The obelisk of his manhood was not immune to the transformation, and I stretched to accommodate him, overfull. I moaned, digging my fingers into the hard flesh of his legs, which had become thick and fluted as the trunks of hornbeams.

"Having second thoughts?" His phantasmal voice caressed my ear.

He was too much, but still I wanted him.

"No," I breathed, "Let me have every part of you."

He rumbled an approval as he drew me to his chest, resting me long against him, my thighs splayed wide over the width of his massive lap. The red mist of depraved magic coiled around us, nipping at my skin with cool touches, creating tideways of magic in all the most sensitive locations.

"Hold on to me, Curse Eater."

I did as instructed, raising an arm behind me to grasp at the back of his neck, thick and knotted with sinew. Saturated in my previous climax, he moved in me, the friction equal measures disorienting and ecstatic. This side of Victor didn't care for restraint; it claimed recklessly, and I could barely do more than cling to him as he plundered my cunt. Despite this overwhelm, or perhaps because of it, pleasure built, my body sensitive from its previous rupture.

"I want to see your face," I gasped.

"Another time."

Ignoring his refusal, I attempted to turn my head, but the monstrous hand at my neck kept me fast in place.

"If you can't be content with just my cock, Curse Eater," he rumbled. "Take my magic. Let it know you."

While he claimed me, his dark energy heightened its rhythmic pull, tumultuous and compelling, powerful but never cruel. His fingers, sinuous and tapered, returned between my slick lips to stroke me. I became a pillar of sensation, exclusively aware of the possessive drive of his unnatural body into mine, and the frenzied rise to my next orgasm.

"That's right, Eleanora. Come apart on me."

He cupped my chin in his palm, tilting my head until it rested beneath his chin, running the rough pad of his thumb over my bottom lip. My tongue snaked along the pointed tip, and in response he groaned, the sound like the earth tremoring. For the second time that night, I splintered, my cry rising above the crash of waves, echoing into the night from the open window. With my release came a flood of magic, raising gooseflesh on my skin and pouring into Victor. In three harsh thrusts, he finally met his ecstasy, his laudations shaking the timber of the dock house as he pulsed inside me, the sensation teasing my still quivering sex, extending the pleasure for a few blissful moments more.

His release relieved his beastliness, temporarily satisfying its cravings. It retreated, returning him to the form I knew best, a better fit against and inside me. He held me, my head resting on his chest, both of us breathless.

He kissed my bare shoulder. "Are you all right?"

"Yes." And it was true. Then, as an afterthought, "Will that happen every time?"

Victor's laugh was genuine and unexpected, warming me through the way no sunbeam could dare hope to. I wanted to hear that sound more times than a hundred lifetimes would allow.

"I've never tested it," he admitted, still chuckling. "Was it unpleasant?"

"I was unprepared," I admitted. "But it was nowhere near unpleasant."

He turned his face into my hair, knotted and wild from our activities, his fingers pressing into the soft swell of my belly, gentle. I turned my head to look into his face, pausing as the low firelight gave me a glimpse at what our magic had unwittingly conjured. Above us, a cloud of unwoven curses lulled in the air, pulled from our bodies through the bedlam of magic we'd produced together.

"Yours or mine?" I asked, delirious, unable to tell if the Drudge lingering among my ribs was reduced.

"Ours," he answered, his lips finding mine.

CHAPTER THIRTY-NINE

We lay on the blanket-draped cot by the fire, entwined with each other. Victor solemnly watched the flames, his fingers tracing absentminded patterns on my hips. He was more at ease than I'd ever seen him, and I could sense the metrical ebb and flow of his magic, mirroring the heartbeat in his chest, though the darkness there lingered, present always.

"What triggers the change?" I asked, careful to phrase the question gently, recalling the self-loathing in his voice.

He inhaled slow, deep, returning from whatever realm he'd been visiting in his mind.

"From what I can tell, any profound emotion: rage, grief, passion. Whatever riles my magic encourages the Drudge. I connected most with rage and grief as a boy—really the only emotions I was capable of. Barrick taught me how to cope with those. When I became a man, passion was a problem as well, and I frightened a few young ladies before realizing it."

"You haven't had any lovers since?"

He chuckled. "Passion isn't a prerequisite for sex. I'm sure you have enough experience to know that. How much passion did you feel for Ben?"

It was intended to sound offhand, but the hint of tension surprised me.

"Surely, you're not a jealous man, Inspector." The counter was playful.

"What about me makes you think I wouldn't be?"

Both of his brows raised, giving me a view of his face that I found even more alluring for its humanity. But I wasn't naïve enough to believe it meant he was teasing. Victor had given me no reason to doubt the kind of man he was.

"Ben wasn't passionate, he was safe," I replied, rounding back to his question, "But he was also kind. I didn't love him, but I regret hurting him. He must think I'm dead."

"I'll send him my condolences." Victor's quip was toneless. He was uninterested in my ex-lover's feelings, and the shadow of his Drudge quivered in annoyance, the vibrations of it never letting me forget it existed. In the back of my mind, I continued to prod at the encapsulation of curses in my own bones, anxious over its lethargic nature. It didn't behave how I'd expected it to, almost as though it lay waiting for something. Biding its time.

"What happened after you left Blackwicket House?" I asked, trusting Victor to know I meant the horrible day that had changed us both.

The silence drew on so long, I assumed he wouldn't answer, but at length, he spoke, venturing into his worst memories.

"When Grigori realized I wasn't dead," he said, "he used everyone believing I was to his advantage. It gave him sway over Blackwicket House and an opportunity to continue his experiments on me unbothered."

"He wanted to make you Drudge?"

Victor offered an affirmative noise.

"Grigori believed curse magic was most formidable, needing a human element to shape it into something commandable, a notion he acquired in the war." He rested his hand on my waist, warm and harboring. "He'd been 26, already a high-ranking officer in the agency responsible for creating cursed soldiers. But the Authority came to power, put a stop to it all."

"For whatever good it did," I muttered.

I gently touched a ragged scar the length of my thumb beneath Victor's collarbone.

"Grigori thought he was doing me an incredible favor, building me the same way he'd once built soldiers. When the Drudge is in control, it enhances strength, makes me difficult to injure, quick to heal, but it's unpredictable and burns through magic like tinder. His previous attempts needed to feed on magic outside themselves to survive, but even then, host vessels didn't last more than a few weeks."

"That's why Grigori wanted Dark Hall children." I made all the horrible connections. "How did you escape?"

He exhaled.

"William."

The name turned something in my stomach, and I regarded the scarring on my wrist, experiencing such an intense surge of hatred that the curse forced upon me unfolded, curious, waiting to see how far my turmoil would reach. It began a slow climb, using my anger as stepping stones.

Victor moved his hand, placing it over the permanent mark his brother had bequeathed to me in his insanity, owning a piece of me even in death.

"Don't feed it, Eleanora." His caution only thickened the venom.

"Good advice coming from you." The words emerged in a hiss.

"Ellie."

Victor brought my ruined skin to his lips, placing a kiss on it. His use of my childhood nickname softened me, and my eyes welled.

"I'm sorry," I said.

"Keep your meaningless apologies." The words were harsh, but his delivery of them affectionate.

"If you're willing, I want to hear the rest," I whispered, and he tucked my hand against his chest.

"Grigori raised the two of us as brothers." Victor ran his thumb over my knuckles. "Until I was eight, I had a vaguely normal life. Our father was busy with the Brom, and Will and I were abandoned to our own devices most of the time. We were both scared to death of the old man, because even minor infractions were met with swift consequences. William took the blame for things, even when it was my fault, and always stood in front of me when Grigori lifted his cane."

Victor's voice lowered, burdened by the misery of his past. His Drudge surged, and he raised his guard. I didn't try to stop him from pulling his defenses into place. They weren't mine to dismantle, but I offered him presence, as he'd done for me, turning my hand, our palms touching. I threaded my fingers through his.

"When Grigori began his attempts at transforming me, William protested, and when the protests began making things worse for us both, he subverted Grigori in other ways, taking curses off me when our father wasn't looking, sitting outside my door in the middle of the night to talk me through wanting to die."

He laughed, the inappropriate emotion an alternative to one he didn't want to express.

"I bet you don't cry."

"No. But I'm a weak man, Jack. You don't want to be like me."

"After a while, Grigori started dragging me along to see your mother. He thought her weakness might be children like her, and he needed help if there was going to be any chance of my surviving what he was doing to me."

"He was trying to weasel his way into her heart using you," I said. Despite my revulsion for the tactic, I recognized it as one that would have worked on me. "If you knew Fora Blackwicket brought you to Grigori, how could you stand to be friends with me when my family was responsible for what was happening to you?"

"Grigori was responsible." He corrected me, the edge of the words kindling with animosity for a man long dead. "And when I was at Blackwicket House, I was in less pain, felt more at home in my body, clear-headed. You taught me to eat curses when I'd only been able to consume and hold them. Before you ever gave me your magic, you were helping me survive."

I slipped my leg between his thighs, moved our joined hands to guide his arm over me. I would never be satisfied with any distance between us. He paused to enjoy my warmth.

"William and I thought we'd make it, but Grigori discovered I could curse eat, that I'd been siphoning all of his work. He raged, slipped outside of himself, overcompensated— too many curses all at once. You know the rest." He said, running his hand along my spine.

Yes. I knew. Grigori had gone rabid with fury, crippled his oldest son, and dragged his dying one to my mother for salvation, believing she would take pity and surrender to his plans. She hadn't. But her daughter had.

"Grigori kept me a year more, tested his theories on how quickly a body melded with a Drudge could heal."

I sucked in a small breath, aware of every ridge of damaged tissue.

"One night, after a hard course of trials with Grigori, I heard William's voice. He'd still been barely able to walk then, so he must have crawled. He told me our father was at the

Vapors and used a key he'd swiped to unlock the door. It took me too long to leave that room. I knew if I did, Grigori would likely murder Will. I wanted my brother to come with me, but he was gone by the time I found the nerve, and I was too afraid to look for him. In the end, my selfishness saved my life, but it cost Will his, just not in the way I'd imagined."

I was familiar with this kind of pain. Acutely. Silence fell, giving way to the waves and crackling of the fire. We'd both loved people whose familiar forms had contorted into something hideous in the wake of our absence, had lived lives that had led us to become distorted ourselves. Our pasts were inescapable, and our futures unknowable, fraught with promises of Authority retaliation. My mind spiraled with thoughts of all the ways things could go wrong, and my magic responded to the growing despair, enlivening William's Drudge. Victor shifted to look at my face.

I met his gaze.

"What are we going to do?" I whispered.

"Spend the night together," he replied, his palm cupping my cheek. "Drown in each other until the sun comes up."

"And after that?"

"After that, Curse Eater," he said, lowering his head to brush his lips against mine, our magic rejoining. "We fight the tide."

We drank each other in, Victor's Drudge making no further appearances, until an hour prior to sunrise when an exhausted, fitful sleep overtook us both. I stirred as dawn broke, uneasy. Victor rose with me, experiencing the same unrest, and we dressed, anticipating Ramsey and Hannah's arrival. He'd closed himself off from me, the stony armor firmly in place. I didn't fault him, nor find myself hurt by it. I preferred him safe. Taking a page from his book, I began gathering my own defenses, difficult with the hulk of the curse in my way. I'd have to learn to circumvent it for now.

Aside from the slip and ruined chiffon dress, I had nothing to wear, but along with a spare revolver and ammunition he'd hidden away, Victor also had extra clothes stashed in the cabinet from the days he'd forgone staying in town during his visits on Barrick's behalf. The trousers didn't work, but a wool knit sweater covered me. As I'd pulled it over my head, there came a fervent knocking.

Victor and I exchanged glances, a brief meeting of our gazes to fortify ourselves before we opened the door to the news Ramsey and Hannah had brought with them. The knocking persisted, urgent as ever, no voices raised. Indicating with a motion of his hand for me to keep my distance, Victor reached for the handle. When the latch was undone, the door burst inward, propelled by the violent force of a Drudge entering the Dock House with the chaos of a wildcat. It crashed into the back wall, scrambling upward, confused, toward the ceiling, where it lost purchase and fell with a crash onto the table below, rolling onto the floor, twisting like an injured animal.

Victor's Drudge had risen in response, but I put a hand upon his chest to delay the transfiguration. Two Drudge in this space was a disaster, and I'd already recognized the creature thrashing by the fireplace, its limbs skimming the embers, scattering them.

Auntie had hunted us down, desperate and wailing, curses roiling from her in weak strands, spent.

Victor was straining to keep himself in check, eager to engage with the Drudge who'd leveled two attacks on us already.

"Wait," the pleading encouraged his affliction to recede a fraction. "She was at Nightglass Estate. She took some of William's curses from me. Don't hurt her."

Victor's brutal instincts made his grip harsh as he grasped

my shoulder to turn me to face the Drudge. It no longer thrashed, but moved in small spasms, breathing hard and fast. The angular limbs softened, shortened, and raven-like claws retreated into nimble, feminine hands scratching weakly at the floor as the body endured the visceral, noisy rearranging of bones and muscle, until it lay still.

The woman faced the fireplace, tattered pink day dress scorched at the hem, battered by magic that had wound it around her cursed form, golden hair tumbling free, ratted by the ordeal and lack of care. At length, she rolled onto her back.

My heartbeat ratcheted in my chest, kicking up a painful pounding that matched the wretched noise that escaped me as I saw my sister's face. I pulled away from Victor, and he released me, recognizing her as I had.

I rushed to her, stumbling to my knees beside her. Our arms were around each other, her limbs so slender, her body reduced to little more than bone, and I kissed her cheeks again and again, for a beautiful, rapturous moment, not caring about anything she'd done, forgiving her for every horrible decision she'd made.

"Fiona," I wept against her shoulder, smelling of honeysuckle and damp loam.

"Hi Ellie," she said in a hoarse croak, the most beautiful sound I'd ever heard.

Chapter Forty

I could have held Fiona for hours, days, never asking questions, but she pulled from the embrace, sat fully, and I took stock of her. Her skin was sallow, the signs of curse rot obvious from the sunkenness of her cheeks, the softness of her collarbone.

"You're Drudge?" I whispered.

"I am." Her eyes glimmered in the faint light of morning. "Hazard of the occupation, I'm afraid."

My face collapsed as I realized what she'd done for me. The Drudge I'd thought to be Auntie, who'd come to me in the hellish inferno of Nightglass Estate and taken the worst of William's curse, had been my dead sister. Who wasn't so dead after all.

"You saved my life."

I sobbed, and she kissed the tip of my nose as she'd done often when we were children, her favorite way of showing me she was the big sister.

"Were you responsible for the fire?" I asked when I could breathe again.

"William's flair for ambiance usually outweighs his common sense." Speaking of William curdled her tone, her contempt palpable. "The candles were already a hazard, I only gave them encouragement. I didn't know you were there."

Her brows knit together in exasperation, as though she'd just remembered she was upset about something.

"Why didn't you stay away?"

"If Victor is to be believed," I said, hoping to defuse her consternation and discourage myself from crying again. "I don't listen well."

Fiona glanced over my shoulder to where Victor stood nearby, giving us distance for our reunion while positioning himself for an advantage if anything went wrong, a reminder of his inherent distrust. His defenses remained in place, but I could sense the dark energy roiling from him, still agitated from Fiona's chaotic arrival. But there was more than Victor's power brushing the hairs on my arms. Fiona's presence was also detectable, sickly.

"Take some of my magic, Fiona." I took her hand. "I can spare it. You look wrung-out."

Fiona's smile was indulgent, like someone who'd heard something critically naïve.

"Magic doesn't help anymore, Ellie," she said.

"But between us, we have plenty of curses," Victor said impassively. "Maybe those will do."

A wave of pain clenched Fiona the way I'd seen it take hold of Victor. Her skin became dappled in the crimson drench of the rising Drudge, then ebbed, leaving her catching her breath.

"Inspector Harrow," Fiona drawled, on edge from what she'd endured. "How good of you to be preying on my sister in my absence."

Victor responded with a hostile laugh.

"You two are familiar with each other?" I said, battling some bitterness over Victor's withholding of this information.

"The good Inspector enjoys harassing women who want nothing to do with him." Fiona's falsely sweet smile dripped with venom.

"She's talking about Thea," Victor replied in explanation.

"Thea never told you about her connection to Victor?" I asked, surprised.

"I know all about it." Fiona's response was bitter, making it clear that she didn't like Victor on principle. "But being what I am, I recognize another Drudge when I see it. No matter what your intentions were, Inspector, you made everyone's lives here harder."

"By making it more difficult for you to murder people, Fiona?"

"That's enough. We're all murderers in this room, for fucksake," I said tersely to them both, stunning my sister. "You should have shown yourself, Fiona. We could have figured something out together."

"Ellie, you were as trapped as I was the minute you stepped foot in Nightglass," my sister replied. "I wanted to warn you at the morgue, and I tried to in the only way I could with Farvem standing outside the door."

The Drudge that had attacked me at the funeral home. I hadn't seen it as a message, but as a lingering symptom of my sister's illness.

"How did you fool Mr. Farvem?" I asked. "He's dealt with so many dead. How couldn't he see you were alive?"

She pressed her lips together, knowing this revelation would wound me.

"It was his idea for me to fake my death in the first place."

"Farvem's?" I echoed, disbelieving.

"Before you arrived, I was staying in the morgue, out of sight. I didn't know you were there until Horatio came barreling in, panicking, telling me you were demanding to see my body. I thought my warning in Devin for you to stay away would have been enough."

"You didn't think I would come after finding out you were dead?"

"You weren't supposed to ever know, Ellie."

"William made sure that I did," I snapped. I was angry with myself for being gullible and so readily manipulated. Fiona was about to speak, and I didn't want to risk hearing an apology I wasn't ready for, so I intercepted. "What possessed you to make a deal with Farvem? The man was insane."

She nodded, resigned to telling me even worse news, and I braced myself.

"I was working with the Veil from the moment the Authority procured Jack for Grigori. I couldn't live with what we were doing anymore, and William was letting his father's ideologies consume him. I was so deep in everything. Farvem offered protection for Thea and the boys if I'd help take care of the Brom."

"But he hated Curse Eaters."

"Because we're unnatural, Eleanora," Fiona said, holding my gaze. "We shouldn't exist here. This isn't our home. He knew that."

"That's not true," I replied firmly.

"It is. Even mother knew it. That's why she raised us the way she did."

There was a bitterness in my sister I was learning to share. My mother had thought cloistering us from the world was safety, feeding us pretty lies about enchanted gardens that could take the burden from our shoulders, when it only held them in time, the same way I was holding the curses I'd collected in my wooden lock box. Then she'd offered Grigori as a single evil for us to focus on, so the overwhelming horde of factions who wanted to eat us alive wouldn't worry us. "By the time he came to me, I was eager to believe Farvem's lies, bought into building a world without curses, becoming normal. All we needed to do was eradicate the right people, and everyone would be safe. He was so sure. He seemed so good."

Fiona pushed the hair from her face, eyes darting around the floor frantically as though she were tracking down the memory of what had driven her to trust the old man.

I wanted to ask about Roark, where he'd come from, where he'd gone, but it seemed a lot to request all at once.

"So you started feeding Brom to the Fiend?" I asked.

"I'd already been doing that," she replied, unruffled by my knowing. "I was furious, lost, and the Drudge had already been forming for years."

She touched her chest delicately, indicating the creature scratching at the walls of her fragile magic, and I finally understood her desperation.

I squeezed her hand to show her I was still there, that I wouldn't abandon her even in the face of these admissions. I felt certain I understood, but she pulled away from me, ashamed.

"I started the work I did because I wanted to, the Drudge *needed* me to."

"Is that what drove you to attack Jack? The Drudge?"

I was freshly aware of the abomination lurking in my own magic, one that had dug far deeper than any I'd held before. A parasite, just out of reach.

"Of course not, I wasn't trying to hurt him!" She was insistent. "I was in the tower and saw William getting out of the car. I panicked. I wanted to hide Jack in Dark Hall, keep him safe for a little longer. I knew the house wasn't going to reject William. It was too weak by then. I'd been feeding off it for too long."

This explained why the house had acted so strangely, why it had eventually grown silent. Fiona had been siphoning curses from it, consuming them for the power she needed when her magic was struggling to bounce back from its scourge. It likely required more and more to remain stable, like a drug. Victor's pitiless comment made sense now. He'd come to that conclusion already, knowing what it took to handle being inhabited by Drudge.

I had so many questions, but Fiona looked tattered, defeated. She knew what she was, and didn't need me to point it out anymore.

"I thought you were Auntie."

I offered this small bit of humor in hopes it would help bridge the chasm between us. Return us to our history as sisters, reminding her we'd once shared so much and that regardless of her transgressions, I loved her.

"I suppose I am," she said, giving me a faint smile. "There was no more Auntie after Mom entered Dark Hall. I naturally filled that void."

Just as I'd thought I'd caught up, Fiona gave me a new revelation to struggle over. Auntie wouldn't have followed our mother into Dark Hall so willingly, not when she'd avoided capture for so many generations. Then a horrible knowing crept in—all those nights Auntie had stood in our room guarding us, keeping other Drudge at bay, mother always making excuses for why she couldn't unravel her, humanizing her with a name, giving us a lullaby to sing when we were afraid.

A song a mother would recognize through the haze of the Drudge.

Oh, Moira, my love

Weeks ago, I would have rejected the suggestion, but with the work Isolde Blackwicket had done our entire lives, there'd been plenty of room for a Drudge to take root. The unease I'd soothed previously returned, and the curse, settled comfortably in my magic, breathed.

"Mom?"

"Yeah," Fiona said, pained. "I didn't know until that night.

She'd changed, Ellie, permanently. I think that's why she did what she did. Why she left."

Fiona was fighting tears again, and she wiped them fiercely from her face.

"I made sure every person I gave to Dark Hall had earned it, that they were all people who'd hurt her or would have. It was going so well for a while. Then Grigori caught on, and Roark disappeared."

"And so you killed Grigori Nightglass. Slit his throat," Victor said casually from his station nearby, strung tight.

Fiona glanced at him, but her eyes remained unfocused.

"Farvem thought if Grigori fell, the Brom would scatter. But none of us had anticipated Williams' willingness to step into his shoes. So it all backfired. William became more aggressive, moved plans forward faster, and tightened his hold on me. It's why we faked my death."

"Grigori wasn't the only one, was he?" Victor asked, his tone sharp and predatory, the one he used to extract information from reluctant sources. It didn't matter that she was my sister, or that she'd been through hell. He remained intent on uncovering the truth of what evil had been moving under the shining exterior of this town.

I prepared to defend her, but color rose to her cheeks, the slightest tinge of pink around her nose.

"Good boy, Inspector." Fiona intoned, full of hatred. "Figuring it out all by yourself."

Thatcher, Patrick, Cora, our Darren—their throats all cut.

"I might have made the connection sooner, but I don't usually include the deceased on my suspects list." Victor offered a humorless smile.

When I found my voice, the words it produced were weighed down with painful astonishment.

"Darren?" I said. "You murdered our father?"

"He brought you to Nightglass." Fiona's anger with Victor for revealing everything lifted her voice. "He traded you for a payday!"

I stood slowly to my feet, needing to move, to feel my body, gone numb from shock. Fiona followed me, wobbling, losing her balance and falling to her knees.

"And Thatcher refused her a train ticket." Victor began stringing it all together at last, his eyes locked on Fiona as she attempted to stand, needing to hold on to the table to pull herself up. "Patrick wanted to gut her in the street. All men who did her harm."

"How could you," I asked her, still reeling. I could have lived a lifetime without Darren's shadow ever darkening my door. But the knowledge he was gone, that I'd held him while he died, because my sister had been feeding the monster in her bones, was difficult to bear.

"Ellie," Fiona rasped.

"He was a terrible man." My voice pitched. "But he was the only one left who knew anything about what we'd suffered."

"I heard what you said to him. Everyone did," Fiona argued. "You didn't want him!"

"But I didn't want…"

"Some people just deserve to die!" My sister screamed, interrupting me, and the Drudge overcame her again, shifting her into the beast which gnashed its jaws, twisting its horrible head on its long neck. When she wrested control and regained her human form, she sank, the effort costing her too much.

I dove to catch her before she hit the ground, and the contact with her body cleaved my anger, reminding me I hadn't lost everything, and had been given something precious back, no matter how broken. I helped her stand, and she leaned on me, gasping for a moment, crying small sobs into my shoulder. I'd become her protector, the last person in the world she could depend on. I needed to put my hypocritical judgment to rest and love her despite everything.

"At risk of being insensitive," Victor chimed, his voice devoid of interest in Fiona's suffering. "I need to clarify what crime Cora committed to invite your retribution."

His callousness reminded me of the man he was capable of being when focused on keeping his own demons at bay. I hadn't considered what it might be costing him to be in such proximity to Fiona's Drudge. Still, my anger flared. Fiona answered him, preventing me from offering a rebuke.

"Cora was keeping track of Jack for the Authority," Fiona rasped. "She used Thea to stay close, to ensure she didn't do anything to disrupt their plans. They wanted to see what William would do, how he'd use Dark Hall children to change the landscape of magic in this world."

"But you helped Grigori with that, before you killed him, you gave him a child from Dark Hall. You stole a boy to support Grigori's plans to create Drudge soldiers."

"Victor," I snarled.

"That wasn't what Grigori was doing, you fool," Fiona said, voice thickening. "And I didn't steal Roark from Dark Hall."

This information interested both Victor and me a great deal.

"Where did he come from?" Victor demanded.

"I made him." She spoke the confession with sober pride.

"You made him?" I repeated. "With William?"

She stared at me for a beat too long.

"Oh, Ellie. You really don't know any of it."

Voices raised from outside, Ramsey calling to us, urgent.

"Why is he here?" Fiona was suddenly on edge.

The door flew open, Ramsey barging in with Hannah close behind. They were agitated, faces tense, eyes sleepless.

"We found them," Ramsey said by way of greeting.

"Then why do you look so afraid?" My heartbeat ratcheted.

"They're locked in the Vapors," Hannah said. She had a long wool coat clutched to her, yellow as daffodils, and she handed it to me as she said, "with William."

"What the hell do you mean?" Victor roared, punctuating the stab of horror that momentarily crippled me. I clutched the coat as blood fled from my face, leaving me woozy.

Hannah chose that moment to notice Fiona, and she took hold of her husband's arms, gripping them with the shocked strength of any woman who'd seen someone rise from the grave.

"Fiona Blackwicket?" Ramsey stared at her, disbelieving.

Fiona had leaned against the table for support, eyes fixed on the two of them with cold distrust.

"William's dead."

She enunciated each word as though saying them strongly enough would keep them true.

"We tracked their magic all night, finally traced it to the club," Ramsey said, off balance by the sight of my sister. "It's strong, they're alive, but I'd recognize William's noxious trail anywhere, and it's there too."

My shock had abated, replaced by a detonation of wrath.

"You're lying. No one's capable of tracking people by remnants of magic that way." I said, the wicked creature in me expanding, glorifying in the wreckage my horror was making of my magic.

Hannah reached to put a hand on my arm, but I recoiled, finding Victor near, his steadying touch not to hold me up but to assure me he was on guard.

"You're not just a driver for the Brom, or an informant for Barrick. And your wife," I shoved a finger in Hannah's direction, and she raised her chin. "She can almost make a body whole again? I've never witnessed magic do more than barely cauterize a cut!"

"It can't do more than that," Hannah said. "Not in this sad little world."

"Hannah," Ramsey barked.

"How are you involved in this?" I insisted, aiming for the tender spot Hannah had revealed. "Are you Authority? Veil? Brom? *Who*?"

Fiona had moved towards me as well, standing silently at my shoulder as I interrogated them. Neither my sister nor Victor was inactive, they were bullets loaded into a gun, cocked and ready for me to pull the trigger.

"There'll be an inquest," Ramsey cautioned his wife.

"There'll be an inquest anyway," she cried, two spots of red blooming on her cheeks. "They deserve to know. They're involved!"

"You're both from Dark Hall." Victor interrupted the back and forth. "That much is clear. Now you're welcome to reveal the rest before we decide you're responsible for Thea and Jack's current circumstances."

Ramsey ran a hand over his face, long-suffering, muttering a string of words in a language I wasn't familiar with, but it was clear as day they weren't polite.

"Make it quick," Victor said, his form deviating beside me as the anxiety of the moment drew too taut, encouraging the Drudge.

"They're Authority," Fiona said in their stead, taking their narrative power, her voice icy as fingers of frost on glass.

"Not the one you're familiar with," Hannah said. "Not the one that's failed so miserably to protect you all."

"What other Authority is there?" I asked.

"The one responsible for annexing this world, removing the magic," Ramsey answered.

My instinct was to reject what I was being told as drivel to cover some worse thing, but Hannah's eyes were pleading, begging me to accept what they were saying despite the implausibility. I turned my face up to look at Victor. He said nothing, but his Drudge ceased its attempts to take the forefront.

"I guess we have no choice but to tell you the rest, but it'll have to be later," Ramsey said, an urgency in him. "We're running out of time. I don't know what William Nightglass has in mind with Thea and Jack, but we have reason to believe he wants to open Dark Hall."

"For what purpose?" Victor remained menacing, just as he'd always been when dragging information from unwilling mouths.

"To release the Fiend," Fiona said with resigned certainty.

My breath stalled, and I spiraled back to the claustrophobic study at the Nightglass Estate, the taste of bourbon on my tongue, the smell of William gagging me.

"Jack's the key." I blurted it out in panic. "That's what William said. He wants to use Jack to open a portal."

My sister's eyes became wild.

"No," she said. "Thea can open the portal. He wants Jack as a new vessel."

"For what?"

"His Drudge."

There was too much missing information, secrets and wounds, all the horrible knowledge my sister had collected without me. And though she was here, there was no time to know it all.

Victor was aware of that too.

"Let's make sure that doesn't happen," Victor replied, taking the coat from my white-knuckled hands, opening it with a snap, helping me into it like a gentleman taking his lady to the theater, not to face a madman she'd already killed once.

"We can't get in," Ramsey said. "That's the problem. We've been working most of the night, trying to break through the doors, a window, anything, but it's all magically sealed, and the magic is strong. More than William should be able to do. Nothing in, nothing out."

"There's a way in," Fiona muttered.

All eyes were on her.

"There's a Narthex."

The flutter I'd felt in Dark Hall, the gentle tug. I'd been unable to open myself to the possibility, but my suspicions had been true.

"We need to go," I said, pulling Fiona's arm around me to help her walk to the door.

"Where?" Ramsey followed us out, ready for any answer I gave him.

"To Blackwicket House."

CHAPTER FORTY-ONE

During the reckless drive to Blackwicket House, I learned some things from my sister, who became more and more lethargic. I'd offered my magic to her, but even the Drudge shied away, refusing to accept it, or perhaps no longer knowing how. She spoke faintly, her words trembling, and I worried she would lose consciousness. I held her against me as we bounced wildly onto the main road.

She murmured about the Narthex, how she'd started building it the night our mother left, how she'd constructed another many years later when she and Thea started looking for a way to remain undetected by William, once a doting lover, grown more fanatical following the Authorities' procurement of Jack.

"He was so wonderful those first years." My sister spoke deliriously as we roared up the drive. "I thought we were going to change Nightglass."

We drove past my sister's open grave, and the charred remains of Victor's car, arriving at Blackwicket House, desolate as an old log, its many inhabitants evicted. I couldn't be sure where they'd gone, but I imagined the tourists stranded in Nightglass were having a very bad time.

"Who helped him meld with a Drudge, Fiona?" I asked gently, knowing there were very few people powerful enough to anchor the Drudge and soul together, like two bodies sharing a heart.

"Roark."

Everyone's attention was captured.

Victor's interest arose from the violent empathy he felt for others in the same circumstances he'd survived, but Hannah and Ramsey's investment was odd.

"I think that's why he ran away." Fiona finished, aware of the unwanted scrutiny. This explained Fiona's blame. Even if Grigori and William hadn't orchestrated Roark's disappearance, they were still responsible, and it was a crime a mother's heart could never forgive.

As we climbed from the car, my sister lost her footing, and I barely caught her before she hit the cold ground. Even as I helped steady her, Victor approached and, without preamble, scooped her frail body into his arms.

"I'm not a child," she snapped, but didn't physically resist.

"We'll get to Jack and Thea faster if I carry you," he said, effectively silencing her objections.

The front door stood wide open, never having been shut when we departed for William's final High Tide. Cold and hollow as a body emptied of its life magic, the house sagged on its foundation. The interior was no better. Within a day, Blackwicket House had become the home I'd expected to find when I'd first arrived, floor buckled from the weather, the foyer ceiling sagging under accumulated moisture, splitting the coffers. Black mildew clung to the walls where patches of plaster had crumbled, revealing lath, and the same shriveled blackberry vines that had grown so prolifically in the tower and entwined among the bones of Fiona's victims in Dark Hall.

"You've been living in this?" Hannah's tone was a blend of sympathy and repulsion.

"It's changed," I remarked as we made our careful way up the steps, creaking and groaning beneath our feet.

"You'd be amazed at what curses can keep together," Fiona said.

Victor placed my sister on her feet when we reached the third floor. She stood more steadily, the proximity to Dark Hall fortifying her, its pulsing thrum recognizable now that the white-noise of curses was absent.

"The Narthex is upstairs." I said. "You'll sense the portal to the Vapors. It's the only other one still active, but I don't know where you'll end up inside."

"The dressing room, behind the bar." Fiona had continued to improve, gauntness reduced.

It was the same room Thea had put the makeshift Curse Eaters in during High Tide. It made sense. The force strengthening Fiona would have amplified whatever small ability the Brom had, making them less likely to void.

Before I could continue forming the half-cocked plan, Ramsey intervened.

"I'm afraid we can't go through the Narthex, Ms. Blackwicket," the grizzled man explained regretfully. "Any Authority stationed in annexed provinces are monitored. We aren't allowed to enter Dark Hall under any circumstances unless we're leaving for good. One exit."

"Then break the rules." Victor's brow furrowed in anger.

"Our Authority does have something in common with yours, Inspector." Hannah's reply was calm. "Annulment. It's strictly enforced for the safety of Elsewhere."

"Annulled by them or me," he growled. "You can choose."

He took a threatening step forward, urging Ramsey to shield his wife with his arm, though she didn't seem threatened. Instead, she appeared endlessly empathetic, inspiring unexpected rage in me.

"Fine," I hissed. "Ramsey and Hannah can wait outside the

Vapors for the wards to be dismantled. I'll go by myself. Victor, stay here with Fiona; she can't be alone.."

I'd already mounted the broken stairs when Victor took me by the arm.

"Like hell you'll face William alone," he said.

"Victor, the Fiend will sense you immediately."

"And it'll politely ignore the portion of William's Drudge you're carrying around, will it?" He asked with some impatience.

There'd be no shaking him.

"I'll keep the portal open," Fiona offered, and when she saw I was about to object, "I need to stay close to Dark Hall, Ellie. I won't be any help at the Vapors. Hannah and Ramsey should go."

A knot of fear tightened in my stomach for what we were risking.

With Fiona clutching me for balance, we ascended the decayed steps, returning to the room filled with my sister's terrible secrets. The cursed plants had been reduced to brown, rustling husks of vines and stalks, mingling with the remnants of blackberry fruit. It possessed the smell of an overgrown graveyard, and the floor beneath us was soft, weaker for the absence of roots holding it together.

The portal shimmered, responding enthusiastically to our combined magic. I sensed the call, the melody of Dark Hall beckoning me. Much like the sea, it was familiar and welcoming, despite the dangers lurking within.

My sister's trophies lay scattered around our mother's hope chest.

"Why did you keep their clothes?" Morbid curiosity compelled me to ask.

"So I could remember how much I hated them all. It helped the cursed fruit grow." No pride or offense existed in her tone, only the resignation of someone who could never change the past, and wouldn't if given a choice. "You should know I never fed on their magic. Of all the horrible things I am, I couldn't bring myself to do that."

It was a shot at Victor, whose abuse of the Brom had never been a secret.

"We all make choices," he replied, but the words lacked their typical steely edge.

Fiona touched the Narthex, and it quivered, connecting to her. She sucked in a small breath, in pain, and I reached to her, but she waved me away.

"Don't baby me. You'll have to go directly after her, Victor. Don't linger. There's no telling how near the Fiend is."

I spared seconds we didn't have to hug her, longing for a day when neither of us would be looking death in the face and asking for a minute more.

"Eviscerate the bastard," she whispered, releasing me and turning her attention to Victor.

"I don't like you, Inspector," Fiona said pointedly. "But you're not the worst thing that's ever happened to Eleanora. Take care of her."

"In Dark Hall? If history serves, it's going to be the other way around," he replied with a note of teasing, as though he'd just remembered that once, he and Fiona had been friends.

My sister surprised us all by hugging him as well. Victor stiffened in the embrace, expression the closest thing to bewilderment I'd ever seen on him. He offered her a graceless pat in return.

"Go quickly." She hurried us, tears in her voice.

We said nothing more as I faced the Narthex. The wall was pliant, and I leaned into it, suspended for a disorienting moment in space, before I found myself upright in the dark.

"Victor?" I whispered.

"I'm here," he said, at my elbow.

It occurred to me, as pointless thoughts sometimes do when you're trying not to be frightened, that this was our first journey to Dark Hall together since childhood. I hoped this one would be an improvement over the last.

"This way," I said, hushed, moving into dark, trusting my magic to guide me. I was unwilling to wait until the corridors fully materialized, uninterested in seeing the bodies again.

But Dark Hall had different plans. Eager to exist with two people inside, it formed in two steps, replete with bones and vines, rendered ever more ghastly by their entrapment in the magical, scarlet flora. Victor muttered an oath.

"It's certainly not the Dark Hall I recall," he said as we traversed the overgrown catacomb.

"It finally matches what everyone's afraid it is." I was bitter about the transformation, growing increasingly resentful that nothing from my childhood had escaped spoilage.

A set of bones shifted as the vines grew, impatient to show off their green leaves, their trumpeted flowers tinkling like bells. Victor reached for the holster at his waist, to find it empty.

"Fiona," he groaned, "That little pickpocket."

"It explains the hug."

I struggled to keep my mind off our surroundings and the looming danger of the Fiend, which often appeared with no warning, as it had the night Thomas had almost been lost to it. "Seems I wasn't the only one Darren mentored."

"He taught you to pick pockets?"

"As any good father would."

To my great relief, we moved out of the morbid copes, nearly jogging, following the pulse of the Vapor's portal. We navigated several turns, passing door after door in quick succession, but no matter how far we went, I still barely felt the itch of the Narthex.

Panic set in, and I suspected that the faster we moved, the

further the portal would drift. I slowed down. I would need to open my magic to sense it, but doing so was an incredible hazard.

"I can't find it. I have to use magic," I breathed. "I don't want to do this. I can't endanger you again."

But I couldn't abandon Jack or Thea, the woman who'd made my sister's life bearable. Facing Fiona and admitting I'd bowed to my fear wasn't an option.

"Eleanora." Victor's hand brushed mine, not taking it, knowing it would impede our ability to run when the time came, and it would soon. "There are a thousand moments I would change if I had the power, but that day isn't one of them."

My heart skipped a beat as I raised my eyes to his.

"Do what needs to be done," he said.

When I was finally able to speak through the rush of warmth and unending gratitude, all I could manage was, "Get ready to run."

As though dropping a garment from my shoulders, I released my guard, power rising with eager exhilaration, unaware of what it might invite. Right away I perceived the direction of the Narthex, like a song playing from another room. As soon as I'd locked on, the Drudge haunting me reared, presenting itself, greedy to experience Dark Hall.

I broke into a run, trusting Victor to follow as the Fiend responded to the presence of the impurity in its domicile, the roar of rushing water drowning out the sound of our breath. But we were already close. On another turn, we entered a dead-end hall, the single door there swinging open to greet us. My magic lunged, colliding with it, a boulder breaking water.

We didn't slow, stumbling blindly through the thick, strange borderland, and into the dimly lit gloom of the Vapor's dressing room, light filtering in from the staff hall. Blood jittery in my veins, I sealed the portal shut behind us.

"We got lucky," I huffed. "But it's active, so we can't go back this way."

In response, Victor caught me in an unexpected, fervent kiss. This embrace wasn't motivated by desire, but by an urgency to express feelings we hadn't been able to articulate—ones we feared for their significance and the pain they promised. I wrapped my arms around his shoulders, committing every sensation of him to memory. We would have delayed the inevitable for centuries more, but we couldn't disregard the miasma of dreadful magic that had begun to close in, as choking as the smoke from the Nightglass fire.

"Stay near me," Victor murmured as we parted.

The hallway was suffused with a low glow from overhead lights whose bulbs had gone dim. The effect was unsettling, creating shadows in all corners of the ceiling and floor. Surrounding us were the uneven palpitations of corruption, the antithesis of High Tide's fizzing, intoxicating atmosphere. But despite this, the theater we entered wasn't empty.

Awash in the familiar blue glow was a full house of tables, each with a candle and cocktails placed out for the guests, none of whom were indulging. Because though there was a body in every chair, none of them were alive. The corpses had been arranged in various ways, hands around glasses, legs crossed, and a woman at the table nearest us had a lit cigarette tucked carefully between blackened lips, her eyes a cloudy white. A drift of ash fell onto her lap. The macabre audience had all been positioned to face the stage, where Thea and Jack sat on the floor, huddled together, disheveled but in one piece.

William was nowhere to be seen.

"There are too many places for him to be hiding," I said unnerved, genuinely afraid as I scanned the scene, my eyes darting to every dark corner.

"He's not hiding," Victor said, low, his Drudge ascending rapidly in anticipation of mortal danger. "He's hunting."

"How right you are." The dockman's accent was abrupt, thick as smoke from a cigar, a sharp pressure against my throat as someone seized me from behind. "And look what I've caught."

Chapter Forty-Two

"Coppe?" I choked against the point of the knife. He must have been waiting in the shadows behind the bar.

Victor's reaction was immediate, a red tide raging forth in response to the threat against my life. I'd never witnessed the full transformation, the visceral sight of a skeleton reshaping itself beneath skin stretched too tight, the wreathing of muscle over its new shape, ultimately contorting into the gnarled, furrowed body of the Drudge. It took mere seconds, but I could only imagine that each was a lifetime to Victor.

"Ah ah," Coppe admonished, unfazed, pressing the point of his weapon deeper. "You stay right where you are. You're powerful, sure, but do you think you can get to me before I slit her throat? Huh?"

I gripped the wrist of the hand holding the knife, my magic responding in fear.

"You hold on too, girl," he snarled as he felt the rise of it, pushing the point until I heard a small pop of flesh, the nip of pain. "I'd planned to savor you, but I'll spill you out in one go if you force my hand."

Thea and Jack had stayed almost motionless on the stage, moving only when Thea wrapped her arms around Jack's shoulders.

"Coppe, you know William's just going to.."

"I'm not Coppe!" The ferocious proclamation was accompanied by spittle flying onto my chin. He calmed as quickly as he'd erupted, voice smoothing.

"To be fair, I guess I'm what's left. You and Thea did a number on him, but he works in a pinch. Being in his head is something else," Coppe inhaled a sharp breath through his teeth, "He's a dirty son of a bitch. Had a genuine soft spot for Jack, though, reminded him of his little brother, dead, I'm afraid. The unlucky boy had a bit too much natural magic for his own good. But I enjoy that memory because it reminds me of you, Thomas."

Victor had been stalking back and forth, keeping a perimeter, looking for a weak spot, but upon hearing the name of his childhood, he paused.

"Yes, Thomas all grown up into a Drudge, just like father hoped for."

"You're not William," was the phantasmic response.

"But it's true, Tommy boy. I wanted to be strong like you, to walk again, to break the old man down, to prove he was nothing. So I tested myself with curses, stretched my limits. I watched father constantly fail, and then finally had an epiphany. The only thing separating the Blackwickets from all the other Curse Eaters Grigori harvested was the fact that they'd cared about you. Isn't that just lovely? Bless you, Ellie."

He pressed a harsh, loud kiss against my temple, and I reacted with vocal repulsion.

"It appears the magic that binds us to power has to be given willingly, wholeheartedly. It's so fucking sentimental, of course it never crossed Grigori's mind."

Fiona's confession in the car now had context.

"You manipulated your own son. Tricked him into giving you magic." I wheezed, trying to keep him talking while I built pressure, holding my guard with every ounce of strength I had.

There was turmoil in his next words, a wave of hurt, deep and sonorous.

"He wasn't my son."

Uncomfortable with his own pain, he increased mine, pressing the knife further into the small slit he'd already made. I nearly lost hold of the reservoir of power.

"With the support of the Authority gone, thanks ever so much to your lover," he continued as though we'd never mentioned Roark, "The Veil will get a foothold, and I'm not interested in playing around with those fools. I need to get the portal open, find somewhere new."

"The Fiend will eat you alive," I managed, lightheaded from the effort I was making, concentrating on timing it right.

"Not if hell is empty and the devil is here. Between the two of us, I think the Fiend will find Victor the tastier option. I'm still working towards such an impressive caliber, and soon, I'll have a much better vessel to guarantee it. Another little fact I discovered - once a Drudge is melded to a soul, the soul goes where the Drudge goes."

"I'll never let you touch Jack," Victor's Drudge had lowered to all fours, readying itself.

"It was my original idea," William admitted, "But I'm not too keen on being a twelve-year-old boy again, so I'm bringing him along for later. In the meantime, I found a much better option. It didn't quite work out, so how lucky we get to try again."

I was released only enough so he could tilt my head, hover his face near mine.

"Now you're going to open your pretty mouth and let me in. And don't worry, you'll still be you...somewhere in there."

He laughed, the sound a light-minded tremolo as if his wits were only just barely there.

His contaminated essence surfaced, and it was time at last.

I released the jolt of magic I'd been building like boiler pressure, force enough to jar the knife-wielding hand away, allowing me to lower my head and bite whatever part of him I could find. My teeth sank into the meaty hank of flesh, just below Coppe's thumb. The hot taste of iron filled my mouth, and the knife clattered to the ground, giving Victor the window he needed.

He struck with precision, magic piercing the disembodied Drudge as it advanced to its new chalice. A screech rang in my ears, and the Drudge abandoned me in its efforts to pull Coppe's body back on like a discarded coat.

In the time it took me to sprint for the stage, William's Drudge had reconfigured Coppe into its monstrous shape, smaller than Victor's by a significant margin, crippled in the legs with knees that bent the wrong direction, a barreled chest, and impossibly long arms, thick as railroad ties. This body composition should have made him slow and easy to outmaneuver, but he moved with a berserk determination, a juggernaut.

He stormed toward me, smashing tables out of his way as he went, jolting corpses from their positions where they fell onto the floor and against each other. Victor caught the thing by one backward leg, dragging it away.

When I reached Thea and Jack, I found Thea dazed, as though she'd had too much alcohol. Fortunately, the boy seemed none the worse for wear.

"He made her do too much magic," Jack said.

The mighty din of the battle continued as I helped Thea to her feet.

"Everything's sealed," she muttered drunkenly.

"We go through the portal," I said to them, buzzing slightly. "The Fiend may be there, but you two are safe. No curses. If something happens to me, you keep going. Thea, you know which Narthex it is."

It wasn't the optimal time to ask how I'd discovered that, so she only nodded.

We took off; me supporting Thea with one arm, and her holding Jack's hand in a vice grip. Victor and William's monstrous forms were still locked in conflict, each a leviathan. As they clashed, William somehow gained the advantage, taking hold of Victor's face with a hand the size of a bear trap before its mouth opened into a wide cavern, attempting to devour Victor's magic.

"Keep going!" I shouted, and Thea and Jack complied, vanishing down the back corridor. I quickly rounded the bar, grabbing the first heavy bottle I came to, slamming it forcefully onto the counter. It took me two swings before it shattered, spilling a wave of acrid-smelling liquor onto the floor where it seeped along the black tile, the grout stained with red. Cora's blood.

My plan was slapdash, unlikely to work. I'd only shaped magic with this intention as a girl, in a much smaller way, when I'd given my pill bug just enough speed to win a race. I lamented never learning what my magic could really do. I'd used it only for tricks and amusements in Dark Hall before repressing it, pretending it didn't exist. My lack of practice had abandoned me with unstructured energy, formless and confused, capable only of being swallowed by Victor's ravenous needs, or released in violent, formless bursts like a scream—exactly what I was going to do now.

I sprinted toward the dueling Drudge, gathering momentum. Drudge were harder to injure, but a distraction was better than nothing. I came upon them in a flurry of furious power, and with a thrust of my arm, I expelled the magic, which acted as a hammer to a firing pin. I stabbed William's Drudge just below its distended ribs with the thick, shattered end of my improvised weapon.

My strategy worked, and William thrashed, letting Victor

go even as I was knocked off my feet, falling across the lap of a corpse before tumbling to the floor, the body on top of me, a thick black bile dribbling from its mouth onto my neck. A dry retch twisted my insides and I struggled from beneath the weight of the horrid cadaver as Victor kicked Williams' knock-kneed form over. It had been busy trying to remove the glass and careened sideways. Understanding the odds, Victor sped towards me on all fours, grabbing me up in one arm as he passed, Drudge form tremoring as it struggled to maintain itself.

We reached the dressing room just as Victor shuddered back into his human body, releasing me. We stumbled to where the portal still wavered from Thea's use of it, her magic not yet completely withdrawn. The awful sound of William's Drudge clawing its way down the hall, scrabbling to get to us, propelled Victor to shove me into the Narthex. For an agonizing second, I thought he was staying behind. But as Dark Hall materialized around me, he appeared at my shoulder.

"Go!" he bellowed, and I obeyed, frantically attempting to drag the remnants of Thea's magic along to close the Narthex. But William, Coppe—whoever the monster was—erupted through right behind us as the portal solidified.

The influx of corruption in the magical byways was blood in the water. The Fiend materialized, a ghastly reckoning for our trespass. It took pursuit, its many limbs and faces tumbling over each other, crashing against doors and walls, shaking the foundation of this in-between where worlds had once touched. The gravity of it was terrifying, a force complicating momentum, dragging us closer. My panic erupted, a squall of magic pouring into my plea to Dark Hall, begging it to yield to my will, as it once had long ago when I'd explored and played in its passageways unburdened.

In response, the corridors undulated, corners merging, doorways disappearing with the creak of lumber as it stole the

Narthex to the tower ever closer. The portal opening flew towards us, and we were caught up in it like fish in a net.

"Close it!" I shrieked as we emerged on the other side.

Fiona was in Thea's arms, her reaction too slow. As her magic lashed back, Coppe had already materialized, along with part of the Fiend. It was caught in the portal, half shut, raging against the accidental trap, stretching the edges with pure might, trying to pull itself free.

Fiona had already driven Thea and Jack out of the tower door, begging them to flee.

William stood dressed in Coppe's body, only a few feet from the grasping tentacles of the Fiend, unbothered. His left eye was a gory hole, bruises spread from his nose beneath both sockets, but the most horrifying aspect of him was the way his skin sat wrong on his skeleton, as if it had been removed then draped back into place by a careless hand.

"Well," he breathed, pleased with himself, just as two ear-shattering gunshots sounded.

Coppe stumbled backwards, clutching the new set of holes in his chest, blood pouring between his fingers.

He looked up at my sister, who held Victor's gun in front of her, pulling the trigger repeatedly, though there were no more bullets.

"You bitch," he gargled.

The Fiend took its opportunity, grabbing hold of Coppe, crushing him back against the wall of the portal, beginning its vicious rending, dragging him through an opening far too small. As the shape of him began to collapse into the hole, his mouth opened, jawbone fracturing as the Drudge roared free. It surged forth, a demon, its many lipless mouths gnashing and drooling curses, teeth long and gray.

The last time I'd seen this horror, its mouths had only been two, but now there were three, a sphere of misshapen howling maws. The remainder of its figure resembled what Victor had grappled with at the Vapors, distended and bent. But now that it had no material body, the physical world no longer hindered it, and as Coppe's remains disappeared, it moved swiftly, engulfing Fiona in a cyclone of nightmares. The Drudge snatched her from the ground where she dangled like a rag doll, gorging on what meager magic still clung to her. It all happened so quickly, I had no time to react other than to reach uselessly as she was pitched aside, her body crashing upside down against the windowsill, feet shattering the panes. She slid down through the glass, lying prone and motionless.

I bolted toward her, tripping on the coiled carcass of a vine, tumbling forward. I was forced to crawl the remaining distance. She was trying to move, her breath ragged. I tucked my arms beneath hers, helping her onto her back, where she coughed, blood rising over her lips in an awful spray. There was no respite, the seething vortex plunging towards us.

Victor stepped into its path, ravaged by what he'd already endured at the hands of his brother's madness. The Drudge didn't slow, but changed intention, striving to infiltrate Victor's defenses, but with paltry results. I realized Victor could do nothing for us but stand there, distracting the Drudge, which seemed obsessed with making a meal of the man who'd matched it.

When its attempted rivening made insufficient headway, it changed tactics, rising into a thunderhead near the arch of the roofline, giant and looming. The Fiend had spread where it could, eager for the influx of cursed magic, just out of reach.

The Drudge opened one of its triple mouths to speak, and Grigori's reviled voice took the air from the tower, gravelly and unkind. My blood ran cold, the fear of childhood overwhelming me anew as though I were still a young girl, listening to a man threaten and manipulate my mother.

"You were supposed to be my greatest success. You ran away, you whimpering coward. Little nothing. Scared of a bit of pain? I'll show you pain, boy!" He yelled, raising his skeletal arm, curses transforming into a cane, scythe-like handle, sharp and cruel. The Drudge swung the ghostly weapon towards Victor, who, driven by an instinct burned into his nature, raised an arm to block the blow, body flinching inward. The phantom cane disintegrated as it made contact with Victor's arm, and the Drudge dove like a wraith, head twisting to give a new mouth prominence.

"You abandoned me," William's voice, wretched and hurt, a lost soul calling from the depths, "Why didn't you come find me? Why didn't you help me? Look what happened because of you. Look what I've become in your stead."

Victor remained hunched, his arm shielding his head, suffering the guilt and horror of his childhood, his Drudge too weak to rise and protect him.

The last mouth was given its voice, and Coppe's rough cadence brought with it a new grating note of detestation.

"You're the torment of all of Nightglass. My family suffered, my brother died, unraveled by Grigori to take your place. You should be dead. You!" It yowled, the sound expanding in the tower as the phantasm dove, clawed hand outstretched.

Victor's psychic barricades had weakened, and despite his best efforts to remain standing proud, he lost his footing, dropping to his knees as the ghast tore bits and pieces of his magic away, clean and corrupted volutions of power extracted with every blow.

I called his name, rising to aid him, but was caught by my sister's hand. Though her grip was feeble, it stalled me enough that I could do nothing as William's Drudge found the soft spot in Victor's defenses, and broke down into a spoil of smog.

I couldn't watch as Victor was possessed, couldn't bear to see him forced to swallow the ghosts of his past.

The tower grew quieter, the uproar diminished to only the clamor of the Fiend and the groaning of the house's frame, the joists and beams struggling.

Victor's back was still to us, and his shoulders rose, squaring off in the way I knew him for, defiant and unbreakable, and I dared hope. But as he turned to face us, it became abundantly clear he hadn't survived the ordeal unscathed.

William's Drudge laughed inside of Victor, his handsome face distorting into something more foul than I'd ever seen.

"This man is damaged," it drawled, lilting the last word with a dripping satisfaction, "And he's really fighting."

I glanced at the portal where the Fiend was almost through. Perhaps I could reach it, give it the magic it needed to open. It would cost us everything. I hesitated, trying to think of a way, any way, we could walk free from this.

The creature stretched its shoulders back, rolling its neck to get a feel for the new body. "The magic in here is peculiar, but tastes so sweet, like you two."

He brushed his thumb over his mouth, simultaneously biting his bottom lip, tantalized, irises the shade of whitecaps breaking shore.

"There are some *very* interesting memories here concerning you, Eleanora," William purred in Victor's voice. "It's a shame I won't be able to bring you with me. And as for you, Fiona, my love. You're a precious, stupid woman. I hope your pride was worth all this. Now, ladies, if you'll excuse me, I need to be out of the way when the Fiend makes its appearance."

The beast in question had pulled itself more than halfway, shaking the house's foundations, which creaked ominously.

As Victor made to escape, I knew what my last choice was. The only choice. The Fiend would soon be in this world, consuming all it could. There was no stopping that. But I could stop William from spreading like a disease through Dark Hall, leaving destruction in his wake in pursuit of more power, more magic. I didn't know what worlds existed beyond this, but I knew they were not prepared for him.

In three reckless bounds, I'd grabbed hold of Victor, and as expected, he turned, ready to fight, to ruin my body with the hands of his brother, who'd once touched me so gently. But he was met with an offering that threw him off guard—all that remained of my magic, every bit of me Dark Hall hadn't used up.

"Oh, that's…" He intoned, low, shivering at the sensation, and in unconscious recognition of my magic, Victor's guard lowered.

"Goodbye, William." I grated, latching onto his Drudge, coiling it around the portion he'd already been so gracious to give me. He tried to wrench away, but it was too late, the natural laws governing this exchange were already in motion. My lungs expanded as I took in a breath that was more than a breath, an invitation to the worst kind of magic. I wouldn't be able to take it all, and even if I had been, there was no time for Victor and Fiona to escape. I couldn't save the people I loved, but I could make sure no one suffered the whims of a Nightglass ever again.

As the first taste of scourge rolled across my tongue, the Fiend crashed through the portal, fracturing the wall, shifting the very structure of Blackwicket House, until the boards began to snap.

In a last bid to survive, William's Drudge released its hold on Victor, using its remaining strength to pull against me, when I was jolted by the impact of a body against mine, Victor tackling me against the wall, sheltering as he had when the house had retaliated against us for my sister's misuse of it. The collision fractured my hold, and the Fiend fell upon us, William's Drudge freeing itself to rise above, clambering high along the sloped ceiling.

My world became an erratic fluctuation of shadowy faces, but through it, I saw William's Drudge crawl like a startled spider down to the ruptured Narthex, where it disappeared inside. Free.

I'd failed.

Victor slid his arms beneath me, holding me up to his chest, tucking my head against his neck. We waited. Waited for the end of us both.

But it never came. The cool plucking hands of the Fiend searched, tugging here and there, chittering and whispering as though discussing something with itself. I raised my head, and in the brume there had formed a single visage, murky and vaporous.

Eleanora, it said, a hundred voices raised in chorus, my name a discordant and ancient sound.

Fiona.

It continued to call names, a current of them, chanted in a reverberating din, until at last I heard another familiar to me.

Isolde.

Upon speaking my mother's name it grew silent, then, like the gentle mist of the sea, it moved on, lingering for a breath above the supine body of my sister, who reached a hand weakly up to touch it even as it billowed from the wrecked tower window.

The tower shook, the beams splitting as the wall the portal had existed in caved in, bringing the tower down with it. The floor pitched, the framework separating, Fiona's body sliding towards the empty air.

"Hold on to me," Victor rumbled, convulsing in a way that had become familiar to me. His Drudge was fatigued, the effort to sustain it for more than a few moments impossible. But those few moments were enough. He leaped as the tower crumbled, catching Fiona as she slipped helplessly over the edge.

Clumsy and fighting for form, Victor crashed back-first into the slope of the mansard roofline below, before tumbling once to the porch cover, managing to land on his feet and jump aside of the falling debris.

The landing was jarring, and Victor was unable to keep hold of us. Our bodies hit the snowy ground with significant force, and we rolled several feet as Blackwicket House continued its disintegration, until the entire middle lay in shambles, its emptiness exposed.

I dragged myself to Fiona, who lay coughing, shaking in the cold. I was in pain, my ribs screaming as I maneuvered myself closer, pulling her onto my lap. Her eyes had been closed, but she opened them, searching for me, struggling to focus. Small wisps of magic slipped from her, and her breath came in a quick staccato.

Voices raised above the sound of the waves on the cliffs below, Thea and Jack rushing towards us, Ramsey and Hannah attempting to keep pace, their age impeding them.

Victor had made his way unsteadily to his feet, his right arm limp at his side, wrist turned at an awkward degree, broken.

"Do you want them to come?" he asked, voice bruised in his throat.

I nodded, eyes welling as I cradled Fiona against me, aware that the time for goodbyes was diminishing, unwilling to withhold something so precious from Thea and Jack.

Knowing my wishes, Victor made no effort to extend the last seconds my sister and I had alone. He limped his way toward us, knelt in silence, a knight bending knee in reverence to coming sorrow.

"Wait for Hannah, she can help you, she knows how... Hannah!" I screamed across the cliffs, knowing it was useless.

"No, Eleanora, please." Fiona took in two sharp breaths, trying to find enough air to speak, "I don't want it. I don't."

"You don't have to die, Fiona." I cried, the words untrue.

"Listen." The plea was desperate, "The night after he gave

magic to William, Roark went to Dark Hall. He's still there. I can feel him. You have to find him."

There were too many questions I'd never be able to ask. I made room for only one.

"Who's Roark's father?" I wanted to know who else besides William she'd trusted enough, or who had been wicked enough to take advantage.

"He doesn't have a father, Ellie," She panted, her mouth bowing into a faint smile. "I made him in Dark Hall. Just like Mother made us. Dark Hall is in our blood. It's who we are. It's why the Fiend leaves us be."

I hadn't been prepared for this answer, for the implications.

"But Victor…" I looked up at him just as the answer became clear. Victor had a part of me permanently entangled in his magic.

"You can't tell anyone, you can't," Fiona insisted. "No one can know what we are. Just find Roark before the Authority does. Before William."

If the Dark Hall magic I'd unwittingly given to Victor served as an inoculation against the harms of the Fiend, it meant William would enjoy the same. The Fiend had never been a threat to him. It had all been pointless.

Fiona seized, blood bubbling from her lips, and I openly wept as Victor solemnly brought a hand to his face, pressing fingers into eyes gone bright with unshed tears. Thea and Jack had finally closed the impossible distance, and the boy stopped to take in the awful scene, huffing with exertion and grief, before he threw himself down, crumpling against Fiona's emaciated, worn-out body, now empty of the curses that had been keeping her alive.

Thea knelt beside him, tenderly taking Fiona's limp hand. My sister gazed at her, drinking the woman in with the awe of someone looking heaven in the eye.

"You were everything," she muttered, the effort difficult. "Take care of our boy."

Jack sobbed into her chest.

Thea, grief overwhelming her ability to speak, could only bring Fiona's thin fingers to her lips, kissing her knuckles before pressing them against her tear-stained cheek.

My sister turned her head, resting it wearily against my chest, her breath slowed, and the desperate heaving calmed. Two tears fell from the corners of her green eyes, our mother's eyes, as they closed. Along with the last of her life magic curling through her lips was a whisper that lingered long after she'd left us.

Love you.

CHAPTER FORTY-THREE

The shore where I'd once stood with my sister and dreamed dreams of leaving to far-off places was now where she would rest forever, buried deep in the shingled rocks.

Hannah had spent several hours healing the worst of our injuries, knitting my ribs together, setting and correcting the bone in Victor's hand, then tended Jack's nose and Thea's black eye for good measure as Victor and I began the long work of digging Fiona's grave. Thea joined soon after, while Jack sat vigil by Fiona's body, stroking her hair, until we were finished.

I comforted myself knowing that my sister had moved on surrounded by people who would miss her, who'd loved her deeply. She'd left an unending list of mysteries in her wake, but she'd also left a trove of golden memories nothing could tarnish. The girl Fiona had been and the woman she'd become would forever remain two separate people to me, and I would choose to hold her close as the girl who'd held me at night when I was afraid, who'd sat with me on the floor to read books by the fire, stolen sweets from the kitchen, and laughed into the wind sweeping off the sea.

The four of us built a cairn to mark her grave, and when we were done, Thea and I sat next to her, watching the waves roll over the beach. I was wondering what shape my life would take now that the Fiend was loose and my sister was truly gone, now that I knew I'd never had a father, that perhaps I wasn't human at all.

Victor and Ramsey had both disappeared, and Hannah stood with Jack near the scraggly tree where Fiona and I had picnics with our mother. They were talking, Hannah pointing to the horizon.

"She was the best thing that ever happened to me," Thea said at length. "And the worst."

At this confession, she cast her eyes down at her fingers, which she ran across the smooth pebbles between us. She was unmade, wrapped in Ramsey's old coat, her face bare and open, hair curling in the salt air. I'd never seen her so at home in her own body, a woman allowed to exist as she was without putting on a show to survive.

"Where will you go?" I asked.

"Jack and I will find somewhere, maybe in the community where I was raised. There's not much out there. Without curses, the Fiend won't bother us."

"What about the Veil? It seems they're in a position to replace the Brom, or at the very least start a war with them. William was pretty certain they were going to be a problem."

"William did always have a knack for having his thumb on the pulse of trouble," she acknowledged, then paused, shaking her head. "We'll just have to do our best. There's no other choice. What about you?"

"I don't know."

I looked over my shoulder, up the slope of the bare, grassy cliff to the ruins of Blackwicket House, the only place I'd ever belonged.

"Will you miss it?" Thea asked, her fingers brushing against my hand in a show of sympathy and in an effort to connect as two people who understood loss. Misery had brought us together. We might not have chosen each other without Fiona, but we were bound by our love for a woman who'd irrevocably changed us both.

"I always will," I turned away from the view with a resigned smile.

"I think I will too," Thea admitted.

"It's time to go," Victor called, he and Ramsey returning, their faces grim. Though Victor hadn't said a word since we brought Fiona's body to the beach, he spoke now with the authority I knew him best for.

Thea and I stood, moving at the same moment to hug each other. She still smelled of jasmine.

"If you ever need anything," I said.

"I hope I never will," she replied.

We approached the gathering of our motley group, and I realized no one among us belonged here.

"It's not safe for any of you to stay here anymore," Ramsey said in his brusque bass, "So we've decided to relocate you."

"Ramsey?" Hannah's voice was surprised, pleased.

"Better to ask forgiveness," he gruffed.

"Where could we possibly go that this won't all reach us?" Thea asked, "Are you going to sail us across the sea?"

Ramsey barked a laugh.

"No, there's nothing out there anyway. What you see there is a line that doesn't exist." He lifted his chin to indicate the horizon.

"That can't be true." I examined the distant junction between water and sky where ships had sailed. "Nightglass was a shipping town. There were always merchant vessels docking at this port."

"From where?"

I didn't know. My mother had talked of other cities far away, but never named them.

"Do you know why they closed this port, Eleanora?"

"The Authority cracked down on illegal magic being smuggled in."

"The Authority—*our* Authority—was responsible for those ships, and they were full of magic, that's true. Magical items to filter some life back to this place. But it didn't work. The curses got worse. So they shut it all down."

"This world is dying, my dear," Hannah picked up the explanation with a tenderness she wielded well. "It has been for a while. It's why the Fiend was so interested in it. Now there's nothing left to be done but close it off for good so its sickness can't spread. The rest of Elsewhere is already struggling; it doesn't need this problem as well."

"Is Elsewhere where I'm from?" Jack asked.

Hannah put an arm around his shoulder like an indulgent grandmother.

"Elsewhere's everywhere we know of, all the pockets of existence floating in Dark Hall, connected by the magic that sustains us all."

Her tone was pious, and not for the first time, something about her disquieted me.

I looked to Victor, searching his face for a sign he believed what we were being told. He offered a tight dip of his head, an affirmation.

"What happens here?" Thea asked. "To this world?"

She seemed to be searching for a reason to stay, to face whatever odds there might be.

Ramsey cast a glance around us, considering.

"The Authority will let the Fiend do its work, clean it out. And who knows, maybe once the fields are scorched, the magic will return. Grow again."

"We're working in a few other pockets, much bigger than this one, that have been nearly magicless for centuries, but are still somehow hanging on," Hannah said. Ramsey eyed her with long-suffering irritation.

"At any rate," he said firmly, making it clear he wanted his wife to say no more. "There's hope as long as someone believes there is. As trite as that sounds, we've found it to be true. You're all welcome to stay if you want, try to ride out the storm."

He looked at me.

"Though I don't think it's a good idea, being what you all are."

Not waiting for us to discuss or ask more questions, he turned toward the waves, and in a long arching motion of his hand, he pushed aside space, cleaving it in twain, and I felt Dark Hall, strong as ever. With very little effort, Ramsey formed a Narthex, and I became aware that the magic I'd sensed in him the night of High Tide had been only a fraction of what he was capable of.

Before us stood a portal, dark and diaphanous as any I'd ever seen, but stable, the simple shape of an arched doorway.

"Were you always able to do that?" I asked, angry that it had been so easy.

"Like we said," Hannah replied. "We get one. One exit. We're using it now, and you're all coming. No arguments."

She motioned for Thea to come forward and stand next to Jack. With a somewhat bewildered expression, the woman did as she was told. Hannah stood at their backs, a hand on either of their shoulders. Jack glanced at me, nervous. I couldn't reassure him.

"Here we go!" Hannah said cheerfully, marching them both forward into the dark.

Ramsey approached to follow, and Victor glanced down at me, waiting.

"Whatever you decide," he murmured.

"You coming?" Ramsey asked.

"You'll excuse me if I have little reason to trust you," I said.

"You're right." Ramsey agreed, scratching his grey stubbled cheek. "But now that Hannah's out of earshot, I'll let you in on something. Neither of you is safe, no matter where you go."

My brows furrowed, and I moved closer to Victor, his body an anchor in this turbulent moment.

"You two," he nodded between us. "There's something strange there. Can't pinpoint it, but word's going to get around, and there'll be people after what you have. Here."

He motioned to the Narthex.

"There. Anywhere you go. But I promise if you come with me, I'll do what I can to make sure whatever's waiting doesn't jump you in the dark."

When we didn't respond, he sighed.

"Alright. I'll give you a chance to figure yourselves out and leave the Narthex open for a few minutes. If you come, you do. If you don't, well…" He shrugged his shoulders. As he was about to step in, he stopped to offer a parting word, specifically to Victor.

"Barrick had one of these too," he said, delivering his news as delicately as he could. "One exit. He was planning on using it with you, son, before everything. He cared for you a great deal, just as you were. I thought you should know."

I could feel the rise of Victor's emotions. Our connection had weakened, reduced by our exhaustion, both curses and magic bearing no strength to present themselves. But this moment, the deep gratitude of love, the ache of loss, it reached me before Victor could repress it. He nodded his thanks.

Ramsey took a last look around, like an old man departing his favorite pub for the last time.

"It'll recover," he said, without knowing, imparting one last hope. "Magic always finds a way."

He stepped through the Narthex.

I regarded the rocky cairn of my sister's grave, awash in the pink glow of the sunset occurring on a horizon that didn't exist, then admired the beach and the cliffs, the home that had made and broken me. I didn't want to leave Fiona, but I knew I was going to. Echoing through my thoughts, swirling along the spindrift of the waves, was her voice.

Oh, Ellie, my love.

A reassuring hand found mine. Victor. Our fingers interwove as he made the same survey I had, before raising my knuckles to his lips, kissing them while holding me in a gaze filled with rare tenderness, the kind he hid from others.

"Don't tell me, after everything, you're afraid of walking through a door, Curse Eater," he said, stroking the back of my hand with his thumb.

"I'm not," I replied, though we both knew it was a lie. I stepped closer to him, closer to the Narthex. "I have you to walk beside me."

"Until my dying breath."

With my sister's voice still on the wind, we stepped together into whatever future awaited us.

Call me back with your sorrows, and in spirit I'll stay.

* * *

ACKNOWLEDGEMENTS

To everyone who believed I wasn't a one-hit-wonder and encouraged me through every step of my imposter syndrome with kindness, humor, and some tough love. To my family, who kept bugging me about how it was going, and helped me through the great computer crash of '25.

To my children, who never stopped knocking at my office door for hugs and kisses, reminding me that there was a world beyond editing.

And to my beautiful little brother, forever twenty-four, who believed in my ability to do anything, and who taught me that strength is learning to swim through the darkness until you find a pocket of sunshine.

Last but not least, thank you to the team that made Blackwicket shine. My cover designer Lena Yang—this book is dressed beautifully, and I couldn't have asked for better. To my copy editor Beth Attwood, who showed me that the em dash isn't scary. And to my formatter Lorna Reid, who is patient beyond measure and has now made sure three of my books have beautiful insides to match their outsides.
And to you, reader. Thank you for being alive.

Kisses,

Bea

ABOUT THE AUTHOR

Bea Northwick is author of the award-winning Gothic Romance THE CRUEL DARK and its novella LOVER.

BLACKWICKET is her first (but certainly not last) Dark Gothic Romantasy.

She is a connoisseur of magical, spooky, and romantic things, owns too much perfume, can't pick an aesthetic, and loves 80s movies. She lives with her family, three dogs, and a black cat in the hot, humid American South, where the palm trees sway.

www.ingramcontent.com/pod-product-compliance
Ingram Content Group UK Ltd.
Pitfield, Milton Keynes, MK11 3LW, UK
UKHW040858150925
7897UKWH00033B/295